MUSIC & LYRICS (THE WILDER BOOKS #4)

SAVANNAH KADE

For Dana and Julie and Eli, my sisters in arms. Thank you for bringing this series to life!

CHAPTER 1

Alex was sitting on his couch with a beer when the woman went stomping past him. She didn't say a word. She didn't have to, her face said it for her.

Her orange hair was scraped back into a tight knot, and her sensible shoes shook the floor as she went by. She was done. He'd seen that expression before. Hadn't he just been trying to ignore the yelling coming from the other room himself? Of course she'd had enough. It was really a miracle she'd lasted this long.

She came back into the room, luggage packed and in hand.

Well, shit. She'd been ready, he realized. Still, he listened to her words.

"Mr. Beaumont, I'm resigning my position here." She handed over a typed and signed paper. It wasn't dated, so she hadn't known she was leaving today. As he scanned it, he saw the words even as she spoke them. "Effective immediately."

By the time he looked up, she was already gone from the room. Then he heard the back door slapping shut behind her. Not that it was a good sound, but it was far better than the discordant yells coming from Sophie's room. That awful sound was probably the worst thing a musician could hear.

He tipped his head back and poured in the beer as though it would seep in and fill all the cracks in his life. It didn't, but the slight buzz of the expensive, local beer made him feel just a little like it did.

It worked, too, until the yelling went quiet and he sat sharply upright at the sign of impending doom. There was no telling what Sophie was up to when she was quiet. But he sat still as though he would hear something, or a crash would come, or maybe she would *say* something.

The last one was never going to happen. Well, not in the lifetime that he could foresee. Probably the reason for the beer. Nothing filled the cracks of failure like a good cold one.

For so long, things had been fine. Golden even. He toured, his wife ran the show here, his daughter was perfect, and things were great. It had all gone to hell one unknowing step at a time. Just one day he woke up and everything was wrong. He could see the path he'd taken to get here, but he hadn't seen it when he'd been walking it. Now he was stuck between the worst options a father could have.

Then Olivia stuck her head into the living room. "Daddy?"

Her voice was sweet, the tones dulcet, her smile soft. She was his perfect girl. "What baby?"

"You need to get Sophie." She began to frown, her lips pressing together.

He nodded and stood up, only then realizing the beer had been a little more potent than he'd figured. He shouldn't have drunk it all. Then again, he couldn't have predicted that Mrs. . . . Mrs. . . .

Shit. Her name wouldn't come to him. Then again, did it matter? The woman had quit. That's what he couldn't have predicted.

But if he'd been a little more sober, a little more on the ball, a little better of a parent, he *would* have seen it coming. She wasn't the first one to leave. She wasn't even the first one to stomp out with no notice.

Then again, if he'd been a better parent, they probably wouldn't be in this predicament in the first place. Maybe it was Bridget's fault. He liked to believe that was possible.

Perfect Alex and Perfect Bridget had made Perfect Olivia.

Then they'd had Sophie and everything had gone wrong.

Catching his balance, Alex followed his older daughter into the back room, just as the discordant yelling started up again. He didn't know if that was a good sign or a bad one.

Looking down at Olivia and thinking he shouldn't leave her in charge of her sister as much as he did, he said, "We'll have to get another one."

She seemed to understand that he meant 'another nanny' and nodded up at him.

But in the meantime, it was all up to him.

He had to go face his two-year-old daughter.

Mariliz Jennings sat across the desk from her last hope.

The stern, older woman frowned down at Mariliz's resume and then frowned harder. It was understandable.

Maraliz had a degree in psychology with a focus on abnormal childhood development, with minors in French and creative writing. It was as though she wanted to be sure she had a career that required she ask people if they wanted fries with that? Oh, and loads of student debt, too.

To say she was having a bad month was an understatement. She was about three weeks away from running out of rent money, and that wasn't an exaggeration. She had the notice—two weeks and five days to be exact. Then she had to either break into the savings she swore she wouldn't touch or find a new craphole to live in.

On the upside, she'd once been a teacher. Not qualified to teach in a real school, because she'd quit before getting the state certificate. She'd worked in a retail shop once—luckily not serving fries—before she completed her degree. Then, after that one year of teaching, she'd been a wife. Which didn't look all that impressive on a resume.

To be fair, her work hadn't been all that impressive as a wife, if her recent divorce was anything to measure by. She'd been told to be pretty, plan parties, play house. She'd done all of that exceptionally well, if her friends were to be believed. She'd also gotten her nails done, spent an exorbitant amount of time prepping home-cooked, organic meals, and filled her boring down time with lunches and more romance novels than a person could shake a stick at. Well, there were no more sticks left; she'd read so many books that all the trees had likely been killed. She was grateful when she got an e-reader and could better hide her habit from Reynold, who thought she should be reading loftier things.

Looking back, maybe he was right. Had she been reading something educational she might have been able to put it on her damn resume. Or, she might not have needed the resume in the first place, because she never would have realized her marriage was so lacking. She might never have found strength from the women behind the pretty or racy covers who stood up for themselves. And Reynold might never have told her she was crazy and should be happy with the good life she had.

She might never have looked further.

She might never have decided to take charge and plan a special trip. That was when she found out her husband had been taking special trips all along—just not with her. Still, he'd told her she should appreciate the nice life he gave her. Mariliz didn't.

Well, until now, when she was her own woman, on the verge of getting evicted from her crap apartment. A woman who had gotten a very nice car in the divorce and not enough alimony to cover everything. Her lawyer hadn't argued well enough that she'd put as much into the marriage as he had. Maybe she hadn't.

At least she learned along the way to sit still and smile when the pressure was on. She used that now. And her nails looked fantastic. She had a lot of free time being unemployed and nail polish was cheap. So she faked calmly lacing her fingers and crossed her legs under the skirt that was only vaguely professional, but definitely not cheap.

She was the best-dressed woman at her apartment complex, that was for sure. So she smiled wide under the last smidge of her expensive lipstick. She needed another tube of it. She needed rent. She needed a paycheck about two weeks ago.

Mrs. Purvey, of the Purvey Child Care Agency—which Mari thought was a terrible name for anything with children— pointed down at the bottom of the print copy she'd been asked to bring. Apparently, Child Care was not part of the electronic age.

"It says here you speak sign language?" It was a question, despite the fact that she said it all wrong.

"I was a certified interpreter in American Sign Language. But I'm not at the medico-legal level anymore." She offered a sad smile. It had been years. Another cool skill that Reynold thought was another way his wife could be crass. Ya know, *working*. Had she tried to get reinstated, she would have surely failed the test now. But, as with many things, at one time, she'd showed promise.

"You do or don't speak the language?" The woman stared at her harshly.

"As a nanny? Perfectly fine." A deaf kid? The thought had no sooner occurred to her than Mrs. Gray was voicing it.

"We have a family in need of a live-in starting tomorrow. The younger daughter is deaf." Another harsh stare, as though she was daring Mariliz to take the job.

"That sounds fantastic." *Tomorrow?* She hardly paid attention as Mrs. Gray listed the stats. Number of kids, ages, genders, etc.

Mari blinked. She could live in. No more worries about rent, or money. Not if she had a place to stay. Then she blinked again. She'd better pay attention or she was going to lose the job before she even got it. In her hand was an info sheet still warm from Mrs. Gray printing it out for her.

"Do you have any questions?" The older woman asked in a tone that brooked no uncertainty that no, Mariliz Jennings did not have any questions.

"I can't think of any." She said, then realized that made it sound like her brain didn't work. She motioned with the fact-sheet. "This looks very thorough."

At last, the older woman looked pleased.

Mari filed that away. She'd gotten very good over the past years at learning and cataloging who liked what, who'd vacationed where, and how to remember factoids as though she actually cared.

Three minutes later, it was over. She was dismissed from the office and found herself on the front steps. She was expected at the address at eight p.m. tonight to introduce herself before the children went to bed, then she would start tomorrow at eight a.m. suitcase in hand.

Holy shit. She had a job. One that paid her for a real skill. She drove off with a smile on her face. It stayed there even though Nashville traffic piled up around her. It stayed all the way to the crappy apartment on the other side of town. Never mind that East Nashville was up and coming. She was too far east and her place was definitely down and going.

Once she made it home, she took one look at the brown, metal front door to her apartment and put the car back in gear.

She was a good cook, but the thought of cooking in that awful little kitchen, with the glitchy electric burners that she hated, was more than she could handle. It was a good news day and there was a meat-and-three down the street. She and her Lexus would stick out like a sore thumb, just like they always did. But they knew her there. They knew she would show up in her designer skirt and happily eat green beans cooked with bacon fat. They would wink and give her extra banana pudding, too.

The meatloaf tasted better with a side of freedom. She read up on the family while she tried to keep banana pudding smears off the page. The address looked nice, Brentwood area on the south side of town, not too far from the agency. That made sense, the agency would be located where there was a high density of families that could afford live-in help.

Once, she'd been that kind of wife. Now she was the help. Maybe she should have had kids. For a moment, she looked up at the old acoustic ceiling and thought about that path. Nope. She would have been tied to Reynold, and even her crappy apartment, with the eviction notice taped to the front door for everyone to see, was better than being tied to a man who cheated on her and didn't even see a reason to be sorry.

She looked back down at the page. Father—Alexander Beaumont. Mother—Bridget Beaumont. Children—Daughter-Olivia-Age 8 and Daughter-Sophie-Age 2.

Fun ages, Mari thought. She had plenty of brothers and sisters and cousins. She understood what a two-year-old and an eight-year-old might be like. She also understood that every single one of them was their own person, even at those ages.

No pets. *Good.* Mari wasn't even fond of goldfish.

Live-in space—mother-in-law suite with private entrance on ground floor. Her own suite! It was probably bigger than her crappy apartment!

At the noise of her spoon hitting Corian, she looked at the plate to find she'd cleaned it. Then she pulled her phone to discover that she had barely enough time to change, fight traffic, and show up at seven-fifty.

Folding the paper into her purse, Mari breathed deeply of the smells of fried chicken and cooked-within-an-inch-of-their-lives vegetables. There would probably not be a mom and pop place like this on the other side of town.

CHAPTER 2

Mari rubbed her palms down the sides of her soft slacks. She wasn't able to remember the last time she'd been this nervous. Looking down at herself she saw a feathery tank top, soft simple pants, and flats. All things chosen to look professional and not too rich—which she wasn't. Also, she wanted to be able to sit down on the floor with the kids if it came to that.

She knocked hard on the door, her knuckles smarting.

Didn't they have a knocker? Or a doorbell? Her house had a knocker. *It also had an asshole*, she thought wryly, and it wasn't her house anymore. She pushed the thought aside, turning her hopes to her new life as a nanny. Plastering an expectant smile on her face, she took a deep breath and waited.

And waited.

No sounds came from inside the big house.

Mari checked her phone. Seven fifty-nine. Not ten minutes early like she wanted, but exactly on time for someone to be here opening the door. Hadn't the family requested she come at eight tonight?

She rang the bell this time, having finally located it in some intricate scrollwork around the door frame. She heard the chimes inside, wiped her palms again, and took another deep breath.

Still nothing.

Looking side to side, Mari checked for signs of life. The garage faced the front of the house, taking up almost half the façade with three identically ornate doors. They were all closed, but an SUV was parked out front of it, so someone was here.

Leaning slightly to the side, she peeked in the beveled glass at the sides of the door. She couldn't see clearly, but of course someone was now coming down the hallway, and she'd been caught looking.

The large door opened, letting conditioned air out as well as a small angry voice. It didn't belong to the beleaguered woman standing in front of her. The curt voice wasn't a surprise, given the expression on her face. "Are you the new nanny?"

"Yes, I—"

"Great, come in." She turned away, cutting off Mari's planned introduction and ignoring the so-nice-to-meet-you smile. "Follow me."

Mari did, even as her heart squeezed. This was not a good sign, but she had nowhere else to go. Mari consoled herself that this woman likely had a job or at least wouldn't be around much if she was hiring a live in nanny. She would have days off, and it turned out she was getting specialist pay for the "foreign" language she needed for this assignment.

She opened her mouth, but another discordant yell came out of the back of the house, along with a loud noise. That would be the little deaf girl. Deaf kids had no idea how loud they were, so they were often not at the culturally accepted decibel level. They banged things, too, not realizing they were doing it.

She figured the woman was leading her back through the house to meet the children, but she veered to the left, to a hallway just past the kitchen. Mari followed her, trying desperately to introduce herself. "I'm Mariliz Jennings. The Purvey Child Care Agency sent me." She winced as she repeated the name.

"Yes, I figured that was you. Who else would show up at eight in the evening?" She didn't look at Mari, and didn't even pause to change the subject. "This is the live-in suite. It's all yours. I even changed the sheets."

Well, if that wasn't a ringing endorsement . . . Mari felt her eyebrows lift up. If this was their mother, she was grateful the girls had a caregiver. Then again, maybe the woman was good with kids? "You're Bridget Beaumont?"

A laugh that bordered on a cackle flew from the woman's mouth. "Oh no, honey. I'm Francesca, her sister."

"Oh." Well, that made her feel a lot better. Mari nodded and smiled, not sure what else to do.

She was about to ask another question when the woman waved her hand around. "That's your personal bathroom. No kids allowed, I suppose. You have this small reading room, and through that door is your bedroom."

Mari was grateful for the bedroom existing, she'd become afraid she was expected to live-in on what looked like a pull-out couch. So she headed over and gingerly turned the knob to reveal a decent sized room with a full sized bed, tall windows, and really nice decor. Not her personal style, but she could certainly live in it. When she exited, she saw the small kitchen built into the wall she'd passed on the way in. Though slightly smaller than her current kitchen, it was a lot nicer.

"Oh that." Francesca replied. "All yours, but you can use the big kitchen, too. Lord knows Bridget doesn't."

Great. Just the opening she needed. "Is she here now?"

Another cackle. Another unsettling twist in her stomach.

"Oh God, no." She stared as though Mari clearly had no clue what was going on. And Mari was beginning to realize she didn't. "Bridget is on a cruise. It's the only reason I'm here now. Next time, she can get her ass home and do this herself."

Ohhh. Kaayyy. Mari just offered a nod, hoping she wasn't agreeing to anything. "And Mr. Beaumont?"

"He left on tour yesterday."

"Tour?" She frowned. *Was he a soldier?*

Now Francesca wasn't just looking at her like she had no clue, she was looking at Mari like she was stupid. "He's a drummer." She waited. "With the band Wilder."

"Oh!" Then *Ohhhhh.* Mari liked them. She'd heard them on the radio. No wonder they could afford a nanny and her own live-in suite. "Okay." She'd get to meet the drummer from Wilder. *Oh!* And probably all the rest of the band eventually. That would be cool, wouldn't it?

"So, let me show you the rest of the house." Suddenly, Francesca sounded a lot nicer, and Mari followed her through the living room, up the wide, carpeted stairway. She peeked in each of the girls' rooms—both neatly kept. There was a music room with a full drum set parked in the middle and some kind of foam padding the walls. It was really cool, but Francesca only opened the door onto it briefly before heading to another.

"Their room," she gave a small snort, "Hall bathroom," then "Guest room."

In the guest room, Francesca walked in, allowing Mari to follow and get a good look. The room was a passable mess and her hostess noticed. "No worries. This is not on you. The maid comes three times a week. She'll get it."

"And the suitcase?" It was open on the bed, the clothing mostly neatly packed with a few pieces rolled and tucked around the edges.

"Mine." Francesca smiled off-handedly, then dug into the purse lying sideways next to the suitcase. "Oh, here, this is the card for you."

Mari took what was clearly a credit card and frowned. She was going to get a wrinkle between her brows just from tonight.

"It's for you. Household account." She went on to describe a few things Mari was supposed to purchase with it, and how much was put on it each week for her to use for the girls. "You know, bring home ice cream, drive-through for burgers, anything you need that the assistant didn't pick up."

Mari nodded and held it tight, not yet having decided where to keep it. She hadn't expected to be handed a credit card, nor to find out that not one but both parents were out of the house. She stood silently while Francesca handed over several items, including a ring of keys. Mari was opening her mouth to ask when she would meet them, when she noticed Francesca pulling the zipper on the suitcase. "Are you leaving?"

"Oh yeah. I'm outta here. It's all yours."

For the first time in her life, Mariliz Jennings actually sputtered. "What? When does Mr. Beaumont get back? Or Mrs. Beaumont? I—"

"That's why I asked you to come at eight tonight. I have plane to catch." She smiled, maybe a little too brightly.

"No! You can't leave." Mari almost grabbed the woman and maybe should have as she pushed by. "I'm not supposed to start until tomorrow."

"You came tonight at eight? Right?" Francesca was already in the hallway looking back at her, suitcase in hand.

"Just to meet everyone. I start *tomorrow*." She stated it firmly and barely held back from putting her hands on her hips.

"Well, I have a non-refundable ticket and I have to go or I won't make it through security. I'm sorry for the miscommunication." She lugged the suitcase down the steps muttering under her breath.

Mari was certain she heard both the names 'Bridget' and 'Alex' in there. She was about to mutter them herself.

While she was shaking her head, Francesca disappeared out the front door with a wave and a "Bye!"

Mari was left alone with two kids she hadn't even met yet. Aunt Francesca hadn't even introduced her to the girls. She could have found her own bedroom, figured out what was in the fridge, and plenty more, but now she had to introduce herself to her charges? Suddenly she realized that no one had even told her when either of the Beaumonts was getting back.

Who were these people?

As she straightened her spine, she heard a faint sound of a car door closing and her spine sagged again. Then she heard a yell from the ground floor and raced down the steps.

CHAPTER 3

Cautiously, Mari approached the noisiest room in the house.

It wasn't the volume that scared her. It was that it sounded angry.

She wondered where the older sister was until she got close, then she heard the voice coming from the room.

"Sophie, no. Don't throw that." The voice stayed calm despite the growl that followed it. "No, Sophie."

Then a sigh.

Mari couldn't figure out what bothered her so much about it. So she paused, listened a little longer.

"Let's play a game, Sophie. Let's play with the toy cars. Toy cars?"

A faint rattle followed, then a crash and a burst of vocal power. Mari was rushing the door when the voice came again.

"Are you hungry? Hungry, Sophie?"

That was it. Why was the girl *talking* to her younger sister? If Sophie was deaf, there was no purpose. And she was too young to read lips.

In a second flash of insight, Mari almost smacked herself on the forehead. The older one—Olivia—was only eight. She'd probably only learned sign for her sister, and like many beginners was probably vocalizing while she signed. It helped newbies keep things straight.

With a sigh of relief that she'd figured it out, Mari turned the knob and realized she had it all wrong.

It all hit her at once. The two girls were as adorable as they could be, and Mari's heart sank. The little one looked at her and let out another horrible sound, angry at just seeing her. The older girl looked at her blankly, but the toddler's diaper sagged.

Time to get to work.

The diaper had to go. But she couldn't do that until she introduced herself. Signing and talking, thinking that might make Olivia more comfortable, she started. "Hi, I'm Mariliz, and I'm—"

"You're the new nanny."

"Yes." She smiled at Olivia, not correcting that she'd interrupted. "And you're Olivia and this is Sophie, right?" She kept her hands moving, eyes on each girl as she turned. This was why she'd had a cross-body strap purse when she was interpreting. Yet another thing on a rapidly growing list.

"Did Aunt Frankie leave yet?"

It took a second for that to sink in, then Mari nodded, "Yes, she left just a minute ago." Then another thought occurred, "Oh, did you not get to say goodbye to her?"

"No, but I didn't want to. Are you fun or strict?" Olivia looked up at her with perfectly round blue eyes and Mari fished for the right answer.

"Both."

"Okay." The girl seemed unconcerned with the answer one way or another—as though she only wanted to catalog it.

"Hey, Sophie." Mari turned now to the little girl who was almost growling at her. "You need your diaper changed."

Something was wrong. Something about the way the little one looked at her. Mari tried again. Same response.

Feeling like she was in an episode of the Twilight Zone, she almost shook her head to clear it, or started looking around for a hidden camera. Then it snapped into place again.

Sophie was tracking her hands. Not looking at her face. And she was wide-eyed.

Mari said it again, both with her words and her hands. "Let's change your diaper."

Same response. The daughter wasn't just deaf, there was something else wrong. Mari was looking for signs of Downs, or fetal alcohol syndrome, or something, when Olivia piped up.

"You can put your hands away. Sophie doesn't sign."

Obviously, but she didn't say it. Sarcasm should not be in her opening conversation with her new charges. "She can read it can't she?"

No response.

So Mariliz turned and looked at Olivia who was shrugging. "Do deaf kids just know it?"

Sounded like something an eight-year-old might think, so Mari let it pass. "No, they learn it the same way you learn English, a little at a time and from the people around them."

She put her hands down, in case Sophie understood more than she was reacting to. This time, Mari faced Olivia and spoke in English only. "She's not making her own signs? You sign to her but she doesn't sign back?"

Sophie was two. Even if she was severely developmentally delayed she should sign something. Even her own, made-up signs.

"I don't sign to her." Olivia said it again. She looked like a little angel. Her hair was braided with ribbons that matched her outfit. Her clothing was high-end childrens' stuff. But her answers were flat, she was only cataloging them. She had none of the bounce and interest Mari would have expected from an eight-year-old meeting their new babysitter.

Then again, Mari had never had a nanny nor ever been one. Maybe the kid had gotten jaded already. "Who signs to her?"

Maybe the parents weren't very good? Or the old nanny was just learning and didn't do it well, or not often? No wonder the little girl was a mess.

"No one."

Holy shit. "No one?"

"She's learning to lip read." Olivia stated.

No, she wasn't. She was two. Mari must have been looking at Olivia like she was insane, because the little girl frowned at her. Great, now she was staring down a kid about poor life choices that weren't even hers.

Then she turned back to the small one who was now quiet, but watching with wary eyes. Trying not to look like she was doing it, Mari took a scan of the kid's head. She wasn't sure if she succeeded in being furtive, because Sophie started to glare a little.

Turning back to Olivia, she asked questions of the only person around who seemed willing to talk to her. "She doesn't have a cochlear implant?"

As the words left her mouth, she realized that she'd asked a kid about a neural device. But Olivia was already on it. In other circumstances—maybe some with some happiness?—she would have liked this kid.

"She's not a candidate for it."

Not a candidate? Little pitchers did indeed have big ears. She hadn't come up with that phrasing on her own. Mari didn't ask why. She wasn't sure of the answer she'd get. Steering the conversation another way, she asked, "Do you know when your dad is coming back?"

"Yes!" This time, the kid smiled. She pulled Mari into the

kitchen to look at a calendar on the wall. A day was circled in red and Olivia pointed. "That day."

Nine days from now. *Shit.* Then she breathed a sigh of relief. "Then when is your mom getting back?"

"I don't know."

"A couple days?" She tested the waters. "Tomorrow?"

"A month?" Olivia shrugged and followed her back down the hallway. They couldn't leave Sophie alone.

A *month???*

Eight-year-old, she reminded herself like a mantra. Bridget Beaumont would be home soon. Mariliz had Alex's number and Bridget's. Though if she was on a cruise, she might not have service. Still Mari could get a hold of the Dad, let him know she'd arrived safe, and that—despite the 'miscommunication'—she had the girls taken care of.

"Let's get Sophie changed."

Sophie fought her the whole time she tried to change the diaper. Mari was stronger and rapidly becoming more stubborn than the little girl, though that was a task. She would have thought the kid would *want* the diaper changed.

In the end, concessions were made on both sides. Sophie was changed on the floor on the mat from the changing table. Mari tried to sign to the girl, but that was difficult with her hands trying to wrangle a rebellious toddler. Olivia watched her the whole time she tried, making weird faces that Mari could not for the life of her decipher.

It was nine p.m. by the time she got Sophie into a clean diaper. She tried again to get information out of the best source. Turning to Olivia, she said. "It's your bedtime, isn't it?"

"It was our bedtime an hour ago." She smiled and headed up the stairs.

Deciding it was her best course of action to follow, Mari tried to pick up Sophie and go along. Sophie did not want to be picked up. She tried to hold Sophie's hand. Sophie did not want to hold hands.

In the end, Sophie followed her older sister and Mari was content with that. There was too much else to do. So she trailed along behind the toddler, in case she missed a step, and peppered the older one with questions.

She learned when school started in the morning and which school Olivia attended. That Olivia had her alarm set. That Sophie had a daycare but had been kicked out of it a week earlier for hitting. *Shocking,* Mari thought and reminded herself that she needed the job. Also, if she didn't do it, who would look after the girls? Clearly, no one else was going to.

She tucked Olivia in, smiling despite the girl's nearly clinical approach to the whole thing. Then she went after Sophie. It was ten p.m. before the toddler finally went to sleep.

Sitting in the hallway, her back literally against the wall, Mari ran her hand over her hair. She'd put it up, but now took it down. She couldn't go home and leave the girls, that had to legally be neglect. She wouldn't do it anyway; it just wasn't safe.

She had to make it through to tomorrow with what was in her purse—a prospect that wasn't too promising. She looked up the address for Olivia's school, then let herself into the garage and tried the car key on the chain. They'd left her a Mercedes to drive. But since she couldn't figure out how to open the garage door, she wound up moving the carseat into the back of her own car. Her car would stay in the driveway until she found a button that didn't need a code she didn't have.

Mari sighed. In another hour, she was as ready as she could be for the morning. There was just one more thing to do. She got the contact list Francesca had handed her and dialed her phone.

◦〜◦

Alex pressed the button on his phone. He'd seen the call from an unknown number last night. There was a message, too. He'd wanted to delete it, but couldn't quite hit the buttons to do it. It had a Nashville area code and might be someone he needed to talk to. So he'd headed out to the front of the bus because it was empty, thinking he could have some privacy.

He simply couldn't handle talking to anyone in Nashville. Even Olivia.

Though he loved his daughters, he couldn't deal with any of it now. He knew they were safe and he wanted to leave it at that. He was between a rock and a hard place—there was simply no way to be a good father. So the only choice left an absent one.

Even if it wrenched his heart in two, he couldn't even tell anyone.

Though he'd been married the longest of any of the guys, he and Bridget didn't have what JD and Kelsey had. Kelsey had JD's back, no matter what. The couple was open, kind, friendly, and clearly still in love. TJ had Norah, and they were new, still honeymooning. Emotional and big, they were the stars of the show. Even Craig found someone. He and Shay were almost the dead opposite of the other two. Intensely private, they lived with the wagons circled. They shared birthday parties and the occasional playdate, but Craig and Shay were the embodiment of 'still waters ran deep.'

Alex was pretty sure that his marriage to Bridget had become the perfect picture of 'shallow waters.' So which of these men could he tell his problems to?

His parents wouldn't understand. They, too, had a perfect marriage. Alex once thought they were the ideal examples of what to do. Only in the past few years had he realized his parents had a steady boat not because they were steady, but because they'd weathered no storms.

He'd been in a slowly building hurricane for a while now. This last phone call was probably just another wind buffeting him. If he was lucky, it was a telemarketer. Maybe it a was a reporting asking about his wife. He never answered. He and Bridget barely made the back pages of the tabloids, if at all. Or maybe it was his mother who would try to explain that he should just wait it out, things would turn around.

Pinching the bridge of his nose, he looked out the window and picked up the phone. Though the new bus was nicer than the old one, longer and bigger, the common area still wasn't that big. He had it to himself until someone else woke up. He hoped he was done with the message before then.

He hit buttons until a sweet-sounding voice came to his ear.

"Hello, Mr. Beaumont." He swallowed. "My name is Mariliz Jennings and I'm your new nanny."

Of course she was. It sounded like Frankie hadn't told her he knew, though it was good to hear that she was installed and functioning. The message chattered on, asking if there was anything she needed to know specifically about either girl. He thought he detected an underlying touch of fury to the message but didn't want to read into it.

Frankie would have given her all the paperwork. This Jennings woman was from the Agency, so he could rest assured she'd been vetted. Between those sources, she had everything she needed, so why was the message still going?

He clenched his jaw when she asked, "So I need you to call me back right away and tell me when your wife is going to return home."

He didn't know when Bridget would get home, and that was only part of the problem. He was stuck on the road for now, and if he was honest, he didn't want to return home either. His bed was empty; his older daughter looked at him like he should be able solve things he just couldn't. His younger daughter hated him, but she hated everyone. And he'd somehow gone from Father-of-the-Year to Massive-Failure.

Just then, JD opened the door to his room, still the front one on the bus, and managed to meet Alex's eyes. "Is it the girls?"

"Yeah." Alex faked a grin as he felt the bands close tight around his chest. He loved his girls so much, and he couldn't help either of them.

"How are they doing?" His bandmate asked, concern on his face. Alex knew that JD saw more than he said. He was only grateful the guitarist didn't call him on it.

"They're great." He flat out lied that time and he felt his chest tighten down to where he almost couldn't breathe.

CHAPTER 4

Alex didn't return the nanny's call until late the following night. Until after she'd called him five more times and left two more urgent messages.

He hoped he was calling the Jennings woman too late for her to pick up. Hoped she'd have turned her volume down and he'd simply leave her a message in return.

Nope. She picked up the phone.

Though her initial "Hello?" sounded groggy, she snapped into full take-charge mode as soon as she realized it was him on the line. "Mr. Beaumont."

"Alex." The correction was automatic. Mr. Beaumont was his father.

"Thank you."

Oh, good. A good foot to start on, he thought, but she didn't return the favor.

"I'm so glad I caught you." He was just thinking that she hadn't actually caught him when she bulldozed the next line. "There was a massive miscommunication and I wasn't ready to start last night but I'm making it work. The girls are fine."

He winced that he hadn't asked first. The girls were always fine. It was the nannies that usually didn't fare so well.

"What I need to know—" she continued as he imagined a sour-faced, middle-aged woman with dark hair bound tightly away from her face. "Is when your wife will be returning home?"

For a moment he didn't breathe. He just rubbed his hand down his face and wished he'd shaved before he'd made the call. Then he wished he hadn't made the call. He inhaled in an attempt to figure out how to answer that question, but she spoke into the gap he left.

"Your daughter said she's on a cruise, and I assume that's why her phone is going straight to voicemail." There was a bit of a question hanging on the end of it.

"Yes." He didn't know why he said it. Olivia said Bridget was on a cruise? Had she made it up? Or had Bridget called and talked to Olivia? Livie was her favorite. Perfect Olivia. Imperfect Sophie. Maybe Frankie had said her sister was on a cruise. He spoke to cover the space he was leaving again. "Bridget's been very busy lately. But you can talk to Nina, who runs the house, and you can call me when you need to."

That should do it.

"You haven't been answering. What if there's an emergency?"

Dammit. That was a good question. But there hadn't ever been one, and he wasn't close enough anyway. Bridget had always handled it. Always wanted to. He hadn't been prepared when she disappeared. "Text me 9-1-1 if that happens. All the doctors, hospitals nearby, that's all in the info packet." The child care agency had made him update it and he'd made Nina do it. All he'd done was sign that the kids had his parental permission to be treated.

He was being a terrible father. He hated himself for it even if there was no other option that wasn't worse.

Sophie never really had a good father, not after about age one. Olivia once had a pretty good one, but since Sophie came everything had gone to hell. He'd gone right along with it. He didn't quite know how he'd gotten here, but he sensed that it was his fault for not seeing the signs. The edges of what had to be a panic attack were creeping in on him.

His hand still rubbed at the stubble on his chin. This time the silence came from the other end of the line. "What else can I help you with?"

"So." She paused. "I'm on my own with the girls until you return home in eight days."

"Of course not." He smiled. "Nina is there, the maid comes three days a week. Olivia has school. If you want you can enroll Sophie in a daycare, too."

He wished like hell this Jennings woman could make that happen. He was pretty sure Sophie had gotten kicked out of enough of them that no one would take her. But no sense bursting bubbles and no sense giving her ideas that might hold her back.

"I see." There was an acceptance in those words that grabbed him in the gut and twisted. They were talking about his daughters.

Just then, another door in the back of the bus slid open. He didn't know whose it was, but he heard it. "I have to go. Good talking to you."

With a cringe he pushed the button just as he heard her resigned, "Good bye."

He felt like shit.

In that moment, the pressure behind his eyes became so bad that he snapped. Bridget had snapped just over a year before. When she snapped, she left.

He'd let her handle everything about the girls, so when she cracked, when she disappeared, he'd been left with nothing but a screaming, angry, mentally challenged daughter no one could calm or deal with. Now his teeth clenched. He couldn't wait for Bridget to return any longer. If anything at all was to be salvaged of his life, his family, he would have to do it himself.

He almost called the nanny back and said, "Yes, I'll be there. I'll answer when you call. You can count on me."

But, as always, he was stuck. He had to figure out a way to be better when he got home. He couldn't do it from here. Before Sophie, he would call Olivia and Bridget when he was away. His older daughter would chatter to him happily and Bridget would tell him that she missed him. After Sophie, Bridget was upset all the time. Then Sophie couldn't talk on the phone. He'd tried video chat, but she got angry. She just didn't communicate.

Though it seemed wrong to not talk with Olivia because Sophie couldn't, it was just as wrong to talk to one of his children but not the other. He felt like he was playing a horrible game of favorites either way he cut it.

There was nothing he could do from here. So he nodded at TJ as his bandmate headed groggily out into the front of the bus, and Alex headed back to get his things. He didn't know how to tell the guys that Perfect Bridget wasn't perfect. That his Perfect Marriage probably never had been. And his Perfect Family would never be perfect again.

He would take over the small bathroom to shower and shave. And he would have to figure out how to be a better father to his girls.

He had to do something to bring Bridget back.

"No." Mari kept her cool on the outside, though on the inside she was boiling.

She could hear Olivia's warning in her ears. *Sophie doesn't get milk on her cereal.* Now she knew why.

When Sophie got mad, she threw her food. She screeched a horrid noise that she could probably feel even if she couldn't hear it. She beat her hands on the table, making Mari wonder if she was going to bruise. And she threw whatever she could get her hands on. Even if it was cereal. With milk.

Olivia had gotten off to school just fine. At least that part had gone okay. Though Nina had shown up to take care of the household affairs—pay bills, get groceries and stuff, apparently—Mari had not known she was coming. So she'd almost screamed when she found another woman standing in the open kitchen when Mari came out the next morning.

"You must be the new nanny. I'm Nina." The other woman wasn't startled at all. She hadn't even waited for a response, just explained her own household duties, that she was only in the house a little and was part-time anyway. "Help yourself to anything in the fridge. Let me know if there's anything you want on the grocery list. You can cook or eat out."

There was a smile, then nothing as she went back to her duties.

Mari studied her for a moment, trying to figure out if everyone in this house was just a brick wall. Everyone except Sophie. Well, and "Aunt Frankie," but neither of them were her favorite people right now.

Mari leaned down and wiped up the mess, wondering exactly what she'd thought her job description would be when she applied to the nanny job. The thing was, she hadn't. She'd been thinking about a paycheck, not cleaning cereal from the floor.

Once the floor was cleaned and Sophie realized that Mari wasn't paying any attention to her, she started eating the cereal again. Her spoon skills were passable for a two-year-old. While Mari wanted to help, the girl didn't talk at all and touching her hand didn't seem like a wise move right now.

So she sat on the opposite side of the table, reading a music magazine she'd found in the mail pile and watching Sophie out of the corner of her eye. Getting Sophie to eat was job one.

This morning she'd put Sophie in the car booster seat, only to have Olivia promptly tell her that the booster was hers. That made sense, it was for a much bigger kid. Upon asking where Sophie's carseat was, she was told it was . . . somewhere. Sophie didn't go out much.

Sweet Jesus, the kid was a shut in. She didn't speak, had behavioral and probably mental problems, and didn't even get out and around. Mari promptly put Sophie into the booster and Olivia into the backseat in a regular seatbelt and barely got the kid to her plush private school on time.

Driving across town to her apartment wasn't a problem, but getting Sophie out of the car, into her apartment, and keeping her busy while Mari packed up as much of her life as she could —that was a problem. Getting Sophie back into the car was even worse.

Then they had to go buy an appropriate sized car seat. Thankfully Sophie was enamored with all the toys and things at the store and Mari got her a squishy stuffed animal for an infant, wondering if it was the right level for her. Then she picked out a seat and never finished a shopping trip so fast.

At the checkout, she was afraid the credit card wouldn't go through, and she'd have to use her own card. If that was the case, they were eating out of the fridge and not going anywhere until Mr. Beaumont—*Alex,* she self-corrected—returned. But the card went through and she and Sophie were on their way.

Everything they did was a lesson in management for Mari. In the parking lot, Sophie didn't want to hold hands. And she *couldn't* listen. She didn't even know any signs, so when Mari signed to her, she would just stop and stare. At least she was watching.

Sitting at the table with the magazine she didn't understand, while Sophie ate cereal she made a mess with, was the easiest thing she'd done since seven a.m. But she had clean clothes and she and Sophie had worked out the logistics of diapers. Mari was already learning that Sophie had different cries for different problems, just like an infant.

When the cereal was finished, it was time to get Olivia from school, and they were off again. Sophie first struggled against the seat, then bounced in it, watching the passing scenery. Mari signed with one hand up in the middle of the car the whole way.

When she was getting her interpreting certificate, she'd had to study this. Some deaf kids didn't get exposed to sign language until they were four or five. Sometimes until they went to special schools. They had memories of before they had words— something most hearing/speaking people couldn't comprehend.

It seemed no one was signing to Sophie. Maybe because she was too challenged to understand it. Or maybe there was something behind Olivia's determined declaration that they were teaching her to lip read—which was utterly ridiculous.

In her head, Mari tried to concoct a best-case-scenario for the strangely disjointed family she'd landed in the middle of. The best she could come up with was that Sophie was language challenged and they didn't sign. Thus they had hired a specialist from the child care agency, and here she was. She was going to do her best.

As they pulled up beside Olivia in the car line—a new experience for Mari—the older girl popped herself into the back seat, and expertly into her own booster. "You got Sophie a seat."

"Yes, she needed one if she's going to come out with us."

"She doesn't come out much."

Mari bit her lip, again trying to remind herself there had to be a best case scenario here.

"She does now!" She said it with a big grin, and without voicing the words, she signed, "Sophie goes everywhere," into the middle of the car. Then she asked Olivia about her day and listened to chatter about math boxes, colored carpet squares, and building energy efficient windmill systems that didn't create a carbon footprint.

Mari wondered what kind of kool-aid the kid had been drinking. Since she couldn't really contribute to the carbon emission reduction conversation, she changed the topic. "Should we get pizza for dinner?"

"Yes!" Olivia shouted with the first real glee Mari had heard.

It occurred to her then that someone must have been feeding this kid millet and quinoa. Well, she wasn't the mom. And if the mom wanted fully organic, spelt-flour food, she was going to have get her ass off that cruise and cook it herself.

They ordered in and then Mari's real work began.

CHAPTER 5

The third afternoon, Mariliz squinted at her pint-sized opponent. "That can't be right, Olivia."

"She's learning to lip read." The girl insisted.

Olivia, or Livie as Mari had taken to calling her, was bright, sweet, and even when she was stubborn it was more just a quiet belief in her own rightness. This was the only thing they butted heads on.

Mari disagreed. She didn't think Sophie was learning much of anything.

Sophie on the other hand was still a terror—which was exactly why Mariliz Jennings was perfect for the job. Apparently only for *this* particular job, but perfect for it. Teaching developmentally disabled deaf kids to speak was exactly what her multi-purpose, would-you-like-fries-with-that degree was suited for.

That and almost a decade living in an upscale house in a suburban neighborhood. She knew all the designers, drove the appropriate car, and knew how to work both the french press and the panini press.

She also knew how to teach a non-lingual style, and how

operant and classical conditioning trainings were used with animals. It was honestly something most parents did with their kids without realizing it. But without language, Sophie's rewards would be different.

Mari had learned the first day that turning her back on Sophie worked wonders. It was the most effective "punishment" to train Sophie that what she'd done wasn't acceptable. Olivia quickly picked the trick up.

As they both stood with their backs to the screaming two-year-old, Mari asked, "What did you do before?"

"Shhhh." Olivia stood stoically, facing away from her sister, very much involved in helping Sophie.

Mariliz fought a grin. A full smile could often be seen from the back of the head. But a slight movement of the lips and Sophie wouldn't know. "You can talk carefully. It's not like she can hear us."

"Oh!" Olivia almost bust into giggles. Then she came back to the question. "We would just distract her or try things until she quit."

Ouch. No wonder Sophie was such a little dictator. The more she misbehaved, the more toys and play she got. Mari was not going to feed into that. She told Olivia. "Look, it's going to be easier for me. I'm new, and she doesn't have any history with me. With you, she knows that the more she misbehaves, the more likely she is to get a toy. You have to stand firm. I don't want her hitting you again."

That had happened the afternoon before and it was the only time Mari had physically pulled Sophie back. It was not okay to hit her sister. "What did your mother do?"

Olivia shrugged.

Bad idea. "Don't shrug. Don't do anything she can see. We are statues. We only interact when she's good."

Mostly, it was already working, but Olivia would have a

longer go of it. As evidenced by the fact that Mari could see Sophie toddling up to her sister right now.

"She's coming for you." Mari warned.

Sure enough, Sophie tugged on Olivia's pants and made a noise in her throat. When Olivia didn't respond, Sophie hit.

Mari saw it in her peripheral vision and whirled on the child. She frowned and said "No," firmly in both languages. Then she said and signed, "You can't hit your sister!"

Sophie wailed then, plopping onto her diaper-clad butt and breaking Mari's heart. *Poor kid.* No one talked to her in any way she could understand. She probably wasn't that bright. They'd rewarded her for being a pain in the butt, because they didn't know not to. Her family just wanted the baby to quit crying. Screaming. Doing that awful discordant yell she did that she couldn't hear. And her father was a musician. It must hurt his heart.

Olivia stayed stoic with her back turned, but from her spot, Mari could see the older girl's chin start to quiver. "Listen first, honey. When you're ready, turn around, squat down and smile. Hold your arms out for a hug. If she hits you, turn around again. But if she hugs you, go ahead."

"Okay." The girl took a deep breath and did exactly as she was instructed.

Sophie ran into her arms and as Mari watched, Olivia almost cried. But she kept it together. A hug from her baby sister meant the world. Mari almost cried, too.

Right then, she realized that everyone had been leaning on Livie way too hard. Herself included.

Livie was the only one who knew what was going on around here. Livie fielded all the questions, ran half the house for Mari still, and was now having to stand stoic against her baby sister. She was holding up marvelously, and she shouldn't have to.

Behind Sophie's back, where the girl couldn't tell, Mari said,

"Livie, I'm going to find a way for the two of us to go out for ice cream tomorrow. You've earned it."

Olivia's smile shone just a little brighter.

~

On the fourth day, it happened.

"Sophie!" Mari yelled with both her hands and her voice. "Yes!"

It was probably the wrong thing to say, since the little girl had signed a vehement "no!" but Mariliz was excited beyond measure.

"Sophie, I'm so proud of you." She signed it as she smiled and hugged the girl close. Probably the kid was confused. Mari had asked her a question, and for the very first time, Sophie answered.

She'd answered, "No!"

Her chubby little fingers had made a chicken-like movement out in front of her with a snap. Mariliz recognized that snap—it was the same one she used when she was making a sharp negative to the girl. But right now, she couldn't be prouder. "Good job, Sophie!"

Though she was signing continuously, exposing the girl to language where before she had none, she was making a point to sign "yes," "no," and Sophie's name as often as possible. So every other sentence or so, she used the name sign for Sophie that she and Olivia had come up with. Mari already had a name sign, she'd had it since she learned the language as a kid, but the two girls had needed them.

It was a badge of honor to have your name sign bestowed upon you, so Mari had named Olivia in a bit of ceremony that the eight-year-old could appreciate. She'd almost done it over ice cream the night before, then decided that the bigger sister needed some time with no references to all that was going on in the house. They didn't talk about her absent parents or her time-consuming little sister at all.

But when they got home, they did the small ritual, with Sophie in attendance even if she didn't understand. Mari then asked Olivia to name Sophie, and they did it all again.

Olivia gave Sophie a "hug" name, while Mari had given Olivia a name reflecting her curls. Both girls seemed happy with the selections and the naming ceremony. Sophie was even seeming to learn her own name. With both Mari and Olivia signing it to her all the time, it helped.

They held up toys and signed the corresponding words as though she was an infant.

Mari had expected her to sign back right away. Sophie had no language, but she had better motor skills than a baby. She played blocks with reasonable dexterity. Her physical capabilities didn't seem delayed. Mari was watching. She scoured the internet for information. Her education gave her a starting point, but she'd never worked with a kid who didn't have language; she'd only read about them.

Once they got going, they would often pick it up like gangbusters. Mari had hopes for Sophie.

The "no" was the first sign she'd seen the girl make. She'd been timid about even pointing at things, which wasn't normal for non-lingual kids. It disturbed her that Sophie didn't even try to communicate other than temper tantrums.

She hugged the little girl for her negative answer and tried to be as positive as she could be. Sophie didn't hug her back, but Mariliz had hopes for that too. Without language, she couldn't really tell Sophie she'd done well, So Mari already had small marshmallows in her pocket. She'd discovered the first day the little girl had a soft spot for them. Mari smiled and handed one over and watched it disappear.

Sophie held her hand out for another.

She looked wary, her happiness at getting the first one already gone.

Why did she look afraid? Mari couldn't tell. But she wasn't handing out the treats for standard generic gestures. She wanted language.

She pulled another one out of her pocket and signed "marshmallow." Then she ate it. She wasn't a fan, but this was important. She was being careful about putting stock in just anything, but she was hoping the first word was a gateway. It was possible for Sophie to have five words by tomorrow.

Sophie didn't say anything.

Mari pulled out another one, signed the word again, and waited. Still Sophie stared up at her, wide-eyed. Getting down into a squat, down closer to Sophie's height, Mari held the candy-colored puff out again. Signed again.

Nothing.

She reached out for Sophie's hand, to help mold her small fingers, but Sophie pulled her hand back. Fighting a frown, Mari forced a smile. Sophie loved marshmallows, but seemed afraid to sign for it.

"Do you want this? Marshmallow?" Mari signed and spoke together.

Sophie watched her hands, not her face. As the language began to gel, as her brain started processing it as language, she would watch faces.

This time Sophie raised her left hand and signed, "No."

Well, *shit.*

Mari almost laughed. The girl said "no." If Mari handed it over, she would be changing the meaning of the word. But she wanted to reward Sophie for using a sign. She offered a hug.

With her arms around the little girl, she looked up and spotted the clock on the wall. *Ack!* They had to leave to get Olivia, and getting Sophie into the car could be a challenge.

"Let's go get Olivia." Mari signed.

Sophie stared blank-faced again, leaving Mari feeling almost like she was signing into an empty room. Still, she kept at it. Sophie had signed. One small word, but it was a breakthrough.

It took five minutes to get the blocks out of Sophie's hands without screaming. They barely made it. Olivia was one of the last three kids waiting when they arrived. It felt wrong to celebrate Sophie's word when she was late getting Olivia. Poor kid. The household revolved around her younger sister. Right then, Mari decided that she was going to start putting Sophie to bed a half hour earlier, and keep Olivia up thirty minutes later.

She made dinner while Olivia worked on homework and Sophie played by banging pans together. Olivia moved upstairs to her room to work. It was bad enough dealing with a kid who liked the noise. Sophie liked the feel of the pans ringing. She was ear-splitting, but Mari didn't want to complain. Yes, Olivia definitely needed some extra time just to herself.

It occurred to Mari that she was taking some liberties with the girls, but she wasn't letting it bother her. Just like she wasn't letting it bother her that Bridget Beaumont still hadn't called her back.

What kind of mother left their kid with a new sitter twenty-four seven and didn't even call to check on them? Mariliz had left four messages on the phone, though she didn't know if any of them had gotten through.

She'd been on cruises before and the cell service sucked at sea a lot of times. Still, she'd called in regularly to let her parents know she was okay. She didn't even have kids—small kids—she'd left on shore. Mari checked the phone call log religiously; Bridget's number never rang the house.

Mari chose to believe that Bridget was getting updated from Alex, but he wasn't calling her back, either. She was leaving messages each night, telling him what they were up to. She would tell him in tonight's voicemail that she was moving the girls' bedtimes. He could protest if he wanted. It was ballsy, but she was feeling bold.

For a man who told her, "Call me Alex" he sure didn't seem to want her to actually call him.

She didn't even tell him about Sophie's breakthrough. Let him come home and be surprised.

CHAPTER 6

A lex rubbed his forehead. He was probably getting a sinus infection. It felt like a drill was pressing into his head at high speed.

Then again, it may be just the normal headache he got going home.

In the beginning, Bridget had been waiting for him. They'd burned hot once.

He would come home and they would have fantastic reunion sex. When they were first married, they lived in his parents' basement apartment. Bridget hadn't minded. But it had been hard to stay quiet, and they moved out pretty quickly.

He was a musician. She'd thrown her undies up on stage and the red lace wrapped around his drumstick mid-air. He'd been caught as surely as the stick was. He'd missed two beats. But he hadn't missed any after the show. It seemed like a fairy-tale romance for a drummer.

Looking back, he didn't know if they got married that night because they were so in love or because it was Vegas and they were enthralled by the idea that they could.

For so long, he hadn't questioned their story. Bridget loved him. They got a house. He bought her a better car. And they burned hot. They had Olivia. They moved to a bigger house in a better neighborhood. Things cooled a bit with a baby, but Alex had expected that.

He looked out the windows as the bus pulled into Nashville. He couldn't count the number of times he and the guys had rolled into town on this bus. And that was after an uncountable number of times on their first bus.

The town was dark around him, so he couldn't see much. His own reflection stared back at him and he didn't really like it. It was normal for them to come in during the pre-dawn hours; they always had. At first it was just him and JD anxious to get back to waiting wives. Craig and TJ had been getting some while they toured, but he and JD had been waiting. They wanted to drive through the night and get in.

Then Craig married Shay and TJ was totally outvoted. TJ found Norah while he was recuperating from his accident, and they were still touring extra to make up for several months of missed dates during TJ's recovery. So the consensus was to get home to wives and kids.

But Alex wasn't anxious to get back now. He and Bridget had burned out.

Every couple had their breaking point, he'd decided. Sophie had been theirs. Bridget made it a year before she cracked. She screamed, she yelled, she basically acted like Sophie. Alex always went on tour, he always had a break. And she said she needed one too.

Bridget went on vacation then. She'd come back refreshed, ready to start over. But they still didn't burn bright.

She went on vacation again. And again. And now he couldn't count the days she'd actually been with them.

Now he was on the bus, almost home to his two daughters. He would call Olivia more—at least once!—next time they went out. Despite deciding to do it several days ago, he hadn't picked up the phone. He told himself the girls needed time to adjust to the new nanny without him interrupting.

JD came toward the front of the bus just then, dropping his bag at his feet with a thunk and grabbing a rail for stability while he stood. "Can't wait to be home."

Though he was committed to sticking to his promise to be a better father, he still felt like crap. Alex nodded and faked a smile. "It'll be good to be back!"

He wondered if his friend saw the lie.

Mari looked up from where she stood at the kitchen island. Sophie didn't. She was still concentrating on banging her pans together, a noise Mariliz had gotten used to.

She hadn't heard him come in. As he was standing to her left, toward the side of the house, she was guessing that he'd entered from the garage and through the mudroom door. Mari loved the irony that there was a mudroom in this house—she didn't think there was any mud in the neighborhood.

The man stared at her for a moment, his sandy brown hair a bit long, old t-shirt clinging to muscles that probably got a great workout over a drum set. Behind him, on the bottom step, sat a worn-out black nylon duffel bag. Something about him looked worn-out, too.

Mariliz Jennings didn't care.

"Mr. Beaumont! . . . Alex." She corrected. "I wasn't expecting you for a few more hours."

Good, she was free at last, and she opened her mouth to say so, but he beat her to it.

"Where's Olivia?" He looked at the back of Sophie's head, but she was engrossed in her work. "Is she up?"

"With this noise? Yes. She's upstairs getting ready."

Even as she spoke the words, the eight-year-old was jumping

merrily down the steps. Dressed for school, but still barefoot, she flung herself into her father's arms for a huge hug. He swung her around until she squealed, then set her down with a pat. "You still have to get ready. You still have school today."

"I know, Daddy!" She bounded back up the stairs, hugs dispensed and her world righted when Mariliz hadn't quite realized it was wrong. But what did anyone expect, throwing her to the lions like they had? She'd done her best, and if she still had a job when she got back this evening, she'd be grateful.

Smiling, she decided to ignore all the seventeen thousand things she needed to talk to this man about in favor of the one pressing issue she had. "Now that you're here, I'll transfer the carseats and you can take Olivia to school."

He blinked at her as though the thought had not crossed his mind. His mouth opened, but then he seemed to think better of it. His hand began a gesture, but quit mid-air. She noticed he still hadn't hugged his younger daughter, or even gotten her attention. Mari did it herself.

Tapping the flat of her hand on the counter in front of the little girl, she grabbed her attention, then pointed a sweep up and back. Saying, *look over there.*

Sophie did, but she didn't move. It was Alex who stepped closer and hugged his younger daughter and rubbed her head. Not the vigorous welcome he'd gotten from Olivia. Sophie barely reacted at all, and Mari fought the frown that wanted to come.

Something wasn't spot-on here. It was likely it was Sophie. The girl wasn't functioning on all cylinders. She hadn't wanted to sign. "No" was useful, and she used it frequently, which was actually age appropriate, Mari noted. But getting her to sign other words was like pulling teeth. On the other hand, Mari had told her, "Go get your bag," the other day, and Sophie had gone to do it. So she understood far more than she was saying.

She and Sophie were still feeling their way around things. It seemed that after two-and-a-half years, her father hadn't found his footing with the child either. That was what bothered Mariliz.

Again, item number seventeen thousand and one that she didn't have time for right now.

Alex Beaumont opened his mouth. "Can you take Olivia to school? I've been up since God-knows-when."

He'd just gotten home. He'd been gone at least ten days. He didn't want to drive his daughter to school? Then again, who was she to judge? Her own father had a nine-to-five job. Maybe Alex coming home was commonplace, and sometimes he was tired. She tried to be flexible. After all, she already planned on the morning loop to drop Olivia off at school.

"Okay, but when I get back, I need to head out. I need all the rest of the day off." She was going to stand firm on that, despite the panic she saw blooming on his face. What kind of father was he?

"Surely you—"

Holding up a hand, palm toward him—she was gesture prone, go figure—she cut him off. "No, I can't. I arrived here for an evening meeting and was abandoned with two children. I'm supposed to work an average of five days a week with evenings and weekends off. I've worked twenty-four/seven for nine days straight. I'm taking today off and you can give me extra days off or hazard pay."

Her heart pounded.

She'd never done anything like that before. If Reynold wanted his party planned, she planned it. If he came in at the last minute and said her colors were stupid, she changed them. If he didn't like the menu, she fixed it. Mostly, Mariliz Jennings did what was expected. But now she was divorced and working a nanny job to make ends meet. She'd also discovered that being a wife or a nanny was the only thing she was apparently qualified to do, and she wasn't going to be a wife again.

She couldn't afford to lose this job, but she was going to damn well stand up for herself for once in her life. Besides, Alex looked shell-shocked. She hated to take advantage of it, but she did it anyway.

Making the decision, he nodded briskly, then said softly, "Hazard pay."

Her eyebrows arched. Was he so afraid of his own kids? Even Sophie the Terror wasn't that bad. She reacted well to being ignored. In fact, she acted attention starved, so Mari had been playing with her, including her in tasks, praising her whenever she could, and turning her back on bad behavior. It was working. Sophie wasn't perfect, she would always be noisy, but she wasn't a complete terror anymore. *Hazard pay, ha!*

First step taken. Hazard pay meant she wasn't getting fired. Mari took another one. "I'll be back tomorrow at seven a.m. to get Olivia to school."

He nodded. The man still looked shell-shocked. She wanted to feel sorry for him. Okay, she *did* feel sorry for him, but not enough to give up her day off. She had an old apartment to clean out. A key to turn in. A life of her own to freakin' live.

"Come on, Olivia." She hollered up the stairs. It was a routine of sorts. She left the older sister on her own for a while, but called her for breakfast each morning. Today, toaster waffles with peanut butter. If Mr. Drummer there wanted to complain, he could make pancakes himself.

He didn't say anything. Just kissed Olivia on her head when she seated herself at the bar, and rubbed Sophie's head as he passed by. Olivia reacted. Sophie didn't.

"I'm going to take a nap." He mumbled. "Knock on my door when you bring Sophie back after dropping off Olivia." Alex picked up the bag off the steps and was halfway up before he turned around and really engaged. "Unless you found a daycare for her?"

"No." Mariliz looked up the steps at him. He looked so

hopeful not to have to interact with his youngest. Curiouser and curiouser. After the first mention, it hadn't even really crossed Mari's mind to find a daycare. Who would care for a deaf girl who didn't speak or understand? How would she possibly interact well with other kids there when no one could communicate? Normal two-year-olds were just learning how to talk and say what they needed. No wonder Sophie was always getting asked to leave.

Alex looked defeated as he nodded and headed up the stairs.

Not my problem, Mari reminded herself as he disappeared, but it kind of was. She smiled at the two girls. This time when she told Olivia to get her things, she signed it. Sophie was watching. Mari wanted to expose the younger girl to as much language as possible, which meant getting others in the house to sign.

Nina had graciously learned "yes," "no," and "pizza" already. Olivia was becoming quite the talker. But Sophie needed everything she could get. So Olivia agreed to sign whenever she was around her younger sister. Mari argued that it would be hard to have people talk over you and not understand. They added the signs for "kitten" and "bowl" to Olivia's American Sign Language vocabulary on the drive in. Not an easy task when the teacher was the driver, too. Mariliz took advantage of the stoplights.

She was about to be free for the first time in nine days, and she didn't know who to call.

CHAPTER 7

Alex watched as Sophie entered the room first, a booster style carseat clutched in her arms. It was Olivia's—she still wasn't ten years old and hadn't hit the requisite weight. Not that he could remember what that was.

Sophie looked like a cherub. Soft, fat, mahogany ringlets tumbled around her head and she turned to look back up at the new nanny.

Mariliz Jennings. He reminded himself of her name. He'd repeated it many times over the past week and a half. He couldn't afford to lose another one. The agency had even told him that they wouldn't send anyone else, not after extending their three strikes policy to five for him.

Each nanny they sent stayed a shorter time than the one before. The last one having lasted only one week before leaving him hanging three days before a tour.

He'd left Bridget a phone message and an email, telling her she had to get home. The girls needed her. She didn't reply. So he was on the hook to Mariliz Jennings.

One, Ms. Jennings had already lasted two days longer than the previous live-in. So hazard pay was hardly an issue. He'd pay her hazard rate all the time if she stayed. Especially if she got Sophie to be reasonable and even cooperate—like she was doing now, carrying something. Not screaming.

Two, he had not expected Ms. Mariliz Jennings to be beautiful. The agency seemed to favor older, staid nannies. He just assumed the same here. Mariliz looked like her name, now that he thought of it—a little exotic and like she'd roll off the tongue.

Shit. He had to put that thought away. He was married. Wasn't he?

As he watched, the woman, whose own hands were full, motioned with the carseat she carried for Sophie to put down the other one.

To his astonishment, Sophie obeyed.

He thought about asking her what kind of spell she had cast, but then he thought maybe she didn't know that Sophie was awful. Hazard pay it was then. She was a miracle worker.

She kissed Sophie on the head and then looked up at him from where she knelt down in front of his little girl. "Mr. Beaumont, I have to go. I'll be back tomorrow morning."

"Seven?"

She nodded at him. He could do this.

The woman started to go, but Sophie grabbed her legs. Mariliz Jennings with her straight nose, high arched brows, and full lips that Bridget would have been jealous of, could have looked snotty. But she smiled at his daughter, leaned down and gave her a hug before extracting herself. She was out the door before he could ask what she was putting in the water.

He watched the woman as she disappeared out the door. She had a nice ass. He didn't berate himself for the thought. He was faithful to his wife in deed, and in his speech, if he wasn't always perfect in his thoughts, could he really be blamed?

Two hours later, he was eying the information packet the agency had sent him. They'd sent it to the house actually, so he hadn't seen it before today. Frankie had looked it over and told him it was fine. But she disliked kids and probably would have told him anyone shy of an ax-murderer was okay. Alex liked to believe she at least had that line.

Skimming the three pages revealed that Mariliz Jennings was single, but divorced. Her car was listed, so he could decide if it was safe for the children to travel in it. He hadn't made that decision, but it seemed she had a Lexus. Her address was on the other side of town, in a not-so-great section. The two didn't go together. Her clothing looked plenty upscale—more so than the previous women they'd hired. He couldn't make heads or tails of her.

Then Sophie interrupted by screaming again. Her head was thrown back, her vocal chords making a noise only someone who couldn't hear would even consider making. Alex wanted to cover his ears, but didn't think that was good parenting.

Hell, whatever he was doing wasn't good parenting. He wanted to call the nanny and ask her what she'd done and why had it worn off? He didn't call her. Couldn't risk offending her, sending her running.

Two hours later, after forcing his child into a clean diaper and praying that the miracle worker would be able to potty train her, Alex tried to feed Sophie lunch. He sliced the crusts off the sandwich, not sure if she even liked that, but thinking it wouldn't hurt. He cut it into tiny pieces so she could pick them up one by one. And he made the mistake of giving them all to her.

Sophie grabbed half the sandwich and stuffed all the pieces into her mouth at once.

Shit. Alex's heart raced. What if she choked? How could he get them out?

He could hold her down and put his fingers in her mouth and dig the food out. She would probably bite him, but that was less concerning than the thought that her struggles would make her much more likely to choke. Instead of acting, he sat there, terrified, while she chewed like a chipmunk.

He grabbed the few remaining pieces of sandwich off her tray in a preemptive strike, and watched with the chunks leaving traces of peanut butter on his palms while he tried to keep breathing. So far, she was okay. Happy even.

Her mouth barely moved, her cheeks were so full, but her whiskey colored eyes looked up at him, watching. He forced a smiled at the girl who looked so very much like him. With her milder coloring, Olivia looked like Bridget. Sophie, on the other hand, was his—his coloring, his curls, his darker skin, his dimple.

Not that he could see that now with her cheeks all puffed out. She'd almost finished it, and as he watched, she swallowed and grinned at him. His heart melted. He loved her so much. Sophie so rarely smiled, and even more rarely smiled at him. He didn't know how to change that.

Then she smacked her hand on her tray, demanding something. He didn't know what. No one ever did. He handed her one piece of the sandwich, then set the others on a paper towel while he stood to wash the peanut butter and jelly smears from his hand now that the danger had passed.

When he turned back, she was smacking the tray again, just as his phone rang. Handing Sophie another piece, he answered it, just barely catching the name. The catch in his heart at operating some semblance of peace treaty with his daughter was fierce.

"Bridget!" He almost shouted it and tried not to calculate the number of days since he'd heard from her.

"Hey, baby." Her voice was warm, then it wasn't. "Ugh. The noise."

Sophie was squealing and smacking the tray. He handed her another piece of peanut butter and jelly sandwich. She quieted for a moment. "Sophie's eating lunch. When are you coming home?"

"Oh, we're not even to Acapulco yet." She sounded like he was being stupid.

"Are you really on a cruise? Get off and come back." He was exhausted from his trip, from having Sophie screaming at him all day, from being the only one here to deal with things, from his life.

"I can't. I'm sure it would put me on some watchlist to abandon the trip. But I'll come by when I get finished."

"When is that, Bridge?" His palm rubbed his forehead, the roughness of his hand at least normal in all of this. He ignored the statement that his wife would "come by" her own home.

"I don't know. I'll look up the dates and get back to you."

He hoped she at least meant it. It wasn't going to happen—he knew that much. She'd forget, or maybe she never intended to do things she told him she would. Alex changed the subject. "The new nanny is working out."

"I heard. She called me and left several messages."

"Did you call her back, help her out?" Even as the words left his mouth, he wondered—*could* Bridget even help her out? His wife hadn't really been a mother in well over a year. Then again, he'd been a pretty crappy father this past year, too.

He had to change that. Sophie banged on the tray and yelled at decibels high enough to hurt his eardrums. Even as Bridget complained about the sound, he got down at Sophie's level and said, "No. I need those ears."

Alex didn't shake his head. He said the words out loud, like he'd been taught, knowing that if he just mouthed them, they might appear wrong and wouldn't help his daughter learn. "Sorry, Bridge, I was talking to Sophie."

"How's she doing?" The raw hope in her voice broke his heart.

"Same as always." He didn't tell his wife that the new nanny seemed to have tamed his child. He didn't want to feed her false hopes. He'd done that more than once before. Even now, he wasn't sure if he truly believed Sophie was improving or if he just wanted to believe it. Either way, Bridget would come home, try for a while, and crack under the pressure again.

"Well, the sun is beautiful here." He waited for her to suggest he join her, but she hadn't said that for a while now. He tried not to count the months.

He tried a second time with his wife. "Did you call the nanny back?"

"You did, didn't you?"

"Yeah, I did." It was the story of the past year-and-a-half. He did it. He arranged the nannies and handled his wife's breakdowns. He handled Sophie as best he could when Bridget quit visiting doctors to get diagnosis after diagnosis.

She was silent now on the phone for a moment before her voice jolted to life. "Oh, they're calling us back to the boat. I wanted to talk while I had a signal."

"Okay, go have fun." He knew she hated that. The insinuation that she was out having fun when she was supposedly just as broken inside as the rest of them. Only she was broken on a cruise ship.

He didn't say *I love you* and neither did she. With a deft movement of his thumb Alex flipped the phone off and stood up to go to the fridge. His bare foot stepped into something squishy and, as he looked down, he spotted all the little squares of sandwich on the floor.

Sophie had demanded them then thrown them. She banged on the tray while he limped away, trying not to spread the mess any farther. Sophie screamed and he calmly washed the bottom of his foot while he ignored his daughter.

In two hours, they would go pick up Olivia and that would help. And how sad was that?

CHAPTER 8

Mari folded clothes into a box she'd wrangled out of the back of her closet. It had only been a few months since she'd moved into this crap apartment, and she'd kept the boxes, thinking she wouldn't be here long. She'd been right about that, if not about the difficulty of finding a job or the fact that she'd get an eviction notice before she moved out.

The clothes were too expensive for her to pack into cardboard or to wear to work with a two-year-old, but for now they were what she had. Her laptop was already at the Beaumonts'—or at her new place as she should probably call it. The new suite had a door to the backyard and a small patio. She could enter around the side of the house if she wasn't on duty. Or her friends could come in.

Friends? It was almost a laugh. She'd call her cousin and see if Missy was free tonight. The rest of her friends had been in the brunch crowd and loved her until the papers were signed and her money was gone. Only Jenny had come through and seen her twice since then. But it was hard letting Jenny pay for everything and even that friendship was slipping away. Mariliz wasn't upset. Jenny was nice, just a good person, but what did they have in common? Not much once Mari's husband and house were gone.

Tired of packing, and wondering what she was going to do with half the stuff, she picked up the phone. "Missy? It's Mariliz."

"Oh gosh, Lize, it's been ages. How's the divorce going?"

"It's gone. I have a new job, and I have tonight off. Want to head out and catch up?" She was grinning at the warmth in her cousin's voice. Mari was the one who'd been an idiot. She'd grown up middle class just like Reynold had, but once he'd made some money, he'd forgotten that. He'd wanted her to forget, too. He'd even complained about his parents' house and their fixed income. Mari had let him. But here was Missy, calling her *Lize*, again, being decent even though she herself hadn't kept up the connection as well as she should have.

"You know I want to go out. Dinner, too?"

"Honestly, I'm free all day. Well, I'm packing." Mariliz sighed, happy now but then remembering the job at hand. She would have been upset to spend her night off alone. "That's something I wanted to ask you. I have some stuff here that I need to store. Do you know a good place?"

"Like a self-store? There's one down the street, but honestly, they were too expensive for the small amount I had when I looked into it two apartments ago." Missy seemed to be thinking. "What did you have in mind?"

Another sigh. "I don't really know—three or four medium boxes? I think I'll take my sound system, and my coffee maker, but I don't need the bed anymore. Or my dresser. So maybe one of those rental units?"

"You need help? I'm off today."

That was Missy. *I'm here, tell me what you need.* "I'll buy you pizza."

Mari had it ordered before her cousin showed up. She was glad she hadn't been such a terrible friend that Missy didn't know where she lived—she'd been by once in the short time Mari rented here. She'd consoled Mari through the lawyer meetings one day before the papers were done. And Mari knew what Missy liked on her pizza.

As Mariliz stood with her hands on her hips and surveyed what was left of the crappy little apartment, she decided that she needed to cultivate better friendships. The ones she'd had, the ones she'd counted on, dissolved faster than sugar when things got tough. Missy was still here, though. At least she'd done that much right.

When her cousin arrived, the workload cut in half. Things were boxed and labeled in Missy's expert hand. "Where does this one go, Lize?"

Missy stood over an open box with a marker in one hand and a slice of pizza in the other. Mari peered inside at the clothing, purses, and about seven bagged pairs of heels. "Those go with me."

"We're about done, you know."

"Yeah. Do you want the coffee pot?" Mari ventured out there, she didn't want to pay to store what Missy might use. "I'm taking the single cup brewer and the toaster oven, but you can have the regular toaster, too."

"That'd be good. Mine is on the fritz." Missy nodded. "I'll put the coffee pot to use. I've got a guest or two sometimes these days."

"Or *two*?" Mari lifted her eyebrows.

"He has a son. Kid's only ten, but he likes to drink 'coffee' with us in the morning." She made air quotes. "It's mostly milk, but his dad gives him a splash."

With a grin, Mari picked up the Mr. Coffee and presented it to her cousin. "You will see far more good with this than I."

They made a box for Missy, including some of the heels Mari was not going to get to wear again before they went out of fashion. Half of the straight skirts she owned went, too. They'd fit Missy and she had a desk job where she could use them. Mariliz sure wasn't going to wear a fitted Vera Wang skirt near Sophie.

"Should we take these to the new digs?" Missy ventured as she folded the pizza box into the last bag for recycling. Everything that could be cleared was.

"I was going to haul it tomorrow morning, but we could. I have my own entrance."

She was thinking she'd have to come back for the bed and dresser, and calculated the cost to store it. "Do you want a bed and dresser? Maybe in exchange for keeping three to four medium sized boxes in your unit?"

"I was hoping you'd ask. The son, Tony, doesn't have a bed at my place."

"Consider it yours."

They worked out details for Missy to come back with the boyfriend and a truck, and Mariliz handed over the keys, realizing this meant she was sleeping at the Beaumonts' tonight.

They took Missy's station wagon to the other side of town because it was bigger, and on the way Mari filled her in. "I'm a nanny now for a family with two girls. The mother's out right now, but the dad is a drummer for a country band."

"Someone I've heard of?" Missy pulled off at the exit.

"Probably. It's Wilder."

"Holy shit, girl! You work for Alex Beaumont? Way to bury the lede." The car swerved.

"Eyes on the road, miss I-have-a-boyfriend. And he's married. With two kids and a nanny." Mariliz shook her head. She'd never understood the whole swooning over rock stars thing. "Besides, we're going in my side door. You probably won't see him."

They pulled into the neighborhood then, and Mari spotted his SUV passing them on the other side. She checked her watch. "That was just him."

"*What?* I missed him." Missy's shoulders slumped.

"He's taking his youngest with him to go pick up the older girl from school." She hadn't been able to see his face.

"Oh well." Missy took the turns as Mari called them and they parked as far to the side in the driveway as they could. They hauled bags first, Mari hanging the peeking hangers right on the rod. She could sort it tomorrow.

The boxes were harder. The two women had to grab either side of them to get them into the car, and now they knew they had to do the same in reverse. This time, it involved a walk on a stone paver path around to the back of the house. The walkway was relatively narrow—clearly for the help—and they fumbled their way along. When they dumped the last one onto the bed Mari laughed. "We are so not professionals. Let's go check the car for stragglers."

They pulled the last few small bags from the car and Missy suggested they at least unpack the boxes. They were arranging the few appliances along the small counter when the knock came at the door to her suite.

Pulling it open, Mari found Alex Beaumont standing there. "Oh, hi."

"Saw a car in the driveway and wanted to be sure it was you." He looked past her at Missy.

Despite the jeans and the dust of moving, Missy smiled and strode up behind her. "Come on, Lize, introduce me to your new boss."

"Lize?" Alex asked, eyebrows climbing.

She shrugged. "Mariliz—Lize, you know. This is my cousin, Missy, she's helping me get my things moved in."

His head popped back. "You haven't moved in yet?"

"No. I worked nine days straight. Unless Sophie and Olivia haul boxes better than it would appear they do, it wasn't happening before today." She offered a half-chagrinned smile. So he wasn't a dick, just clueless.

Seeming to get himself together better, he held out a hand to her cousin. "Nice to meet you, Missy."

Mari let him know that she would be staying in the house that night, but she wouldn't be on duty until seven a.m. He was nodding in return, clearly, finally understanding she had things to do that didn't involve his family, when Sophie let out a discordant scream in the background.

He winced. "That's my cue."

With that, he was off, and Mari closed the door and turned to find Missy staring, dumbstruck at having met a star. Then her cousin shook it off and said, "What was that noise?"

"That was Sophie." Given the look on Missy's face, Mari knew she had some explaining to do.

Three hours later, they had draft beers in hand and chicken fingers on the table. Luckily, between the work and the bar and hanging with her cousin, Mariliz knew she'd be worn out and sleep well.

There hadn't been time with the unpacking and changing to go out to tell her what was going on. So now Missy pointed at her with a chicken finger. "Okay, Lize, what's going on with the new job?"

She had to laugh. "You know how I have that useless degree in psychology and languages? Well, who knew there was a job for me out there?" She took a bite of a French fry that had to be sprinkled with a mixture of salt, spices, and crack cocaine, then ate another and another, before managing to talk again. "The younger daughter is deaf. Probably learning disabled, too."

"Really?" Missy was leaning forward, ready as always for the gossip. She plucked a fry from the basket. "Do go on."

"The older one, Olivia, is bright, charming, well-behaved and more. But Sophie doesn't speak."

"Duh. You just said she's deaf. Maybe you lay off the beer." Missy pulled the glass away, but Mari wrangled it back without spilling. They were each limiting to one and she was damn well going to drink it.

"No, she doesn't even sign. No language at all that I can figure. She's really slow, but I think she's mostly just frustrated. I'm already seeing an improvement." She took a sip of her reclaimed beer.

"Don't do it, Lize." Missy gazed at her sadly. "You're such a dreamer. You thought Reynold was a good guy, that marriage would make him better. Hell, you learned a language almost nobody speaks, just because. You probably can't fix this kid."

"Well, I'd rather try and fail than just sit back and let Sophie be miserable." The beer didn't taste so good with that thought.

"Do you have any idea who you work for?" Missy squinted at her.

"Sure, Alex and Bridget Beaumont."

"Have you seen Miss Bridget?" Missy had stopped eating, she looked serious. Then, as she saw Mari about to answer, she spoke again. "Oh, shit. You have no clue, Lize."

She pulled out her phone and started pulling up pictures. She spent a moment pulling up a tabloid on her phone. Then she scrolled to the stories furthest down, but when she held up the screen, the image shocked Mari.

CHAPTER 9

M ari pulled herself from sleep with an inhuman effort. She'd tossed and turned all night and it felt like she hadn't slept at all until around five-thirty. Just half an hour before she had to get up.

She had to shower. She needed it after yesterday. Last night she'd fallen face-first onto the bed, grateful beyond measure that Missy suggested they unpack. The boxes had been sliced and laid flat and shoved against the back wall of the closet.

At the time, it was just a place to put them until she could take them to the recycling center. She didn't think her new employers would appreciate the big boxes sprouting out of their weekly trash pickup. Now, though, it seemed like a good idea to have them at hand, even if Missy was right and she was already getting too attached to her charges.

Drying off after the shower, she tried to keep her thoughts focused, but they wandered to the pictures Missy had showed her. Bridget in a bikini, looking thin and tan and fabulous on a beach. She also looked very alone. The caption had read, "Where's Alex Beaumont?" and there was an insinuation that he was out on tour while his wife vacationed.

It seemed now that the insinuation was correct. There was an older piece—also buried in the fine print slush—about Bridget checking into a spa for a month. But the questions there were about Bridget's health. Apparently, she'd been treated for the famous celebrity ailment of 'exhaustion' just a month before. Was the spa really a spa? Or maybe a treatment center?

There wasn't too much out there from before TJ Hewlitt had gotten married. His wedding to Norah Davidson barely two years before and a subsequent jump in album sales made the band even more famous. TJ and Norah were followed by the paparazzi occasionally, mostly those pictures just commented on how happy the two looked and speculated at Norah possibly being pregnant. Gossip—that's all it was.

But since then, the cameras had turned to the other band members a little more, too. So, while she never made front page or a big story, a search of the name "Bridget Beaumont" turned up enough tabloid musings to turn Mariliz's stomach.

Putting her one cup of coffee together and waiting while the machine hummed, she sat at her small table and thumbed through a magazine she borrowed from the end table in the living room.

She admired hairstyles that were too fancy to wear anywhere she would go now. She looked at shoes that would never fare well at the local playground she intended to try out later this week. She thought Olivia didn't play with other kids enough, and Sophie didn't at all. It might be Mari on the jungle gym with them until they made friends. She read more, stories about men dating in the real world and women starting businesses.

None of it applied to Nanny-Mariliz sitting in the not-that-big suite off the kitchen of the rich and famous. Still, as she tossed the magazine, she felt more content than she had in a while. It was Friday. Tomorrow she had the girls all day, and she intended to take them to the library. Sunday she was off and she was considering just lazing in the small apartment and reading, hitting a coffee shop when she needed to get out. Maybe a craft store to find a hobby.

The coffee maker beeped, reminding her to turn it off, and she rinsed her cup. Six-forty-five. She'd show up early to work. As she turned the knob, Mari thought, *you can't beat the commute!*

The main house was silent, but she flipped on the light in the kitchen and started a pot of coffee. Didn't she just do this? But Nina would have a cup when she came in. Alex might drink it. Worst case scenario, she'd suffer another one herself. Pulling out packets of oatmeal, she started heating water and setting out Olivia's lunch. She wondered at what age Olivia should start doing these things for herself. Then she wondered if she would be here for that decision, and if she'd even be a part of it. It was sobering to think she was the children's hired help. She wouldn't last too long at this if that were truly the case. Still she would have a work history, and she had a much nicer roof over her head these days. She'd figure it out.

She made a peanut butter and honey sandwich and bagged some carrots by the time she saw the minute hand hit the top of the clock. Heading upstairs, she knocked softly on Olivia's door. "Time to get up, honey."

The endearment came so easily. Olivia was a doll. "I'm up already."

Of course she was. She had an alarm clock, and she set it and checked it each night. Mariliz wondered if the girl had been this responsible all along, or if it had happened when her sister was born and her mother checked out.

Because that's what it looked like from the tabloid pictures Missy pulled out the night before. Bridget Beaumont was constantly on vacation. Or at a spa. Or getting treatment for "exhaustion" that she couldn't possibly have because she didn't *do* anything.

Turning away and shaking the detrimental thoughts loose

—what did she really *know, after all?—*Mari knocked on Sophie's door before sighing in disgust. *You just knocked on a deaf kid's door, Mari.* She turned the knob and entered the dark room.

Sleeping, her curls tumbling around her head, Sophie looked like an angel. While she could be one, she could also be a beastie. She was butt up, her thumb in her mouth, and Mari hated to wake her but wanted to establish a schedule. No one had given her one—well, no one besides Olivia. The eight-year-old shouldn't have that kind of power or responsibility.

First, she went back to the door and blinked the lights twice, leaving them off. Then, putting her hand on the little girl's back, she shook her gently. The lights should be about the same as calling to a hearing sleeper. Sure enough, Sophie blinked, coming awake at a reasonable speed.

The little girl stood up in the crib she was getting way too big for and held her arms out to Mari.

"Oh, good morning, baby." She hugged the little girl tight and then picked her up, setting her out onto the floor and praying the whole day could go this well. "Shall we change your diaper?"

She spoke and signed all the time in front of Sophie.

Sophie signed back. "Diaper."

"Yes! Good work! Diaper." Just like any mom or dad, she was inordinately surprised at the word. It was word number eight. Soon the cascade would come. Even if she was only mentally one-year-old, even if the cascade was slower than it was for other kids, it would come. Mari fought to keep her smile bright —what if it didn't? That would mean Sophie had more problems than she even expected. She was going to ask Alex about it today.

Mind made up, she signed her way through changing Sophie's diaper. She now gave the girl items to hold, naming each as they worked. Including Sophie kept her out of trouble and made her happy. Win-win. They walked across the hall and knocked on Olivia's door again. "Let's go down for breakfast."

Peeking into the hall, dressed far too adorably for mud or trees or anything else Mari thought an eight-year-old should associate with, Livie bounded into the hallway. Of course she was a morning person. "Oatmeal?"

Sophie liked the kind with the dinosaur eggs. They were sugar-coated and the coating dissolved, revealing dinosaur candies. Olivia ate the same kind in solidarity with her sister. So Mari poured hot water over the portions and handed each girl a spoon, watching Sophie carefully so she didn't burn herself. Mari signed, "Hot, hot" and pointed to the oatmeal.

Sophie nodded.

Did she understand?

When the little girl had revealed all her dinosaur candies, she blew on the cereal. She was cooling it down. She understood that the food was hot, maybe she understood the sign. Maybe she just remembered. That was the thing about language, psychologically, there were a lot of things that looked like it, but weren't real language. Kids often said "Dada" because they were rewarded for doing so, not because they had named their fathers. It was only after repeated uses in conjunction with their dads, and not calling their moms or the babysitter or other men "Dada" could you actually say the kid had real language. Mari wanted to believe that Sophie understood her signs, that the cereal was hot. But she couldn't prove it yet.

Once again, she reveled in the idea that her degree had actually taught her something useful. Then again, half her job was making food, and cleaning messes. So, it was still a little do-you-want-fries-with-that? She handed Olivia the pink, thermal lunchbox with matching containers that fit perfectly inside. It was a far cry from her own Scooby-doo metal lunchbox and plastic thermos. "You need your food and we have just a few minutes to head to the car."

Olivia was agreeing, as always, when Mari spotted Alex

coming down the stairs. He was barefoot again, wearing jeans and a t-shirt from some band she'd never heard of. Given the fading of the dyes, he either loved the band or the shirt itself. It flummoxed her, the man of the house in clothing more suited for a teenager. Her father had always had a button-down shirt and a tie on. Reynold would barely leave the house without a full suit. His idea of "casual" was khakis and a polo shirt, still a far cry above Beaumont's jeans. Mariliz was pretty sure she saw a rip in the knee. It was hard to remember this man was her boss.

He ran a hand through shaggy hair and grinned at her. "I can take Olivia in. Just need some shoes."

"Daddy!" Olivia popped up, abandoning her breakfast to run and hug him. Mari didn't know whether to chide the girl to finish or let it be.

She watched as Sophie didn't move. Just kept eating small bite after small bite of the oatmeal. She'd quit when she ran out of dinosaurs. It was light years ahead of throwing cheerios and milk, so Mariliz let her.

What bothered her was that Sophie didn't move. She wouldn't have heard her father come down the stairs. But she was facing Mari, she had to have seen her react. Then Olivia had popped up. Sophie couldn't have missed it, but she didn't turn to see who was there. Just kept looking into her bowl and picking out bites with candies.

"Livie, will you finish your breakfast? Or at least put the bowl in the sink." Mari didn't even have to move it into the dishwasher, though she did. She made Olivia and Sophie do it, too. To her, it always felt wrong, even when it was her own maid she'd hired herself, to leave an unnecessary mess behind.

"Sure. Get your shoes, Daddy!" Olivia popped up

Sophie still hadn't reacted. Mari had to. Looking up as Alex Beaumont emerged from the mudroom, feet stuffed bare into disturbingly cheap-looking sneakers, she popped the question.

"Can I have some time with you later today? I have some questions about Sophie."

She didn't sign the words. Didn't want the girl to think they were talking about her, even though they were.

"Of course." He grinned at her, touched his fingers to his forehead in a sign-off, and ushered his oldest out the door.

At noon, Mari made lunch for Sophie. And Alex Beaumont still hadn't returned.

CHAPTER 10

Alex let himself in the door to the mudroom, noting that it wasn't locked. He thought it should be. As Sophie got older, if she was home, he would need it to be locked. She wouldn't hear anyone come in. Then again, there was hope that as she grew, her skills and temperament would improve and they would be able to fit her with a cochlear implant.

Sophie was almost stone deaf. At her age, and with her aggression problems, she wasn't a candidate for the life-altering therapy. It involved hearing aids linked to cords that snapped onto electrodes planted into the patient's brain. It was that diagnosis, not even getting the cochlear implant, that had cracked Bridget.

Now he got to explain it to the new nanny. He'd told part of it to the last one, thought it was in all the papers the agency was handing out. So what did Mariliz want with him?

After he dropped Livie at school, he hit the coffee shop and read the paper from one side to the other. He called his mother, something he usually did when he returned from tour, but hadn't gotten to yet. He checked for messages from Bridget—there were none. And apparently she *was* on a cruise.

Alex went to the studio and laid down some tracks JD had asked of him. He told himself it was necessary. Wilder was their livelihood. He surely wasn't avoiding the sitter whose looks grabbed him in the gut and whose questions twisted it. By the time he hit the grocery store—telling himself that "Lize" wouldn't know what he liked and he should just get it himself—he admitted he was actively avoiding her.

The groceries were a kind of self-stop. He'd have to go home when he finished or his ice cream would melt. So he opened the mudroom door with plastic bags hanging from his wrists and fingertips, thinking that Bridget would have used the cloth bags he'd forgotten. Saving the world was chic these days.

Swinging right, he noticed the house was quiet. He took a deep breath and looked around the place, even though the circulation was getting cut off in his fingers. He hadn't enjoyed being home much in the past year. The house was never peaceful. Sophie was noisy, the nannies were mad, Livie was sad at all of it. And he was full of self-loathing over things he could do nothing about.

"Let me get that for you!"

The voice nearly made him jump, but he kept it together. Just who he didn't want to see. "Hi, Mariliz."

He liked "Lize" but figured it was far too familiar, even if she had just jumped in and was now lifting grocery bags out of his hands. The other employees around the place seemed to have a "not my job" attitude, and he wondered if/when Mariliz Jennings would figure that out. Not yet at least.

She was opening his bags and starting to put things away. The ice cream she put into the freezer, the milk into the fridge, but she asked about his favorite energy bars and whether he wanted the sports drink to chill or not. They worked side-by-side for a moment before he commented. "The house is quiet, what did you do with Sophie?"

68

"Put her down for a nap. She needed it, you know." She looked at him like she wasn't sure he did.

"Sure, but she'd never go down. The kid just refused to sleep during the day." He shrugged as though that was an adequate explanation for almost two-and-a-half years with Sophie.

Mariliz only nodded, as though she knew she had some magical power that he and his wife didn't. Right now, in the quiet, he believed she did. She startled his thoughts with a question. "I'd like to get Sophie a toddler bed. Is that something you can do? Should she pick it out herself? Should I do it?"

Then she stopped herself, hands on hips. "I'm sorry. I'm not even sure that's something you want for Sophie. But she's going to be too big for the crib soon."

He snorted, at both the idea that Magic Mariliz was deferring to him and that Sophie might "be too big" for the crib. "She's been too big for it for a while now. But it makes it harder for her to get around the room and hurt herself with something or get into trouble."

"She can climb out of it, you know."

He knew. "Have you seen her? It's pretty impressive. She's determined. Puts both hands on the top rail, then jumps until her body weight topples over and hangs there until she decides to drop to the floor."

Mariliz's mouth hung open. "She does gymnastics out of the bed? That's *not* safe."

"Nope. She tried pulling the release latches first, like she'd seen us do. But she can't reach both at the same time, and if you don't they lock back. I guess kids have tried that one before."

Mariliz nodded at him. "That's interesting. So she saw you using the locks and then tried that herself first." Something crossed the woman's face, but Alex couldn't tell what she was thinking. "That's a pretty smart move. What did Sophie's tests reveal?"

This was what he didn't want to talk about. He didn't know if

Sophie's handicaps or her problems were his fault or Bridget's. Though they couldn't be. Bridget had taken great care of herself while she was pregnant both times. They'd hit the jackpot with Olivia; there was no reason to do things differently the second time. Had they gotten too lax? Forgotten a vitamin? He shook his head and stuck to the facts he knew. "She's profoundly deaf. A lot of deaf people can actually hear a little, you see—"

She raised a hand at him, stopping him. "I know this. I have a degree in childhood developmental psychology and I've worked with deaf kids before."

"Oh, so you know—"

She cut him off again. "It was in my application. Didn't you read it?"

Mariliz Jennings stared at him like he was nuts. And he was. *Shit.* "No," he confessed. "I didn't. Frankie did, though, she didn't tell me you were a specialist. No wonder you're so good with Sophie."

His heart unwound. The clenched feeling that had ratcheted up with each of Sophie's diagnoses, with each of her bad days, released just a little bit for the first time.

Mariliz smiled at him in response. "We're doing well."

That was an understatement. He wondered if she judged him—them—for not getting more qualified nannies before now. He scrambled to explain, but she cut him off again. This time telling him not to worry.

"The agency was pretty excited when I walked in. I got this job during my interview. I don't think they had anyone qualified before me." She put her hands on the counter. "But what did Sophie's mental tests reveal?"

That brought on another sigh. "They know she's deaf. They think she's developmentally disabled. And she's highly aggressive." That's what hurt him the most. That at the tender age of six months, his baby girl was routinely hitting people. "She yells all the time. Partly because she can't hear herself, partly because she's pretty angry. No one knows what to do with it."

Alex thought he could stand the hurt of Sophie's diagnoses, but it killed him that no one really thought they could do anything *for* her. "They hope she'll grow out of it, but there's nothing on the books like her."

Mariliz nodded at him, her look concerned but understanding. She didn't seem to place any blame on him like others had. Now, looking back, he wasn't sure if they actually had, or if he'd just taken it on himself. Well, there was more than one doctor who insinuated that Sophie's anger was his and Bridget's fault, that her deafness was, too.

Something in him cracked and he started spilling everything. He'd walked in here hoping to miss the nanny all together. Then, when cornered, he'd thought he'd pass some facts along and get the hell out of dodge. But this time when his mouth opened, a flood passed.

"We went to doctor after doctor, hoping for a better diagnosis. We don't know if she can ever get a cochlear implant —it may not even work for her, but she'd have to be able to handle it as a patient, too, and she's nowhere near ready. We can't even truly test her." He took a deep breath. "When she was little, we think she had colic. Then we thought she screamed because she was deaf, and now I think it was both."

"Colic alone is really hard on families." Mariliz commiserated as though she knew. "It's my understanding there's really nothing you can do but wait it out."

"We didn't even try to treat it, because we didn't know." He sighed, pausing, not really thinking if he should share this. He needed to do it if there was any hope for him and his girls. "We tried to wait it out like the doctors said, but Sophie got worse and worse. We tried so hard, and honestly, it just broke Bridget."

He looked up at this woman who was his hired help. He shouldn't be giving her bad impressions of Sophie. Mariliz was the only one who'd gotten through to her. "For a long time, I harbored hopes that she'd have a breakthrough. That she'd connect with her mom, or with me, and things would start getting better. But it didn't happen."

Now he looked away. Though she stood still and watched him, sympathetic, maybe starting to understand what she'd stepped into, he couldn't look at her. "I couldn't be a good father to Sophie, because it steals so much time and energy from Olivia. And I can't be good to Livie without it being so clear that I don't know how to be good to Sophie. I really thought about putting her in a hospital, an institute, just to save the rest of us. Instead, I wasn't brave enough to do anything."

He put his head in his hands and cried. For the first time in all of it. Horribly, unprofessionally, in front of the person he'd hired to help, he just couldn't stop it. Bridget had cracked over a year ago. Screaming and throwing things and saying how she couldn't do it anymore. She couldn't handle Sophie, and the stares, and the noise, and that it never got better and never would. She accused him of going on tour and abandoning her with a baby that screamed all the time for no reason. Leaving him with this damaged child and no hope.

Maybe he had. So when she left, Alex shored up, curled inward, and did his best without really doing anything.

He felt a hand on his shoulder. Soft heat radiated through him from where she so simply touched him. No one had touched him to console him. Livie really hugged him, but she was a child. His mother politely hugged him upon his entering her house. His father patted him on the back and told him what a man should do. Sophie accepted pats on the head. Most days. No one consoled him. Not until now.

He wanted to lean into the touch, but was too afraid it would go away. He was too afraid to peel his hands back and reveal the tears that had to be obvious anyway. So he stayed as still as a crying man could. When her touch lifted, he made himself take a deep breath. Without looking directly at her, so he didn't have to acknowledge the tear-tracks on his face, he spoke to her. "You've made a difference, a real start with Sophie. She's not any better with me, but she's clearly responding to you. At one point I would have been jealous. Now I'm just grateful."

"Don't worry about it." Her voice revealed a deep sympathy. Maybe it was real, maybe if she specialized in this, Sophie wasn't the first case she'd seen. Maybe she could tell him more. First, he had to tell her more. "I've been a crappy father. I'm going to start being better. I'll figure out what you're doing with Sophie and I'll duplicate it."

Just then, a cacophonous cry came from upstairs. A thud and a knock were followed by a hand smacking on the door when she couldn't reach the doorknob.

He looked up at Mariliz with a wry grin. "You think she should be out of the crib?"

"She obviously gets out anyway. On the upside, she'll never be able to sneak around on you. We can clearly hear when she's up. I'll go get her."

He laughed with her and took advantage of the insinuated chance to run a wet towel over his face. When she came down the stairs with a smiling Sophie in her arms, he grinned at them.

Then he saw her lift her free hand as she spoke to his child. "Do you want some milk?"

Everything in him froze as he watched her. All the ease of his confession, all the guilt he'd unburdened in the last half hour froze inside him to sub-zero temperatures. He wouldn't crack like his wife had, he'd shatter into a thousand pieces right here. She'd ruined everything.

Looking up at the nanny, he barely got the words out. "What have you done?"

CHAPTER 11

M ari stared blankly at the man in front of her.
His mouth was open, stunned yet angry. Sophie sat
frozen in her arms, as though she'd only just now seen her
father and was suddenly afraid. Mariliz hugged her close,
suddenly afraid herself. Something was very wrong here.

"What do you mean *what have I done?*" She frowned and held
her ground, noticing that her ground was the bottom of the
ornate staircase.

"You're signing to her. You can't do that."

"I can." She didn't understand. Clearly she *could sign* to his
daughter. "I was a certified medical-legal interpreter at one
point. Though I'm not at that level any more, I assure you I'm
perfectly capable of speaking to a toddler and her family."

"No." He shook his head, almost violently. His breath came in
gasps she didn't comprehend. Like he was having a panic attack.
"You can't sign to *Sophie.*"

"But I have been!" The girl squirmed in her arms, the tension
of the room clearly getting to her. She didn't cry or hit, but
Sophie was definitely trying to get away. When Mari didn't put
her down, Sophie did ball up a fist.

Despite being confused as hell about the situation, Mari saw it coming and held the toddler away from her, deflecting the worst of it. Not knowing what to do, she set the girl down on the floor. Sophie went for the stairs.

Mari jumped up and cut her off. She didn't want to grab the child, having learned from experience that just made her angrier.

"No, Sophie. Stay here." She signed.

Sophie made a face and Alex nearly yelled. "Stop signing to her!"

She tried not to flinch. The only saving grace was Sophie's deafness. She couldn't hear her father yelling. If Mari didn't react, the girl wouldn't know. So she smiled. Even though she wanted to cry.

She was about to get fired. She was about to have to hand Sophie over and derail the work of the past twelve days. Using her finger, she pointed to a spot on the floor. She signed any way and this time she didn't speak the words. It was the only concession to her anger and her fear. "Sophie sit here. I'll bring you some toys to play with."

Sophie did as she was told, brightening a spot in Mari's heart even as it cracked. Mari smiled. Damn, the kid wasn't as slow as she seemed. Not only had she learned, she surely saw that Mari's smile was faked. Mari held a hand up to Alex Beaumont. Palm out, she held him and his nonsensical arguments at bay while she got two pans for Sophie to bang. Why she'd chosen the noisiest things possible, she didn't know.

He flinched even as she handed them to the child. Even before the cacophony began.

Now, what to do? She took a deep breath as though that would stop the shakes that had come on. It didn't. "I don't want her to see this conversation, but I don't want to leave her alone."

"Come over here." Both his voice and his gestures were angry as he motioned her ever-so-slightly around the corner.

It hit her then. One of the things that was off was that Alex never used his hands around his younger daughter. He didn't point, tap, ask, gesture at all. All the things that normal hearing people did as emphasis or in question, he did none of to his youngest daughter. What it meant, Mariliz didn't quite know, but she had to find out.

"Why are you signing to her!" It should have been a question, but it was nearly growled.

"Why aren't *you*?" She shot back. "Sophie's two! You've had plenty of time to at least learn the basics."

"She can't sign!"

"Obviously, she *can*." Mari shot back, wondering when she'd grown such a set of *cajones*. She'd never been like this with her father or mother. Or with Reynold. But she had to defend Sophie. No one else was doing it.

"You'll ruin her!" He fired out.

"For what? Were you hoping she'd medal in the tantrum Olympics?" She shouldn't have said it. As soon as the words fell out of her mouth, she wished she could put them back. He'd cried over this child. He loved Sophie. Probably more than she did. He had to. He was Sophie's father.

His white face told him she'd severed something major with her hit.

"I'm sorry." She whispered it. Her heart sinking in her chest. She was no longer worried about her job. Only that she'd delivered a near-fatal blow to this man and that his daughter was suffering. "I'm so sorry."

He didn't respond. For nearly a minute he just stared at her, blank-faced and she wondered how much pain was hiding behind that careful absence of expression.

Mariliz tried again, more calmly. "Why can't she sign? What do you mean?"

"Teaching her signs will keep her from learning to lip read! She needs to learn to lip read." He was breathing heavily. His hands moved frantically—ironic for a man who was telling her not to move her hands.

"So you've not only purposefully *not* taught her to sign, you don't even point or gesture at all?" She was starting to catch on. And she was very afraid.

"No. If she starts using some other method, she won't lip read or speak!" His lungs heaved like a runner after a sprint and Mari felt her own breathing rate pick up. It was all wrong.

Then she realized, no one had looked at Sophie. Turning, she tipped her head around the edge of the wall. No sound came from the corner, and Mari saw it was because Sophie was watching the wall, waiting for something from them.

Mari raised her hand to tell the little girl "play" then put it back down and opted for a smile. She couldn't go against the parents' wishes, even though she desperately wanted to. This wasn't her child. *Shit.*

She smiled again and turned back to Alex Beaumont. He was close enough she could reach out and grab his shoulders. She did, her palms hitting the soft knit of a high-end long-sleeved t-shirt today. Jeans again, these nicer. Socks in the shoes this time, she saw. Mari watched his chest rise and fall with his panic. Her brain tugged aside, thinking what a nice chest it was, that the muscles under her hands were warm and strong.

She pushed her thoughts back to the matter at hand. He certainly wasn't looking at her that way. And he was married. *Married!* She reminded herself. Her own husband may not have respected the sanctity of the union, but that didn't mean she was going down that path.

Opening her mouth, she tried to get Alex talking before he got worse. "Why do you think she's going to learn to lip read or even speak before she's five?"

He stared at her. Wondering why she'd pulled that age out of the air. She hadn't. But she waited.

"Her doctor told us that was the only way."

"Only way for what?"

He was still speaking in disjointed puzzle pieces that didn't all fit together. He'd seemed reasonable before—granted her experience with him was limited, so she couldn't say for sure. She needed him to be reasonable here. For a moment, she considered telling him he wouldn't like what she had to say. Instead she figured she had to listen first.

"For what?" she prompted again.

"Deafness cuts you off from people. She won't be able to communicate with others if she can't speak their language." He was pleading with her. As though she'd broken his child.

She was getting a better picture now. And she was afraid she was either going to have to leave Sophie and this family on this cruel and horrible pathway, or she was going to have to break him of his ideas. Neither option was good.

"You're right. We have a saying, 'blindness cuts you off from things, deafness cuts you off from people.' It's hard that way." She nodded.

He nodded back at her as though she understood. She did. And she didn't. "Who told you to train Sophie this way? I'm sorry, it's not in anything—any paperwork—I received. I didn't know. Clearly, you have a plan and you're working it. Who set it up?"

"Sophie's doctor."

Her doctor *suggested this?* She didn't ask that. "Her doctor specializes in deafness? The doctor signs?"

"No, he has therapists, they do speech therapies and lip reading training with the patients."

"But they don't sign?"

"No, it interferes with learning to lip read." He kept repeating that as though if he said it enough she could erase all the education she had on deafness.

"They work with congenitally deaf cases? With infants? Kids?"

He'd said 'patients' as if Sophie might be the only kid. Mariliz wouldn't be surprised if that was the case. "I don't know. Bridget went."

"You haven't been back? I don't have these appointments on any calendar. Have I been missing them?" She was purposefully trying to redirect the conversation from the fact that she'd been teaching his daughter sign language.

He panicked again. "I don't know. Bridget set it up, then I . . . I didn't know—I—I—"

She pushed on his shoulders again, moving him back against the wall for support. But it didn't seem to be enough. This time, she gently grabbed his shoulder and steered him to sit in one of the seats at the bar.

She'd thought sitting him down would make it better.

It didn't. While she waited for his breathing to settle, Mari glanced over her shoulder at Sophie. Not a single sound had come from the pans. Instead, the two-year-old sat wide-eyed and watched the adults.

Mariliz tapped him on the shoulder. "Look at her."

CHAPTER 12

A lex got himself together enough to look at his daughter. Wide ringlets hung around her face. She didn't want her hair cut, and unless they sedated her, getting scissors near her wasn't safe for anyone.

Mariliz's whisper cut through him. "That's unnatural for a toddler to sit that way. It's like she's in shock. Or waiting for the explosion."

He saw now. Maybe only part of it. But that's what other people saw when Sophie was out. He didn't take her out and about much. It was hard with the stares, the sympathy, the fact that they couldn't accomplish anything because his daughter screamed and they had to leave before anything got done.

He whispered back, not because Sophie might hear—she couldn't—but because it was all he could muster. It was all he could make his chest move it was constricted so tight. "I didn't follow up with her appointments after Bridget left. Maybe the nanny did it?"

He didn't know. He only knew that it was taken care of, that Sophie was going regularly for a while . . . and now she wasn't. "I don't even know when her last visit was."

The words and thoughts fell out of him like pieces tumbling away. He'd been a terrible father. The choices he'd had to make were awful, but it seemed he made it worse each time he tried not to choose. He looked up at Mariliz, catching the sympathy in her eyes. They weren't just brown, they were hazel. He'd ask her about it someday. Someday when his brain wasn't looking at her eye color as an excuse for not facing the mess he'd made. "What do I do?"

Her hands braced his shoulders again, and he wondered if she thought he might fall out of the chair if she didn't hold him up. He wondered if she was right.

"First of all, stop beating yourself up." She stared back at him, glanced at Sophie to check on her, then looked him in the eyes again. "This—Sophie's behavior—isn't on you. But I don't think you're going to like what I have to say."

Her expression was grim. He'd hit a wall. What did it matter what she said? It was all bad, right? He only shrugged.

"I'm sorry I taught her ASL against your wishes. I didn't know." She shook her head, offering her own shrug before her explanation. "I did call repeatedly and ask you and your wife for more information. No one responded."

So, don't beat himself up? Because she wanted to do it herself? Alex just stared, at this point he wasn't capable of much more.

She went on. "I'm a specialist. I speak ASL—"

He translated that mentally, American Sign Language, not signs for English. A whole other language. He'd learned a little along the way.

"—as a second language. I don't do speech therapy nor do I teach lip reading. I don't know how. It would never have occurred to me to try." She glanced back at Sophie again.

This time so did he. She still sat there, watching them. Alex almost couldn't stand to look. He couldn't reach her, no matter how much he wanted to.

Mariliz moved her head, gaining his attention again. "Sophie will be fine. But in my expert opinion, *not* if you continue trying to teach her to speak."

That rattled him. "It's the only way she'll be able to communicate with people!" Mariliz had agreed with him! Why was she changing now?

"No, it's the only way she'll be able to communicate with the population at large in their language. I don't know where this doctor came from, but what he has prescribed for Sophie . . ." She sounded like she was carefully choosing words. "It doesn't match what is known about lip reading and speaking for the profoundly deaf."

"What do you mean?"

"Most people don't learn to lip read until well after they learn sign language. They don't learn to speak words until they understand the words and what they mean." She started raising her voice, getting more passionate. "They can't understand sounds without letters! And letters don't exist without real concepts of things." She pointed at the bar, "How would you even know that that was Tay-bul?"

"It's not a table, it's a *bar*." He said, suddenly feeling punch drunk and angry. "And how did you or I learn that in the first place?"

"We heard it. And we heard ourselves say it. We can match it and fix it. But we understood it first. She can't."

"Sure she can!" He was getting frustrated, she didn't know what she was talking about. He mouthed the word "table" followed by the word "bar" to make a point. "You understood that!"

"Yeah, I did." Then she grabbed his shoulders and mouthed "table" twice, followed by "bar" four times.

"So what? Table, table, bar, bar, bar, bar! She can learn it." He was getting frustrated with this woman who'd set them all back. Even if it was really his fault.

"No Alex. I said *Table, Stable*. Did you see the difference?

Watch. *Table. Stable.*"

Oh shit. He couldn't tell.

She didn't stop. "Then I said car, star, gar, and dar. I didn't even say 'bar.'"

His heart fell. Why didn't his arms just fall off? Why didn't his skin peel? It would be easier than these piercing pains. Mariliz Jennings—sweet and beautiful—didn't let up.

"You want a two-year-old with no language and no reference to tell the difference, when you can't tell it. And you've been speaking it for what? Thirty-plus years?"

He nodded. "Dar isn't even a word."

"I know." She said as though she agreed with him, but she didn't pull the punches. "And you *still* couldn't tell. Lip readers have to use context, heavily. Sophie doesn't have any language. How will she get context? Even in her childlike use of words— which probably doesn't include 'gar'—ball, mall, and small all look the same. Almost identical."

She was right.

How could he ask that of a kid? A baby practically. But what was left? Isolation?

"Honestly, lip reading seems to be a skill or a talent, that some people have and some don't. She might never get it." Mari shrugged sadly. "Speaking is the same way. It's all trial and error. You *hear* your mistakes. A deaf person needs a trained therapist for hours and hours to help correct what they can't hear. It's not anything you and your family can teach her."

She paused and let that sink in.

It was even worse than he thought. Sophie might never learn to lip read. How horrifying was that? He'd seen deaf people at the mall. He'd seen sign language interpreters at shows sometimes. The occasional conversation in sign. Never mind that everyone stared. No one understood what they were saying. Because no one spoke the language.

There were no good choices for his daughter.

He was about to say so, when she spoke again. She looked chagrined "Look, I don't know how you wound up with a physician who thought he could teach this to a toddler. But I've never heard anything like it and I've been in this business—in the community somewhat—since I was in high school. You should research it more. But I, personally, would never believe anyone trying to sell me this therapy."

"So what options are there? Let her sign and talk with only her family?"

"Yeah. For now. I'll take her out and about. Olivia's already learning it."

He cringed. Livie knew what they were doing with Sophie. She knew the training—she helped. "Livie?"

"She told me you weren't signing with Sophie. I'm sorry, I thought she meant you didn't know it. This is not on her!" Mariliz leaned back and turned to check on Sophie again.

Alex saw his youngest, at least now she was leaning against the step, sucking her thumb. Still she watched them with eyes that seemed all-seeing. The problem was, he had no idea what Sophie saw.

"I just assumed you wouldn't hire an ASL interpreter as a nanny if you didn't want the kid signing. I'm sorry."

"Enough apologies." Clearly, she hadn't meant to hurt them. It didn't help either.

She nodded, but picked up her standard and charged forward again. "You can learn ASL. Bridget, too."

It seemed as if she'd thrown in his wife's name as an afterthought, and he tried to picture Bridget signing to their youngest. He couldn't make the image come to life.

Mariliz didn't pause for his thoughts. "There are advances every day. I just saw an inventor made sign-to-voice gloves. There's hope." She took a breath. "If she learns to sign, she can communicate easily, freely, and complexly with everyone who knows how to sign. That's me. It's starting to be Olivia. It can be you and your wife."

"That's not much." She'd be a shut in. It wasn't what he wanted for his daughter.

"Actually, there are a ton more people out there who *do* speak ASL. There's a deaf community in every major city. They'll welcome her as one of their own. There's a whole college in DC just for deaf students. She won't starve for friends or education or understanding." Her mouth clicked shut. She seemed to realize that she'd implied Sophie was starving for those things now.

Alex looked at her again.

"The doctor told us to smack her hands." He didn't know why he said it. "I went to the meetings with the therapist the first several times. He said that if she gestured at all, she would use that instead of speech. We weren't to hand signal in any way. We look right at her, mouth the word clearly, but not overly so, and speak at a normal speed."

Why had he never tried it himself? Wouldn't he have seen the difficulty? He didn't know. He was exhausted. He wanted to sleep. For a thousand years. Or at least sixteen. At least until Sophie was grown and he was not responsible for decisions he wasn't equipped to make. "If she learns sign? What then?"

Mariliz Jennings didn't speak for a moment. Where was her charge ahead attitude now? Why wasn't she selling him her beautiful American Sign Language that no one knew how to speak?

She whispered. "You've already seen it."

His head snapped back to her.

"She's less combative. She has choices, some control over her life. She couldn't even say if she liked one cereal or another, now she can." Mariliz shook her head, raised her hands as if to say she didn't know. "Maybe she's not combative, maybe it's not a real disorder. I don't know, maybe it is. But how could she not be angry at the world? She's two and a half. Other kids are speaking sentences, she couldn't even point to say she wanted the toy car."

Tears ran down the nanny's face. She truly believed this was the best course for Sophie.

He stilled for a moment while his mind churned. Sophie *was* less angry lately. She played with Olivia sometimes. He'd seen her eat without throwing things. Sophie hugged this woman. She'd never hugged him really, but she'd run up and offered a hug to this woman who'd lived in their house only a little over a week.

Turning to look at Sophie again, she blew the girl a kiss. And Sophie smiled at her, then looked to him, her expression turning wary. His heart shattered into a thousand pieces, when he hadn't thought it could break more.

Mariliz Jennings spoke softly while he watched his own daughter, still sitting too quietly. "If you won't let her sign, I can't stay. I can't smack her hands if she tries to communicate. I'm happy to help try to teach her to speak words on top of learning to sign. I don't know how good I would be at it, truly, I have no training in it."

"But you'll stay if she can learn ASL." He didn't ask.

"If you want me to. I'm sorry I messed up your plans. I can't change that." She wouldn't take the blame either. She didn't deserve it and he wouldn't lay it on her. "You have a choice to make."

They sat that way for a moment before he said, "Show me."

He watched as she walked over to the little girl and sat cross-legged on the floor. He must have trailed too slow because she patted the ground beside her, motioning for him to sit.

"Sophie." She said it, then turned to him, showing him her hands. "This is her name-sign. Sophie. Try it."

He did. It was awkward, but his daughter startled at the sight of him signing it. Alex did it again. "Now what?"

"Sophie," she signed while she talked, moving much too fast for him. "Go get a toy. Get your favorite."

Sophie blinked, but finally moved. She looked at Mariliz oddly for a moment, then toddled off.

"She understood all of that?" Alex was in awe.

"I don't know. Let's see what she gets." So it wasn't a science yet. The miracle worker was still on trial and error it seemed.

Sophie came back with a red toy truck from the bin in the corner of the room.

"That's her favorite?" Alex asked.

"Again, we've only been at this a week. Thank you!" She said and signed the last part to Sophie. "Car." She signed again. "Car."

Alex watched as Sophie did it, too. She looked at him as she did it. As though waiting for him to smack her hands. *Jesus*. It was what a *doctor* had told him to do! He'd never even smacked her, just moved her hands away. He felt like an ass anyhow.

"You sign it, Alex." Mariliz demoed it again, and he tried.

Sophie handed him the car. He learned the sign for thank you.

"That's her ninth word!" Mariliz Jennings grinned just before she went for his jugular. Turning to Sophie she pointed at Alex. "That's your Daddy. Can you sign *Daddy*?"

CHAPTER 13

Over the next few days, Mari watched Alex light up with Sophie but struggle with the signs. Kids tended to pick up the language quickly—as they did with most languages. But adults struggled to file it, to remember the words, to catalog the alternate grammar.

Luckily, Alex was a drummer. She hadn't thought of it before, but it meant his hand dexterity was great. She'd watched grown men struggle to make their fingers form the complex signs, but Alex didn't. It was a good thing, because letters and fingerspelling were the easiest way for speaking adults to communicate and they required the most manual dexterity.

Mariliz didn't teach him those first. The only letters he learned were "S" for Sophie's name sign and "O" and "M" for Olivia and Mariliz.

"Daddy!" Olivia signed as she spoke. "I want a kitten!"

She had the whole thing down, and Alex was nodding, watching his daughter's hands, trying to figure out which sign was which.

He didn't quite have it. "I saw *I, want,* and *kitten.* Where's *a?*"

Yet another issue in so many. Mari reminded herself that it

was a foreign language and just as hard to learn as any other, even if the sign for "house" was to shape a little house with your hands. "There is no *a*. No *an* or *the* either. They don't exist in ASL. You can say one. Like 'one kitten,' Olivia."

"Two kittens." Olivia signed to her father, this time without speaking. "I want two kittens."

"So she said she wants two *kitten*?" He looked to Mariliz again.

"Yes. No 's' on the ends of the words. The plural is obvious. The girl wants two kitten." She shrugged as though it wasn't as monumental as it was.

Mari leaned down and signed to Sophie. "Two kitten."

Sophie clapped and signed "kitten, kitten."

"How many kitten?" Mari asked her in sign only, then repeated it to Olivia and Alex.

Her apt pupils replied with two fingers.

"At least the numbers are easy. Except for three." He frowned. "And over five. Never mind."

Sophie clapped her hands and said, "kitten, kitten," again.

Okay, so she didn't have answers yet for how many, but she was hitting the cascade. Her ten words had bloomed to twenty in just two days, and Mari quit counting at fifty. Mari thought it might be because of Alex signing with her. It was big for both of them.

Olivia stayed ahead of her little sister for language and word acquisition, but Mariliz wasn't sure how long that would last. Olivia and Alex learned for Sophie. Sophie learned for everything. It was her only communication, and in the end, she would be the victor. One of these days she would teach Mari a new word or two.

"So we can get a kitten?" Olivia jumped up and down.

"I thought we were learning sign. I didn't know we were having a serious discussion about pets we don't want to have."

Alex looked at his daughter. Then he looked at Mari who showed him signs for 'conversation' and 'learn.'

"Kittens, Daddy." Olivia said, until Mari motioned for her to sign. "We need kittens, Daddy." Then she turned to her sister. "One for her and one for me."

"Did you put them up to this?" He looked at Mariliz, then added, "I don't even begin to know the signs I need. Livie's got a week on me and Sophie's got the drive. You're the professional; I'm clearly the straggler."

He was. She'd been signing to him all week. Every time Sophie was around, and sometimes when she wasn't. All three of them needed good demonstrations of each sign in order to get it.

Olivia picked up her baby sister this time, despite the fact that Sophie was a good, bubbly size. Sophie let her, and even signed 'kitten' to her again while her sister held her. Then she signed, "Olivia, Kitten."

Livie hugged her. "We need kittens, Daddy." She made a comically sad face and worked to coerce Sophie into doing the same.

Mari laughed as she fought the swell in her heart. "Alex," she whispered. "She put two signs together."

It was a linguistic milestone, but Alex almost brushed it off. "You didn't get that excited when I put two signs together."

She frowned and hit him with the throw pillow. "You already have language! And you're not as cute as Sophie."

She smiled while she delivered the line, trying to cover for her brain telling her *yes, he is.* He laughed, the dimple coming out in his cheek, the same one Sophie had. He was a good sport, sitting in the evenings with his daughters, all doing basic signs. Olivia was playing him hard for the kittens and he clearly didn't want to answer.

Her own extended family was big enough that Mariliz understood parents not wanting to commit one way or the other. 'Yes' wasn't retractable, and Alex didn't want to have to say 'no' either. She tried to step in.

"New word. Ice cream." She pointed at Olivia who set her sister down then signed it. Then Alex, then Sophie. They all clapped when Sophie did it. Even Sophie. "So let's get some ice cream!"

Maybe she was violating Dad's directives, but honestly, he didn't seem to have many. He'd traveled a lot, and even admitted to her the night before, after putting Olivia to bed, that he hadn't been involved with the girls near enough in the past several years. Working with Sophie was heartbreaking; it had always been easier to let the nannies run their lives. At least he wasn't stepping back now. And he didn't complain about the ice cream, just jumped into the fray like he was a third kid.

Mari headed toward the kitchen to open the freezer where she'd stashed a half gallon of chocolate swirl the day before. The other three followed, Livie settling herself on the tall bar stool. Sophie needed help getting up into her chair and she raised her arms to Alex who didn't make a big deal out of it, but hugged her a little tighter before strapping her in and sliding the high chair up to the bar like her sister. Over Sophie's head, he mouthed, "Thank you." His eyes looked a little wet.

When she finished her ice cream, Mari excused herself to let Alex put the girls to bed. She'd managed to successfully change their bedtimes, giving Olivia an extra hour each evening. It only seemed fair, as Sophie was home during the day. But she said good-night to them all and left Alex to it.

When she heard the lock click into place on her door, her heart sighed out in relief.

The lines between her job and her personal life were blurring. Though she showed up promptly at seven each morning and basically clocked in, clocking out was not as simple. There was no agreed upon time anymore. She'd had the girls twenty-four seven for almost the first ten days. Now, with

Alex Beaumont not working a nine-to-five job, there was no delineation of her on or off time. He didn't come in the door at five, loosen his tie, and take over at five thirty.

Though he often ran errands or headed in to rehearsals or out to interviews, he was just as often around. She was working, supposedly, but he was in the room. Sophie had gotten over her reticence with him and now toddled up to him and waved her hands. Alex understood some of it, but signing with a toddler was confusing. Just like hearing kids, they had their own versions of things because of motor skills, quirks, and more. So often she heard Sophie waddle away, then Alex call out "Mariliz?" when he didn't understand something his daughter needed. She felt she was always in between the baby and the man.

And the man was getting to her.

He smiled with that dimple. He laughed more now, the sound setting up a deep resonance in her heart. Sometimes when he couldn't get the signs right, she would mold his hands. That was normal, nothing she hadn't done before teaching new signers, who often couldn't make their hands form the right shapes easily. Touching his hands like that made her feel things she shouldn't.

The problem was that she liked him. She really liked this guy.

At first, she'd hated him. Hated him on behalf of the girls he was neglecting. But she'd listened, and so had he, and he'd made changes.

It made more sense now, all of it. Sophie was wary of him because he'd shut her down each time she tried to communicate. Her only allowable form was screaming. Bridget and Alex hadn't realized they'd trained that into her—but they had. If the girl couldn't sign or even point, and she *couldn't* speak, all she had left was tantrums. Alex had been stuck between a rock and a hard place. Though Mari thought that speech doctor was off his freakin' rocker thinking a toddler could learn lip reading, it sounded like Bridget and Alex Beaumont had been convinced it would work. Also, the argument for lip reading was mixed with liberal doses of truth —if Sophie signed, she'd only be able to communicate with those who spoke American Sign Language, which was truly a small portion of the population.

To make things worse, Alex had been left to make these hard choices alone. Where was Bridget Beaumont? Mariliz still hadn't seen her or even talked to the woman. Why didn't she help her husband make these decisions? Mari assumed Alex was speaking to his wife, but she hadn't heard a single utterance about "Mom sends her love," or "Bridget wants me to ask you/tell you . . ." There was nothing. How long was that cruise?

She sat on her small couch, probably picked out by Mrs. Beaumont or maybe a decorator, and watched a dull TV show. Always a fidgetter, Mariliz liked to keep her hands busy. She was currently working a cross-stitch. This one said "Sophie" in big bold letters. Another was slated for Olivia, the colors matching the decor in each girl's room.

As she looked down at the partially completed piece, Mari wondered if she should finish it. She wasn't the girls' mother. She wasn't even family. She was the hired help who didn't seem to know when to tap out and take her time off.

A knock at her door only confirmed that. She knew before she turned the knob that it was Alex. He was the only one in the house still awake besides her. He was also the only one tall enough to knock like that, and she hadn't set any boundaries. She should have said something, instead she smiled up at him.

"Can we talk about the kittens?"

Seriously? She had a vote? "Um." Mariliz struggled. He'd caught her in the middle of an epic self-war about her place in things and lobbed a hand grenade like that? Surely Bridget would come home and what would the wife think? Mari knew what she would think if she was the wife. So she straightened her back. "Maybe tomorrow. During work."

"Oh. I'm sorry. Sure." He nodded and stepped back. "Good night."

His smile was tight and so was hers. She'd drawn a line in the sand and politely pointed out that he was over it.

"Good night." She clicked the door shut and fought the urge to lean against it, afraid he might hear her movements. Breathing heavily, she listened to the side of her brain that reminded her he was a married man.

The other side asked, *Just how married is he?*

CHAPTER 14

M ari didn't see Alex again until mid-morning the next day, and then he told her he was heading out for some business at the studio. So she was somewhat surprised when he showed up just after Sophie went down for her nap.

In the kitchen, checking lists for the week's needs, she was startled to hear the garage door. Sure enough, she could hear and almost feel him in the mudroom, then in the kitchen with her. She shouldn't be this aware of him. It was dangerous ground she was treading.

"Hey." He stepped up, far more casual than she was feeling. "Is this a good time?"

"Yes, it is." She put the pen down and smiled. She didn't want to be a bitch, and it wasn't his fault she felt the way she did. Her work had been odd hours and very casual in arrangement, but if she wanted to fix it, ultimatums weren't the way to do it. He'd caved the first time over the hazard pay, but then—aside from the money—she hadn't really cared if she lost the job. Now she did. "What did you want?"

He paused a second, took a breath in and grimaced. "It's about kittens."

She almost grinned. "Yeah, you said that, but I don't understand why you're asking me."

"Because, I'm around right now, but we're out on tour again in two weeks. Only eight days, but it's eight days of you being in charge. Of two girls . . . and maybe two kittens." He shrugged as though it he didn't know what to do.

"Okay, that makes sense. Is it just down to me? Or are there other factors?" Her hands were flat on the granite counter top, her shoulders braced while her mind churned.

"There are lots of factors. I'm not a pets person. Bridget hates the hair on the furniture. I'm not going to change a litter box or remember to feed the thing, and Olivia really isn't old enough."

"There's a 'yes' in there somewhere?" Mari marveled. That was plenty of reasons not to get a cat in her book. She didn't say it yet, but she was *not* changing the litter box.

"That's the problem." He looked chagrined. "Olivia always had me wrapped around her finger. Bridget was the voice of reason. Bridget taught me to tell my daughter 'no' sometimes. But all I ever did was tell Sophie 'no' and not even in terms she could understand."

Oh crap. He might break her heart right here at the kitchen island. She wanted to shut this conversation down or she was going to sink deeper than she already had where this man was concerned.

"She hugged me the other day."

Mariliz could hear the catch in his voice. There went the quicksand, shifting under her feet. She tried to steady herself, but failed.

"I want to tell her yes. There are two of them ganging up on me now. So while I want to be upset that they're trying to manipulate me, honestly—" he held his hands out, palm up, like what-could-he-do? "—it's the most wonderful thing I think I've ever been asked. And I kinda hate cats."

Mariliz threw her head back and laughed—not a delicate, feminine laugh, but a deep, soul born gale. She couldn't breathe. The poor man had been had. His daughters tuned him up and played him as well as he played the many instruments around the house. He knew it, too. Despite being played, he was happy about it. When she finally wiped at the tears that were leaking from the corners of her eyes, she took a breath and told him. "I won't change the litter box or de-fur the couch. But I'll buy cat toys and help build carpeted tree-houses."

"Oh man, I didn't even think about having one of those things in the living room." It didn't seem to change his mind though. "I'll change the litter box. Make Olivia do it with me, and I'll bump the maid's pay to do it, too." He was pulling out his phone as he talked.

"You'd better ask her first." Mari warned.

He held up the phone. "Already calling her. She's the last link in the chain."

Wandering off while he talked, Alex left Mari watching his jeans-clad butt mosey away. Her brain told her to not watch, but it didn't work. For a moment she thought, if his wife would just show up, that would help.

Even as she was thinking it, he turned around with a grin on his face and hit the button on his phone. "She loves cats. I think she loves the pay bump, too."

"Then I guess there are kittens coming." Mari braced herself, thinking of tiny creatures mewing at her, trying to climb her leg, being plucked from the furniture. "Can I strongly encourage Livie to clip their little nails?"

He was nodding when she had another thought. "They'll be indoor cats?"

"I read up on it on the internet last night. Less likelihood of car accidents or fights. I'm not up for getting my girls a kitty then burying it!"

She shuddered at the thought, but he was speaking before she finished the motion.

"I also scoured the literature for cochlear implants and teaching sign to deaf kids like Sophie." His face fell. "It was all there once I dug for it. Everything you said. But I never found it before. I looked for lip reading, but not sign language, because we weren't going to do it."

The squeeze in her heart shouldn't have taken her by surprise, but it did. He was trying.

"I feel like such a . . . actually, I don't think there's a word for it. I tapped out on being a parent. I don't know if I can even ask you to understand. I hated pushing Sophie's hands away and shutting her down. I know she would just sit and stare at me or hit me, but," He took a deep breath. "I thought it was the right thing to do. Anyway," he shook off the melancholy of the moment, "Olivia and I decided we wanted to go out for a sign language dinner."

"Oh, that's a neat idea." Mariliz tried to turn the corner as fast as he did. Maybe he just couldn't deal with the past. The good news was, Sophie might never remember the time when her parents wouldn't speak to her.

"Will you come?"

"Oh, I don't think I can." *Don't think I should.* She would love to go. And that was exactly the problem. "I need a night off."

"Yes! You do. In fact you need several, and some days off. I'll be out of town again soon. How about the four days just before I leave?"

Alex picked Livie up at school and they chatted about her day. She talked about what she was learning in class and what was coming up. It all sounded like a bit much to him.

"Do you have homework tonight?" He hated that he had to

ask his third grade daughter that. Sometimes it seemed like way too much for an eight-year-old.

"No, Daddy. We have state testing this week. So no homework."

State testing sucked. He hadn't had to do it, not like his daughters did. And he'd grown up in this state. Everyone else in the band was an import, but Alex Beaumont was home grown. "Well, let's take advantage of that. Let's have our sign language dinner."

"Now?"

"Sure. I'm hungry and we're all in the car." He grinned at her in the review mirror.

"Mariliz isn't here." Livie protested.

He understood. The woman was a bright light. Fun to be around as an adult. Stable for the kids. And she'd given Sophie a new future. Not the one he'd planned for his youngest daughter, but one he could certainly live with better, one that was actually achievable. Her smile was getting to him. Bridget had better get home soon. Though he had no idea what that would look like.

"Mariliz needs a night off." Maybe Livie didn't understand that Mari wasn't family. "We can do it without her."

His daughter seemed to see that Sophie was looking at her oddly and she started signing to her little sister. "We'll try. So no speaking at all?"

"Nope. Just sign language. You and I will see for a night what it will be like to be Sophie."

"Okay." Olivia shrugged her shoulders. She seemed up for the challenge if not excited.

They picked a chain restaurant with hopes that Sophie wouldn't be too noisy for the place. Also, it was only four thirty, the usual crowd shouldn't be in yet. Alex took a deep breath and really wished he'd pushed Mariliz to come with them. As he approached the front station, Sophie in his arms and Livie by the hand, he suddenly realized he couldn't even say how many.

Letting go of Livie, he held up three fingers. The hostess, made an odd face at him and repeated, "Three for dinner?"

He nodded. But he was *hearing* her. Not the point of the evening. Getting frustrated, he wondered what the right thing to do was. He noticed Olivia motioning to the hostess for a pen and paper. She was given a crayon. Alex watched with pride.

My little sister is deaf. She held the paper up to the hostess, then scribbled more. *My Daddy and I are trying to go all night without speaking. We will sign. Is that okay?*

The hostess smiled brightly at her as she nodded and motioned them to follow. She didn't speak, only held out a hand to the table as if to ask if it was okay. Alex nodded at her and realized he couldn't ask for a high chair. He started cataloging words he needed from Mariliz. He should have brought a sign book! Not that anyone would understand it.

Again, the hostess seemed to pick up his frustration. She pointed at the chair in Sophie's spot and then to Sophie herself. Alex nodded, and held tight to his daughter. Even if he could sign, he had a toddler in his arms.

The woman set out the menus. One for him, a kid menu for Olivia, and a plastic table cover for Sophie. Then she returned with the highchair and he settled his younger daughter into it, wondering if he would survive the evening. It had seemed like a bright, shiny idea when he and Livie dreamed it up. Live one meal as Sophie would. Understand her situation, so they could help.

But he hadn't even ordered a drink yet and he was already frustrated beyond hell and back. This was exactly why they'd wanted Sophie to learn to read lips and speak. This was awful. He was about ready to tap out when it hit him.

This was why Sophie screamed and hated him. He'd trapped her in this world for two years. He'd done worse—the hostess smiled and pointed and *tried*. He'd shut his daughter down. She couldn't lip read. Hell, he couldn't tell the difference between words even after Mariliz had told him exactly what she was saying and he already spoke and understood English.

Leaning over, he kissed Sophie on her little head. It was a wonder she'd forgiven him. He'd tormented his own daughter, but she smiled at him when he kissed her. Kids were resilient, people always said. He wasn't. He was feeling that awful pressure behind his eyeballs and deep in his chest and fighting it hard, when the server came up.

"Hello." She signed. "My name A-N-N-A. I sign little-bit. I try help."

Her signs were slow, but clear. *Holy shit. Jackpot!*

While Livie and Sophie lit up like firecrackers, he signed back. "Me two."

He frowned at the number two on his fingers, trying to remember. There was a sign for "me too," one sign. Livie signed it for him. Sophie signed it, too, and the server nodded and laughed.

She signed again. Over his head, words he didn't know, but she was clearly asking for drinks. Livie ordered chocolate milk. Then Sophie did, too, a mile-wide smile on her face. It occurred to Alex then that his daughter had never seen anyone sign other than him, Livie, and Lize.

He motioned a needle in his arm for a coke. He knew that sign.

The server, Anna, nodded and turned away while Livie gasped out "Daddy!" then covered her mouth as she realized she had broken the rule for the night. "She signs!" She used her hands that time.

Yes. He nodded at her. Mariliz said all forms of non-verbal communication were a go with a toddler. Yes. He nodded again.

Suddenly, he had hope for Sophie.

He didn't have any for himself though.

CHAPTER 15

"What happened to you?" JD leaned over and Alex knew he should have worn long sleeves.

"Kitten. Kittenzzz. Two of them." He shrugged. TJ was running a few minutes late and the other three were standing around, JD drinking a coffee he'd brought, Craig eying the cat scratches.

Craig had dogs. Two big rotty-pit mixes that would protect a home from all comers. Craig also had sons. He raised an eyebrow. "What are their names?"

Alex didn't want to answer. "Lilac and Poof."

"*Lilac* and *Poof?*" Craig was incredulous. "What strange punishment is this?"

"My girls asked me if they could get kittens and I said yes." That part at least he could stand up to.

"Both girls?" JD asked this, his tone low, curious. JD paid attention to the kids. He knew about Sophie, and Alex suspected he'd put together far more than he'd been told.

"Yes, both. Remember when Bridget's sister Frankie came in? Right before we left last time?" He tried to skirt the issue that Frankie came because Bridget wouldn't. He plowed ahead.

"Well, she found us a new nanny, and the new nanny taught Sophie to sign."

JD jerked his head back, right as his brother TJ came through the door. TJ's personality was as big as his stage presence, and he didn't hesitate to hop into the conversation even though he'd missed everything before that. "I thought you weren't doing that with Sophie."

"Well, Frankie didn't tell the nanny—"

"Frankie's a stone bitch." TJ interrupted. "I can't believe you left her with your kids."

TJ didn't even have kids. Alex bit his tongue on that one. "Well, the new nanny, Mariliz, is a specialist. A sign language interpreter, and she assumed she was there to teach Sophie ASL."

"Wow. That derailed a lot of plans." JD commented. That was just like JD—no judgment in it, but definitely sympathy.

Alex took a deep breath even as he settled himself behind the drum kit. "I was furious. But then my daughter asked me for a kitten." The pride that swelled in his chest was almost more than he could handle. Setting down the drumsticks he'd just picked up, he spoke and signed at the same time. "Mariliz is teaching all of us to sign."

"Look at you, ASL-man." Craig mocked, using his hands.

"Holy shit, dude. You sign?" Alex was floored.

"A couple deaf kids in foster care. I learned a little." He shrugged and played a chord. As if it were no big deal. As if his knowing sign at all wasn't monumental. *Still waters*, Alex thought. They'd only recently learned that Craig grew up in foster care.

But notes were filling the air and Alex was being swept up in the music, the feel of it always took him over. He hit the rim of the snare three times to feed into the beat and then laid into the kit. His breathing synced up with the song and helped keep the speed of his hands steady.

He wasn't a songwriter—that had been fine at first, TJ hadn't been either. Alex hadn't had the adversity that the rest of them did, though Craig had lived something on a level worse than a country song. Alex's middle-class upbringing involved parents who took him to music teachers and supported him when he decided to be a professional. He'd lived in the basement apartment at their house and hadn't struggled quite the way the other guys did. He'd seen their concerns, but he'd always been fed and clothed. No surprise kids, no crazy love drama. Just Bridget and her red underwear and the easy knowledge that they wanted each other and they wanted the same things.

The music had always taken him away. But this last year it had been an escape. It still was.

Things were definitely better in the house. The girls were pleased with their kittens. Lilac was Livie's favorite color—so she just had to name the little white ball of fur that. Sophie made a sign like her fingers splaying out for her kitten, a surprisingly fluffy little gray tabby. When Alex asked Mari the next morning what that meant, she told him maybe puffball, or poof. Sophie was gleeful calling the kitten to her.

She and Mariliz had been on the floor playing with the kittens when he'd left to come here. Olivia had been heartbroken at having to go to school, but he reminded her she had her kitten like she'd wanted, and she could play after she got home. His daughter had perked back up. So had he.

It was definitely better.

But it wouldn't stay that way.

～

"Missy, I'll come get you." Mari was lying on her bed about to get ready. They'd decided they would meet up, but not exactly how they were going to do it.

"I'm on the other side of town. Just meet me there." She could almost see Missy waving her away.

She was going to protest when it occurred to her that Missy might have a guest over and didn't want Mari to pick her up, or maybe drop her off. Though Mari hated arriving at a bar alone, she agreed and hung up.

Another hour. She didn't need that long, so she had some time to kill. She'd tucked herself back here as early as she could last night, too. Trying to put some professional distance between herself and Alex Beaumont. She'd cross-stitched and watched a truly bad movie. She turned out the lights, climbed in bed, and read a book until she fell asleep. Then she had a sex dream about her boss.

Bad move, Mariliz, bad move.

She'd woken in a dead sweat in the middle of the night. Her breath soughing in and out, her thoughts and her body on fire. For the entirely wrong man.

Mari didn't know who the right man was, but her boss wasn't him. If it wasn't enough that he signed her paychecks, maybe it should be that she lived in his house. Or that he was *married*.

Rolling herself up off the bed, she decided that she couldn't stay here any longer. She turned on her curling iron and began raiding her closet. She wasn't quite sure about the bar they were going to, only that Missy recommended it. *Nice but slightly slutty should do it*, she thought, pulling out a relatively short skirt.

When she was ready, keys in hand, she slowly made her way along the side of the house, the cobblestones threatening her ankles as she went. There were two long windows over here, to the office at the front of the house. Sure enough, as she went by, the light was on and Alex was in there at the desk.

He had his phone to his ear and offered a polite boss-like smile and wave as she went by.

SAVANNAH KADE

See? She asked herself, *he can behave like this is a professional relationship. So can I.*

The bar boasted both a neon sunshine and a boot over the front door. Mariliz read that to mean "country" and figured her heels would hold up to some line dancing. They weren't that bad, it was that the paver path around the side of the house could steal a heel right off a shoe.

Of course, Missy wasn't here yet. Mari headed to the bar and got the bartender's attention. "Margarita please?" At his look, she filled him in. "Rocks, salt."

Biding her time while he mixed the drink, she wondered if the future Mr. Mariliz Jennings was in here. Before, she'd liked that Reynold was going places. Now, she realized he'd never cared if those places were with her or with some other willing woman. She was just grateful she didn't have kids. Then she thought maybe she didn't have them because she'd liked her husband less and less with each passing year of their marriage. With all the times people joked about the old ball and chain, she'd thought that was just the way marriage was.

She'd been bored. When people joked or even complained about how crazy their spouse made them, how much they wanted to throttle their husbands, Mari thought she didn't feel that way. Ultimately, she realized she didn't feel anything. When she tried to fix that, well, she'd gotten a surprise.

At least she'd gained her pride back when she left, and she certainly wasn't bored now. As she made her way over nearer to the edge of the small stage, she heard a voice at her ear.

"Hey, darlin'. Want to join us?"

Her initial response was 'no' but when she'd looked to men in ties and suits, she'd found Reynold. She'd also known about the husbands of several other women in her group. They openly admitted their husbands cheated. That was the wrong pool to dive back into. So Mariliz at least turned her head and looked.

A mixed group of men and women, some couples, some

singles. "Sure, thank you." She decided to take it as a kindly offer rather than a pure come-on. By the time Missy showed up and found her, Mari was ready to say as polite a 'thank you' as she could and duck out of the group. There was no boyfriend material there, she was now certain.

"New friends?" Missy asked as she wound her way to the back of the room and a small, empty table she'd spotted.

"Not really." Mari set her drink down. "They were polite enough, but after talking a few minutes, it was clear we have nothing in common. Nothing."

In fact, they'd ticked her off, making comments about the people passing by and generally being petty, though they were being nice enough to her. She'd refused a beer from two of the single guys in the group.

Mari hoisted herself carefully onto the tall stool, trying not to flash anyone with her short skirt. "I'm limited to the one drink tonight. Driving."

"Me, too." They ordered some food and were waiting for it to arrive when Missy leaned closer. "So tell me about the job."

"Oh god. You would not believe it." Mariliz felt her forehead settle into her hand, like a reactionary gesture. "It's crazy. I taught the baby some signs, because—obviously—they hired a caretaker who's fluent in sign language. But it turns out, they didn't want her learning sign!"

Her voice was rising as she spoke and she hoped Missy didn't notice.

She did. "So what's the problem. She learned a few signs?"

"They were trying to teach her to lip read and speak." Mariliz was still stunned by that sometimes, but reminded herself that not everyone had her background.

"Can a baby even do that, Lize?" Missy just looked confused, her expression changing to grateful when the fried cheese arrived.

"No. But they had some doctor—a really highly regarded

speech therapist who works with deaf people—convince them it was the way to go." She shook her head, feeling sorry for Sophie again, even though it seemed the worst had passed for the girl. "People will believe what their doctors tell them. And the doctor gave them hope she could live a relatively normal life."

"But now the dad's learning ASL?"

"Oh, Missy, you should see him. The girls are all over it. Sophie is happier. I mean, she still has tantrums sometimes, but she's more like a normal two-year-old. She's learning so many words. Olivia's the fastest, and Alex is having to work to keep up with them!" She smiled at the thought of it.

"You said he left you stuck with the kids. So hot dad is doing better. Have you heard from the mom?" There was something in the way Missy asked it, but Mariliz had too much margarita to grasp the subtle things. She didn't try.

"No. No word from Bridget. I don't get it." She shrugged. "But Alex has really stepped up. That's why I'm out tonight. He's on tour in another week, so he's giving me more days off." She took a breath in. "He bought his girls kittens because they asked for them in sign. I don't think he's all that fond of cats, but he's nice to the kittens when the girls aren't around, and he bought them a five-tier climbing house-thing—"

"Oh, Lize." Missy put her hand on Mari's arm. "You've got it bad."

"No. No, I don't . . . shit. It's the alcohol. I can lie to myself better when I'm sober." Her mouth twisted in a wry grin as she accepted what was clearly becoming fact.

"I have news that isn't going to help."

CHAPTER 16

Mariliz lay on her bed, staring at the ceiling. She could hear the comings and goings of the house. She could hear if Sophie cried out, if Olivia got up and wandered the halls at night. Sophie was the one who needed the most looking after, and thankfully she was the loudest.

She considered sleeping with her doors open so she could hear better, but with Nina and the maid coming into the house on their own in the mornings, she didn't want to. Too creepy to think even one of them could watch her sleep.

It was only ten p.m. but she was exhausted from not sleeping regularly, hence the ceiling staring. She wanted to believe she would sleep better tonight, but there was no reason to think it.

It started a week ago, when she'd been out with Missy. The alcohol, the company, the smoky bar all combined to make her honest for a moment. She'd admitted—out loud to her cousin—how she really felt about Alex. Since she hadn't admitted it to herself before that, it was a bit of a blow.

She told herself it was just physical attraction; the man was hot after all, how could she *not* react? He was a nice guy, and she was a little lonely in that department, if she was confessing. It would make sense that she would latch onto the nearest hot guy. Even the sex dreams were explainable: who didn't have sex dreams about the people around them? And she'd been spending a lot of time around Alex Beaumont. But usually you would wake up from a sex dream about your boss and think, "Oh, that was *weird*." Instead, Mariliz woke up and thought, "Oh, that was *hot*," and wanted to go right back to sleep.

She took her time off to herself. Hung out with Missy, though that didn't help at all. And tried to pry her feelings away from the inappropriate attachment. It didn't work.

Missy had been no help either.

When she'd pulled out her phone at the bar, her cousin had confessed, "I've been digging up the gossip now that you work for them."

"Please, Miss. You know most of that isn't true. It won't even mean anything." Mari protested.

"You need to see this." Missy held up the phone. Though the pictures were small, they were clearly gossip rag shots of a blond woman in a serious liplock with a shirtless man on a yacht. It read, "Is that Bridget Beaumont? Wife of Wilder drummer Alex Beaumont . . ."

Mari didn't read the rest. "That's probably not even her. You know all those pictures showed up of Tiger Woods' wife and it turned out she had a twin."

"Bridget Beaumont does not have a twin."

When Mari gave a pointed stare, Bridget held up her hands, palm out. "I checked! Even her sister, Francesca, doesn't look like her."

"Well, I've seen pictures of her around the house. Bridget isn't blond. At least not now. Probably some old photo." She sipped her margarita only to find she'd hit the bottom. She wanted a second one—desperately—just a few minutes later.

Missy shook her head, and Mari knew there was bad news coming. "One—I had to dig for this. The Beaumonts really aren't front page material. None of Wilder made much news before TJ's accident. So why would there be an old paparazzi photo of her? Two—she *is* blond now. And it's the only time she's been blond. It's recent. There are more photos."

The phone and the photos her cousin had loaded to make her case revealed a brunette Bridget at an awards ceremony with Alex just six months prior. A history of photos showed she'd been brunette all along, but suddenly blond within the past month. And the close ups? That was the woman in the family portraits around the house. And the lip lock? It spoke of a lot more than just kisses.

Shit. Double margarita and triple shit.

She'd been thinking the same thing for a week now. Somehow, she'd managed not to open her mouth, not to tell the man who was quickly becoming a real friend, despite her disturbing crush, that his wife was cheating on him.

Did he already know? Should she tell him?

No. No she shouldn't. It wasn't her place. She was just the help. Mari wasn't positive about the pictures even though the magazine named Bridget as the one standing on a yacht in a blue bikini. It sure looked like her. But the gossip rags didn't sell without juicy tales, and as long as they asked a question, they didn't have to prove who was in the photo.

Her phone rang and her left hand slapped out onto the night stand to pick it up. She pulled it to her ear without looking. "Hello?"

"Hey, Lize." Alex's voice came through despite the noise in the background. "Just calling to check up on my girls. We finally got a moment."

He'd told her yesterday that he wouldn't be able to make any of the possible times both the girls would be around today. "They're great. Sophie got more new words today. She's starting to string them together."

"That's fantastic." She could hear it in his voice. He was proud of his daughter. "How is Olivia's school project going?"

"Two more days to work on it, but we knocked out another section tonight, and she only has one part left. One day to check it or for buffer. And the teacher said I could come and video the presentation for you."

"Thursday? I'll keep my eye out for the video. I'll make sure I get it downloaded." His bus had wi-fi, she knew.

"Aren't you onstage right now?" That was a dumb question. Obviously he wasn't talking to her on his cell while the band was on. She looked up at the ornate iron scroll clock someone had matched to the curtain rods in here and saw that it was, indeed, ten at night.

"Only eight here." His voice came through right as she was putting it all together. "How's my mother? Is she pestering you?"

Pestering wasn't the right word. "Well, she's calling daily—"

"You mean on the phone, not at the door, right?" She could hear the fear in his voice and laughed at him.

"Yes, on the phone. She has sign language tapes—VHS which she struggled to find, mind you—and she's learning words and making your father learn them, too. She's coming over tomorrow to play with Sophie while I run errands and then she's going to take Sophie while I go to Olivia's class to film her presentation."

"Are they ready for that? Sophie and Mom, I mean?" The fear had changed to worry.

"I'll keep her if you want me to. And I do think she'd benefit from seeing the older kids in class, but I don't know if she can— no, I'm confident she *can't*—keep quiet during Olivia's presentation." For a moment, despite the fact that they were talking casually about her job, she wished she had the old phone cord to wrap around her finger while she talked. "In my personal opinion, they'll be fine. Your mom has that bin of toys, and Sophie won't be able to get into any trouble because your mom or dad won't let her out of their sight. They'll probably feed her too much ice cream. She's already learned that she can get anything she wants from them now."

"You're right. You're right." He was nervous. Then again, he had a history with his parents that Mariliz wasn't privy to. Still things looked good to her. When they'd talked about the possibility of Mari filming so Alex could see Olivia's work, they'd also talked about Olivia not needing her noisy little sister stealing her show. "They seem really happy to have their granddaughter back. They haven't gotten to enjoy Sophie much after the first month or two. Once she started screaming, they couldn't keep her."

"Well, your mother was just pleased as little peaches to get Sophie for the afternoon."

"Her words."

"Exactly." Mari paused for a second, out of items on her agenda even though she loved the sound of his voice, his laughter, his excitement about his kids. This man was so different from the one she'd met first.

If only Bridget would come around. Mari almost hoped she would, so she could see the two of them together and get her face slapped with the fact that she was the nanny. Maybe then she'd latch onto a more appropriate crush.

"I need more videos." He was saying.

"You learned all the words from the last one?" Her phone dinged.

"I just sent it to you." He'd taken to emailing her videos of him signing. This was after she emailed him videos of her signing various words, followed by full sentences using the new words.

"Hold on." She opened it and fought a laugh. He looked so serious, concentrating on what his hands did. She read his sentences back to him while she watched. "The cat sat on the roof. The kittens enjoyed the grapes. Dogs don't like chicken—

that's a lie, my dog loved it." She added her commentary, then continued through the remaining first-grade level sentences he produced in sign. "Okay, tomorrow you have to use time. Like, 'yesterday I went to the store.' 'Tomorrow I will' . . ."

"Oh! Yes."

"And you have to start practicing questions, too." She added, as though she were his teacher. "When you get back, we need to find a family class. There's a pizza lunch for the local chapter of TAD."

He was already learning about the local support groups, though they hadn't gone yet. "When?"

"Saturday. Noon. I know it's the day you get back, but these particular meetings are only monthly. If you want to meet other parents in similar situations, help the girls meet others, you should—"

"No, I don't think I'll be up for it. We get in around four a.m."

She knew that. The lunch was at one. Still, something in his tone told her he was going to say no even before she gave him any details. He seemed fine with her taking Sophie out and about. Sophie had met other deaf kids at one of the meetings; Mari had even set up a playdate once with another deaf toddler. They had another date for the following week.

"Send me another video. I'm ready." He changed the topic.

She'd thought about this, last night while she made today's video. She sat on her bed, spoke words, then signed the equivalent. Her phone would sit propped on a pillow. She'd give him sentences to decipher and he'd email his return video the next day. It was all well and good—except she felt a little odd making videos of herself for this man she had a disturbing crush on.

"Alex, you need to start getting words off the web. You can buy DVDs!" She'd decided to stop sending the videos.

"I tried the online ones. Those people are creepy. And I got a DVD and it wasn't the words I need." He sighed, as though she was putting him into a tough spot instead of the other way around. "Please?"

"Okay." She did know what words he needed. She could feed him what Olivia and Sophie asked for each day. Then again, she could text him a list and he could look it up on the internet, too. While the signers online often were a bit creepy, she should have held stronger against him. "I'll send you another one in a bit."

He thanked her, told her he had to go and checked one last time. "You'll have the girls at seven-fifteen for me?"

"Yes. I promise." She knew he would have to get up at five a.m. his time to make it. But he'd missed today and would otherwise miss tomorrow. Saying goodbye, she set the phone down by the bed before remembering she'd promised him a video.

With a sigh, she propped up the phone and pulled her hair around behind her shoulders so he could see. She refused to do her makeup again, though it had to have all worn off today. She didn't even brush her hair. She wasn't trying to catch this man.

Ten minutes later she sent out the video, even though he was probably out on stage already and wouldn't see it for a while. She made a quiet circuit of the house, so as not to wake Olivia, and found everything as it should be. Checking the locks, she felt herself yawn and was grateful.

When she climbed into bed, she stared at the ceiling again. At least this time she wasn't wondering about Bridget. Now she was wondering about Alex.

He encouraged her to take the girls out into the community. Attend meet-ups, find other deaf kids, families. Sophie had met deaf gentlemen and women at the local Y, where a small subsection of older deaf people met up for conversation, crafts, and general community. Some had set up chess games in a corner of one of the rooms. The little girl had loved seeing the others sign to her.

Alex loved hearing about it. But when Mariliz invited him along, he always had something else to do. He'd taken Sophie and Livie out to dinner, and they'd only used sign. Olivia had even spent the whole next morning telling Mari about it—about how the server had signed to them and everything. So it wasn't that Alex didn't want to be seen in public signing.

But something was off.

CHAPTER 17

lex ignored the weird look JD gave him as they said goodbye, the four men scattering throughout the parking lot. JD had been giving him weird looks all week.

When he was in a mood to be honest with himself, Alex understood. Part of it was that the four men were like brothers —they loved each other, they had each others' backs, and they could shred each other if they tried. On the bus, they lived in such close proximity that nothing went unnoticed.

He understood that most grown men didn't have that kind of relationship, that kind of bond, with anyone. As special as it was, he'd always been the odd man out. They loved him; he knew that. But he was the least outgoing, happy to mostly stay quiet and speak when needed. He didn't talk all the time like TJ or have bouts of moodiness like Craig. He wasn't as warm as JD. He was a damn good brother and loyal to a fault, though. He knew that about himself.

Maybe that was why JD was giving him weird looks. While JD had always made it clear he was available if Alex needed to talk about Sophie, about the problems they'd had, about Bridget leaving, the guitarist had never pushed.

Now, they were all keeping up with him talking to the girls like he used to with Olivia. Craig came on video behind him and signed a little on camera to say hello, shocking Mari and the girls equally. Then the next day, the brothers—JD and TJ— pestered him and Craig to show them some basic signs so they could pop in and say hello, too. They were even pushy about it, but he'd been excited. He was happy to be happy with his kids. The clench in his chest was partly gone these days. He was happy his bandmates wanted to make his daughter feel as welcome as possible, even though it meant they had to take time to learn something just to say hello.

Then, the way they'd all walked to the back of the bus, Craig leading the gaggle of them while he kept chatting, seemed odd. They were talking. Craig nodded and had that "I told you so" look. Alex had dismissed it.

Yesterday, JD had come by the main area and signed hello and a few other words before he ran out of vocabulary. But as soon as Alex signed off video chat, JD was back. He'd said only two words: "She's hot."

"She's the nanny." Alex had replied curtly before realizing maybe he should have said he didn't notice. But he had.

JD only nodded before heading back to his own little cubby of a room.

The problem was, Alex understood. Lize *was* hot, but she *was* also the nanny. TJ had been the last of them to get married, right around the time the problems with Sophie were coming to a head. They were supposedly all settled. But Alex wasn't. Not anymore. They each ducked into their own little room to talk to wives, whispered voices coming low through the not-quite-soundproof doors. They'd all learned to live with it.

Being in each other's back pockets meant they all knew he was now ducking into his room to talk to Mariliz. His conversations with Bridget had slowly turned brittle over the past two years. Only as he'd picked up the phone and felt that hot, honeyed melt when he talked to the new nanny had he realized just how distant his wife had become.

He *wasn't* cheating on her. A crush on the nanny was no big deal. He didn't act on it. And it was almost inevitable: Lize *was* hot. She'd also saved Sophie. She had him betting on Sophie now.

So he threw his bags into the back of his car and tried to ignore how excited he was to be going home. He wanted to sleep in his own bed again. It was his, even if he was in it alone. He was happy to see his girls—Sophie would hug him, he knew it. Livie would be happy to see him, she wouldn't have to hide from her sister and he didn't have to feel guilty about time with her. He also had quality, happy time with Sophie now. If he was also excited to see Lize again, that was just because she was the only other adult in the house who did more than thank him for the paycheck. She was fast becoming a real friend. No, she already was that.

He was pushing his way in through the mudroom door and kicking his shoes off when he heard a door open.

Ducking softly through the kitchen, he caught a sleepy-eyed Lize opening her door.

"Oh, good." She blinked softly, her hair tumbling in waves around her shoulders. She breathed in, not really awake. "Just wanted to be sure it was you. See you in a bit."

She started to close the door to her suite, but he made it there just in time to put a hand out and stop her. "Go back to sleep. You have the day off. I've got this."

She blinked rapidly as she tried to process. "I—thank you."

Though her eyes still weren't quite open all the way, a smile graced her lips and punched him in the gut. But she closed the door on him while he stood there trying to figure out what had just happened.

His own eyes fell closed and his head tipped back. It was the videos: the videos she sent of her signing. That's why he liked them so much. No makeup, her hair not brushed. He could tell she filmed most of them sitting on her bed. It seemed intimate, like how she must look when she first woke up.

Now he knew.

He knew he was in deep shit.

Grabbing his bag out of the mudroom, he headed upstairs to try to catch another hour of sleep before the girls got up. He'd barely crawled into bed before he heard the alarm and rolled over to see that he had, in fact, slept, even if it didn't seem to mean anything. He wished he could sleep more, but he was still in a bit of a honeymoon phase.

Lize had taught him about flicking the lights for Sophie—how it was the equivalent to knocking on Livie's door. He was in a fight to learn as many words as he could, improve his Sign Language skills as much as possible, because he was nowhere near an adult level. Sophie needed adults speaking around her. As it stood, she had one adult and two first-graders. It was as far as he and Livie had advanced.

Alex tried not to kick himself for not doing this sooner. He hadn't known; he'd been operating on the advice of doctors. And it had been hell, but it was much better now. Sophie wasn't perfect. She still screamed and had temper tantrums, but she was *two*. The sheer normality of that warmed his heart in a way he'd never expected. So he got up early and made Olivia breakfast with sleepy eyelids but a smile in his heart. He gave Sophie a small bowl of dry cheerios.

After they dropped Olivia off, he drove to a breakfast restaurant he liked and when they got home he sat at the bar in the kitchen with Sophie pulled up next to him. He opened the container of bacon, egg, and cheese biscuits. Putting one back for Mariliz, he set his on a plate and broke one up for Sophie.

Trying to stay quiet because Lize was probably still asleep just on the other side of the door at the back of the kitchen, he proceeded to teach his daughter "bacon" and "egg" and was working on the next one when she ate a piece and pointed to the biscuit.

He shrugged at her. She shrugged back and giggled.

Grabbing his phone, he tried for the video online dictionary. After a minute he frowned. They just spelled it. That was disappointing! He looked up "bread." Better. He signed that to Sophie who signed back to him, giggled, and ate it.

The tap on the bar top startled him, but got his attention. Mariliz was standing there in jeans and a t-shirt smiling at the two of them. She didn't speak but signed *good morning*. Sophie squealed at her.

"I hope we didn't—" he started, but she interrupted him with a shake of the head. Nodding, he started again with his hands. He could now talk with his mouth full, that was a plus. His signs were halting as he worked to put the simple sentence together. "I hope we not . . . wake you."

"Nope. I slept in. So nice. Thank you." She smiled and signed back, fluidly, beautifully. Then she turned to Sophie. "What are you eating?"

"We got you one. There." He signed to her and watched as she lit up at the silly gift. She plucked off a bite and watched Sophie. Like a champ, his daughter moved her chubby hands into approximations of "bacon," "eggs," and "cheese." Then she pointed to the biscuit and shrugged.

So his version of "bread" didn't cut it for her either.

Mari signed it for them with a smile and he burst out, "We looked on the phone—" then he sighed. Every time he spoke without signing, he was cutting his daughter out of the conversation. It wasn't habit yet, especially when he'd been away for over a week. This time he signed. "Sophie-and-I looked at phone. Dictionary. Fingerspelled."

Both the online dictionary and his lack of skills frustrated him. Sophie signed "biscuit" happily, her frustration over. Apparently her breakfast was over, too. She struggled to get down, but pointed one hand and smacked the other on the table for attention. When he didn't respond fast enough, she smacked her hand precariously close to his biscuit crumbs and signed "Daddy, down."

It was the sign for "Daddy" that made him forgive the rest. Unbuckling her, he let her toddle off into the corner to play with the toys in the bin. He turned back to Mariliz. "We'll have to start teaching manners soon."

"Like today." She popped another piece of biscuit into her mouth, standing there on the other side of the island.

"Do you want to come sit?" She was eating standing up. On her day off, nonetheless. But she refused. He changed the subject. "I don't want to punish her. I just got her back."

"You don't have to punish her to correct her. Not until she rampantly disobeys. It's not hurtful to teach her the right thing." Mari shrugged again. "At her age their brains are soaking up everything. The longer it goes on without correction, the more you make bad manners a habit she has to unlearn. Make it easy. Demonstrate the correct way, stop her when she's wrong. That's all."

He nodded.

"I know you're letting her get away with a lot because you just got things together, so to speak, but it's not the best thing. I think it will cause problems later." She stopped for a minute, her gaze in the corner of the room. Weird.

"What?" He asked.

"I'm not her parent. It's your choice. That's just my advice." She offered a half smile that seemed a bit forced.

"Your advice has been the best advice I've gotten all along. It's welcome." He hoped she understood that. He'd had some tough choices. He still had them. But she'd been the one consistent thing that made the world better for him, and he didn't know how to tell her that.

"Can I offer one more piece of advice then?" She looked wary.

"Of course."

"You can't do it now, but . . ." She took a breath. "I don't want to get your hopes up. I just—"

"What?" He pressed.

"I think you should get Sophie re-tested in about six months. Let her get some language under her belt. I think *you* and Livie need to get in some classes and get some language from someone other than me."

His heart clenched. He wasn't ready for that. No classes. Not yet.

Though it seemed he wasn't fooling her, that she'd caught on that he was actively avoiding classes, Lize continued. "But, later, I think you should re-test her. I think it's possible that she doesn't actually have any learning deficits."

CHAPTER 18

A lex was stunned.
He'd stayed that way all morning. Lize left to run her own errands, leaving him with the bombshell she'd dropped. She said she didn't want to get his hopes up, but she had. There was no way around it.

Mariliz Jennings had a degree in childhood development. She knew what was normal and what wasn't. She'd casually pointed out a few things over the past week that Sophie had done. She'd say, "That's perfectly normal for a two-year-old," or even, "that was pretty bright of her."

He'd been proud papa, no doubt. Now Lize seemed to believe it was possible that Sophie was normal. When he pressed her, she gave up the goods and said, "Honestly, if you asked me to gauge her right now, *today*, I'd guess that she's actually pretty bright."

He'd countered, tamping down his own spark of hope. He spoke only English, not wanting Sophie to hear this, in case she was as bright as Lize suggested. "But she tested below level on every test."

Once again, she'd blown him away. She pointed out that

intelligence tests on kids are hard to determine with any accuracy in hearing, communicating children. That often kids who test as low functioning turn out to have amazing skills that appear later. But she'd brought up some very pertinent facts. "Sophie was only tested when she had no language. The things she was asked, she didn't understand. And she couldn't communicate what she thought."

He'd absorbed that, but Lize kept talking.

"It's pretty rare for a kid to be below level on *everything*. Just like bright kids have strong and weak areas." She polished off the biscuit as though she wasn't turning his world upside down again. "It's the fact that she was significantly below age level on every test that made me think it was wrong in the first place. I would have thought that looking at those scores if I had never met her."

There was a brief pause of silence before she continued. "But I have met her, and she's fast with the words. There's not a lot of data on that though. Not a lot of kids who go completely without language for that long to compare her speed against."

She didn't see the knife twisting in his heart, and Alex fought to hide both it and the anger at his wife that came with each thought about it. He focused back on the woman in front of him.

"Sophie does things that are above level. If you look at what she builds, it shows a strong understanding of shapes and relationships. She rejected your sign for bread, knew she needed a different one to distinguish the biscuit. I just think you need to get her re-tested. Later. That's all."

She'd thanked him for the food, ducked back into her room, and left out her personal door. He hadn't seen her again, though she'd left him reeling. He joined his daughter on the floor for a while, gave her a sippy cup of milk and fought sleep, like any other parent.

They played with the kittens until Sophie wore them out

and they climbed up high to sleep in peace. He envied them, but put his daughter to work scooping out kitten food into little bowls, sweeping up spills, and more. It took forever, but that was okay. It was *normal*.

When he was about to tap out, he had an idea.

He looked up the online video dictionary for the word he needed, then signed it to Sophie. She didn't understand. Alex signed it again, and motioned for her to follow.

Pushing up onto her feet, Sophie tucked her cup into the crook of her arm. Alex noticed that she often did that. The milk was cold, and he didn't think it could be comfortable, but he saw now as she asked "Where, Daddy?" that the move allowed her free hands.

Maybe Lize was right.

He headed down the hall with his baby chick following him. Normally, he kept the door to his studio closed to keep dust and children out. Now, he added kittens to the list, not even wanting to think about what a cat could do to his drums.

When he opened the door, he watched Sophie's face. She frowned.

This was his Sophie. She made his heart swell at her progress. She made it feel deep fear at what that progress might mean. She made it fall when he thought about the fact that he was a musician and she would never hear music. She could never feel what he felt when he played.

But she liked to bang things. Lize said she felt the vibrations, and drums had that in spades. So maybe she wouldn't—*couldn't* —like them for the same reasons he did, but maybe she could like them for her own.

He led her inside and closed the door behind them. Pulling out a set of sticks, he sat down behind the kit. As his daughter watched, curious, he tapped the rim of the snare three times to give himself a rhythm and started across the kit.

His eyes closed while he played.

He always did. He knew where everything was. Sure, he opened them periodically, checked where the guys were on stage. Banged out a quick riff when TJ tossed the spotlight to him. But mostly, he closed his eyes and *felt* it.

When he turned to look at Sophie, she was staring at him, wide-eyed. Her milk cup stayed tucked in the crook of her arm, her other hand was stretched out to push into the plush wall cover. She pulled it back to sign, "Again."

With a smile, this time he watched her while he did it. Less than five seconds of sound, but Sophie reacted.

"Again."

They went back and forth like that for a while. He started playing different beats and realized Sophie could tell the difference. She detected a difference in the cymbals, not just that he was hitting something that looked different.

When he added in the bass drum—didn't know why he'd waited on that one—her eyes and mouth went round with excitement. So, using the foot pedal, he only played that.

Sophie set her milk down and squealed and clapped at him.

When he did it again, she clapped in rhythm, nearly stopping his heart. They played that way for a while together, until his phone buzzed. He checked it—nothing important—but noticed the time. Five minutes to nap time.

He was awake now. He wanted to keep playing. He was having fun with his daughter, and he had so much time to make up for. Mariliz would have said she needed to go down for her nap, stick to a schedule, but he didn't want to. So he mostly ignored the time, calculating when she would absolutely have to lie down in order to get up in time to fetch Olivia from school.

He set the buzzer and held his hand out to his daughter. She ran up to him and let him pull her up on his lap. Why have her be a bystander? Putting the sticks into her little hands, just like he'd done with Livie years before, he directed her to bang out her own beat.

Sophie made as much noise as the drum kit. It was almost as though she enjoyed the feel of air passing through her vocal cords, though she would likely never hear the sounds she made. He started thinking, if she wasn't learning disabled, was she maybe also not inherently aggressive?

He would say she was still more aggressive than Olivia, but the difference between now and a month ago was night and day. Maybe in another month, she wouldn't feel so trapped. Maybe if they started working on etiquette with her—score another point for Lize—it would get even better. They'd always made sure Olivia knew polite ways to get what she needed and wanted no matter how little she'd been. There hadn't been a chance until now with Sophie.

The doctors had been concerned she'd rip out any earpieces she had to wear with the cochlear implants, that the wires wouldn't be safe on her. Maybe that was wrong. Maybe if she tested better, maybe if she wasn't so aggressive, maybe if they found some residual hearing, she could get a cochlear implant.

It was a damn lot of maybes. But it was better than they'd had.

He felt her tug at his hands, wanting the sticks for herself. Praying she didn't jab one directly into the surface, he took a breath and handed them over.

She giggled and he wondered if he'd just heard God . . . Or Satan.

Breath held, he waited.

Sophie banged out an imperfect sound in perfect time. This time it was Alex who signed "Again."

They played that way for a while, Alex sitting with Sophie on his lap so his daughter could reach most of the drums herself. It didn't matter that his legs fell asleep. He was a Daddy again.

He directed her into some basic patterns, which she either didn't pick up or ignored in favor of her own creations. Slowly, her sounds got a little better. Or he got used to them. But he was a musician in his heart and soul, while he could be lying to himself, he really did think she was self-correcting a bit. Who knew?

On a whim, he pulled out a second set of sticks and started joining her. Whatever beat Sophie laid out, he worked with it. He hit the far left cymbal she couldn't reach, added the bass drum with the foot pedal, and basically hit around where she was aiming.

It was exhausting, but fun, and when he checked his phone, he found they had only ten minutes left. Putting his hands softly over hers, he signed to his daughter. "Ten more minute. Next nap."

She started to protest, but he stopped her.

"Ten more minute. No cry. Can play tomorrow. Okay?"

Sophie nodded though her lip quivered. So he signed to her "Ten minute. You play!"

They laid out beats that rocked him, even if it was discordant. Then, suddenly, Sophie stiffened.

"Wrong?" He signed at her, grateful he had enough signs to get by with the basics. He *needed* class. He had to get ready for it. Sophie didn't deserve him copping out. But was it really the right decision? It would open a whole new can of worms.

It was a choice for a later day. Sophie wasn't answering. Just staring at him.

"Sophie," he signed again, "What's wrong?"

She was looking at him strangely still when the door opened. Alex looked up to see Bridget staring back.

CHAPTER 19

Alex froze. It was the fact that Sophie wasn't happy to see her mother that bothered him the most.

He knew Bridget had all but abandoned the girl when she couldn't deal with the constant screaming, crying, hitting, and more. It only got worse as Sophie got older. It didn't shock him that Sophie only stared at her own mother as though waiting for the other shoe to drop. It saddened him, but didn't surprise.

He hoped to turn that around. Prayed he could knit his little family back together.

"You going to come greet me properly?" His wife taunted him with a saucy look on her face.

And wasn't that part of the problem? He'd sat there staring at her, too. No desire to jump up and kiss her. No relief that she'd returned. Only concern at how things would go. "Of course, baby."

Standing, he tucked Sophie into his arms, abandoning all the sticks scattered across the drum surfaces. Sophie stayed stock still, even as the phone buzzed in his pocket.

Smiling, for he truly was happy to see her, Alex kissed his wife on the cheek and then reached into his pocket to turn off the phone. "It's time to put Sophie to nap, so we can pick up Olivia on time."

Bridget smiled and said, "It looks like you've found something to soothe her." But she didn't reach out for her daughter. Didn't even offer to help put her to sleep. "I'm going to go grab a drink. Travel was harsh. Come get me when she's asleep." And she walked off.

He understood. Sophie had broken her. The baby had cried, screamed, hated her own mother. Eventually, Bridget had cracked. Everyone had a tipping point. Hell, he'd cracked, too, but he had come back. These were his kids. It wasn't as if Sophie had done it on purpose.

He smiled at his daughter though he wasn't sure she bought it. He laid her in her "new, big-girl bed" and read her a short story he knew all the signs for. He was up to four of Sophie's books now and working his way rapidly toward six. Of course, Mariliz Jennings could read his daughter all of them. And his wife could read her none. He pushed the thought aside.

Sophie went docilely to sleep, which worried him. She usually tried all the tactics: she was thirsty, she had to read another book, something was interesting on the other side of the room. She only signed "Goodnight" to him as he pulled her little crocheted blanket over her.

It was her favorite. A fact he had only learned recently.

Heading downstairs, he found Bridget popping the top on a diet coke from the back of the fridge. As she poured the drink over ice into a tall, slim glass, she started peppering him with demands for information. "I didn't hear anything. No fits. Frankie said the new nanny is a specialist. Is it working?"

"Yes." He was opening his mouth to say more but she won the battle for air and he stood down.

"How is Olivia doing in school?"

"She's getting all As and Bs." He put a smile behind it, this was almost as tense as talking about Sophie.

"No, she has to get straight As. I thought you said the new nanny was working out." She frowned and picked up her drink.

"I think Olivia's fine with As and Bs." He countered. His older daughter was happier now. "She can work on the grades in a few years. We'll start her in middle school and she can be a straight A student in high school."

"She won't get into a good high school if she doesn't have the top grades." Bridget countered.

This was an old argument. He didn't know why he kept having it. Then he did. "Look, Bridget, I caved on this one before and the old nanny rode Olivia night and day about her homework. She hated it. I want her to have a childhood."

"She has one. And she'll have a better one with straight As!" She wasn't angry, just frustrated with him.

"I disagree. She needs to get out, join a sports team or something. She's lost a lot of time because of Sophie. It's hard having a baby sister with special needs." He was frustrated, too. But he'd seen Livie more recently than Bridget had. She was happier now. They all were. Bridget could be, too, if she'd let herself be.

"We've all suffered from Sophie's special needs, Alex." She looked down, the glass suddenly empty. "But there's no box for that on the application. Olivia will need to haul her own weight on that, regardless of Sophie."

"Not at eight. She's had plenty of responsibility. And it's a private school, they want our money, Bridge. They'll keep her around. She's a good student." He was leaning on his hands on the other side of the bar.

She turned away, clinking the ice down the drain, leaving the glass in the sink. When she turned back, she sighed at him. "Look, why don't you stay here with Sophie, and I'll go pick up Olivia at school? I'll surprise her, she'll love it."

"She will." He was just agreeing as Bridget picked up her purse and began rummaging through it.

When she pulled out her sunglasses and parked them on her head, he figured it out. "You're leaving? You have a half hour before you need to go."

"I want to meet up with Amanda and Paisley. Then I'll get Olivia." She was out the door before he got himself together.

She'd made plans with her friends, but she hadn't told her husband she was going to be home.

Mariliz had come home about two that afternoon. Missy was at work that day, and she didn't really have anyone else to call. Making the most of the unexpected full day off, she'd slept in, then hit the coffee shop. After that, she'd looked around, thinking she might try to join a gym. Though her paycheck wasn't huge, room and board really offset most of her needs. The hazard bump Alex had bestowed upon her meant she could afford a few more things.

It wasn't like when she'd lived with Reynold and just spent whatever she wanted whenever. Only when he'd stopped her a few times, told her to tone down the spending, had she ever thought about the money that slipped through her fingers.

In college, she was very budget conscious, and she didn't have much problem getting back into the swing of that now. She'd spent several hours at the mall, eventually polishing off a burger by herself at a food court table. Before, eating alone would have killed her. But now, after having kids hanging on her most days, it seemed kind of blissful.

After lunch she toured two gyms, but then, as she looked at the third and wrinkled her nose, she noticed the salon next door. No gym. Mani/pedi instead. She could always join later.

She left in foam, salon flip flops with massaged legs and hands and decided that a nap was in order. She could read or be lazy, and there was something delicious about it.

The flip flops didn't fare much better on the pavers around the side of the house than heels did, but she made it inside and stretched out, only waking later to the sound of voices. She thought she'd heard the door slam, but maybe not.

When she looked at the clock, she realized it was just past time for them to be getting home from the afternoon school run. So she stretched, thinking it felt wonderful and languid to roll awake with no alarm. And she wouldn't have to eat her dinner alone. Alex and Livie and Sophie would be glad to have her. Her hand was on the knob to enter the kitchen when she heard the strange voice.

"So! Olivia tells me that you and the new nanny have been teaching Sophie *sign language!*" The last words were irate and Mari yanked her hand from the knob as though it burned her.

"That's what I was trying to tell you before." Alex's words seemed calm in response even though Mari could tell he was practically grinding his teeth. "Sophie's well behaved now, she can communicate, *that's* what's working."

He didn't deliver it with the pride and push that she'd expected. Mari thought she should bury herself in her bedroom, put two doors between her and the argument. Maybe turn up the TV.

But for all its fancy brickwork and scrolled staircases, the place wasn't all that soundproof. Turning on her TV would tell them all she was there. And despite knowing she shouldn't eavesdrop, she desperately wanted to. So Mariliz did something she shouldn't.

She turned her back to the door and slid softly down to sitting. She wouldn't press a glass or even her ear to the door, but if they were loud enough for her to hear, so be it.

They were.

"You can't do that! She'll never be normal now, Alex!"

"Bridge, she was never going to be normal anyway. She's deaf!" He fought back, his tone more controlled than his wife's.

"She could have gotten close. She could have learned."

"No she couldn't. We tried to teach her to speak, Bridge, and look what it got us."

"So you wait until I'm gone then you just throw away the advice of the most respected physician in the whole South? What is that, Alex? I worked so hard to get him to take her as a patient!" She slammed something on the counter and Mari sent up a prayer of thanks that Sophie was asleep and Olivia wasn't home to see this.

"Where did you find that doctor, Bridget? I know how many you went to. You stayed with him because he told you what you wanted to hear. He convinced you he could make Sophie seem normal, didn't he?"

"He's the best in the South." Bridget countered.

"He's never worked with—let alone had any success with—anyone under seven. Seven, Bridget. Your daughter wasn't even seventeen months old." He paused and sucked in a breath. "I let you do all of it. You liked being a mom, and you were good at it. So good." He had to acknowledge that. "But you didn't do this one right. You missed things, and I did too. But I'm learning now. No one can learn to lip read when they don't even have any language. It's impossible."

Oh no. Mari heard some of her own words in the argument. This was not good.

"We agreed, Alex, we *agreed*!" the female voice shot back.

"No, *we* didn't." His voice cracked. "It's my fault. I get that. It was easier to let you handle it, so I did. But you *told* me how we were going to raise her. You never *asked*. I went along because I didn't want this family to blow apart, but it did anyway."

"Only when you went behind my back and got some nanny to teach her a language that no one knows." Another loud slam came, but Mari had no idea what it might be. It didn't sound like anything had broken at least.

"I didn't! I wasn't even here, if you remember. Frankie

installed her and left her with no instructions. Frankie picked her." He breathed in and Bridget started to say something, but Alex didn't let her. "She's a specialist. She's fluent in ASL and why else would a family with a deaf kid hire a sign language interpreter? So she taught Sophie sign. That's all."

"Clearly, that's not all. She ruined *everything*."

Mari sucked in a breath then had the sudden fear they'd heard her. It seemed they hadn't. But how had she ruined everything? It was working. Sophie was happy. Olivia was happy. Everyone was happy, except Bridget.

And Alex. He'd been pleased, but holding back. He'd known. He'd known his wife would react this way.

This time he was silent, as though there was no repercussion he could come back with.

Bridget yelled again. "Why didn't you tell her no? Why didn't you stop her?"

This time there was no stopping him. He had the lungs of a musician, Mari had seen him on TV holding court on the drums and then singing at the same time. He bellowed.

"Why didn't *YOU*?"

There was a huff, a noise, then a door. A moment later Mari heard the garage door start to lift, but she didn't know which one of them had left. She didn't know who she would find if she turned the knob or if she should even venture out to check on the girls.

Tears tracked Mari's face as she sat there against the door. She'd fucked up. Royally. She'd come into this very broken house and made it all sunny. But she hadn't paid attention to the shadows. Olivia *told* her they weren't teaching Sophie sign language. When Alex agreed with what she said, he'd been reticent.

Still, Mariliz had pushed. She told him "you have to choose." She meant between having a daughter who signed and having an angry, uncommunicative beast who didn't.

She hadn't realized. That wasn't his choice: she'd made him choose between his wife and his daughter.

Her hand came up to her mouth as her tears broke loose. Her sobs almost masked the sound of a tapping knock at the glass sliding door that led from her bedroom to the back yard.

CHAPTER 20

S tartled, Mari popped up from her seat at the door where the rest of the house had gone disturbingly silent.

The tapping at the glass came again, and she rushed into her bedroom to pull aside the curtains that covered the sliding door. She looked up, expecting to see Alex, but it was a worried Olivia who waited on the other side.

Hoping the girl couldn't see her face in the darkness of the room, Mariliz held up one finger and let the curtain fall closed. She wiped at her face and hoped she hid it but was pretty certain the eight-year-old would see through her.

She slid back the door to the warm night air and tried a smile. "Hey, Livie."

It didn't matter that she'd wiped her face. Olivia threw herself at Mari, hugging her around the waist, sobbing into her shirt. "I'm sorry. I'm sorry."

"Oh, baby." She stroked the girl's head. "It's hard when parents fight."

Hell, it had been hard on her and they weren't her parents. Then she had another thought. "How did you get back here?"

A sniff, a breath. "I went out the door at the back of the playroom."

Okay, so she'd snuck out the back and just come through the fenced in yard to this door on the side. Mariliz's heart beat a little easier. Then, "Where's Sophie?"

"In her room, in bed." Another sniff. "She can't hear them, but she knows."

"Yeah, they made noise. She can feel it even if she can't hear it." Mari sighed, hoping the little girl wasn't awake. What a thing to sit through, not knowing what was getting said or what was coming. "Are they normally like this?"

After a month in the house, Mariliz had to ask the kid. She still hadn't seen Bridget face-to-face.

"Only sometimes." But Olivia looked up at her and changed the subject back. "How can you *feel* sound?"

That was a kid for you. Or maybe she just wanted to be distracted. Mari obliged her. "You know when the music's really loud and you can feel the buzz? Or when your dad's in his room and you know when he's playing and when he's not?"

Olivia nodded.

"Sophie feels that even more than we do. Or at least she pays attention to it better than we do." Mari ushered the girl inside, hoping not to attract the bugs and motioned for them to sit on the bed. Thank God she'd made it after her nap. "She doesn't hear anything, so she pays more attention to the other information she gets. So that buzz from noise, she understands that. Especially when that buzz happens and everyone looks up. She can follow that."

Olivia was nodding, understanding, but then she looked away.

"What is it, honey?" As soon as the words left her mouth, Mariliz wished she could call them back. Who knew what the girl would say now? What kind of awful position could Mari be put into? How should she answer if Olivia wanted information about her parents? And, oh, those pictures of Bridget—Mariliz prayed they weren't true, but felt in her gut that they were.

"You're going to be mad at me." Olivia looked away.

"Why would I be mad?" Not what she'd expected. Her thoughts raced in a different direction, though they didn't get very far.

Livie was crying again, but to her credit, she got the words out. "I told on you."

"I don't understand." Told on her? Tattled? For what?

Now the girl was sobbing in earnest, hiccups punctuating her words. "I was so surprised when Mom came to get me. I was excited."

She was pleading now, her voice, her eyes turning to Mariliz.

"She asked how we were, and I told her you were here and we were all doing better. I told her you taught Sophie to sign." Her eyes were now wide as saucers.

"So? That's true. It's okay to say that." It hadn't been her fault.

"But I knew. I knew she'd be mad about it. That her doctor told us not to let Sophie do it." She sniffled again, fat tears rolling down her face.

"It's okay, Livie. You didn't make the decision. I did. That's on me. Not you."

"But I told her that I told you not to. I was afraid."

Ah, there it was. The kid had thrown Mariliz under the bus to save her own ass with her mother. Jeez. Poor thing had probably been shaking with fear since the afternoon. Mari decided to address that, even as she wondered why she was the one doing this and not the child's mother.

"I forgive you, Olivia."

She'd meant to say more, but the girl threw herself at Mari and hugged her, leaving new tear stains on the shirt. It took a minute for Livie to cry herself down to a level where Mariliz could talk to her again.

"Did it make you feel bad when you said it?" she asked, stroking the blond head, her own skin, colored with her mother's Brazilian blood dark against the pale hair.

Olivia nodded.

"It shouldn't make you feel bad to tell the truth. It's okay to tell the truth. But if you feel bad doing it, maybe it's time to stop and think about why you're saying it."

"Okay." Olivia nodded against her waist and Mari hugged her tighter.

"Don't worry though. Your dad would have told her. I would have said so. It's the truth. You don't have to be ashamed of the truth."

"So I should tell her that I think Sophie should keep signing?"

Oh, way to go Mariliz. Now you really stepped in it.

After evading the answer to that question, Mariliz sent Olivia back the way she came. She added a directive. "Why don't you check in on Sophie? Give her a hug? Ask if she's okay."

Olivia nodded and slid out the door.

Lordy. She did not want to tell Livie what to tell her mother. Especially when the girl was prone to blurting out "Mariliz told me . . ." That sounded like it would not go over well.

Though Mari stood behind everything she'd said and done— no shame or regret there—she did want to have the opportunity to say those things to Bridget herself. Not have Olivia blurt out ahead of time what had happened. The girl hadn't been in on some of the conversations with Alex about why Sophie could sign or what benefits Mari thought it might have.

She stared at the ceiling feeling completely unable to sleep until she jerked suddenly awake at five seventeen a.m. Still in her clothes on top of the covers, and not feeling rested at all, Mari went about getting ready. She was on duty at seven a.m.

Her heart felt heavy, a thudding against her ribcage instead of the normal energy she felt. She showered, carefully dried her hair, and today she ate her breakfast at her own counter, not sure what Bridget Beaumont would think of the nanny coming out to eat with the family.

It would be a fine line between being professional for Bridget, and keeping things normal for the girls. At that point, Mariliz questioned herself and decided that no, she hadn't been *un*professional at any point—well other than in her thoughts about Alex, and that just had to stop—but she had gotten casual.

It happened because she'd been left alone to flounder with the girls with no time off. It happened because Alex encouraged it. After last night's fight, she didn't think Bridget would. Hell, she might not even have a job.

Getting fired was suddenly a real possibility. She had to start planning for it.

At six fifty-five, Mariliz turned the knob into the kitchen to find the lights off and the place empty. Flipping the switch, she started looking around for breakfast. She had time, and it was possible Alex or Bridget was going to drive Olivia in to school, so she started eggs.

The act of chopping ham into cubes, dicing pieces of spinach and onions and mushrooms soothed her a little. Nothing fully released the tension, but it helped.

At seven ten, she worried about going upstairs and waking Olivia. What did Bridget consider part of her job? Things had changed when Alex had gotten home from tour, and they were changing again. But how?

Just when she was about to give up, she heard footsteps. Olivia came slowly down the staircase, her sister's hand tucked in hers as she led the little girl down. Mari's heart sighed. That, at least, hadn't changed. Olivia loved her little sister. Sophie had always had a soft spot for Livie, but now, she seemed to think her big sister hung the moon. Mariliz prayed Bridget's ideas wouldn't take that away from the girls.

Instead of commenting on that, she piped up. "Great, you're ready."

"I even changed Sophie's diaper." Olivia beamed.

"Excellent." There was no need to delve deeper and see if she'd done it out of loyalty to Mariliz, as redemption for spilling the beans, or even just to keep the household quiet. Actually, unless Livie just decided to do the dirty deed on a whim this morning, Mari didn't really like any of those motivations. But there wasn't much she could do about it. She was just grateful that she didn't have to traipse upstairs—right past Alex and Bridget's bedroom door—to wake the girls. "How about omelets?"

She had everything ready and took an order from Olivia, making Sophie wait this morning. A lot of times, she gave Sophie her food first, just to keep things calm, but as she and Alex had discussed, Sophie understood things now, and it was time to learn to wait her turn.

Besides, it was Olivia who had to get fed and get to school.

"You're next. Tell me what you want in yours." She signed to the toddler and watched the eggs as the kid immediately signed back "cheese!"

It helped her find a smile this morning. As did Sophie, when she eyed her sister's omelet, but turned up her nose at the mushrooms in it. She waited just fine. Again, Mari had the hopeful thought that later tests wouldn't turn up any mental impairments. But these were all secondary to the low buzz of tension as she waited for Alex and Bridget Beaumont to come in.

She was getting their shoes on when Alex came down the stairs. Today his jeans weren't ripped, his shirt didn't have a band logo on it, and he was already wearing shoes. "I've got her. I'll take Olivia to school."

"Okay." She smiled as though that was the best thing ever. While she couldn't justify her desire to take Livie to school and run away for "errands" with Sophie for a few hours, being abandoned with Bridget wasn't her cup of tea either.

But there was nothing she could do about it.

CHAPTER 21

A lex knew his daughter was bright, but he lied to her anyway.

"Everything's fine with Mommy. She's sleeping in. She'll probably pick you up after school." He smiled, it felt as forced as Olivia's return fake-grin looked. He hoped he at least faked it better than she did.

"Bye, Daddy." She hopped out of the car, almost like her butt was on fire.

He let her. Poor kid. School was probably her only haven right now. School was stable; home wasn't. She'd been through so much, none of it her fault—either directly or indirectly. Olivia had a solid home once, then she didn't, then for a few shining weeks she did again. Now it was washed away, like a big wave destroying her sand castle.

He'd known the wave was coming. He should have warned her. But how do you tell an eight-year-old that their mom is going to be upset when she gets home? That she's going to be upset that everyone's happy. How could he explain that Bridget wasn't upset *because* everyone was happy, she was upset by *how* it had happened.

A horn honked behind him, telling him to get his butt out of the lane and pull forward so other parents could drop their kids off, too. They probably had real jobs to get to, or yoga class or something.

He pulled forward, waving an awkward "I'm sorry" as he had his epiphany.

Alex sighed. He'd had so many lately, he was shocked he hadn't had an aneurism to go with them. Yet another thing he'd always let Bridget handle: talking to Olivia about important things.

It wasn't that Alex didn't talk to her, but he didn't decide to initiate it. He answered questions, but never sat her down and said, "You need to know . . ." to his daughter. He was going to do that, first chance he got.

Because when he looked down the road now, he was only fifty-fifty on whether Bridget was in his future or watching his taillights. He had to tell Olivia why and how he'd screwed up. He had to tell her the truth; she could handle it better than the lies.

He wasn't where he wanted yet, but he admitted that he liked what he was becoming. He had some control over his world, even if he didn't have any over Bridget. He found himself heading to the coffee shop, not wanting to go home yet. As he stepped in the door, he realized he was leaving Mariliz alone with his wife and that there was a good possibility that neither woman would fare well with that.

Bridget would probably still be asleep. He hoped she was anyway. So he got two to-go and headed back to the car. He didn't like the dread at the possible storm he was aiming into, but he could live with himself now. He could live with knowing that he wasn't leaving Lize to fend for herself when none of it was her fault.

He pulled into the driveway, and let himself in through the mudroom balancing the drinks. He heard the voices even as he entered. For a moment, he was grateful that the conversation was calm, polite. Then he heard the words.

"When did you get your degree?" Bridget was asking as he rounded the corner and saw the two women through another doorway, seated at the dining room table.

The table was empty between them and he wondered if that was symbolic. They didn't seem to hear him, so he went in search of Sophie and found her in a playpen in the living room. A TV show she wasn't watching made noise across the room, but he didn't turn it off. She had several toys and a book and she looked up and smiled when he came in.

In case that didn't melt his heart, she stood up and signed "Daddy, me pick-up," as he set the coffee down.

A full sentence.

Her first? It was three signs, did it count? He would have to ask Mariliz.

Alex plucked her from the mesh contraption and signed to her one-handed while he bounced her a bit. Her smile lit him up and reminded him why he was fighting. He was kissing her on the cheek when the words from the other room came to him.

"So your degree is almost a decade old. You aren't up to date on what's possible." Bridget was stating this like it was a fact as she dismissed Mariliz. He'd expected it.

"No ma'am." The counter was as polite, and as cold, as the comment. "I've gotten back up to speed. I've researched all the current material. And I've attended the local meetings of Tennessee Association for the Deaf and more."

"Sure, but they want signers. They want more people to speak their language. You're a sign language interpreter. You're biased." Bridget spoke without raising her voice, but the subtle fire wasn't to be missed.

"TAD isn't about signing. It's about all kinds of deaf-ness. They welcome the hard of hearing, too, and most of them don't even know sign." Alex set Sophie back down then, asking her to stay. Sadly, she accepted that, and he saw it as another sacrifice they would all have to make until things were settled.

Picking up the coffees, he headed into the other room to do his part and put in his two cents. He wasn't ready for Lize's own steely response.

"You're biased, too. You want Sophie to be normal and she's not."

Bridget didn't respond, but Mariliz filled in space.

"Look, if there was a way to get Sophie communicating with English, I'd be all for it. But she's two. That doctor convinced you to let him try to teach her as an experiment. She doesn't deserve that."

"She doesn't deserve a life where she can't talk to anyone." Now Bridget was getting mad. Alex could hear it in her voice. "You're not a mother. I don't expect you to understand."

"Exactly!" Lize countered, the gloves coming off as he entered the room. "She doesn't deserve a life where she can't talk to anyone! She couldn't talk to *anyone!* Now she *can.* She can still learn to speak later. She'll probably learn it faster now, and she won't get institutionalized in the meantime."

"I did research it! You don't know what you're talking about." Bridget stood up, hands flat on the smooth mahogany table top. She'd bought it to host dinners, not to fight with the nanny. But, Alex thought, she wasn't hosting dinners at it anymore either.

He tried to soothe things over. "It doesn't matter if she knows what she's talking about."

Both women looked at him, standing there, a coffee cup in each hand.

"It doesn't matter who the research supports. What's done is done. Sophie knows sign now and I don't know how to send her back to not communicating at all."

He looked Bridget in the eyes. "You and I both had a chance to stop it before it happened, and neither of us did. Mariliz just did as she was asked. So did the childcare agency. None of that matters anyway; none of the blame or numbers matter at all. All that matters is Sophie. And Sophie is happier now."

Bridget sat there open-mouthed. Mariliz crossed her arms and tried to be cool. He could see she was trying not to gloat, just a little.

"Sure." His wife responded coolly, still on her feet. "She signs. We all learn a whole new language—"

"We're her parents, Bridget. That shouldn't be a problem." He felt his heart hardening as he thought about her wish not to put herself out. Then he tamped it down before it could show. Bridget had put herself out for Olivia, and even Sophie early on, time and again.

"No, Alex, it's that no one else will learn this language for her. It's that she'll only be able to talk to her family."

"She wasn't able to even talk to us before." He countered, watching Mariliz out of the corner of his eye, glad she was staying silent now that he was in the battle.

"What about school? How will she get along in classes?"

"Maybe she'll have an interpreter."

"So she can't talk to any of the other kids? That's not okay!" Bridget was righteous in her anger.

"I don't know! But it beats not being able to talk to anyone. Maybe the class will learn signs, maybe there's a class in sign language! There are options." He knew. He was trying to stabilize his family first, but he'd been trying to look ahead, too.

This time it was Bridget who crossed her arms and faced him. "Did you know that Tennessee School for the Deaf is in Knoxville?"

"I do." He nodded.

"How are you going to make that happen? You work in Nashville. How does that even do anything but pull her apart from us, Alex?" Her anger made her seem as though she'd slapped down four aces.

"I don't know. But I'll make it work. She's my daughter."

Bridget's arms uncrossed. "She's my daughter, too."

Did she think he didn't know that?

She stared at him, and he tried not to buy into the stalemate. All he could do was shrug. Even as he did it he realized he was holding two coffees still in his hands. With a sigh, he handed Mariliz hers, only realizing as he did it how it looked.

Bridget's eyebrows went up.

"You drink diet coke in the mornings, Bridget." He said flatly.

"Yes, I do. I think I'll go get one. I have a hair appointment anyway." With that she brushed past him.

Alex didn't even turn to watch her leave, just listened as she stomped angrily out the door. Instead, he watched as Mariliz took a tentative sip of the coffee he'd brought her. He thought about the fact that it was hazelnut flavored and that he knew that she liked it that way.

"This is perfect," she commented. "Thank you."

Ironic. The coffee was perfect. He wasn't. His daughter wasn't. His marriage was so far from it that he couldn't even think of the two things together anymore. And the perfect cup of coffee had just driven another wedge into the imperfect.

He sat at the table across from Lize, taking the seat Bridget had just vacated. "Can I tell you something?"

"I'm sorry!" She blurted out as she set the cup down a little too hard. "I should have told you about Tennessee School for the Deaf, about it being three hours away." Her face was red, mortified.

He reached out and put his hand over hers for a moment before thinking better of touching her. Before he thought about how much he liked the feeling. As he pulled his fingers back, he told her, "It's not your job to teach me the basics about my daughter. I appreciate all that you have taught me, all the ways you've been willing to step up, fill in the gaps, and more. But it's my job to learn as much as I can on my own."

He paused, "You're the resident expert, so I'll still have questions. I hope that's okay."

"I'm not the expert. I know more than average on this, but expert is too extreme. Bridget had a point." Mari looked down at the table top.

"You're the one in the house who knows the most. The only adult who can speak to Sophie like an adult. The only one who can read her all her books. You still hold the title."

"Thank you." It was little more than a whisper.

"What I wanted to say," he started, "was that I'm behind you. I'm—"

He paused. "Shit, I promised myself this morning I'd be as honest as possible with everyone."

"So you may lie tomorrow?" She almost smiled.

"No," he grinned back, "this morning I made myself a promise to be fully honest from here on out. And in that light, I'm not positive my family can be put back together."

"Do you want it to?" There was something under the words that he couldn't decipher. Or maybe he just told himself he couldn't.

"It's the easiest. The best thing for the girls. And that's the point. I'm behind you on this, because it's what's right for Sophie. It's not about you or me or Bridget; it's about Sophie."

It was hard, saying his peace like that, but he felt better having said it. His heart sighed with relief, until she said, "And Olivia."

CHAPTER 22

Mariliz picked up Sophie out of her playpen and took her out for the morning. She decided a bounce house was in order. They picked the room that allowed for very tiny kids and parents to go along.

"Your little girl is adorable." The woman leaned over as Mari bounced next to Sophie.

"Oh, she's—"

"Is she deaf? I saw you signing." The woman cut in, as her eyes cut across to her own son—grandson?—on the other side of the huge inflated mattress. Though there were blow-up cartoon figures and some obstacles, most of these bounces didn't have much in the way of places to get lost or climb too high.

"Yes." Mari signed back and spoke.

"My grandson is deaf," She signed, too. "Hello little girl." She turned to Sophie.

Sophie lit up like firecrackers.

"My J is deaf, too. Would you like to meet him?" Then she turned to Mariliz and said "Jackson" as she made the name sign again. Waving her hands over her head for a minute, she flagged down a boy not much older than Sophie, but jumping on his own.

He popped over and signed, "What, Grandma?"

"This little girl is deaf, too. She can talk to you."

Now the little boy lit up. It took a minute, but Mariliz eventually felt comfortable stepping down off the bouncer and watching as the two went off just a little distance together. Jackson was very conscious of having a younger kid in tow.

Mari turned to the woman. "He's being very careful with her. That's really cool. I'm just the nanny, by the way. I'm Mariliz."

"Brenda." The woman said back. "It's nice to meet you."

"Likewise. I always forget that a lot of people can sign a little, and more are fluent than you know." Unless she was invited into the conversation, Mari never introduced herself to signers when she saw them at the mall or out and about. Maybe she should tell Bridget. "Can I send a picture to my boss?"

"Of course." Brenda smiled.

They chatted while Mari snagged a shot of Sophie following gingerly behind the little boy, thinking what a world of difference there was between two and almost four. She sent it to Alex and asked him to forward to Bridget if he wanted. Mariliz wasn't quite ready to make that decision herself. Didn't know how "look, we found a signer at the bounce house!" would go over.

Bridget hadn't made up her mind on things. Mariliz didn't know if she'd still have a job at the end of the week, and she also didn't know if she'd want it anyway. But she didn't think she could leave Livie and Sophie even if it meant staying with Bridget.

The two women chatted while the kids played, the conversation coming around to Jackson's dad.

"He's a police officer." Brenda said. "I help out a lot. Lisa, that's his mom, died in childbirth. It left Jackson deaf—luckily the only lingering effect. Well, and a little asthma. But that's from being a preemie."

Oh, Mariliz hadn't quite thought that progression around to her son felt quite natural. She didn't get to open her mouth before Brenda spoke again.

"Thad—that's his name—Thad's a police officer." She beamed. "Is it too forward to say you're just his type?"

Mariliz laughed. At least Brenda wasn't trying to hide it. "So you're thinking a set-up?"

"This is Thad." She pulled out a picture before Mariliz could protest.

Thad was very good-looking and very fit if the picture was current.

Mariliz still hadn't spoken yet when Brenda continued. "Thad doesn't like when I set him up. And I admit, I have been setting him up with just everyone. He's dating on his own again, but nothing has worked out. Oh! Not that—"

Mari waved her hand to cut the other woman off. "I get it."

"Thank you. He might forgive me for the set-up if he shows up and you're there."

Another laugh came out of her. But it wasn't a bad idea. She'd been locked in with the Beaumont family for over a month, tied up in Alex and Bridget's problems when she probably shouldn't get too invested. She should be dating. She was single, too. It might go a ways toward alleviating some of Bridget's dislike. Also dislodging some of Mari's own feelings toward Alex, the inappropriate ones, wouldn't hurt.

Just then, Sophie fell on her little diapered butt and started to cry.

Scrambling up the side of the bouncer, Mari picked her way over and gathered up the little girl.

"Is she okay?" Jackson signed to her.

"Yes. It's not your fault. You were wonderful. I think Sophie's just tired." She held the little girl as she sniffled and buried her face in Mari's shoulder, and Jackson followed them off the bouncer, back to where Brenda waited, worried.

"She's fine. She just fell and she's tired." Turning to Sophie, Mari signed, "Did you have fun today with Jackson?"

Sophie nodded and squirmed to be put down. As soon as her feet touched the ground, she ran to the little boy and hugged him. Unsure how she would pick her melted heart from the rough carpet fibers at her feet, Mari smiled at them then winked at little Jackson over Sophie's head.

Brenda thanked her for reassuring the little boy, then traded phone numbers so she could set up a coffee date for Mari and her son. As she buckled a nearly already asleep Sophie into her carseat, Mariliz wondered what she'd just done. Then decided that she had to get back out there. She didn't need to date—but she did need to get out, make new friends, and not be cooped up with Alex and the girls all the time.

At home, she found Alex waiting for them. He took the sleeping Sophie and tucked her into bed, leaving Mariliz to make lunch.

"Is Bridget here?" She asked when Alex emerged. She'd seen no sign of the woman.

He shook his head.

"I'm making a grilled sandwich, want one?"

They wound up eating an awkward lunch together, with Alex confessing that he'd wanted to play drums with Sophie again.

"So let me get Olivia," Mariliz volunteered. "Then you can play with Sophie when she wakes up."

"I think Bridget is getting Olivia today. I'll double check with her."

They didn't say much after that. Alex tapped on his phone until he said, "Yes, Bridget's getting Livie. So I'll just wait until Sophie wakes up." He polished off his sandwich and stood up with a small smile and thanks.

Later, he found her cleaning up the kitchen counters and stopped her.

"You don't have to do that. We have a maid."

"Sure, but I made the mess, shouldn't I clean it up?" She sprayed the counter again, only to find his hand over hers.

The warmth of it turned her heartbeat to a languid, easy rhythm that she shouldn't have been paying attention to. "No, you shouldn't."

"Hmm?" She hadn't quite followed that.

"Don't clean it. The maid is hourly, and she depends on the hours. She'll take all the work we can give her."

"Seriously?" He wasn't making that up?

"She has a kid off to college next fall, she's a single mom, trying to keep him in football gear and all. So no, don't clean."

Mariliz sighed, hating to leave the counter half done. "All right. So now what?"

"Take the afternoon off." He grinned.

She puttered around for a while, read, watched a show and did her cross-stitch until she was out of TV shows and bored. When she finally checked back in to see if Alex needed help, she realized they were still the only ones in the house. "Where's Bridget? Olivia?"

He looked up at her and shrugged.

Instantly on alert, she blurted. "Are they all right? Do we need to—"

"Bridget picked her up at school. When I asked, she said she had Olivia and they were 'out.' I don't know anything more." He shrugged again.

Mari frowned at him, uncomprehending.

"She's safe. But otherwise I don't know." He looked around the room as though Bridget and his older daughter might peek out from around the corner and say it was a joke. Mariliz had barely met the woman, but she was pretty sure it wasn't. He paused a beat and changed the subject. "Let's make dinner."

Though she was still confused about his willingness to forgo figuring out the situation, she agreed. She set Sophie up with a set of velcro vegetables and wooden knife to "help" with dinner while she chopped up a salad and let Alex make the main dish.

"Fish, huh?" She looked at him squeezing lemons and sprinkling herbs. She hadn't seen that coming.

"I can make about ten good dishes and about six of them are reasonably healthy. Four are definitely for football games or such." The dimple was back again.

Mari decided to make enough salad for four—in the hopes that Bridget and Olivia would return for dinner. She was chopping green peppers when she heard the ping of an unknown text. Bridget?

Wiping her hands, she pulled the phone from her pocket and pulled up the text.

—This is Thad. Apparently my mom set us up for a coffee date. Tomorrow morning at 11 okay?

Oooh. The man spelled out "okay." He was either awesome or a dinosaur—picture of hot cop notwithstanding. Turning to her boss and mentally reminding herself he was her boss, Mari asked Alex. "Can I go out tomorrow morning for a few hours?"

"Sure. Don't see why that can't be time off." He shrugged as he flipped the fillets. Mariliz noted that he had made five, also enough for his wife and child to show up.

"Thanks." She texted back and hoped the thrill of having a date turned into the thrill of meeting this actual man. Who knew? Shoving the phone back in her pocket she looked up at Sophie who was asking for real veggies to chop.

Mari handed her a few strips of green pepper to play with and went back to the salad. For a moment, she looked up at the girl. This was an entirely different child than the one she'd met just over a month ago. She was reasonable, gentle, and even—Mariliz was getting more convinced every day—bright.

"If you're thinking about how far Sophie has come," Alex

seemed to see through her, "then thank you." The last words were almost whispered.

She turned to him, finding him almost misty-eyed. It hit her, what he'd given up to get this. His wife was angry about him changing things on her, when really it had been Mari who'd inadvertently done it. Right now, he didn't know where his wife and older daughter were, only that they were "out." He was trusting that they were safe. Instead of dwelling, Mari aimed to lighten the mood.

"I'm just the paid help. It's my job."

She felt his hand at her waist as he gently moved her. She fought to keep from showing her reaction.

"It's not *just* your job." He was looking right at her, too serious for the dimple to show, his whiskey-colored eyes deep enough to drown in.

Mariliz hoped he wasn't saying what she really hoped he was saying. What a mess.

"It may be your job, Lize," he continued, "but it's not *just* your job."

"Thanks." She nodded, offering a small smile as she moved to escape the touch that shouldn't affect her the way it did. He'd called her "Lize" like Missy did, and it felt too good. Did he know he'd done it?

She reminded herself that no matter what he might think of or about her, this was still a job. It was still her paycheck, and she still loved these little girls. So until she got herself fired or was willing to tap out, she needed to stay professional.

Coffee date tomorrow. Coffee date tomorrow. Hot cop. Hot cop. She ran the words through her head as a mantra.

Mari managed to make it through dinner without letting her heart trip up any more. Sophie ate pieces of veggies in her salad but mostly liked playing with the green peppers and politely throwing the thinly sliced red onions onto the floor. Alex ate two pieces of the fish, keeping up chatter about needing to eat healthier when he was home because of all the crap they got out on the road. The other two pieces sat on the counter with the remainder of the salad that hadn't been served—a reminder that half the family wasn't home for dinner.

The door opened from the garage just as Mariliz was eating the last piece of her fish. With her mouth full, she wasn't able to respond to Bridget's drawled greeting, "Well, isn't this domestic?"

CHAPTER 23

Alex woke to find half the bed cold and empty. If he was being honest, it was pretty cold even when Bridget was in it. His wife had been home four days, and they hadn't done anything more than kiss. Even that hadn't been more than perfunctory.

Sitting up and rubbing his eyes, he decided to count the number of times he'd kissed his wife since she'd returned home. One—when she'd showed up and seen him with Sophie playing drums . . .

Shit.

Oh, two—when she went out the other morning and pretty much demanded a kiss on the cheek. And three—one peck she'd laid on his mouth when she arrived home from being out all day with friends and she'd seemed pretty happy.

Shit.

Always good when your first morning thoughts involved bad revelations and swearing. He blinked a few times. There were big decisions coming. In fact, it felt like his life was nothing but big decisions. If he wanted to pinpoint when he started having to make them, it was when Lize first showed up.

Then again, that was the turning point of things looking up, too. Before that, everything had been on a slow downward trajectory. Sophie kept getting worse, and growing bigger—meaning her temper was getting bigger, too. It was one thing when a baby threw things and screamed, it was another ballgame when a toddler did it. He'd been afraid of her getting older and known it was inevitable.

There had also been a moment when he realized that Bridget wouldn't come home to see the new nanny installed. In the past, she at least made sure the person watching her girls had been interviewed by her. That she knew who it was. When he found out that—instead of coming home before he left—she was sending her sister was when he realized that she wasn't really coming home.

The spa visits and the vacations had become her real life, with home as short interludes in between. Then again, he'd tapped out, too. So who was he to withhold forgiveness?

Alex rubbed his hand over his face as though waking up a little more would make his life better. It didn't. He brushed his teeth, wet his hands and ran them through his hair so it didn't stick up on end, washed his face and then dashed for the alarm clock as it began to beep.

Just as he slapped the button it occurred to him that there was no one to bother with the alarm. Bridget wasn't asleep in the room. He didn't know where she was, and the fact that he wasn't really bothered by this bothered him more than anything else. Sophie couldn't be woken by a beeping alarm, and Olivia should be getting up anyway.

Pulling on an old Wilder t-shirt and jeans over clean underwear, he padded down the hall for the thing that really made him smile.

Alex opened the door to Sophie's room to flick the lights, and saw that she was sitting up on her bed. She lit up.

"Daddy, Daddy," She signed at him. "Pick me up."

"Morning, Sophie-bug." Lize had been teaching him endearments for the girls. Or she had been using them and Alex had pestered her until she told him what she'd been saying. "Oh, diaper wet."

Sophie scrunched her face and moved to be set down. Running to her changing table—which she now never used— she pulled out the mat and spread it out before laying on it. Alex fetched a diaper and told her in his still awkward sign, "You big girl, Sophie. Time no more diapers."

She scrunched her face as he balled up the overnight diaper and held it out toward her. "Diapers are yucky."

"Yucky diaper." She signed back.

"That's right. Time for big girl undies." He grinned at her, then at himself. He *knew* all the signs. For the first time he talked to his daughter without censoring his speech against words he didn't know. Or thinking, *I have to ask Lize how to say X.* He was proud of both of them.

Sophie however, looked at him like she was not entirely sold on the idea. His heart melted all over again. He remembered thinking that Olivia was a sweet baby, but she just kept getting to be more and more fun as she got older. She became expressive, she had opinions, she was funny. He and Bridget had decided to have a second child in part because of that fun. Finally, he was seeing that with Sophie. She was making faces for him, expressing herself. He knew her favorite color. And now, he knew what to say to get her to want to potty train.

"Just like Livie."

"Like Livie. Big girl undies." She signed back, lighting up again.

He put a clean diaper on her and picked her up and said, "Go to the store today for big girl undies."

"Yes!" She clapped at him then squirmed to get down. He watched her reverse her way down the steps, his daughter that he now knew was fiercely independent. When she safely hit the bottom, he turned to Olivia's room and knocked.

"I'm awake."

"Just checking." He said through the door.

"Oh, hi Daddy!" She threw the door open wide and hugged him before retreating into the room. "I'll be ready for breakfast in a few minutes."

He noticed the guest room door was closed and figured Bridget was in there. Alex decided not to bother her and headed down the stairs. He'd been glad to see all the makeup was off Livie's face this morning. It had been a dual shock, his wife being a bit of a bitch at dinner and seeing his eight-year-old in full, adult makeup. In fact, many adult women didn't wear that much, he thought.

Bridget said it was just for fun. That they'd gotten their hair and makeup done and gotten some pictures made. Of course, they'd already had dinner together.

He didn't resent mother and daughter spending time together, hanging out and having fun. He resented Bridget not asking him about it. And he resented the hell out of the fact that he was pretty sure she hadn't even touched Sophie since she'd returned home.

Downstairs, Mariliz was holding Sophie in one arm and stirring oatmeal with the other.

"Dinosaur." Sophie told her.

"Yes," Lize stopped stirring just long enough to say, "Not yet. Too hot."

He caught all of that, too. He needed more signs. He knew that, even if he still wasn't quite sure how to go about it. Once the girls had eaten and Olivia got her things together, he drove her to school, chatting without sign about what she and her mother did the night before. He tried to keep smiling and not show the kid that he was angry about it. It wasn't Livie's fault at all.

Once he dropped her off and waved goodbye, he bee lined for the coffee shop. He needed something. Some time. Ten minutes to himself. As he sat there nursing his coffee and his sore feelings, he picked up his phone without paying attention. He called Mariliz. "Are you good there with Sophie for a while?"

"If you're back by ten thirty?" She sounded chipper, not strained. Bridget was either still asleep or long gone. He agreed, hung up, and called JD.

His friend answered, and Alex only gave him two words. "Bridget's home."

"Are you with her?"

"No, I'm at the Daily Grind."

"I'll be there in twenty minutes."

Alex looked around. He lived on the other side of town from his parents—a good thing, really—and from the rest of the guys —not a good thing. He saw that now. Had he come north for coffee, some part of him knowing he would call JD and want to talk? Maybe.

He waited, his thoughts drifting, then suddenly, his friend was across from him, nursing a tall cup and sliding a second one Alex's way. "I was wondering when you'd crack."

"Oh, I cracked." Alex tipped the second cup at him, enjoying the heat again. "Lize is at home with Sophie and maybe Bridget."

"You call her Lize sometimes."

"Shit. Yeah, I do." Alex looked away. It hadn't escaped his own attention, why had he thought he'd hidden it from JD?

"It's not normal to have a pet name for the nanny." JD always said these things without judgment.

"Bridget's been home for four days. I don't know what to do." Alex shrugged and drank the coffee as though it would help with anything other than caffeine.

"What do you want?"

"I want my family to be happy." That was an easy one.

"Does that family include Bridget still?" JD asked casually.

"You know, I like that about you. You ask the hard questions as though you're asking if I like pizza. And the answer is, I really don't know. I feel like I have to forgive her, because I was just as bad. Even so, I don't *feel* like forgiving her."

JD set his cup down for a minute, thinking. Alex noticed that his friend hadn't shaved. He'd probably just thrown on his clothes and headed out, knowing he was needed. That was just JD; he was everyone's rock. "Thing is, you don't *have to* forgive her. You can hold onto it all you want. And you do get to forgive yourself. We all wondered what was going on, and you didn't seem to want to say. We've all been there, so when pushing you gave us nothing, we waited. Thing is, you're changing. You've made moves to correct what you messed up. You get a forgiveness pass. Has Bridget done the same?"

Jeez. What a great question. "No, she hasn't. Nothing." That was probably why he was still so mad at her. And he was furious. It wasn't that he didn't want to forgive her, he was actually nowhere near that stage. He still wanted to throttle her. "Not only is she not making things better, she's making them worse. She came in last night with Livie in makeup, after they disappeared for hours. She was snotty to Lize in front of me. Shit, I know, I did it again."

He took another drink as though to punctuate his rant. "Then, when I left, I guess she thought I couldn't hear, because she asked Lize 'are you fucking my husband?'" His eyes went wide, still unable to determine if he was more upset about Bridget's audacity or the fact that she seemed to be able to see something between him and the nanny.

JD set his cup down, giving his full attention to his friend. "So you have a thing for the nanny. I don't fault you that—she's beautiful, seems smart and friendly—"

Alex bit his tongue. He wanted to tell JD all of Lize's good qualities. Though if he was defending his attraction or waxing poetic he couldn't tell. So he stayed silent.

"But are you head over heels for her despite being in love with your wife? Or is something missing there?"

It was a hard question for a man, the kind only a good friend could pose. JD put himself out there asking it, so Alex put himself out there, too, and answered honestly. "There's nothing between me and Bridget right now."

JD knew how they'd once been. He'd been there at the beginning. Almost ten years ago, when the red undies had flown up on the stage and Alex had appeared with his new wife in tow at the bus that night. He listened politely and patiently as Alex explained all that hadn't been happening. That Bridget had slept in another room entirely the night before.

There was some silence after that, each man contemplating what he'd just digested. Alex had thought of all of this before, but having JD there helped put it in perspective. Helped him not feel quite so guilty for being so mad at Bridget and so drawn to Mariliz. He was thinking he should be getting home, in case Bridget was asking Lize more hard questions, when his brain wandered around to what he didn't want to think about.

Lize's answer to "Are you fucking my husband?" was not only "no" it was "I'm dating a cop."

He hadn't known. And he didn't like the feel in his gut of the jealousy twisting there. He didn't tell JD that.

It was JD who broke the silence. "So do you want to scrap the marriage you have and start over? Or do you want to put it back together?"

Wasn't that the million dollar question? The truth was, he didn't want to do either.

CHAPTER 24

The coffee date had gone wonderfully, Mariliz thought. No massive sparks had flown, but really, it was just coffee. Thad was as hot as his picture and as sweet as his mother made him out to be. He came off a little shy, but began making decent small talk relatively quickly. She liked him.

Mari couldn't say if she *liked* him, but she was willing to see how it went. There were no better options on her table, and she needed to get her head out of the gutter, that was for certain. So she said yes when he asked if he could call her again. If he could take her out on a real date.

She was looking forward to it, and she hoped not just for the fact that it kept her from being a liar. She knew her motives were twisted, and she was having trouble identifying the individual pieces of them. But she'd told Bridget that she was dating the cop; Mari *wanted* it to be true. At least now it was, in a sense.

She was gratefully still off the clock—Alex had showed up in time to get her out the door and they'd traded Sophie off almost like a busy family. Alex looked different, but he'd given her the rest of the day off until Olivia came home, then said something about all of them having dinner together.

Having no idea if "all of them" included Bridget, Mari was a bit apprehensive. Still, she reminded herself she shouldn't be afraid of her boss, and technically Bridget was her boss as much as Alex was. Not that she'd had a single real conversation with the woman about how Bridget wanted Mariliz to interact with the girls, what her real duties were, or where the boundaries of nanny/family were. Nope, Bridget had only yelled about Mariliz then to her face accused her of "fucking my husband." Not only was the sentiment crass, the words were, too.

Well, you wanted to, Lize. She reminded herself. Then the voice in her head came again. *You still want to, at least part of you does.*

Sad, but true. The sane part of her knew that getting involved with any married man was wrong. Getting involved with your boss was a mess. Getting involved with someone in the house you lived in was sticky at best. Getting involved with anyone Bridget claimed as her own was possibly fatal. So many strikes against him that the feelings should have been entirely overridden by sheer sense.

But nope. There was that damn dimple. The focus in his eyes when he looked at her—*Damnit, Mariliz. Stop it.* It didn't matter what signals he sent, her feelings were her feelings, and she had to fix them.

There was a strange line between wanting to go home and take a breather and knowing that "home" wasn't really her home. Should she stay out? Burn time until later? She didn't want to. She wanted to claim her own home, have her own place. Even if it was just a suite of rooms off the kitchen of another family. Mariliz clearly hadn't thought out all the ramifications of being a nanny before she'd taken the job.

The girls were wonderful. Alex was relaxed. The house was in a much nicer neighborhood than her apartment had been.

She had access to a big kitchen, a yard, so many things that were worth the slightly smaller size of the space. But living inside someone else's house was a little odd. Loving someone else's kids was also something she hadn't been prepared for. Honestly, she hadn't thought much about her own kids. She and Reynold had been so cold and so set that it had only occurred to her as something for later. Now? Now she didn't think of her own kids either. She thought of Livie and Sophie. Working with Sophie had been so rewarding.

Mariliz slung her purse over her shoulder, ran an errand, and headed home with her bags. The rooms were her house, and she wouldn't stay out.

When she pulled in, the garage doors were closed, so she didn't know who, if anyone, was home. Traipsing around her paver pathway, she leaned over to avoid where the bushes had started to grow a little out over the stones with the season. She thought the yard guy was coming tomorrow. At the door, she unlocked the sliding door and passed through her bedroom into the sitting room.

She was putting the small drinks in the half-fridge when she heard it.

Not again.

Mari closed the fridge door and she sighed. You would think a nice house like this would be more soundproof. But she heard it clear as a bell.

"You didn't let me decide, Alex. You made the call to change what we were doing on your own!" Bridget was yelling.

Mariliz prayed Sophie wasn't watching. That had to suck for the kid, to put it mildly. Then again, most toddlers probably didn't understand what was happening when their parents fought.

"I've told you." Mari could hear the weariness in his voice. "I didn't decide. It just happened."

"Well, you didn't decide to fix it either, did you?" The words were biting, accusatory. Mariliz suddenly realized she hadn't heard any kind words from Bridget, maybe ever. Alex was being awfully careful, she thought. Then again, Mari was completely biased. And that was part of the problem.

"How would I have 'fixed it,' Bridge? Push Sophie away? Tell her that I don't want to listen to her?"

"You can't *listen* to her Alex, she doesn't *speak*." Bridget retorted.

"Yes, she does. I'm sorry she doesn't speak your language. But you're her *Mom*. You need to learn hers."

There was a beat of silence. Mariliz sat frozen on her little sofa, thinking that she shouldn't be listening, and that she couldn't not listen. It all affected her. Much of it was *about* her. So she quit acting like she wasn't really doing what she was doing and softly walked to the door and put her ear against it.

Maybe they were done.

Nope.

"You don't know, Alex!" Bridget railed. This time, there was a sound of tears in her voice. "You don't know what it was like being the only parent here. Trying to be good for Olivia during the day, and up all night with Sophie, screaming at me, hitting me . . . hating me. She *hates* me, Alex." She hiccuped a little, her voice catching. "You left me here, for weeks on end. And even when you were home, you left all these horrible decisions to me."

"Whoa! You *wanted* to make them. You told me you had it all under control. You found the perfect doctor and it was all going to be better."

"Well, it was an act!" She yelled, something hit something else, but nothing seemed to break. "You should have helped!"

"How was I supposed to know it was an act? I'm sorry, but I did what you told me to do!" He yelled back.

For a moment, Mariliz picked sides. He was right. He wasn't psychic. Then again, she hadn't been here for any of it. Then, the other voice came, and Mari felt her heart twist. Just the thought of being Bridget hurt deep inside.

"She hates me, Alex. I didn't know what to do with her. My baby hates me." The words were soft, wrenched, painful just to hear.

"Bridget." Alex's voice was softer, calmer now. "I didn't mean to leave you alone, I didn't. I thought it was what you wanted. I'm sorry."

Now, step away from the door now, Mari counseled herself. It was one thing to listen to a fight that she couldn't not hear. It was another to listen to this couple make up.

But if she listened, maybe she could convince her stupid heart to knock it off. To fall for the sweet cop who wanted to get to know her better. So she didn't move. She shamelessly eavesdropped on the dulcet tones of Alex's musical voice and tried not to wish he was using it on her.

"We both did our best, and it sucked. But I didn't change things for Sophie once she learned sign, because she was better. She was happy. Livie was happy. Sophie didn't hate me. And she doesn't hate you. I did all the same things to her that you did—"

The yell was discordant, cutting through the softer tones of Alex's soothing voice.

"I didn't *do* things to her! I tried to give her a *normal* life!"

"We did things to her, Bridge." How he stayed calm was a marvel to Mariliz. "And she's not normal, she's deaf. She'll never be normal. I get it. Olivia was easy and she was perfect. We were perfect, and Sophie was difficult and awful and it hurt us all."

A pause came while Mari tried not to let tears run down her face. As she took a deep breath, trying not to make any noise that would alert the two fighters she was there, listening, she glanced up and saw the clock.

Oh shit! Someone should have left to pick up Livie about ten minutes ago. Scrambling, not caring if she was heard, she grabbed her keys and purse and booked it out the door. Luckily, when she arrived, the car line at school was still long. Though she was near the end of it, Livie wasn't left wondering if someone was coming for her.

Offering the brightest smile she could muster, Mariliz fought the urge to take the girl for ice cream and hide for a while. She still hadn't seen Sophie. And even though Bridget and Alex may have forgotten to get their daughter, she didn't have to hide from them.

Her phone chirped, and she held a brief, terse conversation letting Alex know that she'd seen the time and come to get Olivia. They hung up with neither of them acknowledging that her presence here meant she'd heard them fighting, realized they hadn't left to get Livie.

At home, at least they were expected. Mari marched Livie right in through the front door, into a house thick with tension. She hoped the girl couldn't feel it. It seemed Bridget and Alex were still fighting right up until the moment the door clicked. Their faces were red, Alex paced with his hands on his hips and a half-finished beer in his fist. Bridget even breathed angrily.

Clearly, nothing had been resolved.

Bridget gathered herself and headed straight for Olivia. "Honey," She forced her tone. "Let's go hang out."

"I have homework." Livie's flat tone, and refusal of her mother's offer worried Mariliz. But it angered Bridget.

"Okay, you do that." Her mother told her, but the words were tight, tense. Bridget slung her purse over her shoulder and headed for the garage.

"I'll get Sophie." Mari volunteered for something to do, even though she wasn't sure where the little girl was, only that she wasn't in the room.

Bridget glared at her as she passed by, then headed out the door. Olivia flinched at the sound—it wasn't quite a slam, but it wasn't normal either. Mari headed upstairs returning with a smiling Sophie she'd found sitting on her bed with a book. "She must have woken up from her nap and decided to read."

Alex nodded at her, then turned to Olivia. "Get a snack if you need. But then get your homework done, okay?"

The girl nodded back at him and disappeared upstairs without grabbing any food. Mariliz wondered what it would be like to walk into the middle of that tension. She tried to diffuse her own by bouncing Sophie in her arms and getting the girl to smile. But even the toddler seemed to be able to feel the strange vibes and she refused.

Alex turned to stare at Mari for a moment, as though trying to make her understand something.

She didn't.

CHAPTER 25

D inner had been a tense affair, the four of them sitting around the table, the conversation moving in fits and starts. Mariliz had looked at both Olivia and Sophie and watched as the two girls watched the grown-ups, trying to figure out what to do.

Afterward, she scraped dishes while Olivia cleared the table. A good big sister, she gave Sophie one un-spillable, unbreakable item each trip and had the toddler "help" her do the job. Mari left everything piled in the sink, as she hadn't yet gotten a chance to ask the maid if she really did want it that way. Mari hoped she wasn't being a complete butthead to the woman.

Since Olivia had only come downstairs just before dinner, Mari first asked, "Did your homework get finished?"

When the girl nodded quickly, she didn't press. Didn't need an explanation that she'd been hiding out. She was smart enough to listen for the garage door and smart enough to know it hadn't opened and her mother hadn't returned.

Deciding she wasn't spending the evening waiting for the door to burst open, Mariliz clapped her hands, then started signing. "It's time for Trouble."

Olivia didn't understand. Sophie didn't either, but she looked to big sis before shrugging her chubby little shoulders. Mariliz fingerspelled the word and headed into the playroom where she was greeted by tiny mews as she opened the door. Both the kittens rushed past her, and Sophie gave chase.

Mariliz looked at Alex, confused. "Did they get stuck in there?"

It was Olivia who answered. "Mom is mad that we got cats. She moved the climbing post in there and keeps putting them in during the day."

Alex rubbed his hand down his face but tried to stop the action before he turned and knelt to his daughter. "I'm sorry, honey. I didn't know. Tell me these things."

She looked away, "I didn't want to make Mom mad."

"I'll handle it. It's not your fault. I said yes to getting kittens. This is between your mom and me."

Sophie toddled back in with Poof tucked under her arm. The tiny cat looked resigned; Sophie looked happy. Olivia nodded to her father then turned to Sophie. Without vocalizing at all, she asked, "Where's Lilac?"

"Pee." Sophie responded.

"Litter box?" Livie asked again.

A nod from her little sister and Livie went off to fetch her own kitty.

Mariliz pulled the game down off the shelf and started setting it up on the table. Sophie began "helping," but Alex didn't move. "Alex?"

"My girls just had a conversation. I don't think I've ever seen anything quite so damn cool."

She laughed. Things were definitely broken around here, but there were little miracles along the way, she thought.

Had Mariliz been playing the game with an adult, or even anyone of reasonable demeanor, it would have been finished and put away before the Beaumonts even got started. Sophie was too young, and mostly terrorized the board. Like a giant, she upended playing pieces and made left-field calls about what was an acceptable move. Mariliz had hoped they could work on counting skills . . . but apparently not.

Alex laughed from his belly more than once at Sophie's antics and Olivia trying to herd the cats. They agreed that the first of the three of them who made it halfway to what the game deemed a 'win' would be declared the grand champion. Sophie had already been declared "The Underminer" by Livie, who handled her sister ruining the game with a good sense of humor.

Mariliz made a few bad choices on purpose, hoping to let Olivia win. It took some doing, but it worked.

"Yes!" The girl yelled as she jumped up to do a victory dance. Sophie, of course, followed suit and the two waggled and jumped around with Sophie a beat behind but having fun.

Checking the clock, she looked at Alex, definitely past bedtime. Should she say anything?

She didn't have to.

No one had heard the garage door opening. No one had heard the door opening or any movement in the lush living room or down the hallway. Instead, Bridget stood in the doorway, with her arms crossed as she surveyed the scene. Mariliz stared like a deer caught in headlights.

Bridget's voice was soft as she stared Mari down. "Haven't you ruined enough?"

Mari gulped—visibly, she was sure. What had she done to this woman, really? She opened her mouth to say so, to say that all the problems had begun long before she arrived, but Alex spoke first.

Livie and Sophie had stopped dancing and stared at their mother. Surely the baby didn't understand, but she knew to watch, knew that bad things were going down.

"Bridget." His voice was low, almost feral. "This isn't on

Mariliz. You made your choices this afternoon. We're making the best of what you've left us."

Oh, hells bells. Mari had missed something big when she'd headed out to get Olivia. Nothing like this had been in the fight she'd heard. It had been nasty and painful, sure, but there had not been choices made.

This time it was Olivia who swallowed. "Mom?"

Mariliz wanted to run to her, grab her and hold her close, cradle her head as though she could prevent the girl from hearing this at all. It was her job to help the girls. Screw Alex and Bridget. Her heart was breaking for Livie and Sophie.

"You're right." Bridget said too casually. "I'm just getting my things."

"Mom!" Olivia yelled and followed her mother out of the room.

Mariliz heard a few words exchanged and Olivia came back into the room, red-faced. "Did you know, Dad? Did you know!"

It wasn't a question, it was an accusation. Olivia didn't use her hands, leaving Sophie out. Whether that was a good thing or a bad thing, Mariliz didn't know. So she picked herself up, leaving the remnants of the game and good time scattered on the table and went to get Sophie.

She passed by Olivia, not sure if she should offer to help, be a shoulder to cry on, or what. If she even apologized—sorry that the girl was having to go through this—would Livie take it as an admission of guilt? She offered a sad smile, the best she could do, and went past with Sophie.

Instead of heading upstairs, across the way from where she could hear Bridget stomping around, she set Sophie down, helped the little girl corral the kittens and played in the corner of the living room. She wanted Bridget to want to say goodbye to her younger daughter if she was really leaving. But Mariliz didn't hold out any real hope for it.

Still, she wasn't going to get accused of hiding Sophie away.

So they sat in the living room and Sophie tried to teach the kittens to sit. Truly it was the most useless endeavor Mari had ever seen undertaken. At any other time it would have been wonderfully comical.

Bridget came down the stairs, a large suitcase clumping angrily behind her. On top, strapped to the pull handle, was the matching, logoed carryon.

Well, shit. Bridget looked like she was *leaving* leaving. Mari took a breath and just then Olivia came dashing out of the back room, her argument with her father cut short. "Mom! Mom, can I come with you?"

"Not right now, sweeting." She hugged her older daughter fiercely, whispered in her ear and then turned and headed straight out the door without acknowledging Alex, Mariliz, or her other daughter. Mari was grateful Sophie wasn't older. A slight like that could have been devastating. Instead, Sophie sat with her back to her mother, and Mariliz tried to keep her face straight, maybe even offer the little girl a smile.

She wondered how she'd gotten here. Just a year and a half ago, she'd been married contentedly, if not happily. But she'd found out her husband was cheating, and now, she was in the middle of another marriage going down the tubes. She'd gotten here one step at a time, she reasoned as she listened to the garage door go up and the car engine start. She heard Olivia crying softly, and Mariliz didn't know what to do.

Livie ran back to Alex who was coming out of the back room, probably purposefully not witnessing his wife leave. "Daddy! Why doesn't she understand? Sophie's happy! I'm happy. Or I *was*."

Alex knelt down and hugged his daughter, tugging her over to where Mari and Sophie sat. They planted themselves on the floor, creating a small circle. Though Mariliz felt uncomfortable being part of the family, it would be worse to get up and walk away when the girls needed to know who was there for them.

"Livie," he started, but didn't use his hands. "Remember when Sophie was little? And all she did was scream? Well, your mom got the worst of that. She thinks Sophie hates her. And that really hurt mom's feelings. She also doesn't understand about sign language. Your mom still believes that Sophie can learn to speak English. I don't."

Olivia looked away. Just seeing her expression felt like ice picks in Mari's heart. The kid was getting tugged between two parents who had very different ideas of what needed to be done.

Then the blond head bent closer to her dad and whispered, "Why does Mom hate Mariliz?"

Alex's eyes cut right to her. It felt like he was staring into her soul and she wasn't ready. She was flayed open from Livie's tears, from Alex being stoic against the hurricane in his house, from Sophie's lack of concern that her mother just went out the door. Mariliz's breath escaped and her mouth dropped open.

It felt like a physical change when Alex Beaumont turned that attention back to his eldest daughter. "She hates that Mari knows sign language. It's hard for her to watch someone else do well with Sophie when she couldn't."

"She could learn." Livie wailed.

"That's what I told her." Her father whispered back as he hugged his daughter. "I'm so sorry."

He picked her up, motioning Mariliz to follow. She heard him telling his crying daughter that not much would change at home. Bridget hadn't been around much, Livie would still go to her same school, Sophie would keep getting better. And he would always be there for her. He smiled at Mariliz over the blond head and motioned for her to put Sophie down for the night.

As Mari finished reading the girl her book, he came in and hugged his pajama clad toddler, kissed her and tucked her in with a smile. Mariliz left them there, heading downstairs for one of the beers Alex kept offering her. She popped the top and tipped it back, glad it was cold. She needed it tonight.

"Grab me one?"

He startled her and she thought she didn't hide it well, but reached into the big, sub-zero fridge and popped the top for him. He sighed deeply as though he needed the oxygen, then he drank as though he hadn't had water for three days. When he finally set the bottle—nearly empty—on the countertop, he looked at her. "I'm going to find a sign class for Livie and me."

She smiled and leaned back against the counter, glad to be in familiar territory. "I can find one for you."

"You know, I think that was part of the problem. I let other people tell me what was best. So I'll do some research, find a few, then consult with you. How does that sound?" He finished the last inch of the beer and expertly flicked his wrist, sending the bottle into the recycling bin.

"Sounds good." She smiled, then her brain put it all together. "Oh my God. You didn't want to take a class because if word got out, Bridget would find out you were signing to Sophie! And you didn't want her to find out that way."

He nodded at her. "I was trying to save my marriage." He sighed. "But she made it pretty clear today that she can't handle Sophie."

"She's just deaf." Mariliz frowned at him.

"I know that, Lize. You know that." He shrugged. "I want to forgive her, but I can't. Something about dealing with Sophie broke her. She won't try again. And I wasn't there." This time he looked right at her again, as though confessing what he'd done. As though he should confess to her. "So I can't say if she's got a point or not. But it doesn't matter. She doesn't want to learn to speak to her daughter."

Mari felt her face move, she was horrified and saddened, and Alex saw all of it.

"She had a perfect child in Livie. And Sophie will never be perfect. I don't know if Bridget can't handle being seen in public with Sophie not perfect, or if she thinks that ASL means she failed. Or if she really believes I'm killing Sophie's chances at a normal life." He looked almost broken. Then he turned, took a breath, and didn't break. "But Bridget won't learn. And I will. I won't sacrifice Sophie for the rest of the family."

"Did she suggest that?" Mariliz was horrified.

"She said once Sophie was boarded at the School for the Deaf, she would come back."

"What!" Mari burst out, then clapped her hand over her mouth, hoping she didn't wake Livie. "Wow." Her eyes darted all over as Mariliz tried to process that. She tried to understand, not all mothers were equal. She herself had never been through a single night with a sick baby—Sophie and Livie hadn't even had a fever on her watch—so who was she to say Bridget was weak? But she didn't understand.

When her eyes settled on Alex again, she realized he was staring at her. His breathing was slow but heavy. The look in his eyes said he was not thinking about anything beyond two feet in front of him.

"Bridget got what she wanted." He said, just a whisper. "Now I get what I want."

He closed the small distance between them, his hands coming around and planting on the counter behind her trapping her in. Though she felt trapped, she felt on fire, too.

It was a dare to keep looking at him. Too hard to look away.

Right in this moment, nothing mattered but this man that she had wanted for longer than she admitted and his mouth closing on hers.

Her breath sucked in slightly as she felt his own breathing change. Her eyes fell closed at the feel of him, the heat of him taking over her space. Every muscle in her body stilled—frozen and burning at the same time. Her hands, braced on the counter behind her, clenched at the edge as though they wished they were grabbing him.

His lips moved over hers, coaxing her mouth open. When his tongue traced her bottom lip, she went up in flames.

CHAPTER 26

The taste of her electrified him. Alex felt everything in him melt and shift, as though he was the skin of a drum and she'd hit him, made him vibrate and come to life.

He'd been dead inside for so long, he craved it, this feeling she tugged out of him.

Leaning further into her, he sealed his mouth over hers, the touch of her tongue on his a straight shot into his whole system. He could sense her in every cell. Still he could distinguish the press of her soft breasts to his chest, the rub of his thighs against hers as he moved his legs to both hold her there and reposition himself.

Pressed fully against her now, with Lize reaching for him as though he was further than a heartbeat away, he moved his hands. Her fingers scooted slowly across the countertop, as though she didn't want to admit she was reaching for him. The touch of her pinkies against the iron grip he clamped the granite with ignited him, loosened his hold. Once free, his hands did as they pleased.

His hands knew how to make music, and they longed to make it on her.

Alex trailed his fingertips up her arms, reveling in the vocalized gasp his touch elicited from her. He brushed the sides of her breasts on purpose, but didn't fully touch. Then he took advantage of the way her head tipped back and her mouth opened as he did it.

Her fingers crawled up his chest, her hands splaying wide across the front of him. She touched him like she was memorizing the texture and scent and heat of him.

He wondered if she needed him half as much as he needed her. She couldn't, but he hoped she did. Her heady kisses drugged him, pulled him under, and he found his hands in her hair, against her head, holding her so he could drink his fill.

Pressing her further into the counter, he knew she had to feel his erection pushing against her. God, he'd wanted her for so long. Held back for so long. Told himself it was wrong. He knew now that there was nothing more right than this. Nothing more right than her moving her hips upward with need and want for him.

Lize felt him. She couldn't feel the ache that throbbed in him, or the near pain at being so close but so far. But she felt that he wanted her, just how much he wanted her, and she pushed closer to him.

Tiny whimpers escaped her sweet lips, making him need even more. More mouth to skin, more sex, less clothing.

Using his hands to turn her head, and his arms locked around her to press her breasts to him and pull her even closer, he slid his mouth along her jaw, inhaling whatever potent pheromones she was giving off. His teeth closed softly over her earlobe as his hands tipped her head back.

He registered everything. Her hair brushing forearms as it swung free. Her breasts moving rhythmically against him, partly from the rate of her breathing and the gasps for oxygen he elicited from her, partly because she was simply moving against him in a rhythm he answered.

His mouth found the sensitive spot under her ear and he explored her with his eyes closed, using all his other senses to take her in. Unable to deny the need to go further, one hand slipped out of her hair, trailing down her neck, over her collarbone, and around the curve of her breast. Stopping there, touching her intimately despite their clothing, he pulled back, opened his eyes and watched her as his thumb brushed her nipple.

Her head had been lolled back, still resting in his hand. Her eyes had been closed, her mouth open as though waiting for more from him. At that touch, she straightened, the sound of air sharply taken in vocalized with a tiny gasp as her eyes flew open.

This time as he moved his thumb again, her eyes held his. The flash of heat he saw there was surely more than just a mirror of his own. The heaving of her ribcage as his touch made her gasp for air only moved her against his hand even more. It was probably the most erotic vision he'd ever had of a fully clothed woman.

This time when he moved in to kiss her, his eyes stayed open. Once, he pushed into her open mouth with his tongue. Twice. Then he crushed her and his own hand between them as he moved his mouth to her ear, this time to tell her everything he wanted to do—to her, with her, every way he wanted her to touch him.

He opened his mouth—and heard the sound of a door open upstairs.

Livie?

Sophie?

It was a bucket of cold water on the steamiest moves he'd ever made.

He'd forgotten who he was. Where he was. What he was doing.

Mariliz stared at him, her mouth open this time with shock and not need at all. "Alex."

The whisper of his name across lips wet with his kisses sent blood rushing south again. "Lize."

"We can't." She whispered again as she pulled back into the counter edge as far as she could. Her hand—just a few moments ago grabbing him and pulling him closer—now pushed at him, tried to make space between them.

Stepping back, knowing he needed to, though he didn't want to, Alex looked away. He looked up, as though he might see Olivia through the floor.

Neither he nor Mariliz spoke while the sounds of a kid running a glass of water and heading back to bed came down from the landing. For a moment his mind muttered at him. Surely Livie hadn't seen anything? What a crap thing for him to do to his kid. He'd meant what he said, Bridget had made her choice.

Though they hadn't said the words that they were splitting up, she had said she wouldn't learn sign. She wanted a normal life for Sophie and thought he was ruining their daughter. He'd been clear: if she wouldn't learn the language their child would speak, he wouldn't be waiting when she got back. He wouldn't be boarding his five-year-old at school either. He'd drive to Knoxville every day if he had to.

The thoughts ran rampant through his head as they stood there frozen, until the door closed. He watched as they both breathed a visible sigh of relief.

He was opening his mouth to speak when she shook her head as if she knew he was going to say more. As if she knew he was still aiming for yes.

"I can't be your backup choice." The words were spoken normally, with strength of conviction behind them, neither whispered nor whimpered.

"I—"

She shook her head at him again. "You're married."

"Not really. Not anymore." He was shaking his own head. Could he just move Bridget aside like that?

It was Lize's touch that he felt, her fingers gliding across the back of his hand. He felt it tugging inside him, the knowledge that she still wanted to touch him, until he realized she was running her fingertip over his wedding band.

"Shit." He started to tug it off.

"No. Leave it." Her hand moved away, surprising him at the coldness of the loss of her touch. "I don't want this to be the reason you take it off."

"You're not." He tugged at it, moving it over the knuckle only to find Lize still shaking her head at him.

"What about Livie? What will she think if that comes off tonight? She's got enough on her plate. Her only stability right now is that her parents are still married."

"And you. You're their stability." He murmured, knowing it was true. Hating it even as he did it, anger glazing the world in a wet sheen, he pushed the ring back into place.

"If we're going to give the girls any stability at all, this can't happen again." She motioned between them and ducked to the side. Before he could comment, she was gone behind the door of her room.

He was still standing alone in his kitchen when the air conditioning came on. He heard it, aware of all the sounds he'd heard that night. Bridget walking out the door for what was probably the final time. It hadn't sounded that different from the other times, but it certainly *felt* different. He'd heard Olivia cry and yell out for her mother. He'd heard silence from Sophie —that was maybe the most damning sound of all, that his youngest daughter had no real bond to her own mother.

He'd heard what Mariliz sounded like when she wanted a man. And he'd heard himself respond. He'd heard her whisper his name, the music and lyrics of their lovemaking a song he could now begin to play out in his head. It was a song he eventually wanted to hear through to the end.

It almost physically hurt to push that wedding ring back on. Should he yank it? Pull the band-aid for Livie, too? She was only eight. He stood in the kitchen, his head tipped back casually while his life lay in ruins around him. He wanted to be honest with his daughter. He hadn't been before, softening all the jagged edges with pretty lies about how "Mommy just needed a break" and "Mommy will come back" and "Soon things will be the same." He hadn't really believed any of it. It was pure bullshit intended to soothe his daughter. And himself. It had been easier to lie than to stand and face the music. But things couldn't be ignored now. He wouldn't put his old family back together by sacrificing Sophie.

Worse, he wasn't working out of pure motive. He wanted Mariliz. Alex couldn't deny that he had an agenda there. Maybe it was time to evaluate how far that went. But it was hard to make a reasonable decision about her when she didn't evoke any reasonable feelings.

She touched him like she wanted to feel him on her skin, as though she couldn't help herself. He hadn't been touched like that in forever. No one had wanted him like that for so long. Maybe never.

Pushing off the counter, he headed to bed, climbing the stairs one slow step at a time. He wondered if Lize was asleep, then he wondered if Livie was, if Sophie was.

Then he lay in bed, tossing and turning.

Only when he woke up the next morning, when he was staring at the ceiling feeling like he'd been hit by a Mac truck, did it occur to him, that he'd never once wondered how Bridget was doing.

CHAPTER 27

Mariliz sat at the bar, nursing a margarita. She could have had a beer, but she had those at home—*at the Beaumonts'*, she corrected. She was trying to fix that in her head, as though thinking it differently would make it different.

"Can I buy you a drink?" The voice came over her shoulder, dripping with honey and interest.

Turning, Mari smiled at him, hoping it looked disappointed. "Thank you, no."

With a nod, he turned and walked away, in pursuit of someone new. She had enough of her own troubles.

Her second date with Thad had gone wonderfully. It would have been perfect had she not had feelings for someone else. He said he would call her and set up a third date—number four if she counted the coffee. He'd kissed her and she'd kissed him back. He'd waited, a perfect gentleman that she should feel far more for, until the end of the second date to even try to lay one on her. Sure, he'd hinted, told her she looked great, made no bones about being attracted to her, but he'd kept his hands to himself, not pushing. So Mariliz had gone out for a second date.

It was easier to tell herself it was okay when she didn't have to face how flat that kiss had felt. Especially when she compared it to the buzz she still had from Alex cornering her in the kitchen and setting all her nerve endings on fire.

If this next date didn't create some sparks, she would have to cut Thad loose. Which totally sucked. She stood no chance with Alex. He was married. It had been a week since Bridget walked out—a week of tension in the house, a week of Livie being nervous and crying at the drop of a hat, a week of Alex being disturbingly polite. Still, he'd not once looked at her like he wanted her. And she'd not heard word one about a divorce.

She'd been cheated on. She did not want to be on the other side of that, even though it was clear he wanted to pull his wedding band off, and even though Mariliz could readily admit now that she did not like Bridget one bit. She wasn't ready to get involved with the woman's husband.

"Wow. You look really down for someone sitting at the bar with a cold drink." Missy's voice was at least welcome.

Mariliz stood up and hugged her cousin, maybe a little tighter than usual. Missy seemed to sense it. "Okay, Lize. I'm getting a drink and you're gonna spill. I have more dirt for you, too. Find us a table out of the way."

Mari headed out to the patio area where the music didn't blare so loud. It wasn't quite as warm as she would have liked, but she had on sleeves and this was better. The space was worth it. She caught Missy's eye, motioning where she was going, as she headed through the doorway and found a table for them.

The slight breeze and the cold drink sweating in her hand stopped her for a moment. She sighed shortly and realized she was bottled up. Everything was on edge. She wanted to shake it off for a while.

When Missy came out and sat down with her cranberry something that was surely fifty-plus proof, Mari steered the conversation. "So tell me how things are going with the boyfriend."

"Oh." The flat response boded poorly. The follow up was no better. "Yeah, that ended a week ago."

"Why didn't you call me?" Mariliz felt her heart crack all over again. Dammit. She'd asked because she wanted good news. But no matter how much she didn't want to talk about sad things, she knew she needed to be a friend. Maybe it would be better if she wasn't talking about her own turmoil. "What happened?"

"Honestly, I think it was the bed." Missy sighed into her drink.

"You're gonna have to explain that one."

"The extra bed for his son? Well, they started staying over a lot more, and I think it was too much, too soon." Missy shrugged. "It might have been okay without the kid, but he got tugged between the two of us. I tried not to, but . . ." She sighed again. "It happened anyway."

"I'm so sorry."

"What about you and hottie drummer boy?" Missy asked as though Mari might have gossip to share.

"Oh geez. It would be steamy, but it's all so sad." She didn't know where to start, but she tried to get all of it in.

"So the wife is out of the picture?"

"Ha. She's not *there*, but to say she was 'out of the picture' would be completely wrong." Mari gestured grandly, almost tipping the now empty margarita glass in her ire and realizing the alcohol had hit her a little faster than she planned. "He said she's gone, but he hasn't said the 'd' word yet at all. He's still wearing his wedding ring, but that's because I told him to."

"You told him to?"

"Yeah," Mari went back to the story, having to admit again just how sizzling hot that kiss had been. "It would kill Livie. I can't do that to her."

"So no more moves on drummer dad. That's a shame." Missy seemed almost as upset about the lack of Mari's love life as her own.

"Not until he's divorced. And even then, do I want to get involved with a man who's got all that turmoil?"

"There are no men who don't, Lize. No men who don't." Missy drained her glass to match Mari's then thunked it back on the table. "I need a mental health day. When do you get a damned day off?"

"Tomorrow?" She really didn't know. "Alex leaves on tour for six days in three days. So tomorrow, next day, then next day he leaves in the morning. Maybe I can get tomorrow off?" She'd counted the days on her fingers like the inebriated bar-girl she was. "Want me to call and ask him?"

"Oh yeah. Drunk dial your boss and ask for time off."

She was pretty certain that Missy was being facetious, but since she couldn't spell it, Mariliz wasn't going to give it any credence. With one eyebrow up, she held out her phone and called Alex. "Hey, Alex. I was wondering, since you're leaving on tour soon. And you'll be gone for . . . Five? Six days?"

"Six days." Missy filled in, apparently better able to hold her liquor.

"Can I have the next two days off?"

"Are you drinking?" He asked, though he didn't sound upset.

"I, sir, am off the clock."

He laughed. The first time since that horrible-wonderful night a week ago. Her heart thawed. "Just don't drive. And yes. Have dinner with us the night before? Make a smooth transition?"

"Of course! I promise to be sober, too." She smiled. She wasn't drunk. Just tipsy. Relaxed. Happy. Tipsy.

"Yes, ma'am. I have faith in you."

She was getting ready to sign off when Missy took the phone. "We'll be by to pick up some of her things, but she won't be home for the next few days. I just didn't want you to worry."

"Thank you, Missy."

Missy hung up then turned to Mariliz with her mouth open. "He knows my *name*, Lize! You talked about me."

"I may have." She hiccuped. "How long do we have to wait before we can drive?"

"I'm sober."

"You had a whole . . ." Mari moved her finger up and down the empty glass.

"Cranberry soda."

"Whah?"

"I was depressed. I didn't want to be drunk-depressed. I'm calling my boss, taking a few mental health days. We're going to the spa tomorrow."

"Oh, you're the best cousin ever!"

"I am."

~

Alex sat on the couch, his one beer in his hand. As the only adult in the house with his kids, one was his limit. But he'd wanted that one.

He'd wanted it to help offset the knowledge that Bridget had walked out the door for good, and for the corresponding knowledge that he didn't really care much. Had she done it a year ago, it would have been horribly painful. But she'd been training him for quite some time to get used to living without her. So the loss of his wife was disturbingly not a big deal.

What bothered him was that the house felt different without Lize in it.

She and her cousin—Missy, he knew—came by the night before and packed a bag for Lize and left. The girls were already in bed, but she didn't say anything to him either. The women went around the side of the house, made a very small amount of noise, and then left. He wouldn't know she had a bag with her if he hadn't seen it himself as he stepped into the office and waved at her as she left again.

When she'd been "off duty" before, she'd been here. She'd slept in her room, often had dinner with him and the girls, even helped him make it. For a full day now, he'd truly been a single parent. He'd done this before, it wasn't the logistics that twisted his insides, it was the feeling. Previously, he'd believed Bridget was eventually coming back. The thought that her loss was a permanent thing hadn't bothered him until Lize left, too. He really didn't think he missed Bridge as much as he missed Lize.

He threw back the rest of the beer and stood up from the sofa in his den, the envelope in his hand. He probably shouldn't have been drinking before he opened it, but he felt like he needed it. Chucking the glass into recycling—where it clinked against last night's beer—he stood at the kitchen counter. Though he knew he was avoiding the envelope, he let his thoughts wander.

"Mew." The tiny sound was followed by another and he looked down to see two kittens at his feet. They were still too small to jump up onto the counter, though they had begun trying. They were soft and disturbingly adorable.

"Hey Lilac, hey Poof." He spoke the words, thinking the kittens needed to learn both their spoken and sign names. "Do you need food?"

He'd stopped thinking it odd that he spoke to the kittens a while ago. They rubbed his legs and followed him over to their tiny dishes. "Those are full, guys."

He didn't call them "ladies," couldn't bring himself to do it. "Whatcha need? Pets?"

He leaned down offering them "pets" as Livie called it in English, stroking the tiny cats until he saw a few spots of fur flying up into the air. He wondered how much dander and fluff he couldn't see. Still avoiding the envelope with the return address of a local law firm, he settled on the floor and played with the kittens until they got bored with the attention and wandered off.

He decided then that the kittens could sleep in with the girls if they wanted. He needed to find good things he could do for his daughters that would help balance out the shit they'd been dealing with and probably would continue to deal with if that lawyer info was what he thought it was.

With a sigh, he picked himself up off the floor and headed back to the counter. He *needed* to know what was in there. So far he'd successfully avoided it for about forty hours; anything longer would just be unmanly. So he ripped it open, finding papers stating exactly what he'd expected.

Bridget was filing for divorce. The mailed papers were a courtesy, he was not being served, not yet. There was a lot of legal jargon suggesting mediation and that Alex simply sign and agree to that up front. They could meet with lawyers and the mediator and work out the terms.

Alex read it twice, glad he'd only had the one beer. If divorce papers didn't sober you up, nothing would. He'd thought this would be the actual thing, the lawsuit. But he realized that if he was going to get served divorce papers he would actually have to get "served" and that hadn't happened yet.

By the end of the second reading he realized two things. One —he wasn't going to just sign it, he needed his own lawyer. And two—he didn't even trust his ex-wife anymore.

Shit. He had no real clue what she'd been up to for the past year. When he believed she was coming back, he'd simply placed his trust in the sweet girl he'd married. Now that girl was clearly gone. He'd seen her become a mother, a caretaker, a bit of a socialite, but he hadn't seen what she'd become this last year. Who was she hanging out with? She must have friends—one surely didn't just go on a one-month cruise alone. But he'd only seen the bill for one ticket. Thinking back, there had been spans of time when there had been no bills. Times when he wasn't paying for a spa or a beach house or mountain cabin or even a car rental. What had she done during that time?

He turned over the possibility that she'd cheated on him.

It didn't put a knife in his heart. Jesus, it didn't even hurt as much as the idea of Lize dating that cop did. It was definitely time for a divorce. He'd told himself for a long time that he could put his marriage back together. But the complete death of the feelings coupled with Bridget's seeming genetic inability to accept Sophie as she was would spell the death of things.

No, he held the death of things in his hands. He wouldn't sign the papers. Not like this. First thing tomorrow morning he was getting a lawyer.

No, first thing, he was getting the girls up and making breakfast, and getting Olivia to school. Then he would take Sophie and get a lawyer. Maybe breakfast first. He could work with her on her food signs again.

That settled, he put the papers away so Olivia wouldn't find them, then he wandered up the stairs feeling far more alone than he had on previous nights when he'd done almost exactly the same thing.

He desperately missed knowing that Lize was on the other side of the house.

The question was, what was the right way to fix things and how could he make it happen?

CHAPTER 28

It was awkward being back in the Beaumont house, Mariliz thought.

She'd had two days off, and though she found she missed the girls terribly, she'd needed the break. Six days solo with two kids was going to be a challenge.

Probably, the biggest problem was facing Alex. Two days with Missy, and every secret Mari didn't even realize she'd been keeping came pouring out. Missy had that effect on her. Or hard cider did. Or caramel corn and chick flicks did. Who really knew? But Mariliz spilled everything. Shocking even herself with how deep her feelings had begun to run for a man who was still married and very entangled in something very messy that she should not be getting her fingers into. Or her tongue.

She reminded herself of that repeatedly, but when she took her deep breath and opened the door to the house, he'd been standing there. Despite all her confessions, all her new knowledge, she hadn't been ready for the punch to the gut just the sight of him delivered.

He grinned at her. "You're home."

"I have been for a little while." She'd come in about an hour

SAVANNAH KADE

ago and took some time to put her stuff away, shower, and loll in her bed reading for a little bit.

"I know, I heard you. But you're really *here* now." He turned back to the counter she only just realized was stacked full of stuff. "I made dinner."

"You made it all yourself? Are these three of your ten dishes?"

His grin told her he was happy she remembered his comment. "No, the girls and I read a recipe book and have made our very first lasagna."

"Do I get some?"

"Mariliz!" The word popped out of the air as Olivia bounded down the steps. She looked up to the top and stomped twice to get her sister's attention, then signed "Mariliz" and pointed.

Alex bounded past Olivia and up the stairs to monitor Sophie.

Mari wanted to look up and be sure Alex got to his daughter before she got excited and tumbled. But Sophie was very proficient with the stairs, and Mari was blindsided by a tackle from the older girl.

"Umph." The air came out of her, but she tried not to show it as she hugged the girl. "Livie!"

"You're back!"

"Exactly when I said I would be." She smiled. She stated the words in a way that she hoped was casual, but wanted to reinforce that she wasn't running off. Especially with Bridget gone, these girls needed some stability, and Mari didn't think she was getting fired now.

Just as she managed to get the words out, Alex hit the bottom of the steps and set a squirming Sophie onto the ground. She ran forward as Mari squatted down for the hug. "Hi Punkin." She signed with one hand. "I missed you."

Looking up at Livie, she added, "I missed you both."

The girls hugged her into a sandwich as Alex stood at the

base of the stairs and watched. "Okay, girls. She's here, let's serve up the dinner we made her."

One by one, things were carried to the table. Mari joined in, even though apparently the dinner was in honor of her return after two days off. "You look like you all survived okay without me."

"We went to class!" Livie piped up as she was seated. She picked up Sophie's sippy cup, handing it over as Alex got the little girl into her high chair.

"You did?" She helped herself to piping hot pasta and some salad and a side dish of green beans.

"Wait." Alex put his hand out, then signed, "We're sorry if it tastes bad. It's our first lasagna."

She laughed at him, thinking how good it felt to be home. The awkwardness was between him and her, not at being back in the house. It seemed the house itself had aired out. The tension Bridget brought with her was slowly fading. Mariliz wanted to ask if the girls had seen their mom, but there would be time enough later to get details.

She cut herself a bite and blew on it for a moment while the family watched her in anticipation. When she finally ate it, they all leaned forward. "It's very cheesy," she managed around the mouthful.

"Is that bad?" Alex asked.

"No. It's not. This is very good." She wasn't lying and she was grateful for that, not sure of how proficient a liar she might be.

She asked how their class was, and they told her about learning new words. They even got assignments.

"We have to talk about baby bears, vegetables, and . . . What was the third one, Daddy?" Olivia turned to him.

"Furniture. We have to be ready to tell some details about three pieces of furniture in our house." He finished for her.

"I'm glad you're going to class. It sounds like fun."

He nodded. "The girls really like it, and it's really helpful."

"We met another family like us." Livie piped up. "They have Mercy, who's my age, and Johnny, who's a little older than Sophie and deaf. I liked Mercy, she was fun."

"That's cool." Mari told Livie even as she glanced to Sophie, who was playing with her green beans rather than eating them.

They spoke of the people they met, what they'd done since Mari left a few days ago. They talked about Sophie's potty training, something Mariliz hadn't realized could be dinner table talk until she was living with kids.

They were cleaning up when the knock came at the door. Mari looked up, but Alex was already headed for the front. From the kitchen, she could just see him in the doorway. She couldn't hear whoever was outside, but she heard Alex.

"Yes, I'm Alex Beaumont."

A fan? She thought. There was something odd in the way he said it. This wasn't someone he knew.

"Thank you, very much." Then he closed the door, returning with a manila envelope as he veered into the office for a moment and returned empty handed.

Mari frowned at him as he came back out, but he shook his head like it was nothing.

Olivia caught it, though. "What was that, Daddy?"

"Just some papers—" He cut himself off as if he'd been going to say more. Deftly, he changed the subject. "As soon as this is finished, let's show Lize how we play drums."

"You play drums?" She asked, then shook her head. "I mean, I know *you* do—" she gestured to Alex, "but you do too, Livie?"

"It's awesome!" Olivia smiled up at her. Then turned to Sophie and said, "Hurry up, we can play drums."

The toddler squealed, convincing Mariliz that whatever it was, it was fun. She followed the family around to the back of the house, the envelope and Alex's cut-off words forgotten as she watched him settle himself on the stool with one girl on each leg. Wrapping an arm around each waist to keep them in place, he instructed Olivia to get sticks and hand two to Sophie.

Though Mariliz expected Livie to handle them like a pro, she was surprised to see Sophie had a decent hand position on them, too. But before she could analyze that, Livie turned to her younger sister and nodded. Together they each clicked their sticks together in a classic one-two-three-four and began playing.

Neither girl could reach the span of the drum kit, nor could either get to the bass drum, which Alex worked with the foot pedal, keeping a low steady beat.

She felt her mouth fall open at the sight and sound and feel of it. Walking slowly into the room she stared at the family as they played. Neither girl was perfect, not even close, but they were pretty solid. Both had the same look of concentration on their faces, and Mari couldn't look away. She was held in place by the rhythm in the air. It pulsed around her with sound and beat and feeling.

She readily admitted that she'd always thought of drummers as time keepers. Though sometimes she would overhear Alex talking music, he would say something like "a Ringo Swing" or that he'd been listening to Janet Weiss, and Mariliz didn't understand any of it. She still didn't, but at least now she saw it was its own music, it had variations she hadn't realized. Even in the girls' work—which she could now distinguish from Alex's much more clean, professional sound—she could hear that the hits weren't always the same. There were notes and timbre changes. Now she almost wondered why the band was keeping him in the back.

As she looked up, she saw Alex grinning at her as the girls came to a stop, their serious faces turning to gleeful grins.

"What did you think?" He asked.

Mari looked at each of the girls and signed, "You two are amazing! That was wonderful. Oh wait—"

She turned and ran off from the room. Since the family was signing, she couldn't hear what they said as she flew down the hall and into her suite to grab her cell phone. Well, there was a downside to everything. No eavesdropping.

Dashing back through the house, as though they would get up and go away and it would be lost forever, she hit the button on her phone for the camera. Heading back into the center of the room, where she could face the man and his daughters, she signed, "Play another one?"

The three had looked confused until she returned with the camera, and they'd been silent while they waited for her. Now, Sophie and Livie grinned again and nodded, the toddler letting out a squeal she couldn't hear. Though Mari could easily identify it as a noise made by a deaf person, it sounded happy. Her heart kicked as the girls clicked their sticks together again and she aimed the phone screen, waiting for the perfect picture.

Later, she didn't know how long she stayed like that, only that Sophie eventually squirmed in the middle of the song and threw her sticks on the floor. When Alex asked, Sophie frantically signed "pee."

So everyone jumped up and ran. Toddlers and potty training. Then it was time for a marshmallow treat for not wetting her father's leg while he sat with her at his beloved drum kit. There were books, tucking Sophie into bed, a tv show with Olivia, then her reading time. It was over an hour-long process to get the kids into bed every night. Alex took care of all of it, because for the next week, it would all be hers.

She relaxed on the sofa in the rec room, enjoying the big TV. She'd been provided with a DVR and a TV of her own, but she'd gotten used to watching in here, rather than stuffed into her own little cave. Mari was just thinking maybe she should get up and head to her own rooms when Alex flopped down beside her, the envelope in his hand.

"What's that?" She asked. "You cut yourself off earlier, when

Olivia asked about it, so it seemed odd."

He nodded, looking more solemn than he did while drumming with his girls. "I was served these papers. I almost told Olivia they were from the studio, but I don't think they are. And I don't want to lie to her. That's something I decided the other night. We lied to her a lot."

"What?" That didn't make sense. Who just lied to their child?

"Bridget and I told her that Sophie would come around, that mommy and daddy wouldn't ever get divorced—even though we could see things falling apart. We told her mommy was on vacation, though I told everyone that lie, including myself. I think Bridget told her we might send Sophie away, and I remember that scared the shit out of Livie."

"She must have thought she could get sent away, too, if she was bad." Mari sat up straighter. "She does have a bit of a perfection complex. Do you think that's why?"

"It's possible." He nodded, "But Bridget had one, too. Livie should have perfect hair, and perfect grades, and all of that."

"Hmmm." The sound came out and Mariliz wished she'd managed to keep even that indication of her thoughts to herself.

"But I think I'm about to become a single parent, so no more lying to the kids." He ripped open the top of the envelope and pulled out the paperwork. "Yup. My lawyer will want to see these."

He set them aside, yanked off his wedding ring and put it on the table on top of the papers. "Thank god. Now I can do this."

Leaning closer, he slid his hand into her hair, up the back of her head, and was kissing her before Mariliz had a chance to react. Or consciously react, anyway.

Her body knew what to do. Before she could have even said she was kissing Alex Beaumont, her mouth was open, her tongue swept his mouth, and her hands clutched at his shoulders. She pressed herself against him as his arms wrapped around her waist, holding her tight.

CHAPTER 29

She got up the next morning and made breakfast as though things were normal, calling Olivia down the stairs as she put the water in the dinosaur oatmeal for Sophie. The little one had been on a kick for the stuff, wanting it every day, to the point where Mariliz felt she had to limit it to just breakfast. But she'd already advanced to stirring it herself, watching the little egg candies melt away to reveal the brightly colored dinosaurs.

Olivia came down to eat, now wanting maple and brown sugar flavor with a sprinkling of mini chocolate chips. That had to be way too much sugar, but Alex told her to let it go.

When she thought about it, he might have a point. She read the labels and it turned out neither option was worse than a bowl of frosted flakes. And the point that the girls needed things that made them happy hit home. They needed to get some of the things they wanted, because the storm of divorce was coming.

Olivia had weathered her mother's leaving much better than Mariliz would have. But that only drove home the fact that the girl had gotten used to not having her mother around. Mari had to wonder further had the girl seen her mother stomp out like that before?

Alex drove Olivia to school, wanting to do it one last time before he hit the road. He returned, packed his bags and hauled them down the stairs. Sophie was playing in the corner. She perked up when she felt the vibrations of her father's suitcase bouncing down the steps.

He sat and played with her for a bit before heading to the counter where Mariliz watched from.

"You ready?" She asked him.

"I guess." She noticed he had the wedding band back on. He noticed her noticing. "I'm wearing it in front of Olivia until I tell her, and on tour until it becomes public. I don't want a magazine announcing my divorce before I do."

"Have you told the guys?"

"Today." He changed the subject. "Can you send me that picture of the girls playing last night?"

"Sure." Pulling the phone from her pocket, she quickly sent it, apologizing. "I'm sure JD's photographer wife could have done it better." She couldn't remember the woman's name right then, her brain was still scrambled from last night's kiss and from the disappearing/reappearing wedding band.

"It's a great shot. Kelsey will be impressed." He grinned when it popped up on his own phone.

Kelsey! That was it. She changed the subject back. "Is there anything in particular you want me to tell the girls about you and Bridget? Anything you *don't* want me to say?"

He thought for a minute, then said, in English, "I want to be the one to tell them about the divorce. So maybe you can say you don't know—"

"But I do know. So I lie to the girls?"

He nodded in concession. "Good point. No one lies to them. So you tell them I'll talk to them when I get home about what will happen. But you can reassure them that you and I will both be here and things will run pretty much the way they have. It isn't like Bridget was here for the past year much at all." He sighed.

"I don't think Sophie will ask after her." Mariliz said it before she realized what an indictment it was. She flinched.

"Lize, don't. That's not on you. Sophie didn't have the same mother Livie did. Bridget doted on Olivia, thought the sun rose and set on her." He shrugged. It was the past, and Mariliz understood there was nothing she could do about it.

"I have to say," This time he smiled. "Potty training Olivia didn't give me as much happiness as potty training Sophie. Seriously, it's all about communication, and for so long, I didn't think I would ever have that with her. So even potty training is making me pleased."

"Oh joy." Her delivery was deadpan, but he laughed at her. That damn dimple popped out again.

Then he got serious. "Is this normal? She was diagnosed as learning disabled and aggressive." He looked over at his daughter. "Now, I'd laugh at anyone who told me this girl was either of those things."

It was a serious question, but the only answer she had was, "There's nothing normal about this. There would be a bunch more data if she'd been signing—or signed to—since birth."

"But hasn't anyone else had this? Tried to go with lip reading? You sounded like you knew something about it." He was looking at her now, not accusatory, but trying to pick her brain.

He wouldn't like what she had to say. "There are cases of kids who didn't have language. While the data is relatively consistent, calling it 'data' is wrong. It's just stories. These kids are brought up that way because no one can get to them. They're in cabins in the Appalachians, or so rural they can't get to doctors to get help. So no one knows sign language to teach the family. And no one really knows what's going on until much later. Usually when they get language."

He was frowning. His daughter—an affluent city child—was being compared to kids with no real medical care at all. But there was more.

"Also, those kids don't compare to Sophie because they were allowed to point and develop some communication."

"So they had language?" He asked.

"No, it's not language. It's communication, but not *language*. There's no ability to express anything in the abstract." She sighed. "There were cases where people tried to teach deaf kids to speak, but it was usually later in life—around ages five to ten —so they had language first. I don't know where Bridget found a doctor who thought it was a good idea to teach an infant lipreading."

There was a pause as Alex turned away. When he turned back, he said, "She's not my wife any more. And after everything, I don't feel I owe her, but please—for the girls' sake —don't repeat this."

"I wouldn't. You don't have to tell me. I'm just trying to answer your questions and understand Sophie." Mariliz held her hands up as though she could ward that off.

He plucked them out of the air and tucked them into his own. "You deserve to know everything. I won't keep anything from you. No lies. No big lies, no little ones. No lying to the girls or you or myself now."

Still holding her hands, he said, "Bridget had a perfect life. Musician husband, money, beautiful daughters. It all went perfectly until Sophie wasn't perfect. So I think Bridget shopped for a doctor that said they could make Sophie at least appear perfect. I don't know if she and the doctor made a pact—if they knew this hadn't been done before, but they were going to use

Sophie as the experiment—because if it had worked, it would be a coup. You were right. I called the office. Sophie was their youngest patient by far. But that's over now. I can't change the past, so I'll change the future."

Tugging at her hands, he pulled her in close. Only for a moment did she think to resist.

His mouth touched hers, his eyes closing as he did it.

It wasn't the heavy make-out session from the night before, just a goodbye kiss that lingered long enough to be truly hot.

"I have to go." He whispered against her mouth, the taste of him on her lips sweet with promise despite what she knew.

"Alex," Mariliz forced herself to pull away. "You can't do this."

He leaned closer to her ear, his mouth now grazing another sensitive part of her. "Then stop kissing me back."

A sound of frustration crossed with want emerged unbidden from her throat as she pulled away once again.

"You're married." She whispered it the first time, then spoke the words out loud the second time. The only other person around was two years old and deaf. "You're married."

"I'm not."

"Legally, you are." She shot back. "Listen, if you're serious . . . Well, come back when you aren't *married*."

"It may be a while." He looked disappointed. Honestly, so was she. But a girl had to have her standards. Apparently, Alex's weren't quite the same as hers. "One last time."

Leaning in, he kissed her softly and she didn't protest. Not when his lips touched hers. Not when his mouth lingered. Not when his hand clenched softly at her waist.

As they pulled apart, slower this time, she looked at him, specifically at his mouth. *Shit.* "I work for you, you know."

"We'll figure it out, Lize." He promised, smiling at her.

She wasn't sure he was right about that, but it didn't matter now. "You have to go."

He turned away then. "I'll call. You'll call. We'll figure out when to do video. Just hold down the fort. This one isn't that long."

Mariliz nodded at him and watched as he hugged his daughter and headed out to the garage. Just as she was thinking that was it, he was gone, Sophie came running up to her. "Kiss! Kiss! Hug." She demanded.

Mariliz scooped her up with a smile and kissed her belly until she squealed then hugged her until she squirmed. When Sophie begged to be put down, Mariliz spoke to her back. "You Beaumonts, wanting to be kissed."

She heard the car pull out of the driveway and realized she was at the start of five long days. Alex had given her the name of a teenage girl they'd met at class, to talk to her about babysitting for Sophie. While Mariliz was good with exposing Sophie to as many different signers as possible, she had also grown to understand why at-home parents went so crazy.

She loved the girls, but she couldn't talk to them about adult things. They went to bed early. They wanted to tell her, in sometimes minute detail, about disturbingly unimportant tasks that day. She listened with a smile, afraid she'd already fallen in love with them, but she would gladly take a break.

Picking up the phone, she called the girl and left a message, realizing too late she was probably in school. But Mari had another option. She called Missy. "Hey, can you come hang out over here Thursday night?"

She worked it out for Missy to arrive after the girls had gone to sleep. Alex would be home the next morning, so after she drove Livie to school, and got Sophie traded to Alex she could nap and make up for however late she and Missy stayed up.

With an evening with her cousin to look forward to and the hopes of getting the new sitter in for a short trial run, Mariliz moved the day along handily. This was going to be fine, she told herself.

That night she watched TV in the rec room and then

snuggled into her own bed with the doors to both her room and the suite cracked just a little.

And at three a.m., she heard the first horrible noise.

CHAPTER 30

A lex pulled open his phone and stared at the picture as the bus rumbled underneath him. It was three in the morning and he'd come awake and for some reason stayed that way.

It happened like that sometimes on the bus. The beds were long enough, if not really big enough, to be comfortable. He'd learned to sleep in them sufficiently over the years. But once in a while, he'd wake up and not be able to get back.

It hadn't happened to him at home. Even recently, the nights Bridget hadn't even come in, he hadn't realized it until the morning. He wanted to feel bad about the loss of his marriage—but he really didn't. He couldn't muster the feelings.

Sure, he felt bad for the girls. He felt the loss of the future he'd envisioned. He felt the pain of change. But he didn't miss Bridget herself. He'd done that for the past year and he was all out of pain and grief and anger about it. He'd stuffed it down until it solved itself. He made a mental note not to solve things the same way in the future, because this solution was going to be a mess. He could feel it.

He wanted to feel guilty about his feelings for Lize, but he couldn't muster that either. Bridget had taken herself out of the equation. Though he had to admit she probably saw that differently. She said it wasn't his place to teach their daughter a language she didn't approve of. To him the issue was that she didn't approve of the language their daughter *could* speak.

While he'd once envisioned growing old with Bridget—he'd once thought he'd gotten so very lucky—he knew that the woman he saw in those visions didn't exist anymore. There was every possibility that she'd never existed anywhere other than in Alex's own mind.

They'd fit together well, so he never questioned if the reason they fit was because they wanted the same things or thought the same way. He felt he'd had more deep conversations with Lize in the past month than he'd had with Bridget in . . . well, at least since Sophie had come along. When he thought back, it had been much longer.

Once Livie had been born, Bridget had seemed to *want* to take over the parenting. She picked clothes and schools and often didn't like Alex's choices. He'd seen that as her being a good protective mother, and now he wondered if she hadn't been edging him out. She said, "Don't feed her that!" and "Don't dress her in those clothes." and "Don't let her spend so much time on the swingset when she has homework."

It seemed he was so often wrong. In the big picture, he was the star, the breadwinner, the one with fans. Bridget ruling the home seemed a bit of an equalizer. He hadn't questioned it.

The bus rocked under him, bringing his attention back to the picture in his hand. It was definitely his new favorite—the one Lize took when he was playing drums with the girls the night before he left.

He had both girls on his lap. *Both.* Two months ago he would never have guessed that he could get them to do that. He'd always hugged Sophie, sometimes to calm her down, sometimes to face her to something and help her see a TV show or look at the zoo animals. But he'd never expected her to be able to behave on his lap with his drumsticks, with her sister next to her. He knew it was just that she'd learned to speak, that people communicated with her and she had a voice now. That was all, but to him it felt like a miracle. This picture was the best example of that miracle.

He thought about getting up and doing something, but chances were everyone was still asleep and he didn't want to bother them. So he lay there, thinking, looking at the picture for a while before he decided to text Lize. He figured she should be asleep and she'd see it in the morning. Surely he wouldn't wake her up.

—hey, I miss you.

He typed it out and thought about it for a few seconds before sending it. Was it wrong? He did miss her. She didn't want him to kiss her, he was legally married. But he wasn't married really. Not any more. When he was alone at night, she was the one he thought of, and that had been true even before Bridget had come home. It was what bothered him most when his wife was beside him—that he wanted the woman in his bed to be the woman in the guest suite off the ground floor.

His phone dinged at him.

—You shouldn't text me that kind of thing. Erase it.

She was awake? Erase it?

—Why?

His phone dinged almost as fast as he sent it.

—Could be used against you in court.

Shit. She was right.

—Sorry. But it's still true. Erasing.

She didn't respond while he went into the thread and deleted the texts, wondering the whole time if that was more damning than anything else. That he deleted them made it seem more like he was cheating. Wouldn't a good tech be able to pull up the missing messages? Nothing ever really went away in the digital world.

—I hope I didn't wake you.

This time he texted something that didn't look like he was having an affair with the nanny. Even though he really wanted to. It sucked that she made sense. When she said it, it didn't sound like it was just about his divorce, it was about her morals and his legal paperwork that was only just getting started.

—Nope. I was up. Rough night.

—?

It took about five minutes for her to respond. Time he spent imagining her lying in her bed, phone in her hands, typing back to him. He imagined tousled hair and a just-kissed look on her face, even though he wasn't there to do it. After a few minutes, he got worried.

—Sorry. Girls are sick.

He sat upright and called her then, waiting tensely while the phone rang. She didn't answer; the call sent him through to a sweet voicemail message that almost had him sweating. Why didn't she answer?

He told himself it couldn't be that bad, or she would have opened with that info when he first texted. Still it was a long five minutes while he waited for her to call back. The ringing of his phone in the small room sounded loud to his ready ears. He answered as soon as the first tone started and headed out into the hallway, trying to get to the front of the bus as quietly as he could. He didn't want to wake the guys, but he was worried.

"Lize?"

"Hey, sorry. Sophie needed me." She sounded tired, but it was the middle of the night so he wasn't surprised.

"They're sick? Both of them?"

"Yeah," He heard her pause and heard a few noises he now recognized as hands touching/clicking/smacking as part of signs. But he couldn't hear sign language. "Sophie started vomiting around midnight and Olivia joined in an hour later."

"Oh no. Do you have it too?" He could now hear the exhaustion in her voice, the underlay of worry.

"No. Nothing."

"Was it the lasagna?"

At least she laughed at him. That calmed him a little bit.

He heard her hands again, and a weak laugh from Livie. "We're in the rec room, watching The Little Mermaid. And no, it wasn't the lasagna. That's what Livie asked first, too. That was two days ago, it shouldn't be the cause. Plus I had plenty and I'm not sick. My guess is it's something they got exposed to from Livie's school or sign class or someone at the park. Who knows?"

"What can I do?"

"Nothing. They're sucking on ice chips. We're watching a movie. Sophie has a bit of a fever but I gave her medicine and it's coming down. So no worries there."

"You didn't give her aspirin?" It was probably the one thing he really knew.

"Nope. I know how to do it, how to monitor. Her fever didn't crack one-oh-two. Kids get fevers. She's fully responsive. Her neck isn't stiff."

Oh, he hadn't even thought of those things. She did have it under control.

"I'm going to call Nina when I can and get her to bring ginger ale, saltines, and more kids ibuprofen. We're all set." In the background he heard her hands again. It was three a.m. and she was home with his kids. She was tired and dealing with too much, and she was handling it all just fine.

"Are you okay? Do you need me to come home?" He was so worried. He was rarely around when he was needed. Once Bridget had taken care of these things. Now Lize did.

"You're on tour. You can't just cancel concert dates or

anything. We're okay. I'll keep you posted. Here, Livie. Say hi to your Daddy." He could hear that she was holding the phone out or something.

"Hi Daddy." The small voice sounded weary. But she was safe.

"I'm sorry you feel bad baby." He didn't think there was anything else he could do except express sympathy. It sucked being far away when he could be helpful at home.

"I'm okay. Mariliz is taking care of us. I texted mom and told her I was sick. She hasn't texted back yet, but it's the middle of the night."

Jeez, he hadn't even thought of contacting Bridget. At least Olivia seemed satisfied with her mom not messaging back yet. "I'm sure she'll see it when she gets up." But as soon as the words left his mouth he wished he hadn't said them. He wasn't sure. He didn't know how Bridget responded to their oldest child while he was away.

"Hold on." Lize's voice came over the line. "I'm going to sign off, the movie is just riveting. But we'll send you a picture."

He said good-bye and hung up, then turned the phone on himself. Setting it up to record, he got a few seconds of him signing "I hope you feel better soon. I miss you." He sent it before looking at the picture that came in while he recorded it.

In the picture, Mariliz leaned back against the couch leaning almost all the way over Sophie who wasn't big enough to fill the cushion. Livie sat on the other side. All three looked like it was the middle of the night. But all three had silly expressions on their faces. Lize's eyes were half closed and her tongue hung out. Olivia's eyes were crossed and her mouth pulled down into a silly frown. Even Sophie had her mouth open and her tongue out. He laughed until he had to cover his mouth and he almost cried.

Even Sophie could participate in this. She was suddenly a

normal two-year-old, heading toward three. Making faces, wanting cookies, trying to potty train.

He didn't hear the door or the footsteps. He only saw the feet as they came into view in the end of the hallway. The voice pulled his gaze away from the picture.

"You okay, man?"

Craig stood there, hair on end, eyes not quite open.

"I'm sorry if I woke you." Alex apologized.

"You didn't. Roads are rough tonight. What are you looking at? Seems serious." He came over and sat down at the other end of the small table with the built-in sofa that wrapped behind it. Typical Craig, there but not in your space. He had very strong ideas of personal space, and he never invaded anyone else's.

Alex turned the phone around and showed him the picture. "They just took that."

"Why are the kids up in the middle of the night?" Craig hadn't moved any closer, and his questions stayed soft, never demanding.

"Lize is up with them. The girls are both sick."

"That's good." Craig said. "Wait, that sounded wrong. It's good that they can make silly faces. When they get really sick you can't even get that out of them. Mariliz must be taking good care of them."

"She is."

Something in his voice must have triggered the other man. "Why do you sound upset about that?"

"I'm not there. Bridget always took care of them. Then the nannies. Now Lize."

"Lize *is* the nanny, I thought."

And that right there was the heart of the problem.

CHAPTER 31

Mariliz was exhausted and ready to nap when she got the message on her phone. Alex was headed home. The tour bus had pulled in and he was on his way. Would she like a coffee?

Part of her wanted to say, "God, yes!" and the other part thought it might interfere with the nap she was going to take as soon as she could hand off responsibility for the kids. Calling it a 'nap' would be underselling it. She wanted to sleep a whole night through and she didn't care if it started at eleven a.m.

Puttering around, she tried to keep herself awake until he got in. When she eventually heard the garage door go up, her heart hit a skip-beat in her chest.

She'd had a chat with Thad the other day, letting him know she couldn't keep seeing him. She said her life was tangled, which was true. That if things changed, she would see if he was still interested, also true. But the fact was, she didn't really see her heart giving up on Alex Beaumont. One day, in the hopefully not-to-distant future he would be divorced. He would be free. He could be hers.

She had her own issues with that. He was married. He'd

kissed her when he was married and she didn't like being on the other side of that. Still, there was a lot of gray in the middle. Her situation was far different from Reynold hooking up with a different woman for sex on each trip he went on. Her marriage wasn't over when he did that, either. Bridget had effectively left the house a year ago. And Mariliz—despite the woman's crass questions—had not fucked her husband. So that, at least, was a world of difference.

Ultimately, though, all her words were still excuses. A man who was technically married was married. He hadn't seen fit to get divorced before, and Mariliz didn't want to be part of that process now. She reminded herself that she was here for the girls. She was here to help the family—whichever members that may be—learn Sophie's language and grow. That was all.

She was not here to kiss the superbly fine and disturbingly amazing Alex Beaumont. When the door opened and she turned to see him standing there, she wanted to throw that whole self-pep-talk out the window. She wanted to sink into his arms and relax.

He already knew she'd been running ragged. He knew Livie was back at school today, finally feeling better. He knew that Sophie had perked up the day before, and was now at the park with another new sitter Mari had found and done a test run with yesterday. He knew how little she'd slept, how much she worried, and what she'd tried to accomplish anyway. The only thing left was to curl up in his embrace and let him hold her.

But she wouldn't do that. So she smiled and tried to say "hello."

"Hi." He held out the coffee he must have gotten for her when she couldn't decide.

She took it but frowned. "Did I not text back?"

He shook his head, but continued to look at her as though he wanted to drink her in rather than the coffee he held in his hand.

Clutching the still-hot cup, she took a breath and whispered to him, "Don't look at me like that."

"I can't help it." He shrugged. "I won't make a move on you. You asked me not to. I said 'one last kiss' and I meant it, but I can't change the fact that I want more than I can have." He sighed wearily.

He was probably as tired as she was.

They sat at the breakfast bar in companionable silence for a moment before she said, "I'm sorry the girls got sick."

"As if that would possibly be your fault."

She mustered a chuckle. "Well, last week I was trying to find a way to forgive Bridget and I thought to myself, *Mariliz, you haven't even stayed up one night with a sick kid. You have no idea what Bridget went through.* So it feels kind of like I brought this on."

"No, you didn't. Kids get sick. I'm just sorry I wasn't here."

Another sip. Another shrug. "It's why you hired me."

"I used to think so."

This time she turned to him, curious. "You don't anymore?"

"Honestly, I didn't hire you."

"That's true." She thought back to Aunt Frankie abandoning her with the girls and all her panic wondering where the parents were and what she was going to do.

"But I thought that's why we paid someone. Instead I realize that's all fucked up. You love them as much as I do. You're here for Livie—which is more than I can say for her mother. You connect with Sophie in a way none of the rest of us can."

She stopped him there. "Only because I'm ahead of you in class. I learned ASL a long time ago. I'm fluent. You will be, too, and soon. So will Livie, and you know now where to find other people who sign, so you can surround her with people who speak her language. Honestly, there are more people out there than you may think." She thought about meeting Brenda and her grandson Jackson at the bounce house. There was an older man in the neighborhood who'd come up one day when she was walking with Sophie. He explained—in ASL—that his daughter was deaf and she was a teacher at the Tennessee School for the Deaf in Knoxville. Maybe Sophie would have Miss Lindy as her teacher there some day.

Alex mused for a moment, but then added to her comments. "That's true. But you're the only mother she's had. We all hugged her and fed her and changed her diapers as best we could. We took advantage of her good moods and played. But it always ended badly; she was always angry sooner or later. All of that is different now. Livie and I becoming fluent doesn't diminish what you are to Sophie. You're not Mary Poppins, needing to find another family once we're okay."

She laughed a little at that, admitting to herself that the thought had crossed her mind. But could she ever love another family like this? No. Definitely not.

"You look tired." He commented and ignored her wry, "thanks" in return. "It's not an insult, just an observation. Here, put your head on my shoulder."

He leaned in, wrapped an arm around her, an arm that felt way too good, and tugged her closer. As soon as her head touched down, she felt the tension that had been holding her upright drain away. She felt the soft touch of his kiss placed on top of her head. "Alex, I can't do this. I'll fall asleep."

"I don't mind."

She pulled back, laughing. "We're sitting at the bar! I'll fall out of the chair!"

"Fine. I'd say, come curl up on the couch with me, but people will come in and wake you up." His hand trailed down her arm, landing on her fingers, holding on to them.

He said he wouldn't kiss her, but apparently that didn't include not touching her. She wanted to say no, but she liked it too much. Loved the gentle hum that vibrated her skin at the contact.

"Go to sleep. I'll be here when you wake up."

"It might be tomorrow afternoon." She warned.

"That's okay. We'll take turns. We'll make it work. That's what families do." He let go of her hand as she walked the coffee cup to the trash then veered almost clumsily toward her own door.

"Thank you." She wasn't sure what else to say and she had to get the door closed before she invited him to lie down with her. She wasn't awake enough for sex, but the thought of his body, heated and curled around her, was heavenly.

It was a heaven she wasn't going to have. But the bed was warm and she was out cold before she had a chance to contemplate his talk of families, talk of simply trading off. As though she didn't have days on and days off. The lines were blurrier than her dreams.

When she finally woke, the room was dark. The only light at the edge of the heavy drapes on the sliding doors was the yard light. It was past sunset, but how far past, she couldn't really tell. Her thoughts felt heavy, as did her limbs and she stayed cocooned in the warm blanket for a while, probably drifting in and out of sleep.

With her brain not fully on, she let it drift to the possibilities. Should she leave? Let the family handle their divorce with a more normal nanny? She could then come back and date Alex— once he was well and truly divorced—without all the entanglement of working for him.

She considered it for a bit. The family dynamic here was twisted, she recognized that. But she didn't know that it was *wrong*. She loved the girls. She could come back and stay with them when Alex was out of town. She would need another job, even though another nanny job wouldn't suit her. Not after all that had happened in just a few months here. She couldn't ride that roller coaster again. And she was confident she'd be disappointed in any kids she worked with next; they wouldn't be Livie and Sophie.

What would Alex do?

She didn't know. Didn't like the options if she left, even though she knew that dating her boss was just asking for all kinds of problems. What would she possibly do for work? It would put her back at square one, wondering what an ex-wife was possibly skilled at and finding out the answer was *not much*.

She couldn't leave yet. Sophie wasn't ready for day care. The girls didn't deserve any more upheaval. So she once again decided to stay. Just like she did everyday when she questioned her motives.

As she rolled over, she heard voices and noises beyond the walls and turned to listen. Though she couldn't hear what was being said, she recognized Livie's voice and its happy tone. So Mariliz rolled herself out of bed and went into her bathroom to brush her teeth and her hair.

She was just grabbing the knob to open the door into the kitchen when she heard Olivia say, "Daddy, can I wake Mariliz for dinner?"

No response came, but she guessed it happened in ASL. Pushing the door open, she announced with her mouth and her hands, "I'm awake."

"Dinner!" Sophie announced with her chubby fingers as Mariliz leaned down to sweep her up and make her give her odd-noted giggle. With her free arm, she reached out to hug Livie to her side. The girls needed all the hugs they could get. She didn't offer one to Alex.

They ate dinner as a family—an odd one to be sure, but they all had their places. They spoke readily and freely. Switching topics at the drop of a hat, the way families do. It was an easy camaraderie she realized now that she and Reynold had never quite hit.

After dinner, they cleaned up together. Alex served up

scoops of ice cream with chocolate sauce and once it was polished off—the one part of dinner that Sophie really dug into —he called them all into the rec room to have a "family chat."

Oh shit. Mari knew what was coming. He'd buttered them up with ice cream and was going to follow that with a side serving of getting-divorced. She held back.

"Come on, Lize. Everyone in. I have some bad news." He signed and talked, though Mariliz wasn't sure Sophie could truly understand or that she even cared, but she liked that he didn't ignore the toddler just because she was young.

They all sat on the floor and Alex focused on Olivia. "I need to tell you, Mom and I are getting a divorce."

Olivia nodded solemnly. No idiot, she merely said, "I thought so."

Alex pulled off his wedding ring, hopefully for the final time. "I want you to know that your mom and I did love each other." He signed as he held it. "We both still love you. And I want you to have this." He handed the ring to his daughter.

CHAPTER 32

Alex sat with Lize on the couch. Side by side, they pressed together, the way any happy couple would.

No more making out, though he wanted to—desperately—but he'd given his word. Until she said otherwise, his hands would stay with him. She seemed to have no trouble leaning into him though, allowing his arm around her shoulder. So he took advantage of it.

Sophie had taken the news without a care. In fact, she seemed a bit confused. What did it mean to announce that a mother who hadn't been home much in all the time she could probably remember wasn't going to be home anymore?

Olivia, on the other hand, had taken the news with stoic understanding. She'd seen it coming. Maybe for a long time. He tried to soothe her, to make it as easy as he could. He'd told her, "I don't think much will change. You and your mom and I won't go out as a family any more, but I can't remember the last time we did anyway. You'll still see your mom."

He hoped that last part would stay true.

But Olivia had stuck it to him. "Will we stay in this house? Will I still go to the same school?"

He really didn't know. Though he didn't want to worry her, he knew if he lied now she'd never believe him about anything in the future. So he told her the truth. "I don't know. It may depend on whether your mom decides to stay in town. How much the divorce costs. Things I don't know about yet myself. Is it okay if I ask you first?"

Livie had nodded. The solemn acceptance of her life turning upside down again made him amazed she didn't hate him. She'd gone to bed, quiet with her thoughts and he'd let her because he didn't know what else to do.

"I think you handled Olivia well." Lize said softly from beside him.

"How did you know that's what I was thinking?" The smile slid across his mouth without thought.

"Just a guess."

The warm weight of her next to him felt right. Figuring it was a night for big moments, and that they could exhaust themselves and sleep in come morning, he asked something he'd wondered for a while. "You were married before, too. What happened? Can you tell me?"

He listened to the words that came out of a mouth he couldn't see. She was facing the same direction as he was. Though he wanted to turn and look at her, he wondered if maybe it wasn't easier for her to talk to him if he didn't. So he stayed still.

Her husband had been Reynold Baker and she'd never changed her name. Her marriage had grown cold through ordinary days and her husband cheated on her repeatedly.

"How did you not wind up sitting pretty in the divorce?" He asked. She'd talked about needing this job. Had she run through the money on that Lexus and those nice clothes? It would be easy to do if she was used to a different lifestyle. It made him wonder what Bridget would do.

"I did fine. I took my car, so I had something to drive. I took a small payout on the condo; I didn't want to stay there. The money's mostly sitting in my bank account. I have a degree, and by the time things ended, I was too cold to be bitter. I didn't want revenge, just my own life with nothing to do with him."

This time she did turn and look up at him. "Do you think that's sad? That I really never want to see him again? I don't hate him, I don't want him to fail, but I truly like the man he became so very little that I wouldn't mind never seeing or thinking about him again."

He thought for a moment. "Yes. I think it is sad. Obviously, you loved him once. So it's sad that it ended without even enough passion to spark a fight. But I'm not sad. You're here now."

She leaned into him again, nodding as he spoke.

He leaned down and whispered, "I won't go cold on you."

Her hand came up and pressed flat against his chest as though she was feeling his heartbeat. Not wanting to have to fight his urges, he spoke again. "I dove right into things with Bridget. We got married the same day we met. We had Olivia only a bit over a year later. I've learned a lot, at least."

"Me, too."

They let that sit in the white noise of the ceiling fan going around and around. Small creaks came from the house settling at night. Their breathing slowly synced together and he wondered if she heard it, too.

He spoke again to break the mood that kept shifting on him. "I've been meeting with my lawyer. I think you should know what's going on."

"Should I, really? I'm just the nanny." She shifted again, this time seeming less comfortable.

"Can we please drop that? We both know you're not just the nanny." He squeezed his arm tighter around her. "I didn't kiss you because you were available. I've been on and off the road for almost nine years. My wife has been almost completely absent for a year. I never once touched or even looked at another woman. So don't act like this is nothing. You're the one I want around when all this is over." He felt like he was yanking his heart out and setting it on the coffee table for both of them to watch, but he asked it anyway. "Is that how you feel?"

"Yes, but how I feel isn't the most important thing here." He felt her shrug but waited for her to speak again.

"Didn't you just say you got involved with Bridget too fast? She's not even out the door and you're lining up your next move, Alex."

That hurt. "You're not my *next move.* I understand it looks bad, stupid, I don't know. But that's not what it actually is."

"It's still what it looks like. What if Livie comes back in a few years and asks about me? When she's older and she sees the dynamics more clearly. Will she think I broke up her parents? I don't want that."

"Then we'll sit her down together and explain that it wasn't the case. I'm not above telling her the truth about her mother. I won't malign the woman, but I will tell her that her mother chose to leave. That her mother's choice for Sophie was an institution or boarding school. I'll defend Bridget's rights, but I'll defend mine to leave the marriage, too. I'll also point out that it was her mother who filed for divorce." He took a breath. Lize didn't need all that. He wasn't sure who did, but she didn't need the diatribe. "I just hope you'll be sitting beside me when that happens."

She didn't really respond.

So he shifted back to his original topic before she launched into her *just the nanny* problem. "Bridget and I are negotiating settlements through the lawyers. I haven't talked to her. She asked for alimony, I offered a lump sum, we're negotiating that."

"Holy crap. That's fast."

"Yes and no. There's a ninety day waiting period because we have kids. The lawyer got an investigator. I won't know anything until the report's in, but if something does turn up, it may change things."

"Oh." Her tone sounded as flat as he felt about it. He'd already waited a year.

"Yeah, but she filed within a day after walking out the door, so we're already into the wait. We're going to have everything laid out, ready to rubber stamp on day ninety. All the judge will have to do is sign. I hope I'll hand over a check and be done."

"Wow. That's as sad as my marriage." He was starting to agree, when she added, "Sadder. You were married longer. You have kids."

Well, shit. She was right. But she was here. He was going to keep her here as long as he could. He'd screwed up once. He wouldn't lose Lize.

He hadn't held onto Bridget because he hadn't really felt it was worth the fight. Lize was. He understood that. They were already a family—as ridiculously fast as that was. He'd married Bridget far too quickly. Though he'd fallen for Lize fast, too, it was with his eyes wide open. He hugged her tighter and sat with her, letting the tough conversations die away in favor of a TV show.

Then when she said she had to go to bed, he let her. *Promises, promises,* he thought.

He slept more soundly that night than he'd thought he would. When she woke up on Saturday he was already up with the girls. They tried to stay quiet and let her sleep in, but once she was up, he and Livie insisted on making waffles. Sophie insisted on "helping."

The waffles were great, and he gave Lize the day off, thinking again how weird it was to have the feelings he did for her, not be able to touch her, and to have to give her a work schedule. She almost insisted on helping clean up. But at one point one of the girls—neither was telling—squeezed the waffle mix and sent a plume of powder raining down on everything, he pushed her out the door. His mess, his clean-up.

He got the kids involved, giving each a task. Sophie's "help" was once again more work than relief, but he watched over her. He didn't think he'd ever in his life been happier to wield a dustpan or a sponge. He was also pretty certain that when Olivia had been this age, he'd been shorter fused, less willing to let her help if it wouldn't yield anything other than her participation. He'd gotten frustrated cleaning messes.

Though Sophie's disability and their handling of it had sucked, and he would never do that again could he do it over, he'd gained a new appreciation. Simply communicating with both his children was a joy. Picking up a kitten tracking pawprints through the powder and being able to hand it to Sophie and tell her to take the kitty away was an accomplishment.

So he cleaned up baking mix and didn't balk when Lize stayed out with her cousin and went dancing. He had no doubt men hit on her left and right, and somehow he had no doubt that she'd turn them down. When he asked earlier, she told him she'd stopped seeing the cop, and he'd lost the fear and jealousy. Since he'd kissed her the first time, it felt as though his own thoughts were now somewhat theirs. It wasn't all in his head. He was banking on that. He had plans.

At least he did until Monday morning when he headed into the studio for a rehearsal. All three of his bandmates were waiting there, not an instrument anywhere to be seen.

"What's going on?" He asked warily.

"You should know, your divorce hit the tabloids." TJ announced.

"Why are we in the tabloids? TJ's the only one who hits the tabloids, and even he's small potatoes." Alex said. It wasn't news to any of them. They knew he'd only been wearing the ring for show.

"Way to be a celebrity." Craig said it like a compliment. "It's very A-list of you to leave your wife for the nanny."

Alex put his head in his hands and tried not to moan. "Of course that's how they're reporting it."

"You should know," Craig added, "Some of the reports make it look like Bridget was wronged."

"Of course they do." Alex commented. There was nothing else he could do.

JD, ever the voice of reason, stepped in. "At least I haven't seen anything suggesting those reports originated with Bridget. How's the paperwork going?"

"So far, so good." Alex reported. They'd negotiated and they weren't done, but he hoped they were close. He just hoped all these tabloids didn't plant seeds or get in the way of the simple divorce he was counting on.

CHAPTER 33

Mariliz sat in the pickup line at the school wondering at the long line of cars. Some of the parents showed up at 2:30 for 3:15 pickup. Was their car a mobile office and they got forty-five minutes of work done while waiting? Because she was staring at the butt of the car in front of her and trying to entertain Sophie. She wasn't getting anything done.

Olivia got squirrely if she was the last one picked up, so Mariliz tried to get in the line early enough to not be near the end. Still there seemed to be a competition to get to the front of the line. Most of them were just sitting, wasting their day, waiting for their kid so they could be the first one in line. Mariliz found irony in the fact that it was actually her job to wait in this line. She was getting paid for this, which in turn made her squirrely.

It had been two weeks since she'd sat on the couch in Alex's arms. Two weeks since she'd enjoyed it so much that she told him they couldn't do it again. He had another sixty-two days of waiting before he could be free, and that was if everything went well. *If* things with Bridget stayed sunny that whole time. Mariliz hoped that was the case, if only for the girls and not for her own selfish designs on Alex Beaumont. But she didn't really have anything to judge Bridget by, not on that count. So it was a real crapshoot in her mind. Alex seemed to think it was going well though.

The cars pulled forward and as Mariliz inched up a bit, Sophie took notice. She squealed and clapped her hands, the unusual sound Mari had come to love. "Yes, baby." She signed over her shoulder, keeping her eyes on the now moving cars. "Get Livie."

"Livie. Livie." Mariliz could see the little hand in her rearview mirror singing her sister's name. She wanted to turn and look at Sophie, didn't think it was a big deal in a line where the cars weren't really moving, but she wasn't ready to risk the wrath of the car line teachers again.

They'd seen her once and told her that if she didn't pay attention she could hurt a child. The explanation that the cars weren't moving, and that the child in the back was deaf and needed to be seen didn't make much difference to the man. Like an angry cop, he informed her he would let her off with a warning but if it happened again she would get written up.

Hmph. Mariliz thought to herself now. *Written up.* Like she was a child at the school. But she hadn't done it again, not wanting to hurt Livie's school record, but man.

She inched forward again, only looking at Sophie in the rearview as she turned the corner and saw the surly teacher standing watch. Instead she looked past him, hoping to spot Olivia in the crowd of kids standing along the sidewalk. She had a placard in the passenger side of the front window. Another teacher stood on bullhorn duty, calling out each kid's name and lining them up. It was reasonably efficient but also pretty damn militant, if you asked Mari. She inched again, saw the woman with the bullhorn read Olivia's name out.

With a heavy sigh—she really hated the car line most days, she couldn't even relax while she waited—she inched forward again. The woman with the bullhorn frowned at her and let the bullhorn fall to her side while she yelled to another teacher up closer to the kids.

"Sophie, what do you want for dinner? Fish or chicken?" Mari liked letting Sophie decide some simple things that didn't matter. Though if she thought she could make up for Sophie's missing years of language, she didn't know.

"Fish!" It was a happy, excited gesture, though she didn't think the girl liked fish that much. Oh well, she would learn that her choices had power. Fish it was—

A knock came at the car window on the passenger side. *Shit.* They were going to nail her for signing again. As if the language itself caused accidents. She rolled down the window and leaned across the seat with her best fake smile in place. "Yes?"

"Olivia Beaumont's already been picked up."

What?

"I'm sorry?"

"Olivia Beaumont has already been picked up." The woman repeated as though Mariliz was slow . . . . or deaf? Maybe she thought the signing was for Mari? Didn't matter.

"So she's gone?" Her brain scrambled as she tried to figure out what to do. "Wait, who picked her up?"

This time the woman stiffened a bit. Suddenly it seemed Mari had the upper hand and the woman was afraid something bad had happened and the school was going to come under fire. "I assure you we only let people with school issued placards pick up the kids."

Like Mariliz gave a fuck about the placard. "Those can clearly be stolen. Who has my—" *charge? student?* Olivia wasn't her daughter. What could she demand? "Who has her?"

Frowning, the woman turned away and looked at the other teachers. Mariliz heard her ask who had picked up Olivia Beaumont, but she didn't catch the words. Her brain was firing at rapid pace. Who could have Olivia? Was she safe? She'd gotten in the car . . . so she wasn't openly kidnapped. Why would she have left? A friend?

Mari's synapses connected—hopefully—just as the woman came back and confirmed her thoughts. "Her mother picked her up today."

"When?"

"She was one of the first in line." The mild, snotty sneer indicated that Mariliz was at fault here. As though being later in line was a crime. As though she didn't know her own schedule.

Well, Mari was having none of that. "Her parents are getting divorced. Her mother isn't the one who's supposed to get her."

"Well, we were not informed of this. And you aren't her parent, so you can't fill out the paperwork. One of the Beaumonts will have to come do it. We aren't responsible for things you don't tell us." So first Mari couldn't tell them the info, then she was somehow at fault for them not having it.

"While you're worried about blame, that little girl just got picked up by her non-custodial parent!" Mari barked. She wasn't sure where that language had come from. She wasn't even sure if what she said was true. Honestly, no one had said anything about custody of the girls, they'd simply stayed at the house with Alex, and with her. Bridget hadn't shown up once. As far as Mariliz knew, she hadn't even called.

"Well, we can't he held responsib—" Mariliz rolled up the window as the woman talked, making her huff in further indignation. Mari didn't care. From the back, Sophie gave an angry grunt that punctuated her thoughts.

Whipping out her cell phone, Mari dialed Alex.

The knock on the window bothered her. She was stuck in this single lane, unable to get around anyone without hopping a curb. She would have to wait three more rounds of pickup to get out. She rolled down the window as the phone rang.

"You aren't allowed to use your cell phone in line, it's distracting—"

"Oh, I'm so sorry, Olivia Beaumont might have just been kidnapped, but let me worry about your ridiculous rule. Why don't you try getting me out of this line?" Alex's phone flipped over to voicemail.

"You can't get out. You can just go through." The woman put her hands on her hips as the cars pulled forward, the last slow kid having made it into the car, the round of pickups ready to cycle through.

Thumbing the button to put the window back up, Mariliz stifled the urge to swear at the woman and took advantage of the moving line to hit the soft curb at an angle. Up and over the two foot patch of sodded grass she went. She probably crushed a few flowers. In the rearview, she could see the woman with the bullhorn put it back up to her mouth. Then she heard the words the whole car line heard: "You can't do that. You're getting written up."

"Suck it, bitch." Mari yelled back. Sophie couldn't hear her, and sadly, Olivia wasn't in the car. She bounced down off the curb into the parking lot that was separated from the pickup line and honked until someone let her in at the light. They'd all seen her hop the curb, so they either realized something was very wrong or they thought she'd snapped. Either way, a few of them pulled back and let her in.

The light seemed to take forever, and she dialed Alex's phone again, only to get no response. Where was he? Rehearsal. But where was HeartBeats Studio? She managed to get it looked up on her phone just as the light went green. She pulled a right hand turn onto the side road and entered the address as she waited for yet another light to change.

She dialed Alex repeatedly as she drove, constantly getting sent to voicemail. She was so frustrated with traffic, with the phone, with not even knowing if maybe it was all legit. Maybe Bridget had been supposed to pick up Olivia and she'd hopped the curb for no reason.

Then again, if she'd sat patiently in line while Olivia was kidnapped she'd feel like shit. She might be overreacting, but she wouldn't regret it.

An angry squeal came from the backseat and Mariliz caught the signs in her rearview. "Where go?"

Sophie may have been trying to get her attention for a while. She didn't know. But the girl had gotten frustrated at not being paid attention to. She was also strapped into a carseat. She couldn't tap someone or stomp on the floor like she'd been taught. At least the vocalization meant she was learning she could make them and that they would get someone's attention even if Sophie couldn't hear it herself.

"We're going to see Daddy." Mariliz signed back then hit the button on the phone again. Once again she got voicemail and she realized it was futile.

She'd seen the building—or the back of it—in pictures of the guys in front of the tour bus and it looked like a bunch of other places around Nashville. The studio had some portion of the building, so when she parked she would still have to get inside somehow and get up to see Alex.

Another red light stopped her; there was one every block here, but at least she was getting close. Scrambling for the phone in her lap she tried again. She got the info with the address of the studio pulled back up as the light changed. This time she made it three blocks before the lights stopped her again. Of course she hit green lights when she *wanted* to stop.

This time, she was ready and hit the buttons to call the number from the website.

"HeartBeats Studio, this is Andrew. How—"

Mariliz cut him off. "I'm sorry. I need to speak to Alex Beaumont. Tell him it's Lize."

"Let me check. I'm sorry, he's recording right now. Can I take a message?"

"No. I'm his nanny." Ugh, she hated that title. "It's about his daughter. I'm almost there. Get him out of the studio. Tell him to meet me down front." She demanded.

At least the polite tone the secretary had adopted changed at that. "He'll recognize you?"

"I live in his house. It's about Olivia. I need to speak to him right away. I hope it's nothing but . . ." She was breathless as she pulled to a stop at another light.

"Okay, come around back." He gave her an alternate address that she tried to put into the GPS system while she talked on the phone and tried to ignore Sophie's ever more persistent noises. "I'll get him and we'll meet you there."

"I'll be there in three minutes." She hung up.

It was easy to find, a relatively big, open lot hidden behind the building by a tall fence. She pulled in and didn't see them, though she did see security just inside the door. Wondering if the man at the desk had been told to expect her, she almost skidded into a spot and was in the back seat, releasing Sophie from the carseat and plucking her up.

She was turning to run into the building when she spotted Alex bolting out the back door. A worried-looking young blond man stood behind him in the doorway. *Must be Andrew*, she had the fleeting thought, but the fear on Alex's face quickly erased that, as she dashed across the lot, Sophie heavy in her arms.

"Sophie!" He said, taking the weight of the toddler from her. "She's okay?" He was looking his toddler over, even though Sophie only looked confused. He hadn't gotten the whole message, or he hadn't listened. It didn't matter.

"Lize?"

Mariliz shook her head. "Olivia."

CHAPTER 34

A lex was at a complete loss.

He'd been petrified at first, when Andrew had knocked on the door that clearly said they were recording. That never happened. That meant "emergency." So he'd run, thinking someone was in the hospital, a car accident, a . . . not this.

His brain scrambled to make sense of it. "So she's okay." It was a statement.

"Yes." Lize looked him in the eye and nodded at him. "As far as I know, yes. I'm sorry if I pulled you out of something important for nothing." Her words began to tumble, and she pulled Sophie back into her grasp. He could see she was clutching the girl a little closer, beginning to doubt her decision. "I just thought . . ."

She was stopped halfway through the parking lot, having not even made it all the way to the door. So Alex held his hands out and embraced them both, trying to calm her.

"Alex, I don't know. Maybe you forgot to tell me Bridget was . . . or I forgot?" She was clearly pulling back.

"It's okay." He leaned into the feel of her, flustered though she was, she was solid. His rock in all of this. "I didn't tell Bridget to pick up Olivia. And I didn't forget to tell you."

Pulling back just a bit, he looked her in the eyes. In his peripheral vision, he could see the guys tumbling out the door of the building almost comically. They'd shoved him out, turned things off, then run behind him.

It was time he stopped feeling like an outsider. He was often the quiet one. Often the one who didn't come for Thanksgiving. He was the one who hadn't struggled like the rest of them. But he was their family, no less than TJ or JD or Craig. They were his. "It's okay. It's Livie."

He pulled his phone out and dialed Bridget as he nearly shouted to the guys across the lot as they came toward him. A disturbed river flowing right his way, they were ready to pray or fight or just get scared or angry with him. He was glad he didn't have to shout the next part. "Bridget picked up Livie at school today."

JD frowned and TJ started talking. "But Mariliz went to get her?"

The phone rang. And rang.

"And found her already gone." Lize was perking up. Realizing she'd done the right thing, that he wasn't mad, that Livie *was* missing, she started talking. "Bridget was one of the first in line. So if you didn't tell her it was okay, then she was deliberately there early to be sure she got Olivia before me."

The call went to Bridget's voicemail and he swore but left a message.

"You're sure?" JD asked as Alex texted his soon-to-be-ex-wife. "Because if that's true, these are some opening shots across the bow." He then asked another question before she could answer. Turning to Alex, he stared. "You're confident she's safe?"

"Yes." Alex could say that unequivocally. That, at least, he knew. "But I don't know that she'll get to school tomorrow. I don't know that she won't get made up like a tart, or eat well, or

... even come home." His heart started tripping. He looked up at the guys. They had kids, but they'd never had this. "Is it kidnapping?"

No one spoke. No one knew.

Finally JD asked, "Does she have custody?"

"It's not even a thing yet." Alex shrugged. "There's a ninety day waiting period. We're part way through it, but we don't have a legal custody agreement."

"I thought you had all the paperwork signed. So what's the custody agreement in there?" JD had his hands on his hips and he paced a small circle as his mind worked. Lize straightened up and began talking with Sophie, one eye on that conversation, one ear on this one.

Alex felt all the oxygen rush out of him. *Shit.* "There isn't one."

"How can there not be a custody agreement?" TJ busted into the conversation while his older brother's frown deepened.

"Just hadn't gotten there yet. We hammered out the house, the money, the cars, all the things. But not the kids."

"Did you just assume you'd get the girls?" JD asked.

Alex slowly nodded. "She hasn't been home in over a year."

"Yes, she has." Lize spoke up, albeit softly. "She was home about a month ago. She was home for a while before I got there." She stepped back as they all turned to her. "I'm just stating facts. If you tell someone she hasn't been home in over a year, they might take it literally. I know she hasn't been there for the girls, but she's been *there*, to the building, several times."

TJ stared at Lize. "She has a valid point. Can you call the police? At least report her missing?"

"Don't you have to wait twenty-four hours?" Alex asked, his heart hammering.

"That's a myth." Craig finally added his two cents. "It's only true for sane adults when there's no evidence of anything more sinister than them walking out. So you can't report Bridget missing, but you *can* report Olivia."

Craig probably knew, and Alex trusted him not to spew random information. Just as Alex pondered the thought that his daughter might actually be "missing," JD spoke up again. "You should probably call your lawyer first. He or she can tell you if you should file a report or what."

Alex wanted to sit down in the parking lot and cry. He'd hated the past year, never knowing if Bridget would come home or not. Then, he'd seen Sophie bloom and hoped he could get his wife to bloom along with her. Now though, he took a moment to mourn the loss of a woman who'd never existed. The Bridget he'd believed he'd loved would have come back. She would have seen that her daughter was miserable, and she would have changed her tactics when Sophie wasn't responding. Instead, the real Bridget had become clear. Whether that was something new, or maybe she'd always been there and he hadn't seen her for herself, he didn't know. Either way, their boat had rocked, and Bridget had bailed. Now, she'd taken their daughter. He whispered the thing he hated most to the afternoon heat. "She won't even ask for custody of Sophie. It will all be about Olivia."

He looked over at Lize, watching her smile at his youngest. He saw her fingers fold and straighten to make the "I love you" sign. His heart melted at the sight of the two of them at the same time it cracked at the thought of Livie. She'd just become a pawn. The divorce that had seemed relatively clean, if not amicable, had just gotten dirty.

Sophie was signing that she was hungry, and Alex realized there were logistics here. She planned to be home with her sister by now, eating their "after-school snack" even though Sophie didn't have school. She probably wanted to be playing with Poof, laughing at Lilac, not hanging out in the parking lot, worried.

Craig must have seen it. "I'll take Sophie." He signed.

Sophie reached out for him. "Craig." She signed, "Hungry."

"Let's ask Mariliz." He signed back as he took the girl. He wasn't snuggly or overly demonstrative with the kids, Alex had noticed, even with his own. But he was competent, steady, and had an honesty kids appreciated. They all loved him. Even Sophie saw it. Sophie, who hadn't communicated with anyone until a handful of months ago, readily told Craig she was hungry. As he watched Lize dig in the back of the car for snacks then hand over Sophie's bag, Alex wondered if he could do it.

Could he let Olivia go with Bridget? Just have visitation for his oldest daughter?

The very thought stopped him cold. He couldn't breathe just imagining it. Touring was hard on him. It was hard on all the guys. But he'd always looked forward to Bridget and Olivia waiting for him. For the past year, it had been Olivia and Sophie waiting. Then, for a short while it had been amazing. What would it be in a year if he had Sophie and Lize waiting for him at the end of the trip? The idea was bittersweet.

Craig was asking about Sophie's carseat and Mariliz was helping.

A hand hit his shoulder, breaking the awful spell he was under. He turned to see JD looking somber. "Let Mariliz drive you. You call the lawyer and head that way. Then do whatever he says."

"She." Alex corrected absently as he nodded. At least he had a plan.

"I'm afraid if you let it go, you'll set some kind of legal precedent that it's okay. But I don't know. I've never done this."

Of course he hadn't. JD had Kelsey. He never would have to do this. Taking Sophie from Craig's arms, Alex hugged her and told her he loved her and to go have fun with Craig's boys, Aaron and Owen. Over her soft curls, he told Craig, "I don't know when we'll be able to get her."

"I have the diaper bag and two boys and two dogs and a spare bed. We'll make it work however. Right, Sophie?" He'd signed the whole thing.

"Puppies!" She signed and reached for Craig again. Alex felt a sad grin on his face.

"Feel free to call in the middle of the night if that's when you want to come get her. No worries, man." He let Lize hug her and kiss her little forehead, then he headed over to his own car and seemed to be calling Shay.

"Let's go." Lize held her car keys. "We'll pick your car up sometime later."

Climbing into the passenger side of her car, he realized he'd never sat here before. He'd never ridden with her driving. His girls had, but he hadn't. Did he really know her well enough to envision his whole future with her?

"I saw the envelope. I'm heading toward the lawyer's address until you tell me otherwise. Go ahead and call." Though she was clearly worried, Lize stayed calm as she cranked the engine. "I've got this."

He pulled his phone as she backed out, saying, "You've got a good crew there. You're really more like brothers."

"Jesus, you've never actually met them before, have you?"

"Not face to face." She pulled onto the main street. "I was so scared to interrupt your session, but all I could think was that if Bridget really had taken Olivia, and I didn't say anything in time, I would regret it forever."

His heart stuttered again as a stronger terror struck. "Do you think she'd take Livie out of the country?"

He almost couldn't breathe. Just then the office answered and he tried to explain quickly without hyperventilating. The secretary was fantastic, but he didn't have time to thank her for interrupting the meeting the lawyer was in.

"Hello. I understand you have an emergency. I have another client in the room. Do I need to be alone?"

He caught that she hadn't addressed him personally, and thought it was because of the other client. "As long as they don't know my name, we're okay."

He explained about Bridget picking up Olivia, and that she appeared to have purposefully gotten in line early. "Wait, I'm putting you on speaker with my . . . nanny about it."

"Hello. How much earlier did the wife pick up the child?"

Lize made a left hand turn and spoke. "She actually got Livie about ten minutes before I was there, but that car line stacks up starting at two-thirty, a full forty five minutes before school lets out. So if she really was one of the first—which the school said she was—then she was there at least thirty minutes before me."

"So it wasn't a whim."

"It couldn't have been, ma'am." Lize sighed and shot him a look saying she was sorry. As though there was something she could have done.

"How long has the child been missing?"

"About an hour." He said as he looked to Lize to confirm.

"Is the child in any possible danger?"

Alex motioned to Lize and replied. "I don't think so, but what if Bridget takes her out of the country?"

"Is that a reasonable concern?" The voice was calm, but it was the steel conviction behind it that comforted Alex the most.

"I don't know. I mean, I'm concerned about it, but I don't know what evidence I have." He sighed. It looked worse every minute.

"There's reason to be concerned." Lize said, with a sad sigh. The information surprised him. Then she surprised him with more that he didn't know about his ex-wife. And it was information he didn't know she'd known.

"There are numerous photos of her out on open water— probably international. As well as some from Mexico and a few other out of the country locations. My friend dug them up from the backs of the tabloids."

CHAPTER 35

It was three days before Olivia came home. Three of the most stressful days of Mari's life. She watched Sophie and took care of kittens. She made dinner because Alex was running around trying to tie up loose ends and find his daughter. They both tried to answer Sophie's questions about "Where Livie?" with honesty and without worry. The problem was they both had it in spades.

"At least we're confident she's safe," Mariliz had repeated to Alex and he to her about thirty times each day. Even Sophie wasn't buying into the "everything's okay" façade they tried to put on.

The first night, they'd picked up Sophie around eleven p.m. They never made it all the way to the lawyer's office. She'd advised them to turn around and head to the police department and file a missing persons report as soon as possible. The sooner the report was filed, the better it looked in court. Any parent truly concerned about their child wouldn't wait to file. She even directed them to the address for the station in their district.

There, they'd been given bad coffee and good advice. They'd

filled out the forms. Tried yet again to contact Bridget, both from Alex's phone then Mariliz's. Then the police station tried her.

As the officer hung up the handset, she turned to them. "Does the mother have a home land line? We recommend it for 911 calls and anyone who has kids."

Alex looked up into the corner of the ceiling. "I don't have an address or a home number for her. She just *left*. She filed for divorce through the attorney. I didn't expect her to come back to town, she's been gone so much of the past year and a half."

Mariliz explained again her evidence that Bridget's move was preplanned. The paperwork was filed, Olivia's and Bridget's names had been put on a watchlist for international flights and at the port authority—not that there were any ports in the area, but because it was Bridget's M.O.

Mariliz spent the next afternoon at the Y with a book, wishing she could do more than just sit there. She'd finally gotten Sophie into a daycare program so she could socialize. The program had been recommended through several parents at their ASL class. Three toddlers were deaf and the teachers signed. It was too good an opportunity to pass up.

Still, she'd stood there that morning with Sophie in her arms. "Alex, I don't want to go out this afternoon. Not with Livie missing still."

"There's nothing you can do here. They have an opening, get Sophie in." His smile only made it halfway. "She needs something normal, or at least fun. All I'm doing is shutting down credit cards. Go."

So she'd sat. She had to stay in the room while Sophie played, sitting in the corner, but not participating. It was a stipulation when they agreed to take Sophie, because she'd been kicked out of every other daycare for violence.

So she'd sat there reading, unable to think of little else but hatred for Bridget. She tried to understand, but the woman had kidnapped Olivia—who knew what she was telling the older daughter now? And she'd created this bad reputation that Sophie was carrying with her. Mariliz was now convinced that Sophie didn't have any more aggression or learning disabilities than any other toddler. But the day care only took her on the contingency that Mariliz be in the room until they felt safe.

It took two hours before the teacher approached her. "I think you're right. She's doing fine."

Mariliz set aside her book—which she wasn't really reading anyway—and wanted to thank the woman for agreeing. "I think the diagnoses were based on her not speaking and missed everything else."

"Well, I'd actually like to ask you to leave the room." The woman posed. "You can't leave the building, in case something does go wrong, but I'd like to see how she does without you in sight."

They'd left that day with four hours of play and good marks. Mari told Sophie how pleased she was that Sophie played well. The next time, she was allowed to leave the building but had to stay within a ten minute radius. The mall was close, but planning four hours in the area was the least of her concerns.

The next day while Sophie played in the corner of the living room, Mariliz asked Alex what was happening. The police called regularly to be sure the girl hadn't been located or checked in.

There had been nothing. Alex had been trying Bridget's phone every two hours. He'd been leaving messages; the police had been trying too. Nothing was getting through.

Mari tried to fix a salad and sandwiches for lunch, but her mind wasn't on it. "Did the lawyer get through to her?"

Alex shook his head. "She got through to Bridget's lawyer, but he's claiming he can't get her on the line either."

Alex was exhausted; it didn't look like he was sleeping enough, though that didn't shock her. His voice pitched differently then, "He assures me that they *must be safe*. He *just can't imagine Bridget hurting the girl*. As if he knows her."

"I'm so sorry, Alex."

"I'm sorry to you, too. I know you love her, too."

Mari nodded as though she accepted his comment. She did love Livie, and the lawyer's comments brought up a new fear. One that Alex voiced almost as she thought it.

"What if they're in a ditch somewhere? If that's why she won't answer the phone for anyone?" His breathing changed to panic just from thinking about it.

"I don't know." She shrugged. "But the odds are against it. It's not like if I had her and you couldn't get us. It makes perfect sense that Bridget took her and won't answer." It was her best attempt to not worry. "The police have a BOLO for her car."

"If she's even still in the state." He sighed. Then he started listing what he'd done. "I closed all our joint credit cards."

"You can do that by yourself?"

"Yeah. They're based on my income, and we set them up that way, thinking we would only be closing them because of fraud or something. The accountant recommended that—with the band becoming more successful and all—we would want to be able to have either of us shut them off at a moment's notice." Then he paused. "The one card had a big cash withdrawal two days ago. I haven't been watching."

Mariliz heard the knife clatter to the cutting board as she gasped in shock. It hadn't occurred to her either. "Didn't the lawyer warn you about this?"

She'd heard about spouses cleaning each other's bank accounts out in divorces. She'd even opened her own first thing when she left Reynold. He'd frozen their joint accounts.

"Yeah, but we agreed that as long as Bridget was doing her usual expenditures, we would keep better tabs on her and show what she was spending on. She broke that pattern. There aren't any receipts on any of the cards since before she picked up Livie."

Mariliz sighed. "At least it's evidence that she knew what she was doing."

He nodded. "I've canceled all the cards, frozen our joint account, and shut off every avenue I can think of for her to get our money. She'll have to work it out through the attorneys." He stood now with his elbows on the counter, his forearms propping his head as it rested in his hands. His chest heaved with a deep sigh. "I didn't do it before. I decided I was letting it all go, and she's been an at-home wife with our money. I always thought of it as ours. So I shared, and now she took my daughter."

Mari came around the island that housed the bar and took a quick glance at Sophie who'd fallen asleep in the corner. The demon she'd first met was now a little angel, thumb in mouth. Sister missing. Mari put her arms around Alex's shoulders and held him as he turned to face her.

"I hate to say it, but do you want to call the guys and go to rehearsal?" She knew he'd canceled all the foreseeable times they had in the studio.

He shook his head. "As much as I'd like to get something done, I couldn't focus."

She hugged him closer. "At least play drums with Sophie then. You'll both enjoy it."

The feel of him in her arms was a wonderful weight. One she wished she could bear more fully. But the way his divorce had just turned from docile to dangerous made it even clearer that she couldn't do anything about it. Her involvement with him could cause ramifications for the girls for years to come.

So they'd gone on about their normal lives—as normal as they could be for the next two days. Alex had taken Sophie to the park for an hour. Sophie had walked the two blocks to the playground, but had been carried, half-asleep back. Mariliz had stayed home to man the phones in case the police called.

Batteries were always charged. The volume on the house phone double-and triple-checked. Someone was always there and answered every sales call, every charity pitch, every wrong number, in hopes that it was Bridget or Olivia. It never was.

On the third night, a car pulled into the driveway, and Mari and Alex froze. Sophie was in bed, they were in the back room, watching a comedy but not laughing. They stared at each other for half a second before jumping up and running to the front door. Mariliz heard the car pulling away and felt her heart catch —who would come and leave and not say anything?

But then the knob turned and as they skidded to a stop at the front door, Olivia entered.

"Livie!" Alex gasped it at the same time Mariliz did. It was hard to hold back, she wasn't the girl's mother. But Alex didn't. He hugged her fiercely, picking her up and swinging her around. "Oh God, baby, I missed you. I missed you so much."

He breathed like a runner having crossed the finish line. Mari felt her own breathing change, too, with the excitement and relief of Livie being home. But because she hung back, she also observed.

Olivia had set a new bag by the front door, she wore clothing Mariliz hadn't seen before. Though she hugged her father back, she wasn't participating in the breathless reunion.

When he finally set her down, she turned and hugged Mari for a long minute, then declared she was tired and wanted to go to bed. Her voice was despondent, prompting another round of questions from Alex.

Was she okay? Hurt in any way? Where had she been? Why did she go?

She said she was fine, she'd been on vacation with her mom and she was tired. She just wanted to go to sleep.

She even seemed a little angry. It had taken only a short

while to ascertain that Olivia didn't think anything was out of the norm. She expected to go to school the next day and Mariliz and Alex agreed that was best. She'd missed three days already. They made it very clear that she was to wait for Mariliz or Alex to pick her up and not get in the car with anyone else.

Then Alex put her to bed and notified the police, then the two of them stared at each other for an hour trying to breathe easy at last and figure it all out.

It was the next day, with Sophie home and Olivia safely ensconced in school—the school now having strict instructions not to let Bridget pick her up—when Alex brought up what she'd been waiting for.

"Tell me about the tabloids."

She shouldn't have been surprised that he was finally asking, but she was. "You can look for yourself."

"But you knew. How long did you know she was traveling out of the country? Did you look her up—look us up?—when you first got here and we were gone?" He was looking at her, almost accusing but holding back. He wanted to give her the benefit of the doubt and she wasn't sure she deserved it.

"I told you, Missy dug it up. I don't read those magazines." She shook her head. "I don't believe half of what's in them anyway—"

"But you knew exactly where to point the police." He stated, his voice a little harder.

"Do you want to let me finish?" She tried to keep the rocks out of her own voice; she didn't owe him this. Despite all their feelings, he wasn't her boyfriend. She waited for his nod and continued. "Missy reads them. She showed me pictures of Bridget when I complained once that she wouldn't return my calls."

This time he stayed silent and listened.

"She pointed out pictures of Bridget on a cruise ship—Missy thought she didn't return calls because she wasn't getting service maybe. She also had tabloid comments that said Bridget was in Acapulco, or the Virgin Islands." As she talked she watched his face harden with the knowledge. "I'm not even certain the information is true—just like I told the police. But Missy started following the story. She said the pictures showed blond hair, and Bridget was only blond in recent history."

"That's true." He commented.

"Why hasn't your lawyer found this?"

He scrubbed his face with his hand. "There's a PI on it, but he hands in a report when he's done. I haven't seen it yet."

"There's more." Mari didn't like this part. "I didn't want to say, I don't know that it's right, and it's not my place to get in your marriage."

"I don't have a marriage, Mariliz!" He was almost angry. "Or have you not noticed that? I have you. Except I don't have you either. I can't have you, because of the marriage I don't have. Because of the ex-wife who isn't ex yet and who steals my daughter from me. So what more could you possibly tell me?"

Her heart sank. She didn't want to tell him this. Didn't want to be in the middle of the marriage he didn't have. "You should look up the pictures yourself. Missy said it looks like Bridget was having an affair. Or several. I think she may be right."

CHAPTER 36

A lex picked Olivia up from school himself the next day. While he waited in line, he tried to get his brain back on the right track. He hoped to get back to rehearsals the next day. He'd set the band back far enough with four missing days. They'd been recording a new album, and everything was put on hold, mid-song.

Though he wished he could just chuck it all for a little while —and he knew the guys would agree—the reason he had to keep going was himself. They'd stopped almost cold-turkey when TJ had his injury, so Alex knew it could be done. But he needed to go the other direction. Though he knew they could stay on track to keep producing, no one could ever predict how much money they would make. How big a hit a song would be. He needed a hit. A big one. And he needed it to roll in the moment *after* the paperwork was signed.

He sighed and rubbed his head. This car line was stupid. Only now he was tense because he was afraid Bridget was in it ahead of him. He'd looked at the other cars as he pulled in, but he didn't know what she was driving these days. And he still didn't know what Olivia had done or where she'd been on her "vacation."

When he pulled forward and his daughter climbed into the front seat next to him, he felt a weight he didn't know he'd been carrying lift. He'd been afraid she wouldn't be here. "Let's go get some ice cream. And talk."

"Fine." She seemed sullen again and it was a quiet ride to the ice cream store. Even he was nervous as he ordered and then parked them at a far back table where they could start letting things out. He took a bite, a breath, and began. "Why did you go on vacation with your mom?"

Olivia looked at him so grown-up, and also like he was crazy. "Because she said it was a vacation."

"But it wasn't." He countered softly. "I didn't know you were going. No one told me you were going."

She still stared at him. "Mom said you knew. Mom said you said it was okay." Her ice cream started to drip and she licked at it, while still looking incredulous.

"I didn't." He shrugged. How did one do that? How did a man give his daughter the information, if not the words, that her mother had lied to her? For a moment, he stopped eating, let the ice cream drip. She was a smart girl. He wasn't going to accuse Bridget of anything. He'd make no judgments, but he was going to give his daughter all the necessary facts. He hated it, but he didn't want to pull her apart. The situation could do that all by itself. "Livie, Mariliz called me, *frantic*, because you weren't in the car line. The school told her Bridget picked you up."

It didn't escape his notice that he was often not referring to Bridget as "your mom" anymore. What kind of mother stole her own kid?

He kept going. "We went to the police station and filed a report that you were missing."

"Why would you do that?" Her own ice cream sat cradled in

her loose hand, almost forgotten. "You knew I was with Mom, right?"

"Yes, we did. But we didn't know where Bridget was taking you, when she was bringing you back, if she was taking you out of the country forever—" his heart still shuddered at the thought, and he resisted the urge to just grab her close and hug her, ice cream and all.

"Mom wouldn't do that." She countered.

"But she did pick you up without telling anyone." Alex fought not to fight back. *Just state facts,* he reminded himself. *Don't hurt Livie worse than she already is. Don't lie to her.* All his missives seemed to contradict each other. "Your mother did keep you for three days without telling anyone. The police called her. Did you know that, Livie?"

She shook her head and grabbed a napkin as she seemed to notice her ice cream had melted everywhere.

"I called every two hours. Lize called her. The police called her. She wouldn't even answer the phone and tell us you were safe. We were sure she wouldn't hurt you. But we worried. What if there had been a car accident? I still don't know where you were, where you went."

"We went to Branson and saw some shows. We stayed in a hotel with an indoor waterslide. She said you changed your mind and cut our vacation short." Her voice was small and sad.

Alex didn't know if that was because she believed him, and realized her mother had lied or if it was because Bridget had her convinced it was all Alex's fault. There was nothing he could do but tug on his daughter harder, and that would only hurt her more. "Thank you for telling me." He sighed as he saw his own hand was sticky. "Let's throw out these ice creams, wash our hands and get new cones. We'll actually eat them this time. You can tell me how school went."

They did that. The second round happier than the first. She was late on a poster project because of the missing days. He promised to help her on it. As they left, the kid behind the counter stopped them. "I'm sorry to interrupt, but are you the drummer from Wilder?"

He wanted to say no. Say he was often mistaken for him. Alex just wanted to leave with his daughter. But Olivia was watching. He couldn't lie to her and he couldn't lie in front of her either. Her trust in him was the most important thing right now. "Yes, I'm him."

"You're Alex Beaumont!" The kid came out from behind the counter. A high school drummer—just like Alex had been—he said he studied Alex's videos from the Guitar Center Annual Drum-Off several years earlier. "You and Shannon Leto, man!"

Alex laughed. He wanted to encourage the kid, but it wasn't the time. "When are you here next? I'll try to get you some stuff. I'm sorry, I have to go, my daughter has some homework to catch up on."

"I'm in all day Saturday. But don't worry. It was an honor just to meet you." He grinned, then added a quick, "Sir."

They headed home, picking up poster board on the way. He grabbed the ten pack, thinking it wouldn't hurt for next time.

"Markers, Daddy." Olivia added things to the basket, turning the poster board run into a full shopping trip.

He didn't mind. He had his girl back. *Shit.* Somehow, somewhere along the way, he'd managed to lose each of them. But they were back now. Olivia had accepted it, even if he wasn't sure this was her top choice.

They made it home in time to work on her catch-up homework together while Mariliz made dinner. The lawyer called him while they were working and he left the scene to take the call in his office. Even as he wondered what it was now, he thought about the room he'd just walked out of.

Lize was making dinner. She asked Livie about her homework, watched Sophie and let her play, but redirected her occasionally. The room felt like a family, like a home. He hadn't had that since the days before Sophie was born. But even then, thinking back, it had been more of a dictatorship. Bridget was a managing type of mother. Mariliz was a guiding one. But maybe that was because she didn't see herself as their mother. He did.

When Alex picked up the phone, he tried to be polite. A lot of the news from the lawyer was bad these days, so he wasn't looking forward to the chat. "What's going on?"

"Bad news."

"Color me shocked." He waited.

"Bridget wants more money in the payout."

He sighed. This didn't surprise him. The lawyer had prepped him for the possibility that snagging Olivia had been a threat against future demands. "She can't have it. I don't have it. Is she willing to sell the house out from under the girls to get her cash? Because that's the only way that's going to happen."

"Well, she also wants custody of Olivia."

He bit back the choice words he wanted to say. Took a deep breath. "No. The answer is no. The girls stay together. If she really wanted her daughters, I'd be happy to discuss it, but she doesn't." He lowered his voice. "I'm not even sure she wants Olivia. Maybe she just wants to stick it to me."

"She and her lawyer claim you can give her the money for the household staff." There was a pause, "I'm just repeating what's in the paperwork. They reason that you don't need a maid and an assistant since the house has decreased by one adult. And they suppose that you should marry the nanny and save that salary. Since they are also proposing that you are breaking fidelity in the marriage with her, one Mariliz Jennings."

He felt his fingers rubbing the ache at the front of his forehead. "I'm not sleeping with her."

"Can you prove it?"

"How would a person even prove such a thing?"

"Exactly," she replied.

He was flabbergasted. Where had the Bridget he'd known gone? Was she this mad about teaching Sophie sign? This upset that her perfect family had become imperfect? She was willing to blow everything up and act out?

"Look. I want to put out one more olive branch. I want to remind her that the girls are at stake and though I want custody, I'm willing to share it. She is their mother. But I need to know what the PI has dug up so far." He went on to explain the tabloid pics Lize had told him about. He'd spent the past night into the late hours looking them up, checking the dates. It had taken some digging, they weren't front page fodder.

He'd almost vomited when he'd seen his wife on a private yacht on tiptoe kissing some model-perfect man in a way that looked far too intimate for a couple not having sex. Her hair had been brunette in the picture. It had been shorter. She'd been cheating on him since right after she left the first time.

He'd spent hours matching the pictures of private cruises and different men to hair color and length to get a time frame. He checked them against her spending and found a few timeframes when she pulled no money from their accounts. Other men had been paying his wife's way. Long before she'd suggested divorce. She'd even come back and slept with him in between. It had been lackluster, but he'd thought it was maybe depression, not that she had already cut out of the marriage.

At two a.m. he'd thought of the STD test she'd asked him to take several visits ago. She'd suggested he was cheating on her on the road, because she was gone so much. She claimed she was ill, exhausted, she just needed to know he wasn't. He'd come back clean, of course, and thought things would get better. They hadn't.

They hadn't gotten better because it had never been about him. She'd been fucking checking for herself. To be sure she hadn't given him anything, and that if she had, she could claim it was the other way around. He'd boiled until four a.m. and wound up napping with Sophie that afternoon to make up for it. He passed all this along to the lawyer. "One more olive branch for the sake of the girls. But after that, I'm playing this as dirty as I probably should have all along."

He wanted to slam down the phone, but the cell denied him the satisfaction.

He wasn't even hurt that she'd cheated. How sad was that? He was feeling stupid and low and he'd been made a fool of. Now he just wanted out.

After the girls went to bed and Mariliz tucked herself into her suite with a regretful half-smile, Alex opened the cupboards. Bridget wanted money? He'd give her her own money.

He pulled down a fondue fountain. It cost several hundred new. That would be worth something on an auction site. The hand crank pasta roller was dusty, but in the original box. Hardly worth the weight to ship it to someone. He'd sell it for probably one very satisfying dollar and hand that to Bridget separately. A set of four silver buckets was polished to a shine to hold champagne at parties. *Fuck the champagne*, he thought, until he found a bottle in the back of the fridge.

He liked champagne, and he didn't really think he could make worse decisions when drunk. He was sober when he decided to sell Bridget's stuff. So he popped the top on the very dry champagne he favored and wondered how much money he was drinking. He took the first sips from the bottle, then realized he should fill the ice bucket. He wrapped one of eight monogrammed towels around the neck and set up the bottle before pouring the cold champagne into a frosted beer mug. He put her set of sixteen crystal flutes aside for the auction site.

Two hours later he'd sorted a shit-ton of things into group one--things he would pack and simply give to her. Clothing, makeup, a figurine collection. He'd also sorted a second group— things he would sell. He would claim it was to replace the thousands she'd cash-advanced off their card. The lawyer said if they could reasonably prove Bridget's infidelity, she would argue the money down. But they had no pre-nup. Hell, they'd had no real wedding, just the little quickie ceremony in Vegas.

Lize found him in the living room adding to the pile to sell. Her hair was rumpled, her t-shirt barely showing the cotton shorts she wore under it. She was everything he wanted and screw the rest.

She blinked at him, but spoke before he could ask the obvious question if he'd woken her. "House cleaning?"

"Picking things to sell. I'm going to have Nina put them online."

"Holy shit."

"Lize," he sighed as he said it, loving the way it rolled of his tongue and lips. He almost sang it. "I'm so far out of that sham of a marriage. Please understand that. I knew I was out a long time ago. And it turns out, I was out even before knew I was out."

"Drinking much?"

"No." Almost the whole bottle, but over the course of several hours. He was feeling it, but he wasn't far gone. "Okay, drinking, but not drunk."

He walked closer to where she stood, almost in her doorway. He was close enough to smell her shampoo, her soap, *her*, before he spoke again. "Just enough to ask you again. Just enough to tell you to trust that there is no way this is turning around. That I'm already getting dragged through it for sleeping with you just because it's so damn obvious that I want to." He paused.

She hadn't pushed him away yet.

"I want you. I always have." He waited until her hand snaked out and grabbed a fistful of his shirt.

He thought she was pulling him closer, but realized she was moving away. Then he put it together, she was pulling him into her room.

CHAPTER 37

Mariliz knew she grabbed his shirt. Knew she'd pulled him inside the room with her. But he was the one who kicked the door shut at the same time his mouth fused to hers.

Was she reaching for him? Or him for her? Probably both. That was the best kind of kiss, when you didn't know who started it and it didn't matter. It was the kind of kiss that didn't have to end.

The wall behind her held her against him and she used it to push closer. The feel of him invaded her senses. The brush of his jeans against her bare legs. The feel of his shirt under her roaming hands—she wanted it to be skin, she'd get that soon enough. The press of his erection against her belly as she lifted higher, trying to line them up.

His mouth sought hers again and again, a kiss made up of need and passion and too many nights denying themselves what they really wanted. If it was going to get splattered across the tabloids or at least the courtroom, Mariliz decided she wanted to enjoy it.

His tongue played her mouth like an instrument, tuning her and distracting her hands from their goal of pulling his shirt over his head. It took three tries before she managed to move it far enough to get his attention and his help.

With a grin, he pulled back just far enough to reach behind him and grab the shirt. Using a fistful of the soft cotton, he hauled it up and over his head, untangling those awesome arms as he went.

She'd thought she would take that moment to breathe, to let her insides catch up with her heart rate. But she couldn't. The sight of him caught her unaware. It was the first time she'd seen him with his shirt off. Despite what the romance novels would have her believe, despite what Missy kept suggesting she "arrange," Mariliz had not once mistakenly stepped out of the shower to find him there. Nor had she caught him half-naked in the house at any time either.

Her hand lifted of its own accord as the shirt hit the floor. She used one finger to trace the outline of muscle, of collarbone, the path down the center of his chest that begged for her touch. He was watching her, she knew, but she was looking at his skin—all that skin she hadn't seen before. A tiny scar graced one pec, a birthmark showed small and slight on a rib. Her other hand joined in exploring him, learning him, holding him mesmerized as she did it.

His breathing increased, she could see it in the way his ribs expanded and contracted. His heart rate rose, too; she could feel it under the pads of her fingertips, she was so focused on him. She wanted to touch and learn and know all of this man in a way that she wasn't sure she had ever wanted to know anyone before.

"Lize." He breathed it out on a ragged sound. The cadence and lilt of the way he said that one syllable reaching deep into her and grabbing her heart. She looked up to see he was staring at her. Or into her.

She loved him. She knew that even if she didn't really know how or when she'd figured it out. She wasn't sure it would last.

She wanted it to, but his life was a mess. If he had to choose, he would have to choose his girls. She loved him for the very thing that might steal him away from her.

So if it was all going to go to hell, she was going to enjoy it. He was hers for the remainder of the night. A quick glance at the clock told her it was past two a.m. Not that many hours left before they had to get up in the morning.

"Lize." He paused until her eyes flicked back to him again, back to watch what her hands were doing as they still touched and molded and absorbed the heat from his skin. "My turn."

His deft fingers crept up beneath her night shirt, probably not surprising him that she wasn't wearing anything underneath. Hot touches traced the underside of her breasts, eliciting soft gasps each time he found some place new. He'd almost touched her like this once before. Still, this was more.

He left a trail of nerves on fire as he reverently slid his fingertips from one spot to another. He used his whole hands, leaving her white hot with wanting. His palms pressed into her flesh, lifted her, molded her, stroked her until she was writhing under his touch.

Then suddenly it was gone. She felt the brush of fabric across her hardened nipples as he pulled the shirt off. She saw but never heard it hit the floor behind him. All sound was eclipsed by the wonder in his tone as spoke.

"Jesus, Lize."

It was all he said as his arm wrapped around behind her, lifting her away from the wall. Her head stayed back, laying against the hard surface as though she was too far gone to lift it. Maybe she was.

Her back arched over his hold and she'd only anticipated what his mouth would feel like on her before that point. She hadn't been ready for the way his lips closing over her nipple would send ripples out across her skin. She wasn't prepared for the way the gentle suction shot lightning through the very center of her.

She saw her fingers in his hair, felt his jeans brush her inner thighs, and didn't understand she was holding him to her, begging for more even as she tried to climb him.

"You like that?" She could hear the grin in his voice.

"Jesus, Alex," was her only response.

He lavished attention on her other breast as his free hand came down to clamp on her bottom. The pressure was enough to push her more fully against his erection, and the guttural sound from his throat matched hers as they lined up.

The wall left her, and they were moving. He'd lifted her, or she'd actually climbed him, she wasn't sure which, but he was sailing through the open doorway to her bedroom and kicking that door shut, too.

He didn't lay her down on the mattress so much as he followed her there. Her legs wrapped around him, his knees moving against the sheets as though he could climb higher against her. The feel of him, even through his jeans, that motion at her core, made her moan and writhe against him until his mouth took hers again and the sounds became his.

When his hands threaded their way into her hair and he pulled back enough to look at her, he looked like he wanted to devour her. "I want you so much, Lize. I want to go slow and show you everything we can be. But I can't. I can't wait any longer." His heavy breathing punctuated his statements with truth. "I want to be inside you."

"Condoms." She gasped out. "In the drawer."

And he was gone. Rummaging through her lip balm, bookmarks and assorted crap until he found the condoms she'd stashed there when she first moved in. *Thank you, Missy*, she thought but didn't say.

He stood then at the side of the bed, the condom in his hand not stopping nimble fingers from popping the snap on his jeans and shoving everything down until he was naked. For a moment, he just stood still, looking at her, watching as her breasts heaved with her own heavy breathing.

God, she wanted him.

She watched as he grabbed himself, erect and heavy, and rolled the condom on. Then he reached for her and she realized she still had her sleep shorts on.

Alex smiled as he managed to reach the waistband before she did. He tugged them down before running his hands up the inside of her legs, pushing them apart. She watched him, prepared for the feel of him entering her, but not for the fact that he never touched her with his fingers.

He pushed her legs wide and used his tongue, sending her head back and her voice screaming. She came then, for his mouth. For his tongue that said he was good with more than just his hands. She came as he pressed against her, hot and wet and searching until he found her again, made her buck beneath his touch. This time her hands flew to her mouth in an attempt to cover up the whimpers and cries she made as her whole body rocked in time with her orgasm.

Then he was on top of her, pushing into her, her legs wrapping around him, wanting this union, too.

He moved slowly despite the obvious fact that she was hot and ready for him, and when he pushed completely inside her they both felt it. Her hips rocked up to him, her hands clawed at his back, her back arched as though she could fuse them together even more closely than they already were.

Their rhythm sped up, eliciting soft groans and gasps from both of them. Finally, Alex moved faster, pushing into her and pulling out with a sensation that shot through to her fingertips and toes with every stroke. Then at last he was only pulling short, hard thrusts as he lost control and simply was with her.

Her head fell back against the sheets and her vision clouded. When he hit the end of his tether and a rough, guttural groan escaped him as he came, he rocked his hips with the motion, rubbing against her until she lost it, too.

"Alex!" She tried not to scream it.

There was no going back from this.

She was his.

CHAPTER 38

He woke slowly, surrounded by the best sex he'd ever had. He could smell it on the sheets they'd rubbed against. He could feel it in the heat of her skin pressed naked against his. He could taste her still lingering on his tongue, and that sensation alone nearly brought him to orgasm.

Lize was asleep, curled warm into the heat of him, her even breathing moving her softly against him. Apparently, that was all she needed to do to wake him. To arouse him. To get him harder than a Greek pillar. He was almost in pain.

But tonight he wasn't going to stay that way. This was no longer only in his imagination. More times than he could count, he'd imagined her coming into his room in only her nightshirt. He'd imagined her seducing him with very little effort. But this, her simple honest reactions, that she'd wanted him as much as he wanted her, had been far better than anything he'd dreamed up.

She rolled and shifted slightly, still leaving him with one arm pinned beneath her head. A simple check of the clock told him he had forty-five minutes then he had to creep upstairs and pretend he'd spent the night in his room. His cold, empty bed was exactly the right firmness, the fan circulated the air exactly as he liked it, and even the comforter on his bed was soft to the touch. It was going to be a terrible disappointment after this.

He stroked his fingertips down her arm and up again. He followed the curve of her shoulder, then the roundness of her ribs, down the dip of her waist to her hip. He wasn't trying to wake her. He simply wanted to feel the softness of her skin under his fingers again.

He followed the same circuit again, this time with an open hand, his palm skimming her curves. At her hip, he paused and lightly grabbed her there, liking the fit of her in his hand. Remembering the way he'd held her to him just a few hours ago, pulling her harder against him.

The memory brought a rush of blood and pressure to his already throbbing erection. It was followed by another wave triggered by the breathy sigh she made. He'd thought to just touch her, not wake her, but now he couldn't do that.

As his hand traced up again, he curved forward, finding the weight of her breast and eliciting another soft noise from her. His other arm was pinned under her head but his fingers felt her hair and she rolled a little further into him, pushing a noise out of him that he couldn't stop.

Was she awake?

Her nipples were hard and he tested them against his fingers, loving the way she whimpered with every breath as he touched her. Christ, she turned him on.

His hand pulled her leg up and over his, then slipped downward touching her where he'd wanted to all along. Already wet for him, she writhed against his touch, moaning as his fingers became slick with the feel of her.

"Alex." She breathed it rather than spoke it. Her hand came around and clutched at his ass, holding him to her.

His hips were moving, rubbing himself against her, his

whole body in motion, wanting to be inside her, feel her sweet heat around him again.

"Condom." She gasped, still pushing downward onto his fingers, still rolling against him.

Jesus, he didn't have enough hands for everything he needed. He had to stop touching her for a moment, her whimper sounding as bereft as he felt while he reached back and slapped at the nightstand until he found the condoms he'd set on top, knowing full well it would come to this.

He worked his other arm out from under her, needing both to get himself covered. When he finally did it, he reached out and grabbed her with both hands, roughly pulling her back against him. He snaked one arm under her ribs, bringing his hand up to fondle her breasts and with the other hand he pushed her legs open and guided himself home from behind.

Her back arched and she pushed against him, his uncontrolled thrust and her wild buck bringing them fully together on the first move. He held her hip, keeping their rhythm as he let the tide of feelings wash over him. Physical and far deeper than that, they pulled him under.

Making love to this woman wasn't just sex. It was a soul deep need, an expression of his love, and an emotional claiming he hadn't really been prepared for. He wondered if she knew she'd claimed him so thoroughly.

His skin tingled and buzzed with the sensations wrought by being inside her, and his fingers clenched at her hip, hoping to push himself even deeper. As her hand groped for his and pulled it from grasping her, he wondered if he'd hurt her.

He was opening his mouth to apologize, hoping she would understand as he groaned, when she moved his hand farther. *Holy shit.* He hadn't hurt her, she was directing him. And he could take direction.

"Where?" He whispered it, but her fingers pushed his into her soft folds. For a moment he touched his own cock as it pushed into her and the thought of that joining almost pushed him over the edge. But he moved his fingers until he found the spot that made her cry out. He circled it, then pressed, then held on tight as she bucked against him.

He didn't stop touching her, setting her off as he watched and felt her explode like a firecracker around him. Grabbing her hip again, he held her as he drove home one last time. As wave after wave of his own orgasm poured from him, through his body, through the base of his cock, everything in him clenched down until he was wrung out. Until his last breath had drained from him. Until she relaxed against him, as boneless as he felt.

They stayed like that, bound together, breathing heavily until the storm they created passed. Until they were breathing like normal human beings again. Until she curled back into him and he could feel her begin to fall asleep in his arms.

It was what he wanted, and what he couldn't have. Not yet.

Stroking her hair with his free hand, he spoke to her. "Lize, don't go to sleep."

"Okay," she agreed, but it sounded like she was still going to do it.

He was breathing against her neck, his lips grazing her skin as he spoke. The sweet smell of her skin and his together pervading his senses. Maybe that was why he said it. "I have to tell you something. And it's the worst time to say it, but I'm going to say it anyway."

"What?" She was awake now, almost turning to look at him. But she couldn't quite make it, not the way he held her. He didn't let her go.

"I love you."

"What?" She sounded confused, not upset, and he grinned into the mass of her hair that was in his face.

"I'm not technically free enough to be professing that. But I'm doing it anyway. I figured if I said it right after we made love, you might brush it off as the heat of the moment, but it's not that, and I'm saying it anyway." Then he pressed his lips together, hating the next part. "And I'm saying it right before I have to get up and walk out and go pretend you didn't just knock my whole world off its axis."

He kissed her shoulder then, pulled her tighter for a moment, then forced himself to roll away. "I wish I didn't have to go."

"Me, too. But I understand." She finally rolled over, looking at him through the dim light of the room. A small amount of creamy glow snuck in at the edges of the sliding glass door, lighting the room just enough to see that the sheet had fallen below her breasts. That she was stretched, languid in the still-warm bed.

He didn't want to go, but bigger things were at stake. So he forced himself into the bathroom to clean up and dispose of the evidence. He scrounged the floor in the dark for any and all of his clothing knowing that his oldest had been in here a few times and might very well understand what her father's shirt on the floor meant. He couldn't risk putting that wedge between Lize and Livie.

When he had it all back on, everything accounted for, he leaned over and kissed her, fighting the overwhelming urge to crawl back in, take her again, and screw the rest of the world. But he didn't. Instead, when he hit the doorway, he looked back at her. "Sometime today, tell me if I can come back tonight or not. Please."

Then he turned and walked into the sitting area, pausing at the door to the kitchen. He assumed the place was empty on the other side. He didn't hear anyone. No one should be up at this ungodly hour.

"Alex." She called out from behind him, the words soft. "You're welcome back tonight."

He grinned at her just before she added, "And I love you, too."

Sneaking up the stairs, he felt his lungs fill and his heart grow heavy. She loved him back. The divorce was awful, but he'd survive. He had her behind him.

His bed was as cold and lonely as he'd thought it would be, but he somehow still woke up with his alarm, indicating he had actually fallen asleep. Of course he had, he grinned to himself, he'd hardly slept at all until he got up here.

For the first time in a long time, he swung out of bed, happy to face the day. Lize did that to him. He could practically feel her under his skin. Sophie giggled at him as he threw out her night-time diaper and helped her climb into her big-girl panties. She was doing a really good job and he told her so. Lize was right—they'd given her a taste of language, and she'd soaked it up faster than any of them. She'd been starved for it, but she was now on the right track. He and Livie just had to keep going to class.

When Olivia came downstairs for school, she looked at him and asked why he was so happy. Before he even answered she asked why all the party stuff was out.

Well, shit. He had not planned to leave it out. He had not planned for Lize to actually pull him into her room and . . . well, he needed to scramble now.

"Your mom wanted more money from me. So I'm selling stuff we don't need anymore. That will help." He didn't add that he was only selling Bridget's stuff. And that he was doing it with a touch of facetiousness.

"All the party glasses?" Livie liked drinking out of the champagne flutes.

"We haven't had a party in two years."

As he watched, her eyes cut to her little sister. He understood that. At first they hadn't had parties because there was a baby in the house. Then it was because Bridget wasn't home to throw them.

"What if we want to have a party? We can have one now." She asked him using typical kid logic.

"Yes, we can. I think that's a great idea. But we won't use these glasses. How about you pick out your own champagne flute? We can go to that place that will write your name on it." He suggested an alternative that he hoped would make her happy to let go of her mother's things.

"Okay." Livie agreed then stirred her oatmeal. This time she looked up at Lize. "Can I have something other than oatmeal tomorrow? I don't think I like it quite as well as Sophie does."

"Oh!" Lize turned and looked at her. "Not a problem. Do you want a waffle instead?"

"This is fine today. Just tomorrow." She looked into the bowl as though it may have answers for her life. "Maybe no oatmeal for me for a while."

She didn't sign, even though she was sitting next to her sister. Did he correct her for that? Or let her have a moment where her hands were free?

After a bit, he had her hug Sophie and he took her to school. He returned with two cups of coffee for him and Lize and then played drums with his daughter until it was time for her to go to daycare.

He was grateful the phone call came in during the time they were both out.

CHAPTER 39

"She said what?" Mariliz was baffled.

She sat with Alex on the couch, surrounded by the piles of things he'd sorted. He'd added a few more items that afternoon. Olivia, aware of the idea but not really understanding what was going on in her parents' heads, volunteered to help.

She brought down dresses she had outgrown, shoes, and even volunteered her dresser—white with pink flowers—suggesting it was too "baby" for her. Her stuff was immediately sold to Sophie who tried to wear the dresses that evening. She was nowhere near big enough.

After the girls had gone to bed, Mariliz fought the urge to pull Alex into her room and try not to scream his name again, but she wasn't sure the girls were asleep yet. Besides, Alex had seemed tense ever since she'd come home with Sophie after daycare.

Daycare itself had gone well; they graduated to actually *leaving* Sophie there. Apparently she wasn't a terror despite her history. That part felt good. But what Alex had told her about Bridget didn't.

The lawyers had been in contact again—with Bridget's lawyer bringing forth adultery charges. They specifically suggested that he'd been sleeping with Mariliz, which was now actually true. She'd sighed heavily when she heard that.

"Look, if the lawyer got those papers yesterday, then they were drawn up *before* we did anything." He pointed out.

"I wouldn't exactly say 'before we did *anything*' but you're right. We knew it was coming." Her heart still sank at the thought. There was a difference between knowing you would get accused and actually being accused.

He was quiet for a few moments while she wondered what was going through his head. When he spoke, the words flayed her.

"Thing is, Bridget wants custody of Olivia." He took another sip of the ice water he'd set on the end table as though the simple motion would take some of the power from the words.

"You'll fight her?" It was the only thing she could think to say.

He shook his head, and Mariliz was stunned. He would let his daughter go to a woman who had abandoned her family that way? Someone who couldn't deal with anyone less than perfect. What would happen when Olivia became imperfect? Her heart nearly stopped.

"I'm going to talk to Livie first. I don't want to take her mother away from her. Maybe it's what she wants." He looked horribly sad at the idea.

It occurred then to Mari just how far this man had come in a few short months. When she met him, he wouldn't talk to her about the girls or their home. Mariliz hadn't even realized just how terrible things had been for them.

Sadly, his reward for becoming a better father—a better man —had been his wife letting him know that she was well and truly gone, his new girlfriend (if she even was that?) breaking the news that his wife had been cheating on him since way back, and his learning that he may need to let his older daughter go. How was he still standing?

"I won't let her have full custody. I'll demand equal time. But I want to know what Livie thinks first. She loves her mother." He shrugged it away as though there was nothing he could do.

As Mariliz thought about it, she wasn't sure there was anything he could. Certainly nothing she could do except support him.

Their lovemaking that night was slower, deeper, and maybe a little sadder. The thought of what was left of this family being torn further apart was hard to bear. But Mariliz loved him, and she would stick it out.

The next day, she and Alex and the girls listed things online for sale, and Alex started an account for their earnings. He said several times that he wasn't going to take an alimony deal—he wanted to pay her off once. Having been through the other side of it, Mariliz understood. She took her portion of the 'family funds' she and Reynold shared and got out. The idea that she would have to come after him for a check every month, or that he could default, or even that she would have to maintain some kind of monetary relationship with a man she no longer wanted anything to do with was too stressful. She agreed with Alex that a clean break was best.

But he had the girls. Sophie was two. It would be at least sixteen years before he could truly separate from Bridget. Then again, she was likely to sign over custody of Sophie completely and without looking back. Alex implied she'd almost already done it. Only Olivia was in contention. But until Sophie turned eighteen, Bridget could come back and want to be her mother. She could try for custody or visitation or any of it at any time. It would hang over Alex's head for years to come.

"I don't get it." He said the next day when Sophie was down

for her nap. "I want Olivia to have a relationship with her mother, but I can't even think about splitting the girls up like that. They're sisters. They have each other through this."

"Yeah." Mariliz agreed with a smile. "Sophie thinks the sun rises and sets on Livie."

"So, I would have to take away Olivia's mother to keep them together. Since Sophie doesn't really have one."

"She has me." She whispered.

"I know, Lize." He came over to her despite the fact that it was daytime, without concern for a PI poking in his windows the way someone was surely tracking down Bridget and Bridget's past for him now, and he put his arms around her and kissed her softly.

Alex let Lize take Sophie out that evening. They had instructions to go to the grocery store, take a while shopping, and at least return with dessert. Once they were safely out the driveway, he sat his older daughter down at the dinner table.

"Livie."

"Dad, I have homework." She didn't try to get up and he didn't know if she really did, or if she'd made some up because she didn't want to talk about things.

"Livie, I'll write you a note for any homework you're missing. We have other things to think about." He tried to stay calm, but the conversation was going to be big. His heart twisted.

"Is this about Mom?"

He nodded. "You know she has a lawyer, and I have a lawyer, and they are talking to each other."

"Because you and Mom can't talk to each other, right?" She folded her hands. "I mean you could, but you won't."

He wondered what she was hearing at school from other

kids who'd been through divorces. He wondered what kind of biased crap these kids might be feeding her. Then again, she'd pretty much hit the nail on the head. "Your Mom and I were talking until she stole you from school. After that the lawyer said I *shouldn't* talk to her. That only the lawyers should talk. Honestly, I'm so angry at her that I really shouldn't talk to her."

He hoped that was honest enough.

"She didn't steal me, Dad." He noticed she wasn't calling him *Daddy*.

"Yes, she did. If your Mom expected you, and I picked you up —even if you agreed—but then I didn't answer the phone from her *or the police* for three days, that's stealing. You have to admit that wasn't okay."

She gave a small nod but didn't look up from the table surface. "So I can't see Mom anymore?"

"That's not what I'm saying. I'm just saying I have to know that you're safe."

"I was fine!" She looked up now, almost glaring with her protest.

"I understand that now. But at the time, no one knew."

"I was with Mom! She won't hurt me." A sheen of wetness formed in his daughter's eyes and he wondered if he could ever convince her of the truth. How could he, when he wasn't even sure what Bridget's truth was?

"I never thought she would hurt you. But what if you had a car accident? What if you ran out of gas? No one even knew where to start looking for you. Livie—she wouldn't answer the phone. She's spent half the last year out of the country. How was I supposed to know if you were even still in the state? You weren't! And if you don't believe me, then know that the police thought your disappearance was serious enough to put out a report for you. The *police* were looking for you and your Mom, Livie. That's scary."

He didn't know if he'd gone too far. He wanted his daughter

to form her own opinions of her mother. But he also wanted her to form the same ones he had. There wasn't a good answer.

His oldest didn't speak for a moment. Just stared at the table. So he told her what he felt he had to.

"I don't think it's right for me to make this decision for you. I'm going to try to let you make it." He said.

"What does that mean?" She looked at him like he was nuts.

She was right. That was stupid. And maybe this whole thing was stupid. She was eight, for God's sakes. Maybe her parents should just decide for her. But that was the problem, and under his new parenting policy, he told her so. "Look, Livie, you're a kid. If you want us to make this decision for you, we will. But I think you're a mature kid, and I think you're a smart kid, and I think maybe you'll make a better decision for you."

"Okay?" She still didn't quite get it.

He wasn't ready to tell her that he and her mom wouldn't make the decision, because apparently they could no longer make decisions together. So maybe he felt safer with the call in Livie's hands than in the hands of several overpaid lawyers and a judge.

"I want you here. I want you at your school, in your room, living with your sister. I think that's the best life for an eight-year-old. And—selfishly—I want you with me. I love you, Livie. I can't imagine not having you here all the time." He paused. Maybe he'd pushed too far with the *I want you here* part. "I don't know what life would be like with your mom. She's been roaming the country and down to Mexico and more for the past year and a half. I don't know how you would go to school."

"Mom has an apartment."

"Where?"

"Here in Nashville."

Well, shit. Why didn't he know that? The lawyers hadn't mentioned it. So here was his kid with better intel than he had.

He ran his hand through his hair, noticing his shoulders and back were tense just from the subject of the conversation. "Can you still go to your school?"

"Most of the time. She said we'll travel."

There they were. The words he'd been waiting, hoping not to hear. The words that confirmed that Bridget had already talked to Livie about living with her. She'd beaten him to the punch. He suspected it for a while, that she might easily have talked his oldest around while she had her for three days. While everyone worried, Bridget poured who-knows-what into his daughter's ears.

"Besides," Livie started in, still not really looking at him. "You're not here half the time anyway."

That hit hard. Even if it wasn't entirely true. "I'm on tour fifteen weeks a year." The band limited them because they all had families now. He knew the numbers.

Apparently, so did his daughter. "Sure, but you have to travel more than that. You do other interviews. Most of those weeks have another day coming and going."

"You have a good point. I did think your mom was home for most of that. So when I was gone, you had people here. But that's changing now, so if you need me home more, I can do that." She was right. The fifteen weeks was the limit they had set for actual touring, but other crap always came up. Stations wanted interviews. He'd done the annual drum-off more years than not. He'd even won. But what did that mean if he had kids at home he wasn't seeing?

She nodded, then said, "I don't think so. But Sophie will."

What? His heart beat hard once and quit.

Livie kept talking. "I told mom not to make Mariliz quit. I told her Sophie will need her when you're gone."

Alex was pretty certain that he was having his first real anxiety attack. It felt like he was breathing through a straw and he couldn't take everything in. Bridget wanted to get him to fire Lize? Sophie would need her? Did that mean Livie wouldn't? What had Olivia and Bridget been talking about?

He didn't have to wait long.

"I think I want to go live with Mom."

CHAPTER 40

Mariliz picked up Sophie out of her playpen with a smile on her face. The world sucked around them, but she had Alex and she had Sophie, and she loved Livie even if the older girl was breaking all their hearts.

She could hear Alex's rough voice in her head. They hadn't made love the night Olivia announced her decision. Instead he'd cried, and she'd cried with him. He said, "It's better than having her ripped apart by a court case."

As though that made it okay. He was trying to do what was right for his girls. Part of Mariliz wanted to throttle Olivia, make her see straight. But she understood that the girl—despite her brains, beauty, and bright smile—was only eight. Still, Alex's words occasionally pinged around in her head.

"Hi Sophie-bug!" She picked up the small child, enjoying the weight of toddler in her arms and she hugged tight. Small arms circled her neck and she wondered how she could love another woman's child so much. But she did.

The problem was, she saw the end coming.

The money from the online auctions had made Bridget mad. No one was shocked by this, but Mariliz wondered if Alex's satisfaction had been worth Bridget's wrath. Or if Alex was right and they were going to incur Bridget's wrath anyway, so he might as well get what he could out of it.

Two nights ago, he'd taken a call from the lawyer in his office. Mari hadn't been listening—well, she had, but not on purpose. Even though she couldn't hear the lawyer, his responses had made the issue crystal clear.

"No. I'm not doing that." His first response worried her. What was he getting asked?

"It's not my fault that I fell in love." That warmed her heart.

"No, Bridget doesn't get to decide who lives in my house." Probably her. But why was the lawyer suggesting it?

"So you're telling me that my stable relationship is going to harm my chances of keeping my daughters from a woman who didn't stay home and had multiple affairs?" He'd gotten hot angry, and she'd gone cold.

"It's because she lives in the house with us? It's because I'm still with her?" He'd paused, mad, frustrated. Mariliz could hear him trying to get himself together. "She's their nanny. She takes care of them. She feeds them and clothes them and gets them to school when I'm not here. That's a hell of a lot more than I can say for Bridget."

Mariliz left the room then, moved to the back of the house, unable to listen to more. Her very existence here was interfering with his divorce, and the effects of that could last a lifetime. What if he lost Olivia permanently? He was already broken up over her choosing her mother. What if Mariliz being there meant he couldn't even get partial custody? If the court decided he was unfit in some way, who would get Sophie? Bridget didn't even speak Sophie's language.

"Sophie bug," She told the toddler, maybe for one of the last times, "We need to get Livie from school."

Though Sophie smiled and clapped her hands, Mariliz had to force it. Olivia was going to stay with Bridget for a week

while Alex went out on tour. It would be just Mari and Sophie—
a disturbing portent of things to come.

She took Sophie through their fifteen minute getting-ready
routine. Things were just crazy slow with a toddler, she'd
learned. Sophie had to sit on the toilet so she didn't have to pee
in the car line. They washed her hands. She had to get her shoes
on—horribly time consuming. Just getting in the car and getting
all those buckles done took forever, even if Sophie didn't 'help,'
but really Mariliz loved it.

It had been a long time since she thought about becoming a
mother. She thought about it a lot now. She even thought she
almost was one, but she wouldn't be soon. It made this long run
of getting to the car worth every second.

They waved at Alex as they walked by his office on the way
to the garage. He was having her park her car in there now that
Bridget's was officially gone. Just another way Mariliz had
stepped into Bridget's space and she didn't like it one bit. But
the garage made sense: her car stayed dry, Sophie's car seat
stayed cool. It was silly to park outside out of a misplaced and
perverse sense of self, but she still felt it.

Once on the road, she signed to Sophie as usual, then they
chatted while they sat in the car line. The teacher with the
bullhorn today was the same one who was running it the day
Bridget stole Livie.

But even though the woman gave her a slight foul look,
nothing went wrong. Mariliz scoffed in the car where no one
could hear her. As if Mari had been the problem, not Bridget
practically kidnapping the girl.

After dinner, Alex was going to take Olivia to Bridget's.
She'd be gone, and in her heart Mariliz wasn't sure she was
coming back. Mari would have gladly dropped Livie off the
next day after Alex left, but Bridget was having none of it. She
wanted Alex to do the exchange, refusing to speak to or interact
with Mariliz in anyway.

That hurt as much as anything. Mari hated being treated like a homewrecker. She would never be anything of the sort. She'd taken the job thinking she'd work with the whole family. Now the mother was acting as though the nanny was responsible for breaking up the family rather than dealing with the fact that she left a long time ago. She had multiple affairs. Alex told her that what the PI dug up was churning his stomach.

It wasn't that Bridget hurt him with the affairs. He said maybe it was a blessing learning about them this late in the game. They didn't have the power to wound so much. But he'd been a naïve fool for a long time, and that bothered him.

On the upside, she wasn't going to be able to rake him over the coals for infidelity, but he no longer held the high ground on that one either. His ground was higher, but the papers had not been signed. And that was Mariliz's problem, even as Olivia climbed into the car and they rolled forward with greetings and smiles that weren't as full as they could have been. Until the papers were inked and dried, Mariliz herself could be a problem.

Though they all made dinner together—Alex wanted her to eat healthy since he didn't know what her mother was serving her—and they all ate at the table together, it was a bit of a somber affair. Livie told them about her school project, impressing Mari with the fact that she could talk the whole thing through in sign without asking for extra words. But even as she watched Sophie admire her sister, Mari wondered how much the two girls would miss each other.

They managed to get in a family game of Trouble with Sophie playing Godzilla to the game board again. But Livie was good natured about it as always. Maybe she needed a chance to get away from having a little sister who was always wanting to be in her things, who required a special language, sometimes threw temper tantrums like any toddler, but screamed like a deaf banshee when she did it. Olivia hugged her before she and Alex headed out. At the door Alex turned and looked back as though he didn't know what he was headed into, and Mariliz thought maybe he just didn't.

He came back with a sad expression and low shoulders just in time to put Sophie to bed. He did it all himself. He was leaving the next morning for the bus and seven days on the road.

When he came back downstairs, Mari could tell the toll it had taken. He should be putting Livie to bed next. Though he wouldn't miss her for the next week—because he wouldn't be here either—he understood things were wrong.

"I want her with you, Lize." He said.

"I'm glad you do, but I'm not her mother. And I never will be." She shrugged. It was the truth. There would always be Bridget. At least for Livie there would be. She tried to change the subject a bit. "Did you see the apartment?"

"Yeah. It was nice." He almost smiled. She knew he'd been worried and wouldn't want Livie in some run down place. He couldn't offer Bridget the house while he was out without moving Mariliz and thus Sophie out. There was no good solution.

"That's one worry down." She tried to smile, but he didn't, and she couldn't return what wasn't there.

"Sure, but as I left I discovered a whole new one." He looked off to the side as though he could see out the window and through the darkness beyond it. "Though she has minimal furniture, the place itself is expensive. Livie's only got a sleeping bag on the floor. Still, who's paying for it?"

"Not you?"

"It's not coming out of any accounts I have access to." He shrugged. "Bridget's not supposed to be seeing anyone. That's her moral trump card. That—despite multiple partners while we were married and while she lied to me about it—she's quit and gone solo. So now she's some saintly mother. But if I'm not paying for her, who is?"

Mariliz thought for a while. "Maybe it's leftover from the chunk she cleaned out when she ran off with Livie. Maybe she's been living on that. Was it enough?" She didn't know. She wasn't privy to any amounts regarding Alex's accounts, and she didn't want to be. She already harbored a deep fear of getting called to the witness stand in his divorce.

"Maybe, if she spent it well, was careful with it." He shook his head, unable to make the whole thing make sense. "But if that's it, it won't last much longer."

"Does she have a job?" Mari just wanted to be helpful, wanted to give him an answer he could sleep with.

He almost laughed, but the bitterness underlying it eroded the sound. "Bridget hasn't held a job since Wilder started making money. So she doesn't have the kind of work history that would land her a job that would put her in that apartment. Or one that could pay that and still be flexible enough to be there to get Livie after school each day."

"It'll be okay." Mari reassured him. He'd broken down and gotten his eight-year-old a cell phone. He programmed in his own number as well as Mariliz's and Bridget's. Then he gave strict instructions that it wasn't for games or texting her friends —several of whom already had their own phones. It was for calling any of the three of them any time she wanted to talk or get picked up or anything at all. So if anything went wrong, all Livie had to do was dial. "You won't be here while Livie's gone. Aside from tomorrow morning, it won't make any difference to you."

"Yes it will." He looked at her. "I usually get on video chat with the three of you each day. I see all of you together." He was looking into her, as though she were the one waiting at home for him. As though she was the thing he needed. But she couldn't be. "With Livie not here, I might not even talk to her at all."

"You're right. And Sophie and I will miss her."

"I'll miss you, too. I always do." He said it as though it was an old thing. As though they had been doing this for years. As though this wasn't the first time they would sleep in each other's arms the night before he left. His hand in her hair was an indication that his thoughts had changed direction. His mouth on hers was a drug that changed her thoughts, too.

Though he made love to her like he was going to be gone for a week, she made love to him like he was going to be gone forever. Intense and satisfying, it had worn them both out, and Alex fell asleep in her arms within minutes. He must have been exhausted just from the worry of the week.

This time there was no waking up in the middle of the night for round two. He barely even pulled himself awake with the alarm. They got up with their usual schedule, keeping Sophie on it, but there was no Olivia to take to school, to prep cereal or a waffle for. Instead they both watched Sophie eat her oatmeal. Though Alex tried to choke down a bagel, he clearly didn't have the appetite for it. Mariliz didn't even try.

He played drums with his youngest, who despite all the attention or maybe because of it, seemed to understand that things were off. Alex could now tell her he was going to be gone for seven days. That she would stay with Lize. That she and Lize would take care of Lilac and Poof. And that Livie was gone, too.

Sophie understood the words but didn't fully get the concepts. "Come home?"

He nodded, and carried her to the calendar and tried to work through that with her. But she was two, and Mariliz wasn't surprised when she nodded but didn't seem to really have it. Instead, Alex changed tack and took her to play drums for a bit.

When they came down, he had about five minutes to get his things out the door and into the car.

"We should drop you off." Mariliz volunteered, thinking Sophie might understand better if she saw him get on the bus.

"Next time."

Her heart squeezed as he kissed her goodbye.

CHAPTER 41

Alex was pissed.

He'd hoped to come home and find Lize and Sophie, happy and waiting. He would then go to Bridget's or she could come to the house and Livie would come back. At least until the custody arrangement was hammered out.

But he was on the bus, headed to the last stop on this leg of the tour, and he was already upset about things he wasn't even home for.

"No. No." He spoke into the phone while he paced in the small space on the moving bus.

JD stepped out in time to watch him sigh into the phone and say, "I understand this isn't your fault. I know you're just updating me. But I pay the bills at this school . . . Don't act like I did this. I'm just as surprised as you."

He hung up on the dean from the school and took a few calming breaths before answering his bandmate's unvoiced questions. "The school says Olivia hasn't attended all week."

JD frowned at him. "And they didn't call before this?"

"I don't know. Maybe they called Bridget? But if they did she didn't give them a good enough excuse or she ran out of them."

He huffed, anger pouring through his veins as he tried to calm down. "I don't know."

He wondered if they'd called Lize, but dismissed it right away. He was more than certain that if she'd heard such a thing she would have called him right away.

"You know," He looked straight at his friend, knowing JD would graciously let him rant and maybe even help. "I've talked to Livie and Bridget. Jesus!" He'd thought they simply hadn't bothered to tell him that she hadn't been going but . . . "They both said school was fine! They lied."

"Both of them?"

Damn JD and his insightful questions.

"Yes, my daughter just flat-out lied to me." At least she hadn't looked him in the eye and done it. It was possibly the only way he'd be more disappointed. As much as he didn't want Bridget to take Livie, staying with her mother while he was on tour was actually a reasonable solution. "I just wanted to go home, and pick her up, and us be a family again. Now I'm mad. Now I'm going to be upset with her and she'll have a thousand more reasons to want to live with her mother."

"A mother who apparently isn't even making her go to school." JD looked away, as though he might think of something, as though the two of them standing in the front of this rocking bus might solve the problem.

Bridget had left a long time ago, and all she was doing now was throwing wrench after wrench into the happiness he'd finally found. When JD offered his sympathy and patted him on the back, he knew his friend hadn't solved the divorce problem yet. Alex called Lize just to hear her voice, to let her calm him down.

"Hey, baby."

"Alex." At that sound he felt some of the tension leave his chest. At least something in his life was right. "How are you doing?"

"Not good." He admitted, even though he was better just for talking to her, just for knowing she was there. While he enjoyed the realization that she had his back in a way that Bridget never had, he wondered how he'd lived so long not knowing when he called if he'd get supported or not. Bridget wasn't mean to him, but she wasn't truly behind him, whether she agreed with him or not. Lize had him. "Bridget kept Livie out of school all week. The school called."

"Wait." She paused. "That's how you found out? From the school?" She paused again. "Was Olivia sick?"

"I have no idea, because not only did Bridget not tell me that they hadn't gone at all, she and Livie talked to me on the phone and said she was doing well. I remember them specifically saying school was good."

"So you would have probably heard if Olivia was sick." Lize filled in. "And they lied to you about school? Oh God."

It was rewarding to hear her have the same anger about the lie that he did. He almost wanted her to tell him he was overreacting, but it was a comfort to know that he wasn't.

"What are you going to do about it?" She asked softly.

"I don't know." He put his hand in his hair, seeing Craig wander now into the main area and get into the fridge for a drink. It used to bother him if the other guys saw him having problems. He was the quiet, stable one; he'd liked being that. He understood now they'd never been fooled. They knew what was going on even when he didn't say, even when he tried to hide it, and it was better this way. The guys supported him and he didn't mind that Craig overheard this. "I don't know whether to confront Bridget about it, and confront Livie about lying to me . . . or hold onto it and use it in court. Do I start recording the phone calls?"

"Wow. That's harsh. But maybe necessary. You should think on it."

"I only have until tomorrow morning. They're supposed to call again." Craig was looking at him with sympathy. Probably hadn't put together the whole story yet, but he popped the top on his soda and slid into the bench seat at the table, ready to talk if Alex needed it.

"Then record it." Lize told him. "If you change your mind, you can go back and erase it. But Bridget only has her for another day and a half."

He nodded into empty space. If they lied to him again and he didn't get a copy, he would be angry with himself for missing it. "I hate this. I used to love her. This never would have occurred to me."

Lize paused for a moment. "Probably none of it occurred to you. I know it never crossed my mind that Reynold and I were anything but flatly content. I wasn't happy with him, but I wasn't unhappy, either. I never thought he would cheat. I didn't see it coming. I hope the fact that you didn't see it coming was because you wouldn't do that. Maybe it makes you a better person."

"Thank you." He knew he'd feel better after talking to her. But even as he opened his mouth to say more, he felt the bus shift under his feet and slow. "We're stopping for food. I have to go. I love you."

Alex talked to the guys as they ate, vented his frustrations with the woman who was somehow still his wife and praised the one who somehow still wasn't. They offered solutions where they could, though they were few and far between. Craig offered what little advice he knew from helping Shay with her custody suits, but even though that was mostly just *get a pitbull of a lawyer and a PI* Alex appreciated it. He'd done both, so it was soothing to hear it had worked out for Shay and Craig. Sometimes they just commiserated.

He played that night, giving everything he had to the stage and forgetting everything at home. Even Sophie and Livie and

Lize. The drums beat a rhythm in his blood and he was just Alex, just the drummer with the band. It was a relief to have something to do that didn't require his heart be peeled out of his body and presented to someone for good or for bad.

The next morning when they hit the road home, Alex got ready to call Bridget at his planned time. JD volunteered his services. "Here you go man. This is my phone and I just feel like I want to leave it here recording."

Alex had frowned until JD spoke again.

"You don't record the call. I do. It's not on your phone. But it's there if you need it. You didn't do it. I did." Then he nodded and walked away, the red dot on the phone showing as Alex dialed.

Bridget answered as she had each time he called. Her lawyer must have explained how bad her not answering anyone for three days had looked.

"Hello." The lone word was still somehow over polite. "Here's Olivia."

She'd never called her "Livie" just as she'd never really used "Sophie." Even as a baby, their youngest had been "Sophia" to his wife. Alex pushed all that aside and protested. "Wait. Bridget. Just bring me up to date on everything."

His wife didn't really respond and, afraid he'd blown it, he scrambled to cover and not make it look like he was recording. "I get her back tonight. I just want to be sure I'm current on any big assignments and if she slept well, ate her veggies, that kind of thing."

"She sleeps fine, Alex." The words were gruff and condescending, as though he was an idiot just for asking.

"And the rest?"

"She doesn't have any big assignments." Then her voice turned away from the phone a bit. "Do you, Olivia?"

"No." His daughter's voice came from a little further back.

Liars. He thought. He wanted to say, *and have you been going to school?* But that would let them know he knew. *Ugh.* Instead he asked, "Everything's been going well?"

"Of course it has, Alex. I'm her mother." The defiance in the tone was off the charts.

"I'm just trying to make a rough transition as smooth as possible for our daughter. No one has said anything about you not being her mother, Bridget." He was actively holding his anger in check now.

"Oh? That little tart you moved into my house, who's mothering my girls? I think you kind of did, Alex." She was pissed. So pissed he could hear it through the miles.

He didn't want to play. He wanted to yell that she was the one who left her sister to hire Lize in the first place. He wanted to rail against the fact that she cheated first and often. He wanted to shout that *now?* Now she had *girls—two* daughters?— when she still didn't seem to want to have anything to do with the younger one.

But he swallowed it all, as bitter as it was. As far as he knew, she thought he was none the wiser about her days on her friends' yachts. About the men she was photographed kissing. About the man who paid for two cruises and a getaway week with her. Bridget acted as though she was holier-than-thou for his "cheating" with Lize. So he held back. "Let me talk to Livie."

"Fine."

He tried to shake off the anger before his daughter came on the phone. But when he took stock, he was angry at her, too. Angry for wanting her mother more than him—which he knew wasn't fair, but it hurt. And he was angry at her for lying to him—which was completely fair. He tried to keep it all out of his tone as he glanced at JD's phone and the red dot recording everything they said. "Hey, baby. How are you doing?"

"It's been two days since we talked, Daddy. I'm still fine."

Jesus. Was she getting her mother's snotty attitude? How

could she not? "I miss you. I like to hear your voice and I like to hear you tell me about your day. So what did you do?"

"We went to the zoo. The kangaroo exhibit is really cool, there are babies now. And you can pet the big ones."

"That's awesome." He said, while in his head he tried to calculate if that proved they had skipped school. "Did you check out the meercats?"

Within a few minutes, she'd slipped up. Not in so many words, but that the monkeys howled in the morning yesterday and she'd been there to see it. Yesterday had been a school day. He talked instead about picking her up.

"I'll drop her off." Bridget had interrupted.

He wanted to protest that she was changing their agreement. "Get her there by seven," was all he said instead. Then he hung up the phone. He didn't say goodbye. Screw her.

So he'd recorded himself being a little rude. He'd recorded her and their daughter actively lying. *Shit shit shit.*

JD came in then and took his phone back. Craig consoled him that it would just be a little longer, he just had to hold out a while. And TJ threw him a soda. They all sat in the front watching Nashville roll up around them.

By tonight, his new family would all be together again. He didn't know for how long, but they'd all be together.

He climbed down off the bus at five almost as the driver set the brakes. He rolled into his driveway at five-thirty and was in a hug from Lize and Sophie by five-thirty-two. It felt like most of the grime of travel sloughed off. But he showered and they made dinner and waited until Bridget showed up with Olivia at seven-forty-seven. He snapped a picture of the car in the driveway, his daughter getting out of the car. He made sure it was time-stamped.

"Jesus, Alex." Bridget snapped. "We got caught in traffic!"

He raised his eyebrows and saved the picture. "It's a seven minute drive."

He hated this.

Livie was mad at him for being mad at her mother. She was eight, and she didn't see the problem. But they made it through the rest of the weekend, and on Monday morning he drove his daughter in to school, then walked her into the principal's office where she finally confessed that she hadn't come all the previous week.

"Mom's getting me a tutor, so we can travel!" She'd shouted it to the office and Alex was grateful that it was the principal herself who pointed out that Olivia wouldn't graduate the third grade if she missed any more days. Luckily the year wasn't much longer.

He left her to her classes and headed straight home, where he unloaded the whole story on a sympathetic Lize. When he finished, she told him she had news. He didn't like the look on her face.

"I found a job."

CHAPTER 42

M ariliz thought she might have hurt him less if she'd stabbed him.

"You don't need a job. You have a job." He stared at her.

"I can't work for you and sleep with you." She shook her head. "I don't have those kinds of morals. I guess it's easy to think that I do, because I've been doing exactly that, but I went looking for another job."

"You can't go." He'd protested, looking stricken.

"I can't stay." She countered. "I can't be here and not be with you. So I have to go."

She could see his breathing was faster. He was starting to panic. Mariliz knew she was leaving him in a lurch, but the problems with the divorce and the girls were going to tear the family apart.

"You'll stay here then. We'll work around your job and you'll stay with me." Even as he said it, he seemed to settle into it. "You can move upstairs in my room." He smiled at her, having found his own peace with it.

She shook her head. "I have to get out of the house. I don't think we can be together."

"What?" He'd almost slammed his hand on the counter—surprise or anger, she couldn't really tell—but he stopped himself. The vibration would have alerted Sophie. Then it all disappeared and he was just hurt. "You said you loved me."

"I do. I do love you. I love you enough to get out of the way."

He was shaking his head. "That's not what I need."

"But it's what your family needs. Bridget is lashing out, and I'm her best tool. The lawyer told you this affair reflects badly. We know it." He wasn't speaking so she kept going. "How this divorce shakes out will affect your money, your girls, and probably even you, for the rest of your lives. You owe it to them to make it as easy as possible. To give it the best possible outcome. And that outcome is without me."

"Bridget cheated first! She cheated so much. I have proof now!" He countered, as though Bridget's problems excused his.

Mariliz took a deep breath. This was hard enough without having to fight him. At least he didn't want to let her go. It was hard, but it might have hurt worse had he just said 'okay' and agreed with her. Then again, maybe it was worse being the one hurting him.

"Bridget's trump card is that she's not seeing anyone now. She's not parading affairs around Livie. You are."

"That's not true."

"It's how the lawyer will play it. And let's be honest, you're screwing the nanny." She shrugged.

"That's crass."

"But it's true enough to get used in court. Sure, you'll counter it with all the reasons it doesn't matter, and that Bridget put us in this position in the first place, but you can't say it isn't true."

He looked at her, sad, hurt, angry, broken. "Don't."

She'd been thinking about this and she didn't see another way. "We can't see each other. Not until things are settled. Honestly, we thought you and Bridget would sign nicely and, at the end of your ninety-day period, you'd go your separate ways. But Bridget's pissed, Alex."

He nodded. It was another thing no one could say was untrue.

"I think it's because you won. She cheated first, but she doesn't have someone. She thinks you don't even know about her, and you already found someone who lives in your house. It's a harsh blow."

"So Bridget's in the right?" He asked incredulously.

"Oh God, no." Mariliz countered again. "But from that standpoint, she's wounded, angry, and losing a fight she started. She's going to lash out at you as badly as she can. And I'm the way she's going to do it. I can't be the thing that hurts you and the girls for years to come."

She was fighting tears. Having to tell him Bridget had won hurt worse than anything. They had to let her win. For their own sakes. For the girls. "I'm sorry, but I don't see any other way."

"When do you start?"

"Wednesday." She said.

"Are you moving out?"

"Tomorrow. I have to give the girls some warning." It was so hard to talk. "I can't give them a lot of warning, or Livie can tell Bridget." She shrugged. The game sucked ass.

"You've known about this for a while." He accused her.

He was right to. She'd played her cards under the table, not wanting to hurt him worse than she knew it would. "I'll be working from home, for Tennessee Council on Deafness. It's the better job, but not quite full time. So I picked up some hours at the day care Sophie goes to. I'll see her there. Please keep bringing her."

Tears pushed at the back of her eyes. Her jaw quivered. Mariliz didn't think she'd ever done anything harder than this. Not leaving her family for college, not confronting Reynold about cheating on her, or leaving her life behind and starting over.

"Where will you live?" The words were flat. He'd quit arguing and got down to the logistics of it.

"With Missy for a while. Then we'll figure something out after a few months." The drive would be a bit of a pain, but that wouldn't hurt any worse than any of the rest of it. She shifted topics. "I want to see the girls. I want them to call me whenever they want. I want to take them out for dinner or lunch or babysit when you need me."

"Who will watch them while I'm out on tour?" Again, the flat voice, the concern about logistics. She didn't know if he'd quit fighting or if he thought he could change her mind if he found a missing piece to her plan.

"I found you two sitters who sign. Either of them can do it." She pulled a set of papers out from the drawer where her own info packet still sat. It was a stark reminder that she wasn't his girlfriend. She wasn't the girls' mother. She wasn't his future wife. She came with an information packet of her own and a background check. Now she pushed similar information about the two sitters across the counter top to him.

"Overnight? For a week while I'm gone?" He was growing bitter.

She understood and didn't respond in kind. "I told them all the details."

He didn't respond and they stood there in silence for a while. Mariliz didn't move, she couldn't. But when she finally found her feet and started to turn, she heard Alex mutter from behind her.

"Bridget managed to steal you from me, too."

She didn't say anything. Just headed into her room to pack. It physically hurt to put her things back in boxes. To hang her clothes together and put a traveling bag over them was like clustering the memories she had here and covering them.

Mariliz only worked for a little while, enough time for Alex to absorb what she'd said, or maybe tell the girls. So she wandered out into the house to find Alex sitting on the couch with an open beer. As she emerged, he stared at her, his blank expression hiding anger or hurt or what, she couldn't tell.

She desperately wanted to say she was sorry. That she'd thought about this long and hard and if she could have found another solution, she would have taken it. Instead she said, "Did you tell the girls?"

"Oh no." He took another sip of the beer. "You made this decision, you break their hearts."

Anger, then. Still someone had to tell them. She couldn't leave tomorrow and have it be a surprise. So she rounded up the girls and sat them down in the play room. Both speaking and signing, wanting to be comfortable for them, Mariliz suffered through the small chairs at the small play table.

"You both know your Mom and Dad are getting divorced and that things have gotten pretty ugly."

Olivia nodded, she was seeing the worst of it. Sophie just watched. Mariliz hadn't yet gotten to the part she would understand.

"Well, the lawyers have a problem with me being in the house." She didn't want to say "Bridget is a bitch." She didn't want to tell Olivia it was because of her beloved mother. Because Bridget had said no such words. She'd just accused, hinted, and sent her lawyer after more money with claims of infidelity. "So I have to leave."

"What?" Olivia looked stunned.

Sophie looked confused. "Leave? Vacation?"

Oh, shit. When she'd gone for a few days off with Missy, she'd taught Sophie the word *vacation.* But that meant *come back in a few days.* Like *tour* did for her father.

With a heavy heart, Mariliz shook her head *no.* "Not

'Vacation.' Move. I'm moving. I will live with my cousin Missy, now. Not here."

Sophie began to cry. She just sat quietly in her seat while her sobs ratcheted up and up. She surely didn't understand the details, but she understood enough.

It suddenly hit Mariliz what she was doing to this little girl. Despite her tumultuous early relationship with Bridget, Bridget had been her mother for a while. Then she'd left. Every nanny who'd cared for her had left. Even Olivia had left Sophie behind. Now Mariliz was doing it, too.

She was doing it so that Sophie and her dad could have Livie back—at least part of the time. She thought Bridget might get full custody of the older girl if it could be shown in court that Alex paid wages to his live-in girlfriend while he was still married. Since Mari had lived there before she was involved with Alex, there was no real way to define that their affair had started *after* Bridget had declared she was out of the marriage.

"I'm so sorry, Sophie." She reached out to pick the girl up, only to get batted away.

She wasn't surprised by the action. Sophie had been acting out more lately, since Olivia was gone more often. There had been a few video calls with her sister, and while Sophie loved them, she wasn't old enough to really talk the way older kids might. Sophie was still a toddler and needed real interaction— and Olivia wasn't there. So hitting Mari now wasn't a surprise.

Turning to Livie, Mari asked her what she was thinking.

"Sophie needs you. You shouldn't just abandon her like that."

That hurt, but she understood. Kids had no filters. She understood Sophie's reaction. Knew that Olivia's concern for her sister was probably part genuine and part projection of her own need for an at-home mother figure. What she didn't know was what she should be saying. Her degree was in understanding development, not therapy. She had no clue if the way she was saying this was right. Or if her leaving—being simply the next person to abandon them—was better than living with screwed up divorce arrangements for the next sixteen years.

"I don't feel I have a choice. You and your dad and Sophie have to live with what the lawyers decide until both of you are of legal age and maybe even after that." She didn't know anything, only that her heart was breaking. And that breaking their hearts in the process was even worse.

"Is this because you're Dad's girlfriend?" Olivia asked. At least she signed, too.

"Partly." Mariliz answered. At least the girl didn't use her mother's more crass language. Mari didn't know if things would have gone down this way if she'd been able to keep her crush on Alex to herself when Bridget was here. Maybe if she'd liked Bridget more . . . Maybe if Bridget had just been more likeable . . .

It didn't matter. This was the way it was.

When the girls ran out of tears and hugs and anger for the moment, Mariliz reassured them that she wasn't moving until the next day—still too fast by everyone's count, but necessary. Then she assured them she would see them both regularly. She knew Alex would let her see Sophie; she just hoped she was telling the truth to Livie.

Then she got up and headed back to her room, passing Alex and the dregs of his one bottle of beer on the way.

CHAPTER 43

A lex was exhausted. The month had been vicious.
His brain played a nearly endless loop of Mariliz with
her bags in hand, walking past him to the garage as she made
the final trek to her car to leave. He'd sat on the couch, the
empty beer bottle in his hand, thinking that he had a good
metabolism and one beer wouldn't even get him tipsy. He was
thinking about Sophie and Livie in the other room and how if
they weren't there, Lize leaving would have set him off. He
wanted to get shit-faced and forget, but it wasn't an option.

He kept thinking about how similar it all was to the last
nanny, handing in her resignation and walking out, him sitting
on the couch and watching her go past, bag in her hand.

He'd thought that time things were bad. He'd had no clue.

He had no idea if the intervening weeks had been so hard on
him because Mariliz had left him without her much needed
support, or if it was because the divorce had managed to get
even more ugly. Bridget was gloating about Lize leaving him.

He couldn't tell if she was enjoying that she'd forced his hand
or if she was happy that he was hurting. Even more, he was
stuck questioning over and over whether Bridget had changed

so much from the girl he'd married or if he'd simply never really known her in the first place. Times had gotten tough and Bridget had altered dramatically.

In the end, it didn't really matter other than to be certain he didn't miscalculate in the future.

He hadn't miscalculated with Lize. He *knew* that. She'd only been there in tough times, no matter how much shorter his time with Lize had been than with Bridget. He knew how she responded to pressure—she did the right thing, even when it hurt.

Though he knew he would go back to her as soon as he could, he didn't know that she would be waiting. They had barely spoken since she'd left.

They couldn't be together, so she didn't want to hurt by continuing to see him. He had to agree; it twisted his heart each time he dropped Sophie at the daycare and saw her. Usually at a distance, they rarely spoke. But just the sight of her turned him upside down. At first, he'd spent much of Sophie's daycare time at a nearby coffee shop, nursing a coffee and a broken heart. He'd learned quickly to find an errand or something to do, because even just the sight of Lize across the room would send him into a tailspin, and his time in the coffee shop would just be depressing.

That she was even there, waiting for Sophie, was a reminder of how she did the right thing. That job couldn't pay well. She was surrounded by a gaggle of toddlers; it was not her dream job. But she'd taken it so she could see Sophie twice a week. He'd watched Lize hug his daughter with so much love when Sophie left the daycare each time. Lize worked a whole shift, just to be with his daughter a handful of hours.

How could he not love her? How was he supposed to get over her?

He had no idea.

Olivia had moved out. Just in case his heart wasn't beaten enough. Bridget won that round, too.

He not only missed his daughter, he feared every day she spent with her mother was another day Bridget was poisoning Livie against him. His daughter asked him to call her Olivia. He obliged. She asked him to send her bed to her mother's. He did.

He called the school every day to make certain she attended. He'd learned to wake up and call early. Twice, she hadn't arrived. He'd hightailed it to Bridget's, banging on the door and waking them, then rushing Olivia to school to get counted.

He'd lectured her in the car on the way. "Your mother used up all your unexcused absences! You have to attend every single day until the end of the year or you won't graduate."

She'd sulked. He hated it. She wasn't a sulker by nature. "I have good grades."

"It doesn't matter what your grades are. It's a state law, you can't pass without a certain amount of attended days. One more miss and you fail, young lady. Think about how bored you'll be repeating the third grade." He hated that he spent a good part of the little time he got with her lecturing her.

Bridget gave her back for a week when she went on a trip. Though he loved having Livie back, Bridget had almost thrown their daughter at him. She was leaving the state, and *if he so desperately wanted Olivia to attend that stupid school then he needed to take care of it*. While he was more than thrilled to have her home, it meant he'd become Bridget's trash system. He didn't want her to think she could just call the shots forever, but he'd never say "no, don't give me Olivia, I'm busy."

He was so frustrated he could scream.

Going out on tour had been a nightmare. That had happened twice. The first sitter had been fine, but she hadn't been Lize and she hadn't been able to come for the second time. The second sitter hadn't worked as well. When Olivia headed back to Bridget's in sync with him leaving, Sophie had gone ballistic.

Not ballistic. It was still nowhere near her old, non-linguistic self. But she had been miserable the whole trip. Despite his video calls twice a day, despite the sitter's utter competence, she was unhappy all the time. He'd broken down and called Lize.

"Is there any way you can go stay at the house with her?" Every muscle in his body ached at the sound of her voice. She'd been gone for almost a month and a half and he was no closer to letting go than he had been the day she'd left.

"Of course." Her voice had answered. Less than an hour later, she'd texted him, "I'm here."

He wanted a picture of her and Sophie, like she used to send while he was on the road. But she didn't communicate any more with him. She didn't think they should—thought anything between them could get used against him in court. So she let the sitter tell him that Sophie was much better with Lize there. Let the sitter update him on what she ate and how she played while Lize did a little work. She told him Lize took two sick days and spent the time with Sophie. She took Sophie to work with her at the daycare center and brought her home.

Olivia was late to school another day. Only now—from the road—he couldn't go get her. He finally got Bridget by ringing the home phone and her cell repeatedly until she woke.

"Just pay them Alex. They'll pass her. She has a tutor."

"It's not about money. It's about state law, Bridget." He hadn't seen any evidence of this tutor, despite the lawyer's repeated requests for receipts. Then Bridget said the tutor was a friend and doing it for free. But Olivia couldn't name her tutor and never talked about him or her and Bridget still couldn't produce any lesson plans.

He seriously wondered if she was on some kind of drugs—which only made him more afraid for Olivia. When the school called to ask him about reserving her place for next year, he told them no. Then, like every night, he went to his small bunk on the bus and worried whether he'd made the right decision, or even just a decent one.

The guys made up for his lackluster work on stage, eventually throwing him only one solo, which he underperformed to the best of his current abilities. He was invited back to the annual drum-off and declined the challenge without even considering it. When he rolled into home late at night he found Lize's Lexus in the driveway and felt his heart lift.

Letting himself in through the garage, he tiptoed upstairs to check on Sophie. The sitter was in the suite Lize used to occupy and Lize should be in the spare room upstairs. Sophie's bed was empty. The guest room door was ajar enough to peek in and see the one woman he'd ever truly loved sleeping curled around the little girl she'd brought to life. Hell, she'd brought them all to life.

He desperately wanted to join them there, become the third person in their little ball of contentment, but he couldn't. So he stood propped in the doorway and watched them.

It didn't last long. Lize hadn't been deeply asleep, it seemed. She knew he was coming. He could tell by the way she slowly opened her eyes and smiled at him there.

Before he could stop her, she shook Sophie awake and silently signed, "Look, Daddy's home."

With the kind of soft, slow movements that a sleepy toddler needed, she lifted the girl and hugged her to hand her off.

He put his hand out toward her, stopping her. "Just stay." Even if he couldn't stay with her, Sophie could.

"I can't. I can't spend the night in the house with you here. You know that." She looked sad, but she kissed Sophie on the head, told her she'd see her in a few days, and handed his daughter to him as she brushed by.

Just that soft, almost-touch was electric.

He needed her.

He would never get over her.

He faced the fact that he might never be in a position to get her back.

As she headed down the stairs and straight out to her car, he held his daughter and loved her. But he hated the fact that he was letting Bridget push him around and win.

If the pawns were anything other than his kids and his shattered heart, he would have fought back long before this. But he couldn't use them that way.

Instead, he'd let the love of his life walk out the door with hardly a word. Again.

CHAPTER 44

M ariliz ended the call, hitting the button on her computer.

Her new job had her on-call for most of three days of the week plus the occasional Saturday.

She sipped her coffee and walked around, taking a stretch. Though her shirt was one of her designer button-downs, her pants were cute sweats with Cookie Monster on them and she was wearing matching fuzzy slippers despite the warm day.

Missy liked the AC set to a lower temperature than Mariliz did. Though she was living here now as a genuine roommate, Mari still held out hope that it was temporary. Alex's ninety-day-wait was ending soon. There was a possibility they would sign the papers and she could go back there. Live with him and Sophie, see Livie sometimes. Also, Missy had lived in this place by herself for a while, so Mari didn't feel as comfortable telling her to turn down the thermostat. The slippers were a compromise.

Her whole outfit was a compromise.

She needed to appear on camera to chat with families around the state. Some spoke ASL only, some were hearing with deaf kids, so they talked on the phone. Some switched back and forth—sometimes she would have a couple on the line and one would speak English sometimes while the other signed. But no one ever saw her from the waist down.

She'd wandered into the kitchen to grab something to eat when Missy's car pulled into the drive and she climbed out.

Shit. She was supposed to be ready. Mari was making excuses and running for her room even as Missy came in through the door. "I'll be ready in five! I promise."

Luckily, the top of her was ready to go. A skirt for the warm outdoor weather and sandals and she was set.

In the kitchen, she found Missy grabbing crackers and cheese slices, then they hopped in her Mercedes just a few minutes later than they intended.

"Okay, here's the first address." Missy was excited. She was looking for a house to buy this time.

The breakup with the last boyfriend convinced her to stop waiting for her life to be more settled and to settle it herself. A promotion at work and the accompanying raise made it possible to buy before the local market went through the roof.

"Turn here." Missy read instructions off her phone and munched her snack. Lize snuck a few crackers from her, having cut off her own trip into the refrigerator. "Left here."

They were on their way out of the area where the apartment was. This part of town was gentrifying, big time, and in order to get a house Missy could still afford if she lost her renter—Mariliz—she needed to be on the edge of the price increase.

They pulled into the driveway, parking behind the realtor's car, which Missy recognized. This was the first step of buying a house that wasn't just paperwork and banks. Despite Mari insisting she didn't deserve a voice in which home her cousin chose, Missy insisted she come along. She hoped to have a roommate just as much as she hoped Lize went back to Alex, so either was a win in her book. Mostly, she wanted a second set of eyes, checking for things she missed, something that might not be favorable about the property.

The realtor introduced himself, holding Mariliz's hand a little extra long. She smiled back but tried to keep it neutral. At this point, dating anyone would really just be lying. He told them a little about the house, but then backed off to the sidewalk.

"I haven't shown this one before, and honestly, the information looked better than the house does." Turning to Missy, he explained. "You said you can accept some small cosmetic upgrades, but nothing major. So look at the porch— see how the roofline just slightly sags? That would need repair in a few years, maybe less. And the back yard is not okay, I looked."

He showed them the back and they climbed straight into the cars en route to the next house.

By the end of the evening there were three houses they liked, but one was easily ruled out for being too expensive.

"I feel bad, Missy." Lize sat on the couch as Missy set aside the listing the realtor had handed her for that house. "If I knew I was renting, you could afford it."

"No, I couldn't. I shouldn't buy anything I can't afford on my own. Even if you do rent, for how long? What if you lose your job? Not that I think you will. It's a gamble that I'll have my job and not get cut back in some way, I'm not taking the extra risk of thinking you'll rent until I get a raise. That's too much of my salary."

So Lize let her chuck that page in the trash even though the house itself had been both their favorites. They spent the evening whittling the pros and cons down to one and the next day, while Mariliz was chatting in sign online and Missy was at work, she put an offer on the place.

Missy went back and forth a few times agonizing over

counteroffers and whether the price was too high. Mariliz talked her into tapping out rather than paying more.

"There's another house you can make an offer on. It's still on the market." She advised. With that, the seller caved and gave Missy her price. They celebrated with beer and line-dancing, and both went home alone together—happy at the deal, but hearts still single.

Alex's ninety-day waiting period came and went, and Mariliz didn't hear from him. She consoled herself that the papers might not still be signed. Ninety days had been the minimum for an uncontested divorce. His was now highly contested. It didn't mean he wasn't coming, but she couldn't count on him coming back either. There was no telling what the agreement could be, or whether Bridget would still be in their lives. Probably she would, with Livie under her primary custody. Thus, she could make Alex's life miserable if Mariliz came back into it. They might never be back together. So she pushed forward with her own life.

She worked, she saw Sophie at the day-care, and she fought to keep herself together, though it wasn't easy mending a crushed heart. Once when she was walking away from her computer system, a call had come through.

"Livie!" Mariliz exclaimed as she picked up, then waited to be reminded that it was 'Olivia' now. She hadn't heard from the older girl in a while.

"Mariliz." She was happy but her voice was low. Mari heard the digital dings as the girl lowered the volume. The room behind her on the screen showed Livie's bed and her dresser, but didn't seem like her room at home. "My mom's asleep."

Mari figured that was her way of saying she was off road on this one. That she might shut the computer or drop the call at any moment and she didn't want her mother hearing. Mari's heart pinged with concern. "What's up?"

"I have a question for you." At Mari's nod, Livie continued. "I think maybe I want to go home."

Her heart swelled, both at her joy that Alex just might get his daughter back and that Livie called it 'home.' But she didn't want to push. "Why is that?"

"I think I need to go to school. I don't get to see my friends much and my mom's friends are . . ." She trailed off and Mariliz didn't need further explanation. At best, Bridget's friends were likely adults. Given what the tabloids had showed of her before she returned home, they were jet setters probably without use for an eight-year-old. Almost nine, she reminded herself.

"I think your Daddy would be happy to have you come home." She offered a smile, still trying not to push.

"I wasn't very nice to him." She sighed and looked away. "All my stuff is here. I would have to go to a new school next year."

"Why is that?"

She explained about missing too many days, how her Dad wanted her in summer school and she was supposed to have a tutor, so her Dad wasn't paying tuition anymore. But the tutor hadn't materialized yet. Mariliz read in her face that missing school was making Livie anxious. Ironically, it was likely Bridget pushing her to perfection that led to a child who would fret about missing school. "What if summer ends and no one will let me into fourth grade?"

"Tell your Dad. He'll make sure it happens. I know he will."

"Mariliz," She was almost in tears. "They set up everything. Money, plans, everything, because I wanted to be with Mom. I don't know that there's room for me at Daddy's!" She caught herself, her voice getting too high, and she began to whisper. "I don't know if he'll forgive me."

"Oh, honey. You're eight. There's nothing to forgive, and if there is, he'll forgive you; I know it." She did know it. "You call him. As soon as you hang up with me, you call him. He *always* has room for you."

She told Livie she loved her as the girl suddenly closed the call. So Mariliz didn't know if she called her father and worked things out. That evening though, she'd had a revelation. "Missy, she said the money was worked out. That her mother had custody. That means the divorce went through. It's done."

Missy didn't say anything. Mariliz had to say it.

"He didn't come." It was well and truly over. She'd broken down then while her cousin held her. They'd eaten a carton of ice cream together and watched a truly horrible movie that was supposed to be a romantic comedy but was just depressing. Or maybe that was just her current world view.

Before she went to bed that night, she told her cousin, "You've got a renter."

CHAPTER 45

Mariliz clicked off another call, but now when she hopped up, she opened the fridge about five feet away and headed out the back door and out onto the patio.

The weather was getting hotter, like it did in July in Nashville. It would get too hot in just a few hours, but right now the sunshine and the porch were soothing her and she was enjoying her bottle of fizzy water that she'd gotten at the posh grocery that sprung up down the street.

She heard the beeping of a call and capped the water tightly before moving inside. It was Saturday morning, and she pulled a half shift to make up for taking Monday and Thursday afternoons off to be with Sophie. The sound indicated the call was audio only, a speaking caller. Even though she wasn't on camera, she needed to be inside. While the street was quiet, there were occasionally horns or kids playing and the noises were unprofessional.

A lot of the people who called were families with a kid with a diagnosis—they needed help. In many cases, the deafness was the result of some trauma that left more than one diagnosis. It was why she'd never questioned Sophie's original diagnosis of multiple learning disabilities and aggression—it was wholly possible. Especially in a family that didn't have congenital deafness, which the Beaumonts didn't.

Here she was, way past Alex's ninety-day mark, still thinking of him. Instead of thinking about it more, she answered the call and talked to the mother of a foster child in Memphis. Mari told her how to get an interpreter for the school and that they didn't have to pay for it. She talked about local programs for after school and where and when to find ASL classes for the new family members. They wanted to adopt the five-year-old boy, but the state insisted on fost-adopt—a program Mariliz had become familiar with since taking the job. The family had to foster the kid and get good marks for some set period of time before they were eligible to adopt a "special needs" kid. A lot of special needs kids wound up in foster care, she'd found out.

She gave the woman her direct number, but told her the names of the two other people in her job, in case Mariliz wasn't online when she called back. This call required about ten minutes of paperwork afterward, making sure the new case was documented and that James or Alicia could pick up where she left off if necessary.

She made it out onto the porch for thirty minutes with her book and the sunshine. As the day heated up, her nice hair started to go flat and she tugged it up into the ponytail holder she kept at her wrist. She waited, wanting to squeeze just a little more time outside until another call came. Today she had a short sleeve top and yoga pants. Bare feet peeked out beneath the long hem, a combination of the weather and agreement on the thermostat in the new house.

She finally had all her stuff put away, finally rearranged her one twin bed—humorous for a divorced woman in her early thirties—and her dresser and night table for the third and final time. She'd made the most use of the twelve-by-twelve room, large for some of the bungalows in this area. Missy's room was twelve-by-fourteen and had the attached bath. But Mari had the soaker tub even if she shared the main bath with visitors. She was not complaining. Aside from a party or a friend for dinner, they didn't have many visitors.

Another beep finally called her inside, only this woman was asking for a Spanish speaker.

"Yo solo hablo un poco de español." *I only speak a little Spanish*. Mariliz got a number and told the woman James would call her back when he finished his current call. She didn't add that he might be taking a lunch or a random restroom break. They all three did it. In the end, as long as they each clocked enough answered calls and enough percentage of the time on the line, no one cared. So when the knock came at the door, she simply clicked off her line for a moment and answered it.

She pulled it wide, a habit she should break, but she loved having a front door again. She was not prepared to see Alex standing there.

Her heart skipped at the sight of him. His t-shirt was relatively new and had a picture of Sophie and Livie on it, but his jeans were all Alex—ripped almost to shreds at the knees, they made her wonder if they were 'summer' jeans with purposeful ventilation.

He must have been looking her over, too. "Lize, you look . . . elegant . . . and comfortable." He pointed to her top then her yoga pants, then tried again. "Amazing. You look wonderful. It's been too long since I've seen you, really seen you."

She stood still for a moment, just looking at him. She couldn't move. She'd given up, and his being here now didn't really mean anything. Then her brain jerked into gear and flooded with the thousand questions she had. She tried to prioritize. "Did Livie come home?"

"Yes, last week. How did you know?" His eyes went wide, then she saw understanding dawn just as she was ready to explain. "You told them they could call you any time. Did you coach her to come back?"

She shook her head. "You wanted her to make her own decision. She wanted to come home to you before she called me. She said 'go home' about your place. I just told her you would take her back and not be mad. That you would have room for her, though I don't know why you wouldn't—"

She stopped herself from the tumbling ramble she'd started and watched as he nodded thoughtfully. "There's so much to tell you."

So she waited, not thinking to move inside where it was cool, she just stood in the doorway, wide-eyed.

"We moved. Sophie and me. Up to the other side of town, nearer to my parents, nearer to the rest of the guys. I sold the house to pay off Bridget. The divorce wasn't final until the last check cleared." He looked away. "But I'm out, free and clear. I'm poorer. I can't afford a maid and a nanny and an assistant again, at least not for a while. I don't have a nanny suite either. But we're on the other side of the same subdivision as Shay and Craig and their boys."

"That's why Livie was worried about you having enough room for her." She put it together.

"Yeah, but she had a room with me already. Always will, no matter what."

She nodded at him. She'd known that, and had told Olivia so.

"We just got her furniture and moved it back. She finished a quick catch-up for summer, her summer-school teacher passed her out of third grade at the halfway mark. That was a big load off all our shoulders. She'll go to the local elementary next fall."

Mariliz nodded as he talked, still stunned that he was here. That his arms were close enough to wrap around her even if he

SAVANNAH KADE

didn't do it. That she could feel him standing near her even if she closed her eyes.

"It's Sophie's birthday tomorrow. We're having her party today."

She remembered.

"I talked to Livie about it, and I want to give Sophie the best possible birthday present." He shoved his hands in his pockets. "I want to give her a mom."

His eyes shined with hope and worry as he looked at her. Mariliz stopped breathing, not even wondering what he was saying, only what she should say.

Only then did it occur to her that she'd left him standing in the open doorway. "Come in."

"I was hoping for 'yes.'" But he followed her inside where it was cooler even if neither of them sat.

Realizing she still wore her headset for audio calls draped around her neck, Mariliz pulled it off and almost flung it onto a waiting side table. "You can't ask me that!"

He nodded, understanding.

"You can't come in here after all these months and ask me to marry you because you want a mother for your daughter." She was calmer the second time she said it and wondered how her heart could break all over again. But her feet were moving and she paced as restlessly as her pulse beat.

His hand touched her shoulder, stopping her. The electric feel of his touch was so familiar. "Please, sit."

She did, looking up at him, still standing, almost hovering while he looked for words. Words that she had no idea what they would really say. But she took a quick breath when he said her name in sign. He kept speaking with no English, just ASL.

"I want you for myself, too. For purely selfish reasons, I want you to be my wife." He paused, then started again.

"Just over ten years ago, I met Bridget and we spoke a common language of music. Livie speaks it, too. Then we got

322

this child who didn't—couldn't—speak it. She couldn't even speak English. And everything fell apart." He took a breath, turned away, still signing, but started over when he turned back and saw she was frowning.

"Then you showed up. You taught us how to speak again. This language—" he gestured to his hands, "This is the language of my family. It's the language of *family* and you taught it to me. I love you. I love you in ways I never loved anyone before you and in ways I didn't know I could love anyone."

He sucked in a breath, using his hands to show her his heart, to put it in her hands. Mariliz couldn't breathe either, waiting.

"I hated that you left, but I loved you for loving us so much you were willing to sacrifice you and me for the sake of my girls. They are *your* girls, too. I hope you know that." He didn't stop, didn't ask for words. Didn't mis-step his grammar. He was fluent enough now.

She tried not to sniff, but felt the tears—happy, happy, painfully wonderful tears—pressing at the backs of her eyes. She still didn't get to speak.

"Livie and Sophie miss you terribly. They tell me so, and I tell them I miss you, too. Yesterday, I signed the new custody agreement with Bridget. I have Sophie completely and I have primary with Livie while Bridget has visitation. The girls want you to be with us again. We need you. Not for ASL lessons, not for a nanny, but because you are a part of our family and we will never be whole without you. . . I went to Missy's apartment last night and almost had a heart-attack when someone else opened the door!"

"We moved." She managed to sign stupidly. Clearly, this amazing man had already figured that out.

"Now Sophie's party is in two hours. I need to be there. I want you to come, even if you don't want to marry me." He signed 'marry me' as 'you marry with me' one sign for the whole thing.

Her heart turned over. "Alex," she nodded.

"Wait." He still signed, not a word passed his lips, as though he was truly speaking the language of his heart. Dropping to one knee, he pulled a ring from his pocket, no box, just the diamond winking up at her. "Lize, I love you more than anything. Please, please, marry me?"

CHAPTER 46

M ariliz only nodded. Tears ran freely down her face as she slid off the couch and onto her own knees in front of him. Ignoring the outstretched ring, she hugged him, holding onto him for the first time in months. Her heart beat frantically even as she relaxed into his embrace. It felt like she'd come home, finally.

After long minutes holding him, she pulled back and took a deep breath. "Yes, yes, a thousand times yes."

His smile lit up her world, that dimple throwing her for a loop as always. But his kiss set her on fire. His hands wound into her hair, his mouth searched hers, hungry, needy, and all consuming.

Letting her hands run up under the t-shirt he'd probably put on for the birthday party, she pushed it up, unable to help herself from touching him. It had been so long, but she still knew him, every plane, every curve, every muscle, every sweet spot.

Kissing his chest as she dragged the shirt up his arms, she heard his gasp for breath then at the last moment, "Wait. Wait."

He had a party to get to. *They* had a party to get to. So she pulled back, even though she was breathing like she'd finished a marathon when she hadn't even started.

He fisted a hand and pulled it through the sleeve before chucking the shirt aside. "Here."

He pulled the ring from where he'd stuck it onto his own pinkie for safety and took a moment to reverently slide it onto her finger.

"It fits." She meant that on so many levels.

"Of course it does. I slipped a string around your finger the first night we slept together." He offered a sheepish half-grin. "I knew. I knew you were the one all along."

Then he scooped her up, pushing himself off the hardwood floor and begging her to tell him which room was hers.

"This one," she pointed, then dropped her feet to the ground and walked him in backwards, unsnapping his jeans as she went. She had him naked in no time and he was peeling her yoga pants even as she reached into the nightstand for a condom.

His hands stopped as he looked at the foil packet she'd easily produced.

"There was never anyone else, Alex. I just kept hoping you'd show up." She shrugged.

"It took too long. I'm so sorry. But it's done now, signed, paid, I'm completely free." He kissed her again, both of them knowing there was time to plan, time to relax together in the future.

Right now, though, there was no time. There was a toddler and a birthday party waiting. He pushed inside her with nothing marking it other than their shared sighs of relief at finally being back to together in the most fundamental sense.

She held onto him as he moved into her, over and over, until they cried each other's names into the air and into the future.

Then as fast as they'd peeled their clothing, they scrambled back into it. Alex had lost his shirt, and Mariliz was looking for some shorts appropriate for a kid's birthday party, but she threw the same top back on, having sacrificed time for other things.

"It's in the living room." She pushed his shirtless self out into the hall then followed as she ducked into the bathroom and checked her makeup.

She heard Missy laughing a hello to Alex. "I see you found the place."

He must be turning red; Missy would have seen his shirt on the floor and heard them! Mariliz took a deep breath and entered the living room in time to hear him invite Missy along.

"It's a toddler party, right? I don't know anyone."

"You know us, and all the band will be there, even a lot of my musician friends and their kids." He paused. "A handful of them are single."

"Well, let me get my purse." Missy hopped up and tailed them out the door.

JD and Kelsey had taken over at Alex's new house for him while he'd ducked across town to find her. At least a dozen kids ran around, most of them signing. Mari's heart flipped over, but before she could say hello to anyone, Sophie spotted them.

With a happy shriek to break eardrums she didn't need, she bolted into Mari's arms. Her smile lit up the world and she grabbed for Mari's hand. Putting her chubby finger directly on the diamond, she pointed, "Mommy. Means 'Mommy,' right?"

She looked to her father, who smiled and nodded. Then she looked to Mari who signed back. "I'm so proud to be your Mommy." She hugged the girl tightly, looking over Sophie's tiny shoulders at Alex and fighting happy tears.

Livie came up, too, and Mariliz stroked the blond curls of the older girl's head while she said, "Mom or step-mom, or whatever you want to call me, I'm always here for you."

She was smiling her way through tears for what felt like hours. Even after Sophie squirmed to get down. After the girls joined the other kids, and she was passed around for hugs to all the guys in the band, and the wives admired her ring and welcomed her to the club, she still felt tears leaking out occasionally.

Alex refused to let go of her for most of the night, but she would have held on to him if he had.

At one point, Missy sidled up to her and said, "I told you I needed to be able to handle the payments on my own."

"Who's the hottie?" Mariliz asked, seeing the guy across the room who was keeping an eye on her cousin.

"That's Jase. He's in a band called Train Wreck. And," She turned to face her cousin, "Phillip called back last night. He thinks we let things go too fast. I have a lot of options right now."

"Yes, you do." Mariliz laughed.

She ate hot dogs and chips. She showed off her ring and accepted congratulations until she thought she couldn't smile anymore. Sophie and Livie periodically stopped by to hug her or tell her they were glad she was back. And at one point, Alex snuck her upstairs to show her his room.

"It's *our* room. I haven't decorated it yet. Nor the living room, nor anything but the girls' rooms and the studio. It's *ours*. And if you don't like it, we'll move." He held his arms out into the plain space.

"I love it. Home is where you are."

He kissed her then, deep enough and long enough that she was afraid they would be missed at the party.

When they came back down, it was time for cake and presents. The crowd sang happy birthday to Sophie with every last person signing. Mariliz was thunderstruck. Alex whispered in her ear, "I told them they didn't need to bring presents, but they had to learn to sing happy birthday to her in her language. Everyone did both."

Sophie clapped and squealed at them, her hat tipped at a jaunty angle.

When the guests began to leave, the guys from the band stayed to help pick up torn wrapping paper and throw away paper plates. JD sent his older kids out into the yard with a trash bag to clear the rented picnic tables and grab anything that had blown up against the fence.

One by one, they headed out. JD rounded up their half-dozen kids, loading them into the van Mari had seen at the corner when they came in. He buckled some in and settled arguments between others like a pro. Kelsey came up beside her then, watching her husband.

"I'm glad you said yes. I've been married to JD almost ten years now, and I've known these guys for forever it seems." Turning to face Mariliz, she smiled, deep and genuine. "I knew when he talked about you that you were the real deal."

She hugged Mariliz as though she'd known her all along. "Craig found Shay and became a father. TJ found Norah, and they're talking about getting pregnant. That's a big deal for them. Long story, one day. Maybe Norah will tell you." Kelsey waved down the block to where her sister-in-law was climbing into a car with TJ sliding behind the wheel. Craig and Shay were turning the corner, walking with their boys the half mile to the other side of the complex. "I always worried about Alex. So quiet, he never talked."

"He always talks." Mariliz frowned.

"Around you. About you. That's just one way I knew. Welcome to the family." She offered the last as she started down the hill to her own clan.

When Mariliz turned to go back inside, Alex was standing behind her, his hand out, waiting. She slid her hand in his and headed up the front steps of the porch into her new home. Into the future that awaited them.

AFTERWORD

I hope you fell in love with Mariliz and Alex along with me. This book has a rich history for me as I became a certified ASL interpreter at the young age of 14. To do this, I studied at the University of Tennessee and learned about reading levels, alternate modality lanuages, deaf culture, and the history of speech therapy and integration. What Sophie deals with in Music & Lyrics is in the realm of reality with cochlear implants gaining in popularity and the issues of hearing parents wanting a "normal life" for their child. This story is particularly close to my heart. I knew I would one day write about a deaf character, and there will probably be more in the future. I hope you enjoyed the ride as Mariliz and Alex fell in love, too. If you did, I'd love if you'd leave a review

PREVIEW OF PERFECT (BREATHLESS, GA - BOOK 1)

There should always be fine liquor on hand, you never know when a gentleman might want some. You never know when you might need some yourself.

"Bailey Ann Mayfair, when are you going to marry me?"

Bailey spun around on the street, looking for the voice that was a pure blast from her past. The sound was both sweet and spun with regret. She peered into a wind that felt far more bitter than it should have, but that was likely just her mood.

He'd asked that same question of her more than once before. He'd asked it in jest and in full sincerity. And now he was asking on the street of Breathless, Georgia, where anyone could hear. But Bailey Ann hadn't seen him in at least five years.

Her eyes searched the street until she landed on him. She didn't recognize him by sight, but she knew just by feel that the broad-shouldered form standing down the street was Finn Malloy. Her face lit up; she could feel it. "Finn! I didn't know you were in town."

She fought the urge to run and throw herself into his arms,

to sink there and let him lift away all the world. But she was out in public, so she couldn't do it. She'd also answered that same question in the negative before—a good indicator that he wasn't going to take kindly to her using him as a crying shoulder if she tried it.

He walked closer, the straight nose and bright eyes so familiar. The broad mouth almost smiling, but not quite. Typical black Irish coloring marked him. His hair was so dark as to be inky, his eyes blue enough to be startling. She'd once told herself she couldn't marry a man with prettier eyes than her own.

Even in his twenties, he'd been slim but cut. Something had happened, and he now filled out that suit he was wearing. She blinked. "You're wearing a suit."

"Yeah," his mouth got closer to smiling, but still didn't quite achieve it. "I do that. I wear a suit."

She only nodded, because what else could she say? That she didn't think he'd been the type? That she'd never seen him in one before? Weren't jeans more his style? It all sounded vaguely insulting and she'd been carefully taught to never insult someone unless she meant it. Tears pushed at the back of her eyes, and Bailey fought them back. "Are you doing something specific here?"

Breathless wasn't the kind of place a person visited without a purpose. It was full of families and homes and schools. The shops were cute, the diner was full-scale Southern with a capital S, and the main street was named "Main" and lined with the basic stores with pretty lettering, but it wasn't a tourist town.

"I'm taking care of my parents' house," he finally answered her, the words not quite sinking in.

"Oh, did they move out? Somewhere flatter?" She was thinking of old knees and all the stairs in the house. It was a kind way of asking if they'd been moved to a nursing home, or more, when she noticed he was looking at her oddly.

"No. The house is all that's left. They died in a car accident about a year ago."

"What?" She stopped cold. "They . . ." She couldn't bring herself to say it. She'd had no idea. How had she had no idea?

Finn nodded solemnly. "Single car. They went into the big tree over on Kellar, but neither of them made it."

"Oh, my God, Finn, I'm so sorry." Truly, she was. But she was just as sorry that she hadn't known. That she hadn't come back and attended their funerals. Mrs. Malloy had no more approved of Bailey being her son's girlfriend than Bailey's own mother had approved of "that immigrant boy." Still, it didn't seem right to not attend. It was worse to not have known.

He just nodded. "After your mother passed, I figured you probably weren't getting the news." He shoved his hands in his pockets, the conversation awfully awkward for two people who'd had some of the most amazing sex she'd known existed. For someone who'd asked her to marry him on multiple occasions.

This time, he was the better person and bridged the silence for them. "When is the service for your father?"

Just being asked, just having to think about it again pushed the tears forward. "Saturday morning at the church." She took a beat before she realized she wasn't being clear. "Our church, First Methodist on South Main. We'll have a reception at the house afterward."

He nodded again. Though she hadn't gotten the news about an accident with both his parents, and though she had family and friends in town at the time, somehow Finn—with no family left around town—had heard about her father passing within just a few days.

She stepped in. "Are you planning to attend?"

It was all so formal and stilted, she thought. This was Finn. Finn Malloy who'd sat behind her in seventh grade English class. Mayfair. Malloy. They'd been placed next to each other that whole year and the next, too. Finn Malloy, the boy she'd accepted a shy request for a date from. Finn who she'd lost her virginity to before heading off to college. Bailey Ann pushed her hands down into her pockets.

"Am I invited?"

It was a silly question and he probably knew that. Of course, he was invited. The whole town was. Breathless wasn't that big. People who'd known Con Mayfair would simply show up at the church and many, if not most, would follow Bailey Ann and her sisters back to the house. "Of course, you're invited, Finn."

"He didn't like me all that much."

"He didn't like anyone I dated," she retorted quickly to put Finn at ease, but realized quickly that her offhand remark bore a disturbing resemblance to the truth. She covered it with a smile and a straighter spine.

Finn graciously changed the topic. "Are your sisters coming in?"

"I don't know if you heard, but Harper Rose lost her husband about six months back." She didn't add that it was a big fat mess and her little sister had slowly been learning that her husband had no money, they didn't own the house, and he appeared to have no real job. "She's got three little girls to bring with her."

Harper Rose followed in the family footsteps but had her kids much closer together than their parents had. Bailey Ann had yet to find the man to make her a wife. So here she was at thirty-four, talking to Finn Malloy who was gracious enough not to ask if she was still single. She was so boringly single that she'd quit her job and dropped everything to come home when her Daddy called her. She didn't want to dwell on that. "Emma Kate should be in soon, too, but she's working on getting her classes squared away."

At least, Bailey Ann hoped she was. Somehow, she was now the de facto head of this little family of sisters.

"Well, I'm here if you need me." He had his hands still in his pockets but gestured with the flaps of his coat. "It was good to see you, Bailey Ann. It always is."

With that, he turned and walked down the street away from her as she watched. From behind, the wool coat covered the suit that had been a surprise. She saw now that he had on polished shoes and his haircut had been far more expensive than the ones he'd had in school. When she'd known him, he'd been a jeans and t-shirt kind of guy.

When they'd dated, he'd been creative—picnics, hikes, drives out of town. Only rarely did he take her to the movies and even less often to dinner. In the beginning, she'd thought it was just Finn. When he wore the same pair of slacks the second time they'd gone out somewhere nice, she'd started to get a clue. Later, when she'd been in his house, she'd understood.

The Malloys didn't have the extra money for those things. They weren't poor per se, but it seemed they'd spent all their money on the house on Sparrow Road. Their son was in a good neighborhood of a small town, and he was getting a good education at the public school, but they weren't eating steak every week. They weren't getting the threadbare carpets replaced or the front door painted. And Finn wasn't giving her the impression that one day he'd wear wingtips with his perfectly cut suit and fine wool coat.

Then again, he'd always been a surprise.

Bailey found her first smile that day and headed further down the street away from Finn. Toward the corner pizza shop to get a slice and a coke. She needed it. The bad-for-you lunch would provide three of the four food groups—salt, sugar, and grease. She could get the fourth—alcohol—when she got home. She'd decided she was going to open the decanter to Daddy's whiskey and take her first drink of it.

Not that she hadn't had whiskey before, but Daddy had never let her drink in front of him, and he'd never let her have even a sip of the stash he kept at the house. Today, she might need the whole bottle. She had a funeral to plan and a man to get off her mind.

Thank you for reading! I love romances with real love and believable characters, and I hope you found all that in these pages. I want to fall in love right along with the characters, and I do, while I'm writing it.

About Savannah

I started writing when I was eight--I hand wrote an 80-page novella that I believed to be (adult) romantic suspense. I'm proud to say, I've gotten a lot better since then. I've grown up to be a nerd at heart! I love neuroscience and people watching, and if you look, you'll find some of that in each Savannah Kade book. Most days you'll find me in my office, looking out my window at a handful of the neighbor's cows, or watching my dogs or my cat roam the backyard.

Follow me, find me, ask me questions! I would love to hear from you.
www.SavannahKade.com
Savannah@SavannahKade.com

www.ingramcontent.com/pod-product-compliance
Lightning Source LLC
Chambersburg PA
CBHW020212260626
47156CB00002B/351